The Elevator Omnibus:
The Complete Trilogy

Also by Sam Kates

Pond Life and Other Stories

The Village of Lost Souls

That Elusive Something

The Cleansing (Earth Haven: Book One)

The Beacon (Earth Haven: Book Two)

The Reckoning (Earth Haven: Book Three)

Strange Shores and Other Stories

Ghosts of Christmas Past & Other Dark Festive Tales

The Elevator Omnibus:
The Complete Trilogy

Sam Kates

The Elevator first edition published September 2016
Second edition published November 2017
Jack's Tale published January 2018
The Lord of the Dance published February 2018
This paperback omnibus, June 2018

ISBN 978-1-912718-13-9

www.samkates.co.uk

For Julian

Contents

Book 1: The Elevator   1

Book 2: Jack's Tale   153

Book 3: The Lord of the Dance   303

About the Author   481

The Elevator

Part 1: Sixth Floor

One

The colour of the sky as I trudged to the office should have warned me that it would be no ordinary day. All greens and purples and tones of black, like a few-day-old bruise. It was eight-thirty on a spring morning, yet the air was as stilled and dusky as twilight. Birds flocked and muttered, unsure whether to roam or roost. I paused and looked up.

Big mistake. The cloud formation above Claridge House, where I had worked for the past eighteen months, swirled and spiralled, the colours and movement combining with my hangover to make me want to heave.

Taking a deep breath, I closed my eyes. And opened them in time to see the flash of lightning fork down onto the roof of Claridge House like the world's largest spark. I might have imagined the puff of smoke that rose from the roof, but there was no mistaking the sharp smell of ozone or the way the hairs on my neck and back of my hands fizzed and jived and stood to attention.

I waited to see if the building would collapse or burst into flames so that I might turn around and go back to bed. No such luck. Cursing the efficiency of modern lightning conductors, I resumed my trudge to work. My system needed coffee. Badly.

The foyer on the ground floor of Claridge House could not have been less prepossessing. Unless perhaps it hosted a service for devil worshippers, complete with goat, chalked pentacle and slaughtered cockerel. Grimy, peeling walls and linoleum floor, a suggestion of *eau de cats' piss* and a few doors leading deeper into the building or to the stairwell. I made for the shiny, battered metal door which opened into the lift.

The display panel alongside the two buttons, one with an arrow for 'up', the other for 'down', showed that the lift was on the Fifth Floor. Muttering under my breath—the lift wasn't ancient, but not exactly in the prime of youth either; it would take a good thirty seconds to descend five floors—I pressed the 'up' button. While I waited, I glanced around furtively, hoping that nobody else would come. The lift car wasn't large; it felt stuffy and cramped with two people inside. I preferred having it to myself when I was in tip-top shape; with a hangover, the craving for solitude was almost as strong as my need for coffee.

The lift *pinged* its arrival at the same time as a draught and sudden swell of traffic noise indicated the main entrance to the building had opened behind me. The lift door began to slide sideways in its uncertain, ponderous way. By the time the gap was wide enough for me to step through, the building entrance had opened a second time.

On the wall of the lift was an array of black buttons bearing these images in white, arranged so:

Beneath the right-hand bottom button, the one with the image of a bell, was a small speaker from which, so I am told since I'd never had cause to test it, an operator's voice would enquire of the nature of the emergency in the event that the alarm button was pressed.

Before I was fully inside the lift, I hit one of the top buttons, the one that bore the number six, then the lower button with two inward-facing arrows that would tell the door to close, and stepped to the back of the tiny space. I gazed at the floor, pretending to be in a world of my own so as not to catch the eye of anyone approaching and be obliged to push the button with outward-facing arrows that would tell the door to open again.

Moments before it had fully shut, a set of fingers curled around the edge of the door, tripping the sensors that prevented it from closing on people and squishing them. It began to slide open and I sighed.

"All right?" said the person who stepped in to join me.

The face was one I vaguely recognised, but only because its owner worked on the same floor as me. He appeared to be barely into his twenties, younger than me by around five years. Red rash on cheeks looked like the result of skin unaccustomed to shaving; red rash on nose an acne hangover from being a teenager. In my uncharitable moments, of which this was one, I thought of him as Rudolph.

I grunted a response and resumed my perusal of the floor. Coffee was calling.

Just when it looked as though the door would close and we could begin our ascent to Six and a caffeine infusion, a hulking document case appeared in the dwindling gap. The case—one of those bulky, black leather numbers which look as if they can hold the entire contents of a filing drawer plus the owner's lunch—was followed by a stiff-looking woman in her mid-thirties wearing a dark power suit. She didn't look at me or Rudolph, but checked out the buttons and hit number five, before turning her back to us. When she lowered the case to the floor in front of her, it made a dull *thud*.

Rudolph had been forced to shuffle to the back of the lift, meaning I had to tuck into the corner to stop from rubbing against him. I felt his gaze on me, probably seeking some sort of buddy-buddy exchange of eyebrow-raising. I wasn't in the mood.

Suppressing a sigh as the door once more began to slide closed, I let it out in an audible rush at the sound of the voice.

"Hold the elevator!" The accent matched the choice of words: American. "Hold the elevator! I'm coming."

No I thought *don't hold it. Let the frigging thing close, for the love of God. I need coffee!*

Power Suit's hand shot out and hit the 'door open' button. In the widening gap between edge of door and lift wall, a flushed face appeared.

"Oh, thank you," it said. It belonged to a well-built girl a couple of years older than me, at a guess, although I'm hopeless at accurately estimating women's ages. It's like trying to pronounce long words after sinking five pints.

Power Suit reached down to pick up her case, causing Rudolph to squeeze himself tighter against the back wall to avoid a potentially embarrassing collision of backside and crotch, then shuffled to her right to allow the newcomer to enter the lift. The American (or Canadian; I'm not good with accents, either) stepped in and pressed the number four button.

My breath escaped in another heavy sigh; the lift would visit Floors Four and Five before I could step out on Six where the coffee machine gurgled my name.

American Girl may have smiled at me, but I had already looked away. Rudolph must have maintained eye contact because she addressed her remarks to him.

"Gee, I hope I'm not putting you out, but those stairs are a killer first thing in the morning." She gave a mock sigh. "Though I really should take them. Using the elevator won't bring back my beach bod." She giggled.

I groaned quietly. A bold, brash Yank was the last person with whom I needed to be in close confinement. My head had begun to throb.

The door had at last managed to close completely. Even if it were to open again, there was no room for anyone else to get in, not unless they were built like a broom handle.

"We call 'em lifts," said Rudolph. He sounded peevish.

"Oh, honey, I know that. Been living here for five years. Married a Brit." She giggled again; it was more irritating than her voice, that giggle. "But, if it's okay with you, I'll carry on calling it an elevator. And if it's not okay with you, I believe I'll carry on calling it an elevator."

I didn't look up, but could imagine her smiling sweetly and Rudolph scowling.

It had grown uncomfortably hot in the lift. I swallowed and tried not to breathe through my nose. If any of my temporary companions exuded an odour, I didn't want to smell it.

With an initial jerk, but then as smoothly as though it were a finely-tuned machine, not a piece of junk on its last legs, the lift began to ascend.

Hallelujah! Coffee, here I come.

Only on hearing the murmur of surprise did I raise my head to look at the panel above the buttons on which, in red digits, the floor number was displayed.

4.

The lift normally stopped on the nearest floor whose button had been pressed, regardless of the order in which they were pushed. Yet it was still on the move, ascending to Floor Five.

The American stood sideways on, facing the wall containing the buttons. She turned her head to glance at me.

"I guess it doesn't want to stop on Four today," she said.

I shrugged and continued to watch the display panel.

5.

Power Suit straightened and took a firmer grip on the document case; she must have possessed biceps like a man's to lug that thing around all day. When the lift showed no sign of stopping she, too, looked at the panel.

6.

There is a god and He is good. I could all but smell the coffee.

Rousing from my slouched stance, I cleared my throat to warn Power Suit that I wanted out. Rudolph had the same idea and took half a step forward; any more and he'd have been treading on American Girl's platform shoes.

The lift jerked to a stop and there followed the usual hiatus while it gathered its wits to let us out.

The door began to slide open.

Two

When I was in my early teens, my parents took me and my sister on holidays to Cyprus, the first time I'd been abroad apart from a day trip to Calais with school. We went in July, taking off from Heathrow in howling winds and sweeping rain, four hours late. It was early evening when we landed at Larnaca Airport. I'll never forget the smell that hit me in the face like a light slap as I stepped off the plane: a warm waft of jasmine and pine and bougainvillea and lemons, a heady, exotic mix which took my breath away.

When the lift door opened at the Sixth Floor, the smell, such as it was, that I had expected was the usual underwhelming combination of mustiness, electrical heat from photocopiers and computers, the occasional whiff of body odour, and a faint but enticing aroma of percolating coffee. Instead, I smelled Cyprus.

The dim, flickering illumination given out by strip lighting dotted with carcasses of long-dead flies had been replaced by dazzling sunlight. The air was no longer stale and recycled (over and over until there couldn't have been any oxygen left in the stuff), but a hot breeze bearing those exotic aromas. Not exactly like Cyprus—there was nothing recognisably *lemony* about this breeze—but as far removed from an office smell as to make no difference.

A metal rail ran around the inside of the lift at waist height, wide enough to lean comfortably against. American Girl reached out and grabbed the rail with both hands, her knuckles white, as though trying to maintain a grip on reality. Her head turned to the door and she didn't look about to move.

I don't recall what Rudolph was doing because my attention was distracted by Power Suit. She uttered a noise much like a *squawk* and took a step back, bringing the heel of her patent leather shoes—not stilettoes, thank goodness—sharply down onto my foot.

"Yow!" I put my hands to her shoulders, moving her to my left, at the same time sliding past her to my right. I stood at the open door and stared out at Floor Six, my throbbing foot forgotten.

The once-beige carpet tiles had gone; the reception desk behind which Sourpuss Sue usually sat varnishing her nails was nowhere to be seen; the door leading through to my workspace—and coffee—might never have existed. The entire building, except for the lift, had vanished. By rights—although there was nothing *right* about any of this—we should have been looking out at a drop of fifty feet onto roads and rooftops.

Instead, we faced a wide vista of countryside. Swathes of thick grass swayed in sultry wind; trees heavy with foliage and fruit quivered and bowed; the land dipped and rose like an ocean frozen in mid-swell. Blue-tipped mountains formed a shark-tooth backdrop.

Where the lift floor ended, the grass began. If I moved forward a few inches, I'd be standing on lush meadow. My foot started to slide towards the doorway.

"Don't!" It was American Girl. She had turned to fully face the opening, effectively blocking Rudolph from leaving. He stared over her shoulder, open mouth and protruding tongue making him look simple.

My foot stopped moving. I raised my eyebrows at American Girl.

"Why not?"

"It could be toxic. Or acidic. Or, or, *alive*!"

"Hmm."

The green stuff definitely looked like grass; plain old grass. I poked out my right foot and brought it down gingerly, ready to whip it back at the first sign of the vegetation behaving in any way that grass doesn't normally behave.

My foot touched the greenery. Nothing happened. I pressed down. It gave in the springy way that lush turf does. It felt firm underneath. My weight swayed forward so that it rested fully on my front foot. Still nothing happened.

"It's just grass," I said.

Before American Girl could raise any more fanciful objections, I moved my back foot and stood outside the lift.

The human mind is remarkably adaptable. I had stepped out of the work lift at the Sixth Floor, but instead of walking through the grotty reception area, making like a guided missile for the coffee machine, I was standing at ground level on a thickly-grassed hillside, breathing in lungfuls of tropical breezes. Yet I wasn't gibbering and pulling out clumps of hair as my mind cut loose from its moorings in reality. Sure, I had no explanation for what was happening, and I was freaked out in an unfocused sort of way, but curiosity and wonder at the unknown outweighed my fear of it.

The same could not be said of my lift companions.

Power Suit must have backed up until she hit the rear wall and then slid down it so that she cowered on the floor, arms covering her bowed head. Bony knees, clad in sheer black nylon, peeked above the document case placed in front of her like a barrier.

Rudolph hadn't moved, though in fairness he was blocked in. He continued to stare open-mouthed over American Girl's shoulder as if his brain had departed, leaving a stupefied shell behind.

As for American Girl, she pressed repeatedly on the button with the inward pointing arrows. Then the button with the image of a bell.

No alarm sounded, no disembodied voice spoke from the speaker and the door didn't move, but I didn't want to take a chance on it closing with me the wrong side of it.

"Hey," I said. "Stop that."

She dropped her hand from the buttons and began fumbling in the small leather handbag, which I guess she called a 'purse', hanging by a strap over her shoulder. Extracting a mobile phone, she began punching buttons and tapping the screen in the same frantic manner.

"No service. Shoot! Anyone else have a cell phone?"

Animation had returned to Rudolph's face. He shook his head slowly, mouth twisting into a sneer. "We call them mobiles."

"Frankly, honey, I don't give a damn what you call them. If you don't have one, you're of no use." She stretched out a leg and poked gently with the toe of her shoe at Power Suit's knee. "What about you, sugar? Do you have a phone?"

Power Suit lowered her hands and raised uncomprehending eyes.

"Do you have a phone?" the American repeated in a rising tone; she sounded on the edge of panic.

Power Suit felt in the pocket of her jacket and drew out a mobile phone. She pressed the screen to illuminate it. "No signal." It was barely a whisper.

American Girl turned large, frightened eyes to me.

I shook my head. "I have a mobile but it's locked in my desk on—" I hesitated and glanced at the countryside "—the Sixth Floor." I had gone straight to the pub from work the previous evening. When the beer flows, I have been known to lose mobiles so had prudently locked it in my drawer overnight. It's not that I have so many friends that anyone would worry that they couldn't reach me.

"What's going on?" Minutes ago so brash, so confident, American Girl now sounded like a little girl on the verge of tears.

"I haven't the foggiest, but I'm going to explore a little and I don't want the door closing with me this side of it. In fact…" I stepped back into the lift in front of Power Suit. "I need to borrow this for a while."

Stooping, I laid my hand on top of her document case. She had replaced her phone in the pocket of her jacket and withdrawn back into herself; she didn't even look up. With a shrug and a grunt I stood, hefting the case. No wonder Power Suit had crouched down behind it; it felt like it could stop bullets.

I placed the case in front of the recess into which the lift door slides open. If the door tried to close, if the sensors that prevented it closing onto an obstruction were somehow overridden, it would not be able to shut tight with that monster in the way. And I didn't think the lift could move without the door being fully closed; it should be a standard safety measure, even in a piece of machinery this old. There was no way to test out my theory so I had to trust to it not being wishful thinking on my part.

"Right," I said, "who's coming with me?"

Power Suit didn't raise her head. If she'd noticed that I'd relocated her case, she didn't show it.

Rudolph's glance flickered to mine and away, like the erratic flight of a moth. He nodded towards Power Suit and lowered his head so he didn't have to look at me.

"I, er…" He cleared his throat. "Someone'd better stay with her…" The parts of his cheeks that were visible blazed red, accentuating the pock marks.

Ah, well, so I was on my—

"I'll come," said American Girl.

My expression must have betrayed surprise and gratitude for she shot me an uncertain smile.

"But I'm scared," she added.

"Me, too," I said, although I wasn't; not then. I nudged Rudolph's foot with mine. "Hey, man. Hey, I don't know your name."

"Jack," he muttered, without looking up.

"Jack, listen to me. We're going to explore. Just a little. See if we can get some idea of what the heck's going on. If the door tries to close or the lift starts to move or you see anything— *anything* at all—out of the ordinary, yell at the top of your voice and we'll come running."

He nodded. I guessed that was the best I would get.

"Ready?" I asked American Girl.

"No." She took a deep breath. "But let's go."

« »

American Girl stuck so close to me that I could smell her perfume. Not unpleasant. Fruity. It mostly masked the musky scent of her fear.

We hadn't taken more than two steps from the lift. Her eyes looked large and dark in a face which had grown ivory pale.

"Okay?" I said.

She glanced back inside where Power Suit hadn't moved from her crouched position in the corner. Rudolph—sorry, Jack—had moved forward to stand near the door from where we should be able to comfortably hear him if he needed to holler.

"I'm okay," she replied.

We'd only taken one more step when I felt her tug on my jacket sleeve.

"My name's Kim," she whispered, as though we were tiptoeing through a hushed cathedral. "Short for Kimberly. You?"

"Matt."

"Short for Matthew?"

I didn't answer. What the hell did it matter?

"Stick close," I muttered.

Could have saved my breath. For the next few minutes, she became my second shadow.

Yeah, minutes. That's how long our jaunt into this bizarre version of the Sixth Floor of Claridge House lasted.

Long enough to nearly die.

Three

Taking a deep breath of scented air, I moved away from the door, curious to see what the lift looked like from outside. Would the car be visible, all aluminium panels, winches and cables?

What came into view was a brick wall, festooned with cobwebs. Puffs of dust lifted in the breeze like tiny smoke signals.

"That's the elevator shaft, right?" said Kim from behind me.

"I guess so. Look how high it is. The gubbins must be inside it."

"Gubbins?"

"Er, you know, the workings. Whatever makes it go up and down."

"Ah. Sure. Okay." She gave a high-pitched, feverish giggle.

I possess a highly developed sense of self-preservation, but I still didn't feel scared. Adrenaline and curiosity had combined to overcome the fear that must have been there, lurking, waiting to turn me into a quivering wreck.

The wall extended to the left a few feet more than it needed to contain the lift car; presumably to hold the recess which allowed the door, consisting of two overlapping panels, to slide out of sight when fully open. On impulse, I stepped forward on the springy turf and placed my palm against the brick. Powdery with dust, smooth and sun-warmed.

"It's real," I said. "It's really here, wherever this is."

"Are we still on Earth?" Kim sounded breathless and I shot her a glance.

Some colour had returned to her cheeks, but her eyes remained wide, like those of a deer about to bolt.

I shrugged. "How the hell do I know?"

We moved to the back of the lift shaft. Another dusty brick wall met us. Grass grew up to the wall. The ground hadn't been churned up as might be expected if the shaft had suddenly sprouted from underground. It looked as though it had always been there.

"Let's take a closer look at those trees," I suggested, nodding towards a small stand less than twenty yards away.

"Ooh, I don't know." Kim's tongue came out to lick her lips. "What if… I don't know, *something* happens?"

"It's not far. I'm going." I set off, my stride more confident than I felt. It was one thing walking around the lift shaft, close enough to touch it; another to walk away from it and safety.

"Oh, shoot!"

Rustling footsteps confirmed she was following. Air shot from my nose in an involuntary snort of relief.

The stand consisted of around a dozen trees, irregularly spaced, each the size of a mature apple tree. Purple fruit hung heavy from boughs, making them bend. The air grew redolent with a rich aroma.

"What are they?" I mused. "Plums?"

They looked more the shape of kidney beans than plums. The one dangling nearest me appeared close enough to reach if I stretched.

"Don't touch them!"

"I only want to…"

My fingers grasped the fruit. The skin felt velvety, like the outside of a peach, the flesh beneath firm. I tugged and it came away in my hand.

"It doesn't seem—" I began. "Urgh!" The fruit dropped to the ground as if it had given me an electric shock.

"What?" Kim took a step back.

"It moved. Something inside it wriggled."

"Aw, Jeez, let's get out of here." She took another backward step.

"No. Wait."

I crouched and peered down. The fruit nestled amongst thick grass, barely visible. Reaching with both hands, I pressed down on the blades around it, flattening them and revealing the fruit. Aware that my heart was racing and with my enthusiasm for this adventure fast waning, I cupped it in my hands and stood.

It moved once more, a small jump, as though I held a Mexican bean. This time, I repressed the impulse to fling it away.

"Come and see." I opened my hands so that the fruit lay flat against one palm.

It twitched again. A split appeared down its length and a line of pale orange showed against the deep purple.

"No! Put it down and let's get back to the elevator."

"Come on." My tone was coaxing and Kim stopped moving away, but refused to come any closer.

Sensible girl.

Imagine a fairy a little smaller than Tinkerbell from the Peter Pan movies. Swap Julia Roberts's head for Freddy Krueger's, *sans* hat. Bat ears complete the resemblance to a gremlin from that Spielberg movie. Change the cute frock to a covering of short, bristly fur; talons instead of hands and feet. No gossamer wings; they've been replaced by leathery, functional appendages, criss-crossed with black veins. No wand or showers of sparkly dust.

The fruit lay in two halves on my hand. The layer of pale orange flesh beneath the purple skin was thin, little more than a veneer. It had acted as a cocoon for the tiny creature that was shaking itself free and spreading its wings. They looked damp.

"Holy shit!" I muttered.

"Matt?" Kim's voice sounded from behind me. "*Matt?* What's happening?"

The creature raised itself to its full height, which couldn't have been much more than an inch. It flapped its wings once or twice experimentally. Or maybe to dry them. When it lifted its head and looked up, revulsion overcame me.

I flicked out my hand, flinging the fruit away.

"Yow!" The yelp of pain came out before I knew what was happening. I looked down at my hand.

The fruit had disappeared, but the creature hadn't. Wings

flapping so quickly they had become a blur, it had fastened on to my thumb, face pressed to the fleshy pad. From the sensation of hot needles boring beneath my skin, it was a fair assumption that the creature possessed razor-sharp teeth.

"Yow!" I yelped again. "The frigging thing's biting me."

I waved my hand from side to side, trying to dislodge my passenger. It was having none of it. Using its wings to help maintain balance, it clung on with talons and teeth. Judging by the excruciating pain in the pad of my thumb, the latter were long indeed for one so small.

"Get it off me! Kim, help!"

In fairness to the American, who must have been scared half to death by my yelling, she appeared by my side in an instant. She stared down at my hand.

"Oh my God what is that?" she said in a breathless rush. "That's disgusting!"

"Get it off me!"

"Are you nuts? I'm not touching that thing."

For a moment, our eyes met and I could see she meant what she said. Can't say I blamed her.

Blinking back tears of pain and fighting waves of revulsion, I brought my other hand across and grasped at the creature. With a hiss, I yanked the hand away, the skin of my right thumb and index finger torn and bleeding where it had been slashed by flapping wings.

My ineffectual attempt at grabbing the creature must have distracted it because the pain in my left thumb eased. The creature pulled away and hovered in the air a few inches from my hand. Blood dripped from its jutting chin down its furry front.

I took a step back in a hurry.

"Ow!" exclaimed Kim. "My foot."

"Sorry. Let's—"

Whatever else I was about to say was lost in a piercing, rising shriek that rent the air. Kim clutched at me, her fingers digging painfully into my arm. Head jerking like a hyperactive pigeon's, I cast around for the source of the sound.

It seems so obvious now, but wasn't immediately apparent to us in our panicked state. Of course, it was the creature that was shrieking.

Tiny mouth thrown wide, revealing row upon row of what indeed looked to be needle-sharp teeth still dripping with my blood, the creature gave full voice, belying its diminutive stature. Higher and higher rose the sound in a shrill crescendo. If there had been any glass in the vicinity, it would have shattered into a trillion, sparkling shards.

Kim released her grip on my arm and we both thrust hands over ears in a vain effort to block out the noise. It rose to an impossible peak, then stopped as abruptly as though a switch had been thrown. Cautiously, we lowered our hands to silence.

"Look," said Kim, gripping my arm once more.

The creature hadn't closed its mouth or relaxed its stance. It made no sound that we could hear but gave every appearance that it was still shrieking.

"No," said Kim. "Look at the trees."

I followed her gaze and my jaw dropped open, throbbing thumbs and finger momentarily forgotten.

Every bean-shaped, purple fruit dangling from the trees shook and quivered like crystal droplets on a fine chandelier during a mild earthquake.

One by one, then in a trickle, finally in a brief but violent shower, the fruit dropped to the ground.

Four

With Kim tugging on my arm, we backed away side by side. The creature, to which I shall refer as Freddy since that film character is indeed who it resembled, continued to hover, watching us, but closed its mouth, the aim of the shrieking apparently achieved.

"We need to get back to the elevator," said Kim, speaking slowly, enunciating each word in her American drawl as though addressing someone whose first language is Latvian. "I have a bad feeling about this. A *really* bad feeling."

"A flying gargoyle chewed on my thumb and *you* have a bad feeling?"

Freddy flew higher, hovering just beyond reach at eye level. The malevolence in its grin was unmistakable. Behind it, rising from the grass, black dots appeared. More and more, like a swarm of flies. Flies as big as tropical moths, with razor-sharp, leathery wings and movie monster faces.

Kim uttered a low moan.

"Run," I muttered. Louder: "Run!"

We turned. Or tried to. She was still gripping my arm. The swarm had grown as thick as a thundercloud.

Panic rising in my throat like bile, I shook Kim off, swirled to about face—she followed suit—and grabbed her hand.

We ran.

A combination of smooth-soled work shoes and thick, springy grass was not ideal for trying to sprint, but at least my clothes—loose-fitting trousers, open-collared shirt and lightweight jacket—did not hamper me. Not so Kim.

Her dark skirt came down to mid-calf with no slit to allow ease of movement. It's not being unkind, merely truthful, to observe that she wasn't a slim girl. While not exactly what I'd call fat, she filled her clothes with little room for manoeuvre. Add a clunky pair of high shoes and her ability to move quickly was seriously hindered.

While I took short, shallow paces in an effort to combat the slippery surface, Kim had no choice through the constraints of her garb but to do the same. We must have resembled cross country skiers, minus skis and poles, which sounds funny now but held no humour at the time.

"Oh, crap!" I muttered, hearing a buzzing drawing nearer. It was the sound of thousands of tiny wings beating against the fragrant air.

Kim moaned. Her grip on my hand held the desperate strength of a drowning person.

"Faster," I urged.

"I'm going as fast as I can."

We had almost reached the rear wall of the lift shaft. It was too warm for heavy exertion and sweat had broken out on my brow. The buzzing grew louder; I imagined I could feel the draught of flapping wings on my neck.

"Nearly there," I gasped.

We shuffle-ran past the brick wall to the front of the shaft, where I tried to turn abruptly on a surface on which I had little or no grip.

Physics took over: lack of friction teamed up with inertia. While my torso tried to turn towards the lift door, my legs continued their forward momentum. With a grunt, I fell flat on my face.

Kim's grasp was nothing if not tenacious. My landing on the thick grass didn't hurt; Kim's tight grip on my hand made it feel that my upper arm had torn loose from its socket, and *that* hurt.

Ignoring the burning pain in my shoulder, I raised my head towards the lift. The leather document case no longer obstructed the door and there was no sign of Rudolph standing in the opening—for a moment, I had forgotten his name. In fact, there was very little opening remaining; the lift door was sliding closed.

"No!"

A brief but bright vision flared in my mind of the door shutting completely and the brick shaft sinking into the ground, leaving Kim and me alone with thousands of peckish pixies with sandpaper wings and razor-sharp teeth.

I lunged with my free arm, causing fresh, hot pain to sear my shoulder as I yanked against Kim's grip. In my panic, I hardly noticed. My fingers scrabbled at the rapidly-diminishing gap and curled around the edge of the door as it tried to close, bringing a fresh gasp to my lips when the torn flesh of my thumb and forefinger came into contact with the metal.

For a second, it looked as though the door would shut on my fingers—perhaps there were no sensors this close to the floor—but it jolted to a halt with barely an inch gap remaining.

Kim's grasp on my hand grew tighter and she shrieked. It was an inhuman sound; if there were words mixed up in it, they were incoherent. I uttered a hissing shriek of my own as she yanked harder on my arm, causing me to slide across the smooth grass, my grip on the lift door becoming a tenuous, fingertip one.

A name popped into my overwrought mind.

"Jack!" I yelled at the gap. "Jack! Help! For pity's sake—"

How I managed to hold on to the lift door, or what would have happened if I'd let go, I'll never know, but hold on I did despite Kim's fresh tug on my arm in an apparent attempt to drag me away from the lift. I swivelled my head, trying to peer back at her without jeopardising further my fragile grasp on the only thing that represented sanity in this crazy place.

As though she had suddenly become charged with static electricity, Kim's shoulder-length hair rose in brown strands and clumps. Her neck bent backwards, cords standing out like veins on a weightlifter's biceps. I struggled to understand what I was seeing until I noticed the corona of madly-flapping wings surrounding Kim's head. The creatures had caught us up; employing their talons to snag and tangle the American's hair, they were using it to pull her away.

Ignoring the pain in my fingers and thumb, I tightened my grip on the edge of the lift door; my grasp on Kim's hand, too, despite the fiery pain in my shoulder.

Her breath came in short, hissing gasps as her head was forced back.

"Hang on," I told her. "I'll try to pull us towards the li—"

My words died in my throat. Using the lift door as an anchor point against which to try to yank us both forward would no longer be an option.

The door slid open, leaving my fingers clutching at air.

It's funny what you notice in the extreme of panic. The sweet scent of crushed grass, that's what I recall of those terrifying moments when I floundered on the ground, one arm stretched above my head seeking in vain anything to hold onto, the other held tightly by a woman about to be dragged away to her death.

The smell reminded me of a summer's afternoon, redolent with lazy heat, chirping grasshoppers and growling bees. For a moment, I hoped that I had fallen asleep in a deckchair in my parents' garden, having just finished mowing their lawn, a cold beer cooling my dry throat, and that this was merely a nightmare.

But the pain in my shoulder felt all too real. The smell of grass grew stronger as I began to be hauled sideways, crushing more fragrant stalks beneath my torso and flailing legs. I glanced back at the lift in desperation.

Two pale faces appeared as the door withdrew into its recess. Jack cowered in the corner of the lift, hands partly raised as though to ward off evil. Next to him crouched Power Suit, once more employing her document case as a shield. But her head was raised and she looked at me with wide eyes.

"*Please.*" My tone was pleading, almost wheedling. It didn't matter; nothing mattered except my relentless slide across the grass.

Kim screamed and my head jerked in her direction. Tears streamed from her tightly scrunched eyes. The hand not holding mine for dear life waved above her head, trying to dislodge flying creatures or clutching at taut strands of hair to try to relieve the pressure on her scalp. Blood flew from her hand; it seemed to make the creatures more frenzied.

My view became obstructed as one of them flitted between us, its gaze fixed on me. Blood still stained the needles protruding from its mouth. Although they all looked pretty much the same, I had no doubt that it was Freddy, the one who'd tasted the flesh of my thumb.

Swinging my free arm, I tried to swat it. It darted easily out of reach and uttered a high noise that must have been its version of a snigger.

Bringing my arm forward had been ill-advised. As my weight shifted, my body slid another foot. Kim's head had become obliterated by a swarming cloud of creatures.

It had taken a while, but at last I realised that my lying about on the grass wasn't helping her much. With a grunt and a fresh grimace of pain, I used her grip to bring myself to my feet. Grasping her wrist with my spare hand, digging my heels into the turf for leverage, I heaved.

She shrieked again and creatures scattered, still clutching strands and tufts of brown hair in their talons. But Kim was free. She buried her face against my chest, forcing me to take a step back.

That's when I felt the first needles of pain in my scalp.

Five

My hair has always grown thickly. Like a bramble thicket. It doesn't lend itself to being long so I keep it cropped. Just as well.

The flying creatures were entangling it and tugging, but were unable to gain much purchase due to the denseness and shortness of the hair, and the smallness of their talons. Unlike with Kim's fine, long strands, they could not gain any leverage from my bristly tufts. It didn't stop the little buggers from giving it a good go.

Hot tears sprang to my eyes, but now my arms were free. I swung them around, open-palmed, slapping creatures, keeping them away from my face and Kim's head. Fresh cuts opened on my fingers from their wings. Blood sprayed.

Kim wore a tweedy jacket. It lifted behind her as hundreds of them snagged it in an effort to drag her back. Many as they were, they were too lightweight. I slapped the jacket down with contempt, scattering hangers-on like confetti at the weird wedding from Hell.

Jerking my head from side to side to make it even more difficult for them to grab my hair, I edged back towards the lift. The biggest problem now was the slippery surface underfoot, made more treacherous where the grass had been flattened during my helpless slide of moments ago.

Freddy hovered nearby, waiting for an opening to latch onto me again. Something in its expression, some hint of malevolence that went beyond its normal expression of ugly malice, told me that it wanted a choicer morsel this time. An eye, maybe.

Kim pulled back from my chest so she could look up at me. Her breath smelled sour with fear, but her face was set in determination. My appreciation of the girl's courage began to turn to admiration.

"The elevator," she said. Her hand flicked out, making Freddy swoop out of reach. "We have to get back inside."

I nodded. "Together."

Waving our arms about like demented bookmakers, we shuffled, Kim forward, me backward. Creatures scattered under our flailing limbs. We were able to keep our footing, despite the slickness of the grass, due to the tiny steps we were taking.

Progress was going swimmingly well and we had almost reached our goal when someone grabbed me from behind.

Letting out a startled cry, I instinctively jerked forward and my feet went from under me, taking out Kim who collapsed on top of me. I fell onto my back, but not onto grass. Instead, I found myself lying on something bony.

"Oof! Get the hell off me," came a voice from ground level.

I twisted my head so I could see upon what I was lying. Or who. It was Jack.

"Get off!" he repeated.

Kim used me as leverage to push herself back to her feet, drawing a grunt from me and another curse from Jack.

I scrambled off him and rose unsteadily, my underfoot grip still uncertain.

There were no flying creatures in the immediate vicinity—this was all happening too quickly to look around to see where they'd gone—so I held out my hand to help Jack up.

"Why did you grab me?" I asked him.

"Only trying to help," he muttered. His bottom lip stuck out like a sullen child's and his gaze darted about nervously.

"Well, er, thanks."

If he meant to say something more, he was interrupted by a low moan coming from Kim. As I turned to her, I gasped at fresh pain. Jack had clutched my forearm, his nails digging in painfully through my jacket and shirt.

I shook him off. Kim stared over my shoulder in the direction of the lift, her eyes wide and disbelieving. I followed her gaze. Jack had already looked; what he'd seen, or rather not seen, had caused him to grab me in panic.

The lift was no longer there.

When faced by a situation that appears to promise certain death, the body reacts in peculiar ways. The stomach tries to climb the torso to change positions with the throat; the bowels loosen, their contents turning to slush; a faraway rushing sound begins between the ears; perspiration springs to hands and armpits as if they've been sprinkled with balmy water.

All these things and more were happening to my body. Unable to help myself, I let out a hot sigh of foetid wind. Not my finest moment, but nobody cared; there were more significant matters to occupy our attention.

The answer to where all the flying creatures had gone was there in front of us. They had gathered together in their tens of thousands and hovered, a living, seething mass. Undulating and pulsing like a murmuration of starlings.

The swarm was barely yards from us. Close enough that wafts of perfumed air puffed into our faces under the combined force of all those madly beating wings. Alone in front, just out of arms' reach, hovered Freddy. Difficult to be entirely sure due to the rictus into which their features seemed to be permanently frozen, but I'd swear it was grinning at me.

Kim stopped moaning. I became aware that she had stepped close to me when I felt her fingers dig into my left bicep.

"Will you both stop grabbing me!"

I jerked my arm to dislodge her grip.

"The elevator," she said, her voice small. "Matt, the elevator. Where's it gone?"

"Buggered if I know." In the extremity of my own shock, I was in no mood to treat her with kid gloves.

"My oh my oh my," she said without pausing between words. "We are all ways screwed."

In no position to disagree with her blunt assessment, I nodded.

"No," said Jack. "The lift's still there."

"Huh?"

"It's still there. It's behind those flying things."

"Huh."

He was right. The creatures were so numerous and had massed in such density they had obscured the lift, like a dark cloud blocking out the sun. In our distress at no longer being able to see it, Kim and I had wrongly assumed that the shaft had physically disappeared instead of merely visually.

"It's still there?" said Kim, her voice stronger but high-pitched, as if she teetered on the edge of insanity. Perhaps we all did.

"Yes," I said, although until I actually saw it, I didn't completely believe it.

"So how do we get back to it?"

The creatures were too numerous, in too tight a formation, to be easily scattered, or so I judged. Jack appeared to agree.

"There's too many," he muttered. "We'll never get through in one piece."

I shrugged. "We'll have to try. Can't stay here."

"And we need to try now," said Kim.

Some additional discordant note in her voice—a hint of hysteria—made me glance around. She was staring behind us. Maybe thirty yards away and closing came a new threat.

If the cloud obscuring the lift resembled a small rain cloud, the one approaching from the rear promised a storm of hurricane proportions. Perhaps fifty yards high and twice as broad, it must have been composed of hundreds of thousands, if not millions, of creatures. Even at this distance, the buzzing of their wings reached my ears.

"Oh Jesus H. Christ." Jack's face, pale to begin with, drained of the last of its colour.

"There must have been more fruit trees out there," said Kim. "A forest full."

"What…" Jack appeared to be struggling with something. He raised an arm and pointed with a quivering finger.

I looked back at the approaching swarm and gasped.

Maybe it was a trick of the light or my overwrought senses messing with my head. If so, Jack was experiencing the same delusion. Kim, too, judging from the disbelieving sounds coming from her direction.

The creatures had arranged themselves into a formation that resembled the outline of a hooded figure. Like a monk. Or Death.

"This is so fucked up," muttered Jack.

"Guys, I don't know why they're impersonating Darth Vader," said Kim, "and I don't really care. We need to get out of here."

In other circumstances, I might have found her observation amusing. I suppose the swarm did vaguely look like the outline of the villain of the *Star Wars* films, but to me the misshapen hump where the head would be suggested a baggy hood, not a helmet.

"Come on, then." I nodded towards the lift. "No time to linger."

Not waiting to see if Kim and Jack were following, I stepped forward. Freddy retreated, its gaze not leaving mine. A tiny black tongue came out and licked some of my blood off its fangs. When it reached the ranks of its comrades massed in front of the lift, it stopped and hovered as though waiting for me.

Taking a deep breath, I tensed and prepared to spring forward, my arms ready to windmill to keep as many of them off me as I could for as long as possible. The rushing sound began in my head and my stomach cramped.

"Here goes nothing," I muttered.

Six

Bravery is not my forte. If I had been a foot soldier in the Second World War, I'd have been examining my boots when the sergeant-major came round asking for a volunteer. Not even in more fanciful moments could I imagine myself storming a machine-gun nest single-handedly, armed with a rifle and a hand grenade. Yet, in effect, this is exactly what I was about to do.

Nothing to do with bravery, though. Everything to do with necessity. Maybe that's what drives most acts of valour.

"Wait!" Kim's voice was low but assertive.

"What?" I shook my head. "No time."

Her hand once more grabbed my arm.

"*Look*," she said.

A ripple ran through the cluster of creatures amassed in front of the lift. More than that: a commotion. As a shoal of fish will swoop and part and reform under attack from a predator, so the swarm moved, pulsing and swaying and thinning as though at random. Or in panic.

The lift briefly became visible through the seething throng along with a glimpse of violent movement. I could only see the cause of the movement for a few seconds before the creatures closed ranks, but it was long enough. My jaw dropped open in surprise.

Power Suit stood at the entrance to the lift, clutching in both hands a flat object the size of an encyclopaedia and the colour of sunflowers, swinging it from side to side, clearing breaches in the swarm that sealed almost immediately. A dark substance stained the smooth, yellow surface of her weapon.

The creatures had turned their backs to us in order to face Power Suit. She must have caught them from behind by surprise, but now she had their undivided attention. This would unlikely turn out well for her. They were too numerous, acting too much in concert, to be thwarted for long by one person and a big book.

"Now's our chance," I hissed at Kim and Jack, "while they're distracted. Let's kick some flying bug butt!"

Whirling dervishes on triple-strength espresso—that's what we must have resembled as we flung ourselves into the fray. Maybe it was the monk-shaped cloud of pixies approaching from behind like one of the Ten Plagues of Egypt lending us fervour, but Kim and I threw ourselves forward as if our lives depended on it, which of course they did. If the larger swarm overtook us, we were goners.

Jack lacked our enthusiasm. The few times I caught sight of him he was hanging back, biting his lip, eyes wide and cheeks chalky. I sort of understood. Kim and I had already been in close contact with the creatures and had, if only through exigency, overcome our revulsion. He, on the other hand, had not had to touch them and he looked like he had no intention of doing so now.

There was no time to concern myself with Jack. We cut a swathe through the smaller swarm, pinwheeling our arms, batting away anything that flew. My hands were curled tightly into fists to limit the amount of exposed skin and I mainly swatted creatures with my jacket-protected forearms.

Power Suit came back into view. Blood trickled from cuts in her forehead, but she seemed to be gaining fresh vigour from our entry into the fight. She swung the object—I could now see that it was a ring binder—like a woman possessed, stunning our adversaries with the force of her assault.

Between us, we scattered the cloud of creatures like a pile of autumn leaves blown by a sudden squall.

"Into the elevator!" Kim yelled and bounded through the doorway.

Power Suit backed in after her, still swinging the binder.

I was about to follow them when Jack pushed past me, making me stumble on the trampled surface. He muttered under his breath and didn't appear to notice me, so single-minded was his intent on gaining the sanctuary of the lift.

The lack of grip on my shoes told. I went down like a novice skater and once more my nostrils filled with the scent of crushed grass.

A dead creature lay by my face. 'Dead' seemed a reasonable description given the copious amount of gloopy, black liquid that seeped from the gap where the top of its head used to be.

"Matt!"

I craned my neck to look at the lift. Kim peered out, a frown of concern creasing her brow. She took a step onto the grass.

"No!" Bringing my elbows up beneath my stomach, I lifted myself to my knees. "Stay there. I'm coming."

"Hurry!"

She didn't need to tell me. The buzzing of the creatures approaching from behind sounded like an out-of-control chainsaw. In an undignified crawl-cum-stagger, I slipped and slid my way to the lift. Kim grabbed my arms and yanked me inside.

Power Suit still clutched the ring binder, now more sticky black than sunflower yellow. Two bright spots flushed her cheeks. Jack had made it to his corner and crouched against the rear wall, his back to the door.

The door that remained open. It took me a moment to realise why it hadn't closed: the document case stood next to it, lid raised, preventing the door from sliding shut.

Although the day remained bright and sunny, it had grown dark in the vicinity of the lift. The larger mass of creatures was nearly upon us. It no longer resembled a hooded figure; merely a huge, dark cloud.

"Close the door, Matt!" Panic lent stridency to Kim's voice.

I stooped and dragged the case into the lift. Before I could straighten, I felt pressure against my nose. The accompanying stab of pain flared bright, making me scrunch my eyes tight and sink back to my heels.

My hands groped at my face, opening fresh cuts to my fingers as I felt the familiar slicing movement of rapidly flapping wings. I forced my eyes open and peered blurrily through tears.

Freddy had clearly taken a liking to whatever my flesh tasted of—beer would be my best guess—and must have been hovering near the lift door, awaiting its chance. It had fastened firmly onto my nostrils, snagging one in each talon, and sunk its fangs into the fleshy tip of my nose. If I had poked out my tongue, I could have licked its belly.

Fed up of being yanked and slashed and grabbed and bitten, I no longer cared about damage limitation. I cupped Freddy between both hands and brought them hard together. Its wings stopped fluttering and I curled my fingers around the creature's body. Not pausing to wonder what further harm I might cause to my nose, I clutched tightly and yanked my hands away from my face.

"Fuuuck!"

Blood dripped down onto my lips and ran down my chin. I held Freddy up in front of my face and squeezed.

It opened its mouth and let forth a piercing screech. I squeezed harder. And harder.

Its head popped like an overripe grape in a gout of sticky goo. With an exclamation of disgust, I flung the small body to the floor.

The screech seemed to have spurred on the approaching swarm. Obscuring the last of the sunlight, droning like an irate nest of hornets, it arrived.

Freed of the document case obstructing it, the lift door began to slide across. It would not have moved fast enough to keep out the swarm had not the creatures paused as if to gather themselves to charge.

Holding my breath, I watched the door move, willing it to slide faster.

The swarm surged forward, coming for the kill. A low, keening noise sounded behind me. There were two women and one man sharing the lift with me, and the sound wasn't coming from the females.

The door slid closed.

A new sound came: a steady *thud-thump* of collisions with the outside of the lift door, increasing in intensity like a drumroll building to a climax.

Rising unsteadily to my feet, I swiped at the blood dripping from my chin, unable for now to touch my mangled nose. I kept my gaze fixed on the door, terrified that it might begin to slide open as it had done three times that morning when all I'd wanted was a fix of caffeine.

I became aware of movement from the corner of my eye. A few stragglers from the original swarm had found their way into the lift, but Power Suit had become masterful in her deployment of the ring binder, swinging it in short, sharp bursts that the creatures, nimble though they were, were not fast enough to avoid. One after another, they smashed against the walls, leaving a greeny-black trail on the shiny surface as they slid to the floor.

As satisfied as I could be that the lift door wasn't about to slide open, I took a step towards Jack, who still uttered the low wail. After all we had been through, the noise was beginning to seriously freak me out.

"Hey! Shut it!" I poked him in the back.

He grunted and hunched his shoulders, but blessedly shut up.

Power Suit lowered her ring binder, looking at it thoughtfully.

"Who'd have thought last month's sales figures would be so useful?" she muttered.

Kim opened her mouth as though to speak, but clutched at me instead as, with a jerk, the lift began to move.

Part 2: Fourth and Fifth Floors

One

My nose and thumb throbbed where Freddy had chewed on me, the cuts on my hands inflicted by talons and leathery wings stung, and my scalp ached where my hair had been tugged, but there was no time to take stock. The lift was already stopping.

Four pairs of eyes turned to look at the floor display.

5.

Power Suit had taken up her previous position at the rear next to Jack. She still held the ring binder, now dripping with gunk. The fiery spots were fading from her cheeks.

"Your floor," I said.

She nodded.

All gazes moved to the door.

It slid open.

Our minds become conditioned to seeing what they expect to see. One of my friends worked on Floor Five for a firm of surveyors, and I sometimes popped down to see him during breaks or to wait for him to finish work so we could go for a pint. (I would rather spend ten minutes in a grotty waiting room than occupying my own soul-less workspace for one minute longer than necessary.) I was therefore accustomed to stepping out of the lift into the reception area of the Fifth Floor, where the layout was slightly different to that of the Sixth Floor even before the latter turned into a pixie-infested rural landscape.

For a moment after the door opened, I saw the familiar worn carpet tiles, tired chairs and water-cooler that never contained any water. Then I blinked.

There *was* water—lots of it—but not suspended in an upside-down plastic bottle. As far as my eyes could see, there was nothing *but* water. A vast expanse which lapped gently against the groove along which the door moved, without seeping over the lip.

The water looked silvery-grey, reflecting the colour of a low, brooding sky. No land or structure or vessel interrupted the calm expanse; no creatures floated on the surface or flew in the air. A light, cool breeze broke the uniformity, creating an occasional ripple which made the surface shimmer like molten glass.

A faint chemical odour came to us on the breeze: tangy, not strong enough to describe as acrid, but almost.

Kim scanned the aquatic panorama, eyes wide and disbelieving. With a grunt, I sank to my knees in the doorway, meaning to rinse the blood from my hands so I could examine the cuts.

"Wouldn't do that if I were you."

The voice came from above. Power Suit had stepped forward and peered out at the water over my crouched form. Even Jack had turned to see what was happening, his face pale and his eyes unable to meet mine. I shrugged and returned my attention to the woman.

"Why, what's wrong?" I asked, as if there was anything *right* about any of this.

"Look at where it's touching the lift." Her arm appeared over my shoulder, finger pointing at the dirty, metallic sill.

Except it wasn't so dirty any more. Where the water lapped against it, the metal shone bright and silvery, as if it had been cleaned and scoured as good as new. The faintest wisps of vapour rose from the water's edge before being lost in the breeze.

Kim stooped. When she straightened, she gingerly held the gooey corpse of Freddy by the edge of a wing. She stretched out her arm and dropped it into the water with a *plop*.

The tiny body dipped out of sight, to immediately bob back to the surface like a ghastly buoy.

We all watched Freddy, hardly daring to breathe.

There isn't much in my bathroom cabinet aside from shaving equipment, deodorant, an old can of athlete's foot spray and a few containers of *Butch* talcum powder which my gran insists on buying me for birthdays even though I don't use the stuff. There is also a box containing sachets of supposed hangover cure. What you do is take a glass of water and empty the contents of a sachet into it. For a moment, nothing happens. Then the water begins to boil, its surface spitting and fizzing, as if it contains a shoal of attacking piranha.

Something similar happened to the patch of water in front of the lift. At first, nothing. Then the water began to bubble. The corpse of Freddy reanimated as it was buffeted by the commotion; it looked as though it was trying to flap its wings to escape the watery grave. Tendrils of vapour eddied in the breeze. Within a minute or two, Freddy became lost in a swirling mass of smoke. A popping, sizzling sound reached my ears; the odour borne on the breeze made my eyes sting.

A low moan came from Power Suit, a gasp from Kim as the smoke cleared. All that remained of Freddy, bobbing gently on the now-slack surface of the water, was a pale, chitinous skeleton.

"Oh god oh god oh god…"

It was Jack, muttering in a low but insistent voice, not pausing for breath.

"Shut up, there's a good boy," said Kim. "That's not helping."

Jack's lower lip quivered. For a moment, I thought he was going to cry. Instead, he opted for spite.

"Piss off, Yankee bitch. Why don't you go for a swim?"

"Oh, darling, I'm from Connecticut. Calling me a Yankee ain't an insult." She smiled sweetly. I felt relieved that her sassiness had returned.

Power Suit sank to the floor, her back to the rear wall of the lift. She still held the ring binder and stared at it blankly as though unable to recall what the gloopy stuff was on its cover.

"Hey," I said. When her gaze lifted towards mine, I held up my bloodied, aching hands. "Thanks for the warning. I would have frizzled these to stumps if it wasn't for you."

She shrugged.

"Erm… I'm Matt. What's your name?"

"Tara."

Jack sniggered. He'd obviously recovered from his shock. I

glared at him and he hurriedly looked away. That suited me; he was getting up my nose and if he started to get lippy, I was liable to thump him.

"Thanks, Tara," I said.

She shrugged again. "Don't go thinking we're all mates here. As soon as that door opens onto what it's supposed to, I'll go to my sales meeting and blank all this—and you people—from my mind."

"Oh, nice," said Kim.

"Nah," said Jack, without looking up. "She's got the right idea. None of this can be real so treat it as a dream or something."

"The blood on my hands is real," I said.

"And your nose," added Kim.

"And your head."

Where the flying creatures had yanked out strands of Kim's hair, bloody gaps showed. A trickle of blood, now dried, had run down to above her eyebrow.

"And that gunk on your binder is real," said Kim to Tara.

Jack made a high-pitched sound and I glanced at him. He stared past me, his newfound poise gone.

"You telling me *that's* real?" he said.

He held out a shaky finger, pointing out of the door.

At first, I couldn't see what he pointed at. Then I noticed something different about the water, maybe fifty yards away.

Something had risen above the surface. Drips tumbled from it like rain. It rose higher, as tall as a two-storey building. It wasn't easy to make out clearly since it was a similar slate-grey colour as the water and sky, but I gained an impression of a shimmering humanoid form, vague mounds on its torso suggestive of breasts, two blank silvery discs higher up that might have been eyes. Those discs turned towards us.

"Oh, man." Kim's voice held a tremor. "What is *that?*"

She reached to the panel on the wall beside her and started frantically pressing buttons. Nothing happened.

Since entering the lift that morning with a yearning to drink mug after mug of sweet, black coffee, I hadn't been in control of anything. Except when stepping out onto fragrant grassland and deciding to examine the fruit trees at closer quarters, I had merely been reacting to what was going on around me, events over which I had no influence. This never felt more true than when looking out from the lift at the apparition that had risen from the grey waters.

"Helpless," I muttered.

Kim glanced at me. "Huh?"

I shook my head.

"Oh, shit." Jack's voice came low, laced with dread. "She's moving."

It struck me that he, too, saw the figure as female, but there was no time to consider it further. She was heading directly towards us, yet other than she drew nearer there was no impression of movement. The water around her didn't churn or dimple, which might have suggested a wading motion of legs beneath the surface; the torso didn't sway; the arms didn't swing. She might have been resting on a wafer thin raft that glided forward silently without raising a ripple.

A sense of impotence swept over me in the face of such alien intelligence. And she *was* possessed of intelligence, I felt sure of it, if only from the calm manner in which she contemplated us with her silvery eyes. Watery eyes. In fact, the entire being consisted of water, which is why we were having difficulty seeing it clearly and how it could move so effortlessly.

It halved the distance between us before coming to an abrupt halt. It towered before us, huge and hairless yet unmistakably female, head cocked to one side.

"What's she doing" asked Tara.

"Sizing us up," said Kim.

"Someone do something," said Jack.

"Suggest something, brave guy," said Kim.

The figure disappeared, sinking into the water—into itself—

like a collapsing waterspout. A ripple expanded from the spot as though a pebble had been tossed in.

"Oh, bugger!" I exclaimed.

"Where's it gone?" said Kim. "Oh guys, where's it gone?"

Before anyone could answer, the surface in front of the lift dimpled. Freddy's skeleton was shunted aside as a patch of water rose six feet into the air, two silvery discs prominent near the top: pupilless eyes, as big as dinner plates, peering into the lift from less than a yard away. If I stretched out an arm, I could have dipped my hand into one.

The surface next to the head began to ripple, take form, rise. A two-fingered appendage, more claw than hand, attached to a diaphanous limb. It reached towards us.

Kim clutched at me and I clutched back, wanting to turn my eyes away from the approaching acid death, but powerless to. Powerless to do anything.

A sharp smell hit my nostrils, blurring my vision. The hand-claw—translucent, undulating—was barely inches from my face. With nowhere to run, nothing behind which to shelter, I stood and wondered what it felt like to be defleshed with acid.

Kim let out a strangled yelp and I was shoved roughly aside as Tara pushed past. She wielded the ring binder in two hands and swung it at the hand-claw like a block of wood. I ducked in anticipation of being sprayed by acid, but Tara must also have recognised the risk and cut the swing short, like a pulled punch. The binder struck the tip of the claw, scattering droplets before it. None hit us.

A brief deluge churned the surface as what remained of the limb collapsed.

Tara drew back her arm and flung the binder.

"Leave us alone, you bitch!" she screamed.

The binder flipped end over end, spilling pieces of paper like oversized confetti, and struck the creature roughly where its mouth would be had it possessed one. The water parted as the file passed through, but immediately closed again behind it. It reminded me of the molten metal from which the cop-robot had been constructed in the second *Terminator* film.

Our respite was fleeting. From beneath a surface littered with pieces of paper already smoking and bubbling, the limb rose again, complete with claw. Not only a fully re-formed claw, but one grown three times larger, the size of the bucket on a mechanical digger. It began to move towards us, slowly, as if its owner had grown wary. It had nothing to be wary of. No ring binder would halt the hand-claw's progress now; it would fill the lift doorway.

But Tara's intervention had bought us precious time; a delay during which the ageing mechanism which controlled the lift could go through its ponderous routines in preparation for moving between floors. With the new and improved version of the hand-claw mere inches from entering the lift, the door began to slide closed. Tara darted back, barging past me, to avoid tripping the sensors.

I continued to stare out as the door slid shut. If anyone else saw what I saw, they kept it to themselves. In the final second before this watery version of Floor Five disappeared, the female figure changed as smoothly as the cop-robot in that film. The hairless head filled out like a startled puffer fish, acquiring faint outlines of nose and thin-lipped mouth. The torso thickened; the breasts flattened. The diaphanous arm grew wider, while the hand-claw shrank and gained a few more fingers; it stuck out from the end of the limb like a hand protruding from an oversized sleeve. An identical arm and hand appeared on the other side of the torso.

My last glimpse was of a pair of silvery, glinting eyes regarding me from beneath the shimmering impression of a baggy hood.

Then the door closed and my stomach fluttered with the familiar sensation of the lift dropping between floors.

Two

Old and decrepit it might have been, but the lift seemed to be coping well with its jaunts between dimensions. That was, and is, my best guess for what we were doing: inter-dimensional hopping. Hardly an explanation, but I have nothing else to offer.

The car juddered to a halt in its usual manner and we all glanced at the digital readout above the panel of buttons.

4.

"I guess it did want to go to the Fourth Floor, after all," said Kim, with a nervous-sounding laugh.

A blast of hot, dry air hit me in the face, taking my breath away, as the door slid open.

We peered out onto a desert landscape. Bleached sand baked beneath a blazing sun.

"Is that..." Kim gulped. "Is that *our* sun?"

I narrowed my eyes and glanced up through my lashes at the buttery disc in the bone-pale sky.

"Dunno." I looked away and blinked to clear my vision. "Looks a little bigger than ours. Just as bright. Perhaps more yellowy. And there's a dark red spot near its edge."

Kim gasped.

"A dark red spot... is that normal?"

I shrugged. I was more interested in the landscape.

The lift opened onto the floor of a broad, roughly circular depression. White sand rose in soft undulations, like gently drifting snow, to a ridge maybe a hundred yards distant. Heat made the air shimmer. Sweat had already broken out on my brow and trickled down my back. I shrugged my jacket off and dropped it in the corner.

Nothing moved except the air. No flora or blanched bones broke the monotony of the sand.

A movement from behind drew my attention. Jack was taking short breaths, hopping from foot to foot.

"Need a pee," he said, noticing me looking. "All that water on Fifth…"

I nodded towards the desert.

"Out there. Don't you dare go in here."

His only answer was a scowl. I turned away, not trusting myself to get into a conversation with him. I hadn't forgotten that he had made me stumble and fall with a few hundred thousand needle-toothed pixies bearing down on us.

"What now?" asked Kim, looking my way.

Quite why she thought I'd have the answers was beyond me.

"We climb to that ridge," said Tara. She pushed past me once more and took a tentative step onto the sand. When nothing happened, she turned back with a twisted grin. "This time I'm coming, too."

Before we set off towards the ridge, I took a quick trip around the lift shaft, not straying from within touching distance of it. Kim and Tara looked at me anxiously as I returned to the open door.

"Any signs of life?" Kim had removed her tweed jacket. The blouse she wore beneath was short-sleeved, for which she must have been thankful, although her long, dark skirt looked like it would absorb heat. A line of perspiration already glistened on her top lip.

I shook my head, dislodging drops of sweat which ran down my cheeks. "No vegetation. No rib cages poking out of the sand. Nothing."

"Which way shall we go?" asked Tara. She still wore the jacket of her power suit and did not appear to be sweating. An ice lady, this one.

"The dip seems fairly uniform and we're pretty much in the centre of it," I said. "The same distance to the ridge, the same gradient in all directions. Probably best to head up from the doorway so we can get back in quickly if we need to."

Kim shot me a strained, quizzical glance which echoed what I was thinking: what were we going to find beyond that ridge that would make us want to get back inside in a hurry?

After positioning Tara's document case in front of the retracted door and admonishing Jack not to let the door close with us still outside—he grunted an acknowledgement without looking up—we set off.

The sand was yielding, swallowing our feet to the ankles, forcing us into a trudging motion that soon told on thighs and calves, and crunched a little underfoot. "It sounds like we're stepping on potato chips," remarked Kim.

Unhampered by a tight-fitting skirt, I had soon pulled a little ahead of the women.

"What do you do?" Kim asked Tara behind me. Before she could answer, Kim continued, "Look, I know you think this is all some sort of weird dream. What's the point of being civil to us when we're not real, right? At least, you know *we* are real, but this situation must be fantasy. Right? I get it. But why not make the dream as pleasant as possible? Humour me. What d'you say?"

There was a brief silence, broken by a deep sigh. "You're right," said Tara. "None of this is real. None of this *can* be real. But I suppose it won't hurt to pretend to like you."

Kim chuckled. "Well, nobody can accuse you of being tactful. So, give. What do you do?"

"I'm a sales manager on the Fifth Floor for a company that manufactures prosthetic limbs."

"That's handy," I muttered, unable to resist.

"Oh," said Tara in a world-weary tone, "we have a comedian among us. Save your breath, funny guy. I've heard them all before." She resumed her conversation with Kim, dismissing me as contemptuously as I probably deserved after attempting such a weak joke. "Of course, the limbs aren't manufactured in Claridge House. That's merely the admin centre. The manufacturing *arm* is located elsewhere."

I grunted. "Touché."

"So," continued Tara, "er, Kim, was it? What brings an

American to the U.K.?"

"Met a British guy when he transferred to Head Office in Hartford. Fell for him hook, line and sinker. We got married and I came with him when he transferred back here. I thought he was the sweetest, most handsome guy I'd ever met. Turned out he was the world's biggest shit. We got divorced and I decided to stay. Changed jobs and now work for the loss adjustors on Fourth. Worse pay; marginally more exciting work."

"You going to settle permanently in Britain?"

"Undecided. The weather's pretty crummy. You married?"

"Not unless you count my job. I'm turning thirty-four next month and aim to be head of division by the time I'm thirty-five."

"That's a shame. There's more to life than work, sweetie."

"Not to me there isn't." A hint of frigidity had crept into Tara's voice.

Kim was either oblivious to it or chose to ignore it.

"What about you, Matt?" she said. "What do you do up on Sixth?"

"I ring people and try to sell them product replacement cover for digital television systems." I shrugged. "The best I can say about it is that it pays the rent."

Sweat ran freely down my back, but that wasn't the reason I felt uncomfortable. It was always the same when anyone asked me what I did for a living. It wasn't the cold-calling and trying to sell people insurance they rarely wanted or needed, so much as the reminder of the aimlessly meandering course my life seemed to have taken since joining the workforce. Aged twenty-six, nearly eight years out of school, I had worked at a succession of jobs without a great deal of enthusiasm or success. The only things I seemed any good at were drinking beer and coffee, and procrastinating. The perfect job, one that I could turn into a career, the girlfriend I'd want to get serious with, the place I'd want to buy instead of rent, was always the next one, the one I sometimes thought about going out to get rather than waiting for it to fall in my lap, before shrugging and going down the pub.

If Kim held an opinion on what I did for a living, she kept it to herself. Instead, I heard her mutter and the next moment she let out a squeal of pain. I turned.

She had removed her clunky shoes and trod barefoot on the sand. It was understandable that she had taken off her shoes. Mine had filled with grit that made it feel I was trudging through drying concrete.

"The sand," she explained in answer to my enquiring look, "is hot as hell."

Tara snorted. "Really? What did you expect?"

She still wore her power suit jacket, though I noted with a stab of satisfaction that her hair clung damply to her forehead.

I grabbed Kim's hand to stop her toppling over while she struggled to replace her shoes.

"Your skirt's long," I said. "Might be cooler if you yank it up to your knees."

Her cheeks were already red from heat and exertion so I couldn't be certain that she blushed. Tara gave another snort, a knowing one, and turned away.

Kim shot me a dark look and concentrated on fastening the straps on her shoes.

"What?" I felt genuinely puzzled.

Kim straightened, jaw set in a firm line. She planted her legs in the sand, shaking off my supporting hand.

"You have a lot to learn about women, honey. It's not summer…" It was her turn to snort; I began to think they had sinus problems. "I mean, where we've come from it's not summer. So we don't bother shaving our legs. You may think I'm a brash American, but I don't expose my hairy legs to anyone."

There was nothing I could think of to say, other than to comment on how ridiculous the amount of weight women attached to certain things that to me were meaningless, especially in the circumstances in which we found ourselves. But I was outnumbered and so wisely, for once, kept my mouth shut.

Three

Sweat oozed from every pore in salty springs, stinging my mangled nose, and my shirt clung to me like damp muslin. I felt as though I'd stepped out of a too-hot shower.

The searing heat and silence, only broken by the *scrunch* of our steps and shallow breaths, grew oppressive. By the time we reached the summit of the depression, we were in need of water.

I hauled myself onto the lip of the ridge to gain the broadest perspective. Tara and Kim arrived moments later, panting like dogs.

A flat, featureless landscape lay before us, unbroken by tree or bush or building or living thing. I turned slowly until I faced back down the slope. The view looked the same in every direction: a broad expanse of pale sand shimmering in a golden heat haze.

Except that the haze wasn't quite as golden as it had been. The sun had slipped towards the horizon, yet the air hadn't grown dimmer. Its quality had nevertheless changed, become ruddier, lending a sinister feel to the place.

I gave a low whistle. "Weird."

"What is?" Kim asked breathlessly.

"It should be darker. Look, the sun's setting, but the air's almost as bright as when we arrived. The light's grown, well, *redder.*"

She laughed. It sounded high and unnatural.

"The elevator stopped at the Fourth Floor of a scruffy office building. We should have stepped out to ringing phones and sludgy coffee, but instead we're standing on a dune with sweat pouring from us in the middle of a freaking desert. Yet you find *that* weird?"

She laughed again in that high pitch I found unnerving. My nose throbbed, my legs felt like they'd been pounded with a steak tenderiser and I had a raging thirst. I bristled.

"Of course I find this desert and that acid sea woman and

those flying gargoyles weird. It's *all* bloody weird. But you stand there in your too-long skirt and stupid shoes and pitch a hissy fit because I notice yet another weird thing? The sun's starting to dip below the horizon and it should be twilight, but it's not. Just because there's lots of other weird stuff going on doesn't make that less weird. And it's a lift, not a frigging elevator!"

Kim's face twisted in a way that I thought meant she was going to cry. Until she opened her mouth and I realised that she was furious.

"Look, buster, this skirt and these shoes are what I wear to the office. The *office*. If I'd known I was going to be playing at Lawrence of freakin' Arabia I maybe would have dressed in shorts and sneakers. Oh, and I'd have shaved my legs because it's what's expected of us by the likes of you. God forbid that we should show our bristled calves to the world while you stand there and let hair grow on your chin like a fungal infection. No, that's fine, mister high and mighty. You're a man and you make all the rules. Well, let me tell you, I'll have bristles if I want them and I'll call an elevator an elevator if I want and *screw your rules!*"

Kim reached down with both hands and rolled up her skirt until it formed a sausage above her knees. She paused to glare at me before rolling it to mid-thigh. The newly-exposed flesh glistened faintly with perspiration. It also looked more shapely that I'd imagined. My anger drained away as though a plug had been pulled.

Before I could utter conciliatory words, Tara spoke over me.

"Shut up, you two. Something's coming."

Approaching through the heat haze, maybe a couple of hundred yards away, came small puffs of sand, heading directly for where we stood on the lip of the ridge.

"Oh, crap," said Kim. "What now?"

"We'd better get back to the lift," said Tara. She no longer sounded like an ice maiden; more like a scared teenager.

"Wait," I said. "Whatever it is, I don't think it's very big. And it's alone."

Unless the surface was more compact and easier to traverse on the open plain, whatever caused the dusty disturbances possessed the ability to move quickly without being hampered by deep, dry sand.

A shape could now be made out, becoming clearer as it drew nearer.

"It's not huge," said Kim. "About the size of my Ronnie—he's a chocolate Labrador—when he was a three-month-old pup."

"Maybe," said Tara, "but that's no pup coming towards us."

She was right, although I didn't know what it was. Rusty-orange in colour, it appeared to be hairless. It had a head and a body but no tail. Forward movement seemed to be achieved in a rocking motion, like the movement of a small boat caught head-on in choppy seas. It took me a little while to understand why it threw up so much sand in its passage: it had not two pairs of legs, but five, spaced equally down its torso.

"Jeez Louise," muttered Kim. "It's some sort of mutant."

The creature drew closer and I could make out its legs more clearly. The front and rear two pairs were jointed and moved in much the same way that a dog's legs move. They ended in trotter-like feet which sank into the sand with each step. But the middle legs were shorter, unjointed, and ended in three broad, flat toes that spread on the sand's surface and allowed the front or rear pairs of legs, depending on its stride, to break clear of the surface and bound forward, while their counterparts sank and presumably gained leverage from the more tightly packed sand that lay beneath the surface.

It didn't look the most gainly motion, but it was effective. The creature was almost upon us.

Tara uttered a low moan. "Look at its face. Aw, look at its face." She shuffled a couple of steps backwards, her patented leather shoes burying themselves in the soft sand that we had trudged up to gain the ridge.

How the creature noticed us I don't know, but it came to an

abrupt halt, rear legs planted in the sand, its front half raised towards us. It did not possess anything that were recognisably eyes. Its face, or at least the front portion of the lump above its body, consisted of wrinkled skin surrounding a gaping maw and nothing else. No nose or nostrils, no ears, no horns or antennae or other appendages. A circle of red, glistening tentacles lined the entrance to the maw as though it had tried to swallow a sea anemone.

"Ugh!" exclaimed Kim. "That's *gross!*"

I couldn't disagree. The red tentacles lining the maw rippled, like fronds in a breeze. It felt like the creature was watching us intently, or perhaps tasting our scent or listening to us through its mouth. It didn't seem to like what it detected for it eased the front part of its body forward, at the same time pivoting on the central legs so it faced a little to the right. Then it resumed its forward motion on a diagonal arc that would avoid both us and the depression in which the lift shaft had emerged.

My breath came out in a heavy sigh. Tara wore a frown that said 'why on earth did I leave the safety of the lift?' Kim looked as relieved as I felt that the pup-sized creature had avoided us.

"Time to return to the elevator," she said.

She'd get no argument from me; even less from Tara, who had already turned and started down the slope.

Kim and I had barely taken two steps in her wake when the pounding began.

Anyone who's ever stood on the grassy enclosure alongside a race course will understand what I mean when I say that the vibrations of something approaching, something big and heavy, could be felt in the soles of my shoes. Not as powerful as the *thrumming* sensation that's experienced when a dozen racehorses go pounding past throwing up clods of turf in their wake, but otherwise there was little difference.

Tara looked back, her eyes as wide as a lemur's.

"The lift." Her voice dropped to barely a whisper. "We need to get back to the lift."

She took a stride with her right leg, leaving her patented shoe behind in the sand. She carried on without pause, only the black nylon of her tights shielding the skin of her foot from the baking heat of the sand.

I picked up the shoe, turning it upside down to let the sand which filled it run out.

"Hurry," said Kim.

The vibrations in the soles of my shoes grew stronger. I became aware of a distant pounding sound, a rhythmic *thump-thump-thump* like the noise of someone approaching from afar beating on a bass drum. It grew louder and our efforts to descend the slope grew more frantic.

A pale face appeared in the lift doorway, peering anxiously up the slope. Evidently Jack could feel the pounding, or hear it, and he beckoned frantically. We didn't need his urging to hurry; we were struggling through the sand as fast as we could.

Going down the slope was easier and quicker than trudging up it. Tara had already reached midway; Kim and I weren't far behind. The American seemed to find the going less arduous with her skirt hoiked to her thighs.

Now and again I stole a glance back, certain that the source of the thumping must appear behind us. The sound reached a plateau, not gaining intensity but not receding either. It seemed to be skirting the depression, causing me to glance anxiously at the ridge.

We had drawn close enough to the lift to see Jack clearly. He had moved Tara's document case away from the door and waved a hand at us in an impatient get-a-move-on gesture. We could also hear him.

"Hurry the fuck up!" His expression was filled with dread. "I don't know what's making that noise and I'd rather not find out."

Tara had closed the gap between her and the lift to around twenty yards—Kim and I were maybe another five yards behind— when we discovered the source of the pounding.

Four

The reverberations through our feet and incessant thumping abruptly ceased. Movement in the corner of my right eye turned my head. A figure had appeared on top of the ridge. A large figure.

For a moment, my legs refused to move.

The figure stood as tall as a horse, but upright on two legs which looked as powerful as a kangaroo's. It was coated in a pelt of rippling hairs, the colour of which shifted, difficult to pin down, like one of those shimmery, two-toned shirts people used to wear to discos in the seventies; if pushed, I'd say it was dirty grey fading to off-white. Mushroomy.

A torso as broad as a silverback gorilla's gave way to a tree-trunk neck and head the size of a small boulder. Disproportionately short arms like knotted rope tapered to claws as yellow as bile. The claws clutched the lifeless body of our friend with five pairs of legs. A liquid the colour of heavily oxidised iron oozed from the gap where its head had been.

Kim groaned. She, too, had come to a halt and her expression must have mirrored mine: extreme apprehension with more than a hint of disgust.

Tara continued towards the lift; she had closed the gap to ten yards. Her movements had quickened, an impression of urgency suggesting that she had seen what was watching us.

If 'watching' is the correct word. Like the lifeless form it clutched, the new arrival did not possess anything that could be described as eyes. Its head cocked at an angle as though straining to pick up sound—the way my heart hammered behind my ribs, it would have to be as deaf as a rock not to hear it—at the same time revealing slits more resembling gills than ears. A hole roughly the size and position of a mouth opened at the front of its head; something protruded, red and glistening with serrated edges.

"What is *that?*" I murmured. "Its tongue?"

Kim uttered a high-pitched giggle. "It looks like a bread knife. An organic bread knife."

Again she giggled—it was *way* too shrill—and I understood that she was close to losing it. I reached out my hand to grip hers reassuringly when the creature moved.

Allowing the headless corpse to fall with a dull *clump* to the sand, the creature started down the slope. Immediately the vibrations in the soles of my shoes began anew and the *thump-thump-thump* sound resumed. I could now see the cause.

As soon as its feet came into view, the creature became known to me as Paddlefoot. Shaped like the head of a broad-bladed paddle, each the size of a dinner tray, the feet hit the sand with that reverberating, thumping sound, spreading Paddlefoot's weight and allowing it to move across the soft surface with surprising speed.

Scary speed. Heading directly for Tara. Jack's pale face darted back out of sight into the lift.

Kim let out a yelp, whether of terror or warning I wasn't sure, and Paddlefoot's head darted briefly in her direction, the red protrusion snapping towards her and quivering. But it did not deviate from its course. It would be on Tara within moments.

She must have heard Kim's cry for she half-turned towards the creature. If she still thought this was some sort of waking nightmare, it didn't show. The panic in her bearing as she attempted to sprint the remaining few yards to the lift suggested she regarded the approaching threat as all too real.

She almost made it. A few yards from the lift entrance her remaining shoe, heavy with grit, came off her heel as she brought her foot down, causing her ankle to twist and pitching her sideways to the sand.

Paddlefoot bore down on her.

Discomforts like thirst, excessive heat and fatigue are thrust aside by a rush of adrenaline. As fast as was possible in that terrain, I dashed forward, Kim a pace or two behind. I'll say it again: that girl was one brave cookie. Despite her obvious fear, she didn't hesitate in hurrying to Tara's aid. Whether there was anything either of us could do was another matter.

My mind raced, thinking about, of all things, grizzly bears. Perhaps a rural myth, but weren't they supposed to stop attacking if they believed their quarry to be carrion?

"Tara!" I hissed. "Play dead."

She had begun to raise herself up on her elbows, but lowered herself back to the sand when she heard my voice. The creature had come to a stop huddled over her; the serrated protrusion poked further from the hole in its face.

Without speaking, Kim and I changed our angle of approach so that we would come in behind Paddlefoot rather than from the side.

The tongue—for lack of a more apt name to call it—continued to extend, red and glistening like a fresh murder weapon, until it touched Tara's shoulder. As if it had been subjected to a jolt of electricity, a quiver ran through the creature, making its colours shimmer.

With the snaking movements of a blind, questing worm, the tongue moved up the jacket of the power suit to the back of Tara's head. Pausing briefly as if to savour the anticipation of contact with flesh, it probed above the collar of the jacket, under her hair and stroked the nape of her neck.

It must have been taking a huge effort of will for Tara to hold it together sufficiently to lie motionless with the creature in such close proximity, but the sensation of its caress on her bare skin pushed her over the edge.

Kim and I both slewed to a halt on the soft surface on hearing Tara scream. She was almost completely obscured by the broad back of Paddlefoot, its fur rippling in rapturous spasms, but I could see enough to know that she was scrabbling towards the lift on her stomach, trying to escape the tongue's touch.

The creature bent at the waist as though bowing to royalty and Tara gave another shriek, this time not of revulsion but agony. Paddlefoot's arms were too short to reach her without bending itself almost in half. It had taken a swipe at her, tearing the back of her jacket to ribbons with its claws.

It drew its other arm back a little—it only seemed to be able to pull them back far enough to clap—to slash at her again.

"Matt, do something!" Kim looked at me with a mixture of helplessness and entreaty.

Without thinking what I was doing—there was no time for reasoned consideration—I raised my right hand, which still clutched Tara's discarded shoe, and brought it down as hard as I could onto Paddlefoot's bent back.

To my surprise, the shoe did not encounter solid muscle, tough as tempered steel. The blow landed to one side of where the spine would be, assuming the creature had one; it felt like hitting a hairy pillow. I wished fervently that Tara had been wearing stilettos, even had it meant my toes being at risk of injury when she stepped back onto my foot on the Sixth Floor. I could have inflicted some grievous bodily harm with a pointy-heeled shoe in my hand.

I brought the shoe down again with all the force I could muster. Paddlefoot straightened.

When looking back on a terrifying incident, it often appears in retrospect to have occurred in a confused mix of freeze-frame and fast-forward motion. The oddest, most irrelevant details are recalled with the clarity of a high-definition photograph; more significant moments pass in a jerky blur.

Thus was my memory of the few minutes during which I engaged Paddlefoot. The way its creamy-grey pelt rippled like the legs of a scurrying millipede is as clear to my mind's eye as if the incident had happened yesterday. Yet the red-hot sensation as the barbed 'tongue' whipped out and wrapped itself around my arm can only be recalled vaguely; it might have taken place months ago to someone else who later told me about it.

One firm whack with the shoe was all it took to make the tongue unwrap itself from my arm and withdraw to a safe distance. There is still a pale weal around my left forearm; it looks like the scar left by a jellyfish tentacle. It would probably have been more severe if my shirt sleeve hadn't protected me from the worst of its sting.

I have a theory about the nature of that creature: I believe it to have been an apex predator, at the top of the food chain in that place, wherever and whenever that place existed. If it had predators itself, it would surely have developed better defence systems. As far as I could tell, its sole protection was its fur coat. Its weapons—the serrated tongue and its foreshortened, clawed arms—were designed for offence; as defensive implements they were useless.

Only its pelt saved it from serious damage. What saved me was the shortness of its arms, the limited range with which it could spread them and its inability to reach behind itself. I was also helped by the impracticality of those enormous, paddle-like feet, which made about-facing in a hurry an impossibility. As it lumbered awkwardly around to try to bring me within reach of its claws, my strategy became obvious.

"Quickly," I hissed to Kim. "Get Tara inside the lift. And stay behind the furry bugger. It's not built for turning quickly and can't do much when we're behind it. If that tongue comes near you, thump it."

"Okay."

"Yell when you're safely inside."

"Be careful."

Kim moved forward, taking herself behind Paddlefoot.

It completed a half-turn towards me. The red tongue quivered, an anticipatory shiver that promised it would yet taste my flesh when I fell to the claws.

Five

S cent. That must be how Paddlefoot detected us. By hearing, too, utilising those gill-like slits at the side of its head. I am, of course, only surmising, but I believe it could smell us through sensors located in its red tongue.

And what a musky scent we must have been giving off. Sweat and fear, a potent mix. If my suppositions are correct, we must have presented vivid olfactory images for the creature to track.

At any rate, it had no problem sensing me, even if it struggled to match my circular crabbing movements which kept me out of reach of those arms.

In my peripheral vision, I became aware of activity as Kim attempted to get Tara to the lift. Then the flaw in my strategy hit me: the more I circled around Paddlefoot to stay out of reach of its claws and the more it followed my movements, the closer it came to facing Tara and the lift.

Oh bollocks!

I risked a glance to my right.

Kim had stooped, her arm around Tara's waist, struggling to support her. Tara had managed to partly raise herself and was trying to crawl across the scorching sand with Kim's help. A bare heel poked out of a hole in the nylon covering her shoeless foot. Strips of shredded jacket flapped gently in the breeze.

"Hurry!" I hissed.

They had almost reached the lift, Tara's fingers inches from touching the raised sill which glinted red where it had been scoured clean by an acidic ocean.

Red?

While my attention had been diverted by Paddlefoot, the last of the golden tint had leached from the sky. Instead of dusk deepening to night, the air had become ruddier, illuminated by a rosy glow as though the sun had not set but remained suspended in the sky with a sheet of scarlet gossamer draped over it.

But there was no time to wonder about the source of the glow. The creature had completed its turn and leaned towards me, its arms swinging…

With an undignified *squawk*, I stumbled backwards. My feet, encumbered by sand weighing down my shoes, caught in each other and I tumbled to the scorching ground. Yellow claws, bearing bloody stains, slashed the air where my face had been a moment before.

In a frenzied effort to gain purchase which flung sand in every direction, I managed to scramble back to my feet. The serrated tongue darted towards my neck—probably to drag me back within range—and I remembered in the nick of time that I still clutched Tara's shoe.

Paddlefoot had not grown accustomed to being whacked with patent leather and rubber. The tongue recoiled under my assault, whipping from side to side like a live cable until out of my reach. The creature bounded forward, moving easily over the shifting surface. I paused for a split second so it would not have time to change direction, then dived to one side.

Heat, thirst and fatigue combined to interfere with my timing. A swinging claw caught the cuff of my trousers, turning it to ribbon, sliced through a sock and scored a groove along my ankle.

"Sod this…" I drew in a hissing breath as pain flared "… for a game of soldiers."

Paddlefoot slowed but did not stop. It clearly possessed cunning, judging by the way it seemed to know that it could turn quicker on the move than while standing still. The pounding *thud-thud-thud* coursed through my body as I lay on the sand, panting.

A sense of resignation fell over me like a damp blanket; I had little more to give.

Other than stare at anxious-looking people, there's not much to do in a dentist's waiting room except flick through one of the tattered Sunday supplement glossies about country homes or fine furnishings that someone seems to think will take patients' minds off their impending treatment. In one such magazine, I read an article about how furry animals stay cool in summer. Apparently, their fur traps air which the sun first has to heat before it can get to work on their skin. Through moderate movement to replenish the air, the animal has a built-in cooling system.

Despite the disappearance of the sun, the sand continued to bake under whatever caused the ruddy tinge to the air. Heat rose in shimmering waves and sweat ran from me in salty streams. When I struggled back to my feet, sand stuck to my sodden shirt like sugar to a damp finger.

Paddlefoot, with its natural cooling system, seemed able to exert itself in that debilitating environment without obvious handicap. It completed its turning arc and came at me again, picking up speed.

And it was learning. As I tensed to leap aside once more, it slowed fractionally, not sufficiently to give it time to follow my movement but enough to deliver a raking blow as it passed.

I sat on the sand, clutching my right arm. The shirt over my biceps had been shredded into strips like coleslaw cabbage. Blood seeped between my fingers and ran down my arm. Paddlefoot's tongue spasmed; it could smell something new. A rich, coppery scent.

"Matt!"

Kim beckoned from the entrance to the lift, glancing from me to the wheeling creature. The document case had disappeared; all that prevented the lift door from closing was Kim. It began to slide towards her.

Paddlefoot completed its turn. I scrambled to my feet, sand caking my bloody fingers, and lurched towards the lift. I hadn't enough energy to attempt the dodging trick again.

The next problem immediately presented itself.

The sensors located along the leading edge of the lift door operate thus: when an obstructing object is detected, the door does not retreat a few inches before trying to close again so that it bumps repeatedly against the obstruction, but opens to its fullest extent and pauses for a few moments before attempting once more to close. The delay is designed, presumably, to allow the offending object to be moved out of the way.

As noted with a hint of caffeine-deprived exasperation when I was anxious to reach Sixth and coffee, the actions of the door sliding closed, detecting the obstruction, sliding back open, then pausing for a deep breath before repeating the process, seems ponderous, frustratingly slow when occupants are anxious to be on their way.

But then it had been a mere irritation. Now the laboriousness of that process was about to get me killed.

The door closed as far as where Kim crouched in the doorway. The sensors detected her and it slid open again, juddering back into its recess.

I continued lumbering towards the opening. The ground vibrated beneath my feet and the *thud-thud-thud* sounded frighteningly near. At any moment, I expected to feel stinging heat in my back as bloodied claws sliced it open.

My tattered corpse would only be the start of the slash-fest. I was leading Paddlefoot directly to the lift where its bulk would block the entrance and it would have captive prey to reduce to meaty strips at its leisure.

"Quick!"

Despite the desperation in Kim's voice, for a moment I faltered. I knew what I needed to do: change direction, lead the creature away from the lift, give the others time to allow the door to close and escape without me.

Even if I were the sort to perform selfless acts to save lives at the expense of my own—it turned out that there *was* one among us capable of such bravery, though I'd never have guessed it then—I wasn't physically capable of leading the creature a merry dance across the desert. I barely had enough energy left to close the last few yards to the lift; none with which to entice my pursuer away from it.

Sweat streamed into my eyes. The creature could have had no problem 'seeing' me; the smell I exuded must have been as strong as runny Stilton.

Kim reached out to grab me as I arrived at the threshold, drawing a hiss from my parched lips when her fingers dug into my slashed arm. Then I was stumbling into the lift's interior.

In the depth of exhaustion, the next few moments were a little confused. The only thing that stood out clearly, cutting into my mind with the precision of a scalpel, was the sound of Kim's scream.

It was later, during a few blessed minutes of calm, that I learned fully what had happened.

After dragging me inside, Kim turned back to the opening. The serrated tongue of the creature lashed her cheek, causing her to scream in pain and revulsion. She struck out and her hand connected open-palmed along the length of the protrusion. Ignoring the burning sensation, or perhaps inured to it through fear, she grasped it and squeezed. When she relayed the tale, she showed me the palm of her hand. A raised, ragged band of scarlet rawness ran along it, as if she had grabbed a poker fresh from the fire. The weal on her cheek was less vivid and paler, like a fading scar.

The creature swayed back, whipping its tongue away. Kim had the good sense to let go or the damage to her hand might have been much worse.

At that moment, the lift door began to slide closed once more, but at the same time the creature leaned in to bring its claws within reach of the American. She jerked back, stumbling against Jack who tried to shove her away.

"Nice," I remarked, shooting him a dark glance. He didn't look at me. "So that overgrown muppet was preventing the door closing?"

Kim nodded. "If it had remained there, or moved closer to

slash at us, the door couldn't have shut."

But the door *had* closed. Through the fog of fatigue and resignation, the next thing I could recall clearly was the sense of relief that the door had slid fully shut.

I raised my eyebrows. "What saved us?"

Kim's expression grew sombre. "The Eye."

Six

While not one for books, I love watching films. Especially the action-filled gore-fests. A smattering of sex and nudity, all to the good.

Not sure why I enjoyed *The Lord of the Rings* films. Not a great deal of gore and definitely no nudity. Instead, a great number of elves (admittedly, some smoking hot) and orcs and hobbits and tree-things, with the odd dwarf and wizard thrown in for good measure. Then, of course, there's The Eye. The leader of the baddies, an incorporeal being of pure evil, is portrayed in the films as a lidless, flaming eye perched on top of a stone tower from where it could see for vast distances across forests and plains to white cities and snowy mountains.

The image of that flaming eye is what came to mind while Kim tried to describe what she'd seen.

"It was red and glowing," she said. "As big as the sun."

"Was it on fire?" My mind was still obsessing with the cinematic image.

Kim shook her head. "Yet it filled the air with red light and heat."

"Black pupil? Round?"

"Round, yes. But..." She hesitated as though uncertain how to describe what she'd seen. "The red outer ring was so bright that it's difficult to be sure, but the pupil wasn't dark. It resembled a silver dollar, but smooth like all the markings had been rubbed off." She nodded. "Yeah, it looked like a huge metal disc."

Jack, who had been watching and listening, chipped in.

"It was definitely silver in colour. Like a polished steel shield."

Kim shuddered. "There was something about that eye. Something terrible. Full of cunning. And knowing. And something worse..." She tailed away as though struggling to find the right word.

"Malice," supplied Jack. "It gave me the creeps. Seemed to look right at me. Right *through* me." He glanced my way, face gaunt and haunted. "It was as she says. Full of cunning. And great knowledge, but not like stuff *we* know about." He shrugged. "Most of all, it was pure malice."

The eye stained the desert landscape and the interior of the lift an arterial red. It rode above the horizon as though orbiting in the same trajectory as the sun but half the circumference of the planet behind, or ahead, of it.

A silvery pupilled eye in the sky sounds like a psychedelic episode, yet no more than flying Freddy Kruegers or acid sea-women or what was to come later—the machine, the fire, the river… but I'm getting ahead of myself.

Our final moments on the Fourth Floor, as related to me by Kim shortly afterwards, went down like this…

When she stumbled back against Jack and felt him shove her in the back (only a small push, she was keen to make me understand, more instinctive than deliberate), she realised she had no escape route.

The creature had drawn back its short arms as far as it could ready to slice her stomach open. The door had begun to close again; when it came to within an inch of the furry bulk blocking the doorway, the sensors would trip and it would judder open.

More out of desperation than in any hope it would prevent the imminent attack, Kim lashed out with her foot. Her skirt had slipped a little from where she had hoiked it up, but not enough to restrict her legs. Her clunky shoe connected firmly with the lower section of the creature's abdomen.

"It was… *squelchy*, like kicking a mound of barely-set Jell-O," she told me later. "My foot went in so far I thought it would get stuck."

I nodded, recalling how yielding Paddlefoot's back had felt when I whacked it with Tara's shoe. "Do you think you hurt it?"

Kim shook her head. "If it even felt my kick, it gave no sign."

She shrugged. "And yet…"

Paddlefoot straightened, almost clonking its head on the door lintel. For one terrifying moment, Kim thought her foot had become lodged in its midriff. She experienced a lurid vision of the creature thumping across the desert with her hopping before it in an absurd effort to stay out of reach of its claws.

"In other circumstances, I would have found that image hilarious," Kim said. "But I thought it would actually happen. Until the creature took a step back and my foot came free. Lucky for me. I jerked my leg back inside the elevator in a hurry to get it clear of the door."

The creature took another backward step. The tongue rose above its head like a rearing cobra, its end curved up towards the eye. Paddlefoot quivered and spasmed as if in ecstasy.

"But I don't think it trembled through anything that felt good. Not this time. It could sense The Eye and didn't like it. Not one bit. In fact, I think that oversized furball was terrified."

The light around the entrance to the lift glowed brighter; to use Kim's words, 'like a flare had gone off'. That part I vaguely recall: an abrupt change to the quality of the air as it grew ruddier, more intense. It made me squint.

"The Eye swivelled to look directly at us." Kim's voice dropped to little more than a shocked whisper. "Not only *at* us. *Inside* us."

"Yeah," agreed Jack. "It was as if the Devil had taken a peek into my soul."

Scattering sand in its haste, showering Kim with grit, Paddlefoot turned clumsily and pounded for the ridge in the direction in which the sun had disappeared. Away from the eye.

It had not taken more than a few steps before it was hidden from sight by the shutting door.

"But I swear," whispered Kim, "that its fur was starting to give off smoke. Like The Eye was burning it."

The sudden flare of light before the door closed brought me out of my dazed state. I blinked and turned my back to the side wall. It felt blessedly cool after the desert heat. As the lift lurched into descent, I surveyed my companions.

Jack stood in his corner, knuckles white where he gripped the side rail. His face expressed a dark-eyed mix of bewilderment and horror, but he was in the best shape of us all.

Tara slouched in her corner, one leg curled out in front, the other hidden beneath her. She was leaning forward, the slashes on her back presumably too painful to allow her to rest against the wall. Her visible foot was covered only in torn nylon. With a grunt, I stooped and placed the shoe which I still clutched onto it. She didn't even raise her head in acknowledgement.

Wincing at the singing, stinging pain in my ankle and arm, I regarded Kim.

"You look like shit," I muttered.

Her hair hung down in lank strands, like the strings of a damp mop. A white line ran across her cheek, interrupting the high colour that flushed her skin. It was difficult to tell whether her blouse had been white or cream, so stained had it become with sweat and Tara's blood. Her skirt had unrolled towards her calves unevenly, giving her a lopsided look.

"So do you," she said.

She made a game attempt at forcing a grin to her face. I tried to return it, but only succeeded in grimacing.

Part 3: Second and Third Floors

One

The lift shuddered to a halt and the forced grin faded from Kim's face.

"I don't care what's on the other side of this door when it opens." Her gaze fixed on mine with an intensity that bordered on manic. "I don't care how harmless it looks. There could be bushes made from cotton candy and lakes of cherry soda, with pink bunnies and orange kittens and… and green lambs, but we *ain't going out there.*"

She looked so fierce that I managed a smile, a genuine one.

"*Green* lambs?"

"It was the first thing that came into my head…"

The lift door began to open.

Before looking to see what it would reveal, I glanced at the digital display above the buttons.

3.

The door slid into its recess with a *clunk*. I took a pace to the lip which marked the end of the lift to gain the best view of Floor Three, or whatever had taken its place. I glanced out, took firm hold of the handrail, looked up, down and to either side, before shuffling back with a deep sigh.

"Don't think there's much hope of going outside, even if we wanted to."

A place of shadow. Erratic pulses of flaring light could not entirely disperse the gloom, but were enough to give a sense of our surroundings. Enough that we could tell immediately that we were not on the Third Floor of Claridge House with its threadbare carpet tiles and tired décor.

The air felt warm and still. I sniffed. It was faint, but I could detect a whiff of electrical discharge. And something else, something warm and alive. Organic.

The lift shaft had emerged from a smooth, curving wall which rose behind and over us, forming a dome-like ceiling perhaps thirty yards in height. Beneath the lift, the wall fell steeply away to darkness. Before sloping out of sight, it bent away, mirroring the curve of the ceiling. Stepping outside the lift would mean a short, sharp slide towards deep shadow.

Had the space been empty, it would have been cavernous and echoing, but a hill or mound rose before us, loosely following the contours of walls and ceiling, to almost fill the cave. The gap between walls and hill was wide enough to allow the lift shaft to have emerged without touching anything; my cursory inspection had suggested that the shaft protruded at a shallow angle so that it occupied the gap without butting against walls or hill.

"Lucky," I muttered.

"Huh?" Kim had also stepped to the edge to look out. She turned to me, her face darkly shadowed in the gloom.

"We're lucky the shaft didn't hit that." I indicated the mound. "We're now on the Third Floor so there are three floors of empty shaft above us. If we'd emerged at a different angle, the top of the shaft would have struck that hill." I pulled a face. "Goodness knows what that would have meant."

Kim glanced back outside. "That's one weird hill. What's with those flashing lights? And what's it made of? Doesn't look like rock or earth to me. It's covered with something. Like a shroud."

I looked again. Kim was right about the shroud. It completely covered the mound, making it difficult to see the material beneath clearly, yet was thin enough to allow light to escape.

Some areas of the mound remained in darkness; others lit up with orange, yellow and white lights which flared briefly but brightly. Sometimes the lights seemed to form a linear pattern, flashing down or up the slopes of the hill like streams. But mostly they appeared randomly.

Kim shrugged and turned away.

"Let me take a look at your back," she said to Tara.

I shuffled around her and watched as she helped Tara gingerly remove the tattered jacket of what had come to look more like an urchin's rags than a power suit. Tara still seemed to be in a daze, complying with Kim's instructions uncomplainingly, but without giving the impression that she knew much of what was going on.

My movement had brought me next to Jack. He had lowered himself into a crouch and stared past me, his expression dour. I did not feel well-disposed towards him after he had shoved Kim towards Paddlefoot and for barging past me on Floor Six, causing me to fall. Still, I reminded myself, no real harm had been done on either occasion, and he had, after all, left the sanctuary of the lift on Sixth to try to help me and Kim. Perhaps I ought to give the guy a break.

"So, Jack," I said, sitting down and leaning back beneath the handrail, "I've seen you around, but don't really know you."

He turned his mournful face towards me. There was something about him, some negative vibes that he gave off, which irritated me. Now, as I write this, remembering the way I felt, how I'd christened him Rudolph because of the rash on his nose, gives me a pang of guilt.

"I work for the IT firm on Sixth," he said with a slight shrug. "Training to be a programmer. Share a flat in town with three people."

"Friends of yours, yeah? The people you share with?"

"Nah. They're wankers. Don't have any friends."

"Everyone has friends."

This time his shrug was more pronounced. "I don't."

I'm not the best at chit-chat, but I was determined to make the effort. There was little else to do.

"What about family?" I ventured. "Parents live locally? Brothers and sisters?"

He looked down at his hands.

"Only child." He uttered a short, humourless laugh. "At least, s'far as I'm aware. Never knew my dad. Not even sure that my mum knows who he was. Too many drunken one-night stands. She kicked me out when I was sixteen. I didn't get on with her latest boyfriend."

"Do you still see her?"

He shook his head. "Had a birthday card off her once. The council forwarded it to the hostel where I lived. She hasn't been in touch since. Last I heard, she'd moved. Dunno where she's living now." He looked at me, his eyes hard. "Quite honestly, I don't fucking care."

"Oh, man, can't say I blame you. How did you cope with leaving home at sixteen?"

Jack grunted. "Drugs. You name it, I popped it, smoked it or injected it. OD'd when I was eighteen. My heart stopped for almost a minute. That made me get my shit together. Cleaned myself up. Got this job last year. Don't know how long I'll have it. The other trainees are *way* ahead of me. While they were still in school and learning code in their spare time, I was running wild, smoking dope and popping ecstasy." He sighed. "Twenty years old, a reformed addict, prospects bleak. That's me."

"Well, it sounds like you've done really well to get off the drugs." It sounded lame and I knew it, but felt I had to say something.

He, too, knew that my words were trite. He looked past me at the flaring, shrouded hill and we lapsed into silence.

It's funny how your perspective can change during the course of a snatched, strained conversation. Until Jack told me about his unhappy background, I'd thought that my relationship with my parents wasn't great. Well, it's not, but it's positively rosy compared to what that poor sod went through.

They—my folks—live in a small village about twenty miles away. The place where I grew up and from which I couldn't wait to escape. They wanted me to go to university. I was ready to leave education for good once I'd bombed my A Levels, but surprised everyone, myself included, by passing the exams. Against my better judgement, I agreed to enrol on a degree in marketing. Don't ask me why marketing as I couldn't tell you; all I cared about was escaping the tedium of village life.

I didn't last a term, or a semester as Kim would call it. Long enough to conclude once and for all that I was not cut out for academia. Using what remained of the money my parents had given me to survive the first term, I moved to this town and paid a deposit on a flat. Yeah—should probably have discussed it with them first.

On the rare occasion that I go to see them, my dad's unremitting disappointment in me is writ large on his face, which makes me feel guilty and seek escape in drinking too much beer. He in turn withdraws into a mute, seething pit of disapproval, which prompts my mum to start talking twice as much to try to make up for his stony silence. That makes me want to drink more to drown out her wittering.

Strange things, families. But at least I had one. Talking to Jack made me realise that I needed to build a few bridges, especially with Dad. I bumped it high on my to-do list. Not that I'd be able to tick anything off that list until we escaped the bloody lift.

Kim finished fussing over Tara's back and noticed me watching.

"Superficial cuts," she said. "Already scabbing over." She wiped a hand across her brow. "My, I could drink the Connecticut."

"Huh? I thought that was a state."

"It's also a river that runs by Hartford… doesn't matter. I'm thirsty."

Her lips looked dry and cracked. Everyone's did, except perhaps for Jack's. Maybe because he hadn't ventured out into that scorching desert on Fourth.

Tara rose unsteadily to her feet. She hadn't bothered to replace the jacket of her power suit. It lay in the corner like a bundle of off-cuts.

"Thanks," she said to Kim. It sounded begrudging; maybe she hated to be reminded that this stuff was really happening. Must be difficult to put bleeding cuts and ruined clothes down to a nightmare.

"You're welcome," said Kim in that sincere way Americans sometimes have.

"What is this place?" Tara took a step closer to the doorway and gazed out, wide-eyed and alert once more.

"It seems to be some sort of cave," I said. "Complete with flashing, shroud-covered hill."

Tara stared for a few moments before stiffening and letting out a sharp gasp.

"That's no cave," she said. "No hill or shroud, neither." She turned to face us. "I know where we are, though it's going to sound bonkers. Full-on certifiable bonkers."

Two

While I scribble in these pages, recounting events which I experienced first-hand, even to me they seem inconceivably far-fetched, the product of an overactive imagination. There can surely be nobody of sound and enquiring mind who will give credence to my words. I don't tell this tale in hope or expectation that anyone will believe it.

Then why bother? you might ask. Good question. It partly comes down to a burden shared is a burden halved. You won't believe my story, but I feel better for the telling. Selfish? Maybe, but there's more to it than that: we owe it to certain people to create a record of what they did if otherwise their bravery and sacrifice will go unnoticed. To honour their memory. That sounds as twee as a Disney song, but it doesn't matter; some words need to be said regardless.

The police didn't believe this tale, either. They reacted, as might be expected, with extreme incredulity and hostility, and there were at least two of us, in separate interview rooms, spouting as near as damn it identical versions.

Yet even in the knowledge that nobody reading this will regard any of it as credible, still I hesitate to recount where we found ourselves in the space formerly occupied by the Third Floor of Claridge House.

Of all the strange events that befell us that spring morning, of all the weird worlds (for that is how I think of them) that we visited on our jaunts between floors, Floor Three was the most bizarre of them all.

I misunderstood what Tara said. "We're inside ahead? That makes no sense." Judging by Jack's and Kim's non-plussed looks, they were equally baffled.

Tara sighed. "It *does* make sense, or as much as anything does in this lift."

I still wasn't getting it. "Sorry. No idea what you're talking about. We can be inside something. We can be ahead of something. But I don't see how we can be inside and ahead at the same time."

"Those walls and ceiling of the cave…" She tutted impatiently and pointed to them. "They're not walls and ceilings. They're the inside of a skull. That hill isn't a hill. It's a brain. The shroud, as you call it, is the membrane that covers the brain."

Jack straightened, eyes bright. "Ah. You mean we're inside a *head*."

Tara looked at each of us in turn as though we were elderly relatives to whom she had been trying to explain the latest technological gadget. "That's what I said. We're inside a head."

"Ah," I said, the penny dropping. "Oh!"

Kim blanched. "Oh, man, that's crazier than alcohol-free wine."

I pulled myself to my feet, wincing at the pain in my arm and ankle. The cuts had stopped bleeding, but every time I moved it felt like they were reopening. The throbbing in my nose from where Freddy had chewed a chunk out of it had settled to a dull ache that I could put up with. The lacerations to the pads of my thumb and fingertips seemed trivial in comparison.

Stepping back to the lip of the doorway, I peered out.

In the flashes of light, the smooth walls of the 'cave' did appear to be a creamy, ivory colour, like bone. The 'shroud' could have been a membrane; suggestions of faint lines running through it like the after-image of forked lightning showed in each flash. Veins, maybe. The surface of the hill contained dark cracks, like crevasses in ice, between long lumps and hummocks which resembled strings of sausages packed tightly and randomly together.

And the flashing lights…

"They're thoughts," I murmured. "Chaotic ones, at that."

Kim raised her eyebrows, but not in a casual gesture of enquiry; she looked about ready to lose it big time.

"Those lights," I said, "must be thoughts. You know, like brain waves or electrical impulses or whatever they are."

"Like on a motherboard," said Jack. His eyes shone. Of all the weird crap that had happened to us that morning, most of which seemed to have terrified him, this was the first time I'd seen him animated. No, more than that. The boy was downright excited.

"I think they're called synapses," said Tara. "And, yeah, I suppose that's what thoughts look like."

"But *whose* thoughts are they?" Kim's eyes darted from my face to Tara's to Jack's to the flickering mound outside as though if her gaze settled in one place she would have to confront the madness of us discussing being inside a gigantic head looking at the thoughts of the head's owner.

Tara shrugged, and drew in a hissing breath as the movement tugged at the cuts on her back. "Who knows? We'd better hope that whoever's they are, he or she doesn't wake up."

Until that moment, it hadn't occurred to me that the owner of the brain must have been sleeping. If he wasn't sleeping, or unconscious, he was keeping his head uncommonly still. (I say 'he' because we later had reason to believe that the owner was male.)

"They're asleep?" Kim looked ashen in the gloom. "How can we know that? They could be dead."

"Don't be stupid," said Tara. "Those flashing lights represent brain activity."

"Huh. Yeah, I s'pose, unless we're inside a zombie…"

"What happens if they wake up?" Jack's earlier excitement seemed to have faded as more practical concerns began to surface.

"Let's hope we never find—"

The end of my sentence was lost beneath Kim's shriek and Jack's yell as the floor of the lift lurched. I grabbed at the handrail with my left hand. With my right, I lunged for Tara as she fell through the doorway.

The lift car had shifted so that the floor sloped at roughly a forty-five-degree angle down towards the gaping doorway. The floor surface consisted of a composite material that provided sufficient grip, even with my smooth-soled shoes, to prevent us from pitching out with Tara, but if it tilted any more then we would go slipping and sliding the same way.

Kim and Jack had grabbed the handrail on the rear wall. Their quick actions meant they hadn't gone bowling into me. If one of them had, there is no way I could have maintained my grips on both the handrail and Tara.

My right hand had snagged her wrist as she pinwheeled her arms in a vain attempt to maintain her balance. Our skin was still damp with perspiration from our adventure in the desert-scape of Floor Four, but she managed to wrap her hand around my wrist. Although soaked with blood which had run down my arm from the slashes on my bicep, the cuff of my shirt remained fastened and gave enough purchase for her to cling on.

But only just. Fresh warmth trickled down past my elbow; the cuts on my arm had reopened. My shoulders once more groaned under the strain of holding on to one of my companions, my hands became slicker with sweat and my grips on both the handrail and Tara's wrist grew tenuous.

She looked up at me, her eyes level with the floor, face white with fear. Her free arm hung loosely by her side; her legs dangled over space. At our new angle, what had been a steep slope beneath us had turned into a dark precipice. If she fell, she would clip the mound (I was still struggling to think of it as a brain) before disappearing into unseen depths.

"Tara!" I hissed through gritted teeth. "Reach for the lip of the floor with your other hand." I doubted she would gain enough leverage to haul herself up—the floor sloped at too sheer an angle—but I hoped she might be able to partly support her weight and ease the burden on my shoulders.

"Can't. Not strong enough."

Her expression told me that she had nothing left to give after the trek across the scorching sands of Floor Four and her debilitating encounter with Paddlefoot. She would cling to me for as long as she could, but was already contemplating a plunge into oblivion.

"*Please*," I implored. "At least try. I can't hold on much longer."

Her only response was a curt shake of the head. And I could feel the cuff of my shirt, sodden with fresh blood, tearing.

An arm snaked around my chest, encircling it, and Jack's voice came from behind. "Can you pull her up if I hang onto you?"

"No. But hang on anyway."

The pressure of trying to maintain my footing on the sloping floor eased with Jack's help, but my shoulder joints still felt likely to pop out at any moment. Tara's expression had become glazed, as though she had mentally resigned herself to whatever lay at the end of the fall into darkness.

Movement to the side caught my eye. Kim had made her way along the opposite wall. She reached the lip and leaned a little way over, looking down at Tara.

"I think maybe…" She let go of the handrail and began to shuffle closer to where Tara dangled.

I had a clear vision of Kim reaching for Tara, slipping and taking Tara with her as she fell.

"No!" It came out almost as a shriek, but had the desired effect of making Kim stop moving. "Don't you let go of that handrail. It's too risky."

"Okay, okay. Keep your shirt on." She stepped back to the wall and took hold of the rail. Then she nodded down to her feet. "Could we pull her up using that like a rope?"

I followed her gaze. My jacket lay crumpled into a ball in the corner where I had left it. Tara's document case had slid up to it. The slight protrusion of wall from which the door emerged had prevented them dropping over the edge when the lift lurched.

"Worth a go."

They were my words, but I didn't believe them. My grip on Tara's wrist had grown precarious at best as sweat continued to burst from my pores. The cuff of my shirt, wet now with blood *and* perspiration, no longer supplied any purchase for Tara's hold on me. All that stopped her from dropping was that our fingers clutched each other around the end of the wrist where the hand started; that broadening of wrist to hand provided the only barrier to our slick skin sliding apart.

My fingers were already being forced wider by, forgive the expression, Tara's dead-weight, and my grip crept unstoppably up her hand. When it reached the tapering point where her little finger and thumb began, her hand would slip from mine like a greased eel.

We never did find out if Kim's idea of using my jacket as an impromptu rope worked. She stooped to retrieve it from the floor and the lift lurched again.

Three

For a few manic moments, the world became topsy-turvy. My stomach tried to jump into my throat as down became up. The pain in my shoulders intensified but I clung on grimly to Tara's wrist. After three or four seconds of tumbling confusion, punctuated by grunts and yelps and shrieks, the four of us lay in a tangled heap on the rear wall, which was doing a passable impersonation of the floor.

Tara lay on top of me, heat radiating off her in waves, our hands still clenched together. I let her go.

Over the top of her head, I could see the flashing mound through the open doorway. Except that the doorway had taken up position where the ceiling should be. The owner of the brain must have turned his head again in his sleep. Fortunately for us, and especially Tara, he'd turned in the opposite direction.

"Will you get off me?"

Knees and elbows dug into my back as Jack attempted to shove me and Tara off. To one side Kim rose unsteadily, standing on the rear wall. She reached down to help Tara up. Then I could move. I stood, a little awkwardly since the wall still sloped, and helped Jack to his feet.

"Is everyone okay?" I asked.

"A bit squashed," muttered Jack.

"I banged the back of my head on the wall," said Kim. "But I reckon I'll live."

I turned to Tara. "How about you?"

She massaged her wrist and stood lopsidedly as though favouring one leg. "My hand hurts where you grabbed me. And I sprained my ankle when I came shooting back inside. It's the same one I twisted in the desert."

"But that's better than dangling over the drop, right?" said Kim, a slight edge to her tone.

Tara shrugged.

"Thanks, Matt," said Kim, the edge sharper. "For saving my life."

Tara shrugged again. "Yeah," she said. "Thanks."

"That's fine." I held up a hand to forestall Kim's next words; even in the dim light, bright spots of colour were clear on her cheeks. "Really, Kim, it's fine."

"Huh!" Kim turned away. "Some people can be *so* ungrateful…"

"The door's closing." Jack's head was raised.

We followed his gaze and watched as the door slid closed, hiding the shrouded hill and flashing lights. I was glad to see the back of them.

"I wonder what'll happen when the lift begins to move," said Jack. "Will gravity return to normal?"

"Oh, shoot," said Kim. "We could be in for another—"

This time, Jack landed on top of me. The rear wall became a wall once more and the floor returned to where it should be.

We extricated ourselves and struggled to our feet. My gaze darted to the floor display.

2.

We faced the lift door as it paused in preparation for sliding open.

I can't recall what I felt at that moment: trepidation at what horrors might await us on Floor Two, or numb resignation that whatever lay the other side of the door there wasn't much we could do about it, so bring it on and get it over with. I think the latter more likely since we had all become to some extent inured to strange and fearful sights.

The door slid open.

I'd never had much call to visit the Second Floor. From what I could remember from my brief glimpses from the lift when it stopped to let someone out, the floor contained the usual drab, partitioned office spaces inhabited by firms of planning consultants, solicitors and surveyors.

It most definitely hadn't been a silent, abandoned city last time I'd noticed.

The lift shaft had emerged into a small square between grey buildings three or four storeys tall. Stone in the same drab colour as the buildings paved the square. The scene was bathed in a muted, rosy hue that seemed familiar. A sun at least four times larger than our own and as red as a ripe rose dominated the portion of sky visible above the buildings.

By my side, Kim gave a gasp; her hand came out to grab my arm.

"Ouch! Will you stop grabbing me."

She let go. "Sorry. For a moment I thought The Eye was back."

"It's a sun, but it looks much older than the one at home."

Some of the paving slabs had sunk, giving an impression of long neglect, but no weeds grew in the cracks between them. In fact, no vegetation could be seen anywhere. Or birds. Or any sign of life at all. No litter or rusting vehicles spoiled the uniform dreariness of the square. Even the air felt still and lifeless.

A dead place.

"Does anyone have any idea where we are?" Kim glanced at us each in turn.

She was met by blank stares and shrugs.

"I don't know where this is," I said, "but I don't recognise it as being anywhere on Earth."

"How d'you mean?" asked Jack. "Apart from that sun looking nothing like ours."

"Well, have any of you ever been to a town or city where there are no street markings? Or street signs? There aren't any signs on the buildings, either. Or inscriptions or decorative stonework. They all look strictly functional without any outward clues of what the functions might be."

"No streetlamps," said Kim. "Or stop lights. Nothing to suggest this place even has electricity."

I pointed up at the rising walls of the structures nearest us. "The buildings have windows, but only above ground level. They look as if they're glazed, but the glass is plain. No company names or logos stuck to them. No blinds or curtains that I can see."

"No shutters," added Kim.

"This place feels totally deserted, yet there's no evidence of war or catastrophe or damage that might give a hint as to why. It's weird."

"No weirder than any of the other floors we've visited. If anything, this place is a lot *less* weird than those other places." Kim drew her arms around herself as if suddenly chilly. "It's also a whole lot creepier than those other places. Even the last one, and *that* was inside a freaking head."

I couldn't help myself; it sounded so ridiculous the way she'd said it. I giggled.

The sound left my mouth, hit the air and died as though encountering a vacuum. Kim shivered and turned away.

There didn't appear to be any danger of being attacked by strange creatures or thrown about by tilting lifts, but I had learned my lesson. I sat with my back to one of the side walls to rest and take stock. With the adrenaline created by the flight from Floor Four and clinging on to Tara on Third draining from my system, pain from cuts and bruises and bites and strains made itself known in rather a strident manner. At least the cuts on my arm seemed to have stopped bleeding. The ragged remnants of shirt sleeve on that arm had started to turn black as the soaked-in blood dried.

Tara, too, had sunk to the floor. She fiddled with the discarded jacket of her power suit, tearing off strips of cloth where the claws had shredded the material and using them to bind her sprained ankle.

Jack seemed the most intrigued by the dead city. He stood at the entrance, gazing out at the silent buildings.

Kim slouched opposite me, looking glad of the respite. Her gaze moved lazily between Tara and me. Now that she was happy no red eye peered down from the sky, what lay the other side of the door apparently didn't much interest her.

Just when I thought this would be the least eventful of floors, Jack walked out.

Struggling to my feet, I called out to him. "Hey, man, where are you going? Probably better that we stay inside the lift."

"There's something…" He continued forward.

"Wait!" I glanced at Kim. "Will you make sure the door stays open while we're out there?"

She straightened, concern creasing her brow. "We're not going outside any more, remember?"

I pointed impatiently at Jack. "He's outside." Jack had stopped moving, but stood facing away from us. "I'm going to take a look to make sure everything's quiet behind us. Keep an eye on the door."

Before she could raise any further objections, I stepped into the dead city.

There was nothing to see behind the shaft except more uneven paving and plain, grey buildings. The stones immediately around the shaft had not been disturbed, as though the brick column had always been there. When I returned to the front of the lift, Jack still stood facing the far side of the square. I strode to his side.

"This isn't such a good idea, you know, after what happened on the other floors."

He didn't respond except to nod in the direction of his gaze.

At first, I couldn't see anything. Then I drew in a sharp breath. Whatever damage being a smack-head had caused to Jack, it clearly hadn't affected his eyesight.

The object he had spotted might once have been bright silver in colour, but had tarnished so that it blended into the grey background.

We approached it together.

Four

We trod carefully, picking our way past lopsided paving slabs. The object stood in one corner of the square in the shadow of the nearest building.

"What is it?" I muttered. We hadn't been walking quickly, but my pace slowed.

Jack didn't falter and didn't respond to my question. He drew nearer and I slowed further, my reluctance to approach such an innocuous-looking item more evidence that the morning's events had knocked a large deal of caution into my stubborn hide.

The object resembled an oblong metal box or an aluminium suitcase, with rounded edges, standing upright on one of its ends. It looked as though a stiff breeze would knock it over.

Jack shuffled around it, peering closely. As I arrived, he reached out a hand…

"Don't!" I hissed.

He gave the top of the box a light shove. I flinched, steeling myself for a resounding crash as the box toppled.

But it didn't fall. It barely rocked once before settling back into its original position.

Jack shot me an excited glance. "It's weighted at the bottom."

My nerves pinged like taut wire. "I don't really care. We need to get back to the lift. The— What now?"

A faint whirring had reached my ears. For a moment, I struggled to pinpoint its source. Then I realised that the box was making the sound and took a sharp pace away from it.

When the box lit up, Jack stepped back, too.

A ring of white pinpoint lights encircled the box, a few inches below its top edge. In the gloom of shadow, they appeared almost dazzlingly bright. Jack and I exchanged a nervous glance.

The lights began to wink out one by one until only the few immediately facing us remained lit. The whirring sound faded. My nerves continued to jangle.

"What d'you reckon it is?" Jack's voice sounded low and breathless.

"How would I know?"

The surface of the box was smooth, unblemished except for the lights. They did not stand proud, but shone through the metallic material as if it became transparent under their glare. I could not see any appendages or protrusions that might suggest the box could cause us harm like some sort of miniature Dalek.

"It's watching us." Jack's words sent a chill down my neck as though an animated corpse had breathed down my collar. "Sizing us up."

"Don't be daft."

A third voice spoke and I jerked, whipping my head around to see who had joined us. But there was nobody there; I could see Kim and Tara inside the lift, the former staring out at us from the doorway, the latter seated against the rear wall.

"It was her," said Jack, indicating the box.

"*Her*? How the hell do you know it's a 'her'?"

He shrugged.

"And if it did speak, what did it say?" The words I had heard, if words they had been, were unintelligible. Gibberish.

The voice came again, the lights dimming at the same time before returning to their previous brightness as soon as it fell silent. The voice did indeed appear to be coming from the box, although I could not make out anything resembling a speaker. It did not sound metallic or computerised, but mellifluous and unmistakably female. I glanced at Jack; to his credit, he tried not to look too smug.

The voice came for the third time and now we could understand the words, if not their meaning.

"Terra One. English. Western Europa. Circa late third century to mid second century BE."

"Huh? Terror One? What's it on about?" Fear interfered with my thought processes.

"Terra," said Jack. "You know, like Earth. It's Latin or something."

"Okay. But I still don't know what it's on about."

Jack frowned. "I think… yes, that must be it. She's analysing our speech. Voice patterns, accents, that sort of shit. She said that we come from the west of Europe."

"Wish you'd stop calling it 'she'. Okay, so it might have got where we're from correct, broadly speaking, but what was all that stuff about third and second century BE?"

Jack shrugged again; it seemed to be his favourite gesture. "Why don't you ask her?"

In these days of voice recognition, voicemail and automated menus, we are accustomed to talking to machines. Yet as I cleared my throat and prepared to address the box, I felt like a complete idiot; I was twelve again, about to ask out the most popular girl in class who would reduce me to a state of shambling, tongue-tied befuddlement. It was a relief when I caught sight of movement near the lift and the words died in my throat.

Kim made her way across the square towards us, glancing about as if feeling vulnerable away from the safety of the lift. A safety that was largely illusory, as the previous floor had demonstrated. I looked back at the lift, praying that she hadn't left the door unguarded. Even if this place held no patent threats, I had no wish to be stranded here.

I needn't have worried. She had left Tara standing in the doorway under, I had no doubt, strict instructions not to desert her post until we were all safely back inside.

"All right?" I enquired as she drew close.

Kim didn't reply. She slowed, like I had done earlier, and regarded the box through narrowed eyes. Her brow bore a frown of deep suspicion.

"What's that?" she asked.

"Some sort of computer," said Jack, excitement in his tone. "Highly advanced. Maybe even AI."

"Eh aye?" My brain still wasn't in top gear. "What the heck is 'eh aye'?"

Kim snorted. "Don't you ever watch shows like *Dr Who*? Artificial intelligence. You know, sapient machines."

Another couple of lights illuminated near the top of the box as Kim approached. They pulsed.

"Terra One," said the mellifluous voice. "English. Eastern seaboard of the republics formerly known as United States of America. Same period."

Kim glanced from me to Jack and back to the box. "That was the computer? She can tell where I'm from just from my voice? How cool. She sounds sweet."

I rolled my eyes. "Don't you start personifying it."

She ignored me. "My name's Kim," she said, addressing the box. "Do you have a name?"

The lights pulsed. "The English speakers called us MIRIAM. It is an acronym. Migration, Restoration and Integration Activation Module."

"Very pleased to meet you, Miriam. I would like to stay and chat. Find out what you meant by 'formerly known as'. But, sadly, we must be going."

Kim looked at me and I realised from her thunderous expression that her apparent enchantment with the box (I refused to think of it as a personality with a name) had been an act. "We need to get back to the elevator, Matt. *Right now.*"

Kim's glare would have stopped a rampaging bull in its tracks.

"Do you hear me, Matt? We need to go."

"Give us a few minutes," I said. "This place doesn't hold any threats that I can see."

"Neither did Sixth until you decided to pick a fruit off that tree."

I felt myself colour, but held her gaze.

"And," she continued, "Fourth was just a bunch of dunes until we decided to go trekking across them." She sighed, but her fierce expression didn't falter. "Whenever we do anything to interact with whatever environment we find ourselves in, it doesn't go so well for us."

My mouth opened to argue further. Then closed.

Instead, I nodded. I knew she was right. Again.

She turned the glare on Jack.

"Wait," he said. "We need to ask her—"

"Look, sweetie, we don't *need* to do anything except get back inside before the elevator takes off again." The high patches of colour had returned to her cheeks. "So far we've been lucky not to have anyone seriously hurt or worse. We ain't gonna push our luck."

Jack's lips compressed to a pale line. "*I* haven't been arsing about outside asking to be attacked by anything with teeth or claws. Now that we've ended up somewhere *I* find interesting, you'll bloody well have to wait for me." He took a deep breath. "I want to know more about this place. Miriam can tell us."

"No! I didn't come out here to engage in chit-chat with a computer, no matter how freaking sweet it sounds, but to drag you two dumbasses back."

Jack nodded at me. "Take that dumbass back if you want, but I'm staying to talk to Miriam."

"Hey!" I began to bridle, but no one paid me any attention. Jack and Kim stared at each other so intently I could almost see their wills clashing like strands of magical energy snaking from combatting wizards' wands.

The stalemate was broken by the box (which I still struggled to think of by name, but that I shall refer to that way for the sake of brevity).

"Kim is correct," said Miriam. "It would be prudent that you return to your transport and leave this place. If you stay, you will die."

Five

When advised by a local to leave their patch as otherwise you'll expire, it's probably a good idea to hotfoot it out of there post-haste, right? You'd think. But Jack wasn't ready to depart and I wasn't prepared to leave him out there alone.

He looked at Kim, his jaw set. "I want to find out more."

"Did you hear what Miriam said?" she asked, disbelief and frustration turning her cheeks the colour of ripe tomatoes. "If we stay, we'll die."

"Just a few more minutes, then we all go back to the lift together. Okay?"

Kim stared at him for a moment, then threw her hands in the air in surrender. "You're crazy. We're all crazy."

Jack's face nearly broke into a grin.

"Get on with it, then," said Kim.

"Um, so, hello, Miriam. My name is Jack."

The lights pulsed. "Hello, Jack."

"Hi. Er, can you tell us where we are?"

"You have been displaced, spatially and temporally."

Jack glanced at me. "Space and time."

I nodded, a trifle impatiently. My mental faculties had recovered from their temporary leave of absence so it was no longer necessary to spell everything out as if I were a kid.

"What is the name of this place?" asked Jack, turning back to the box.

"This city is named Ultimus. The last city."

"But *where* are we? As in, where in the universe?"

"The planet we are on is named Terra Two. It is in the galaxy named Bruder after the Swiss scientist who discovered how to make interstellar transition possible."

"Interstellar transition…" Jack's voice had taken on a dreamy quality. "How far away are we from The Milky Way?"

"In excess of one thousand light years. The Bruder Galaxy was unknown by humankind until they arrived in it."

"How is it possible?" asked Kim, who sounded interested despite herself. "Interstellar transition, I think you called it, how is it possible?"

The lights pulsed, taking on colour, becoming a rich yellow. For a moment, I thought the box wasn't going to answer.

"I suspect," said Miriam, "that a comprehensive explanation is not required for that would take many of the temporal units you call minutes."

"The couple of sentences version will do. Was it wormholes?"

"No. Nor bending space or any of the fanciful notions wistfully imagined in the period you are from. At least, not precisely. The succinct answer would be that the solution Bruder came up with was a combination of all those things and more. None of them, yet all of them."

"Terra Two," I mused. "Earth is Terra One?"

"Yes."

"What happened to it?"

"I can show you."

We looked at each other uncertainly, then at our surroundings. There was nothing even remotely resembling a monitor or screen upon which images could be displayed.

"Observe," said Miriam.

The entire square beneath our feet lit up. As though the paving stones had turned to glass, we gazed down on a scene that looked so real we might have been standing on a nearby hilltop. The only distortions in the clarity of the image were caused by the occasional slab that had sunk out of alignment with those surrounding it.

Kim gasped and grabbed my arm. For once, I didn't shake her hand away. Its presence felt comforting, an anchor to stave off the sensation of vertigo that might otherwise have made me stumble or throw up.

"I know that place," she muttered. "I've been there."

A landscape of sunlit craggy hills and low-lying plains opened up below us. Grasslands and rocky escarpments, lakes and rivers, waterfalls and darkly-forested slopes all combined in vivid shades of green and brown and turquoise to present a spectacular vista.

"It's Yellowstone," said Kim. "My parents took me when I was twelve."

"Look," said Jack.

The scene, so tranquil at first, became busy with movement. The air grew thick with birds on the wing. The ground trembled beneath hooves and paws of lumbering bison and bears, loping grey wolves, elk and mountain lions and coyotes on the gallop. Smaller mammals—skunks, raccoons, rabbits, chipmunks— scurried alongside, prey and predator united in a headlong rush from the park.

The ground shook more violently, but not under the thunderous passage of fleeing wildlife. Plumes of steam and scalding geysers shot into the air; yellowish clouds of gas formed and spread. I could almost smell the sulphurous fumes.

Chaos erupted. Plates shifted, shattering the status quo that had so long held this landscape in peaceful check, creating the conditions that would allow hell to be unleashed. Explosions flung earth and splintered trees hundreds of feet into the air. Lakes and pools boiled. Gases compressed for millennia expanded and combusted in violent concussions, sending molten rock and ash skyward.

The picture postcard image became a flaming, churning terrorscape. Although it still rode high in the sky, the sun over Yellowstone grew dusky. Soon it was obliterated entirely by the dust and ash clouds that filled the air.

The image faded and the surface of the square returned to mundane paving stones. Maybe it was an after-impression of the explosive scene we had witnessed, but the air seemed redder, more fiery, in the light of the massive sun which dominated the sky.

Kim's hand dropped away from my arm. She sobbed quietly.

I turned to the box. So did Jack. He looked ashen.

"When did that happen?" I asked quietly.

The lights pulsed. "The Event occurred in the year 2279, as reckoned in your period."

"And the people of Earth, er, of Terra One? What happened to them?"

"In the decades immediately before the Event, seismic activity at Ground Zero had increased to such a level that the Event could be forecast to a degree of accuracy with less than nine percent margin of error. Humankind was prepared. Bruder had fine-tuned his discovery sufficiently to provide an escape route. More than two-thirds of Terra One's population chose to leave."

"What about the other third?"

"They chose to remain."

"They all died?"

"That is not known. It is likely that many will have perished, but the possibility that some yet survive cannot be entirely discounted."

Kim stopped crying. Even in that baleful light, which lent an unnatural ruddiness to our cheeks, she looked wan; more potato than tomato.

"Guys, we need to get going." Her tone lacked the tenacity with which she had addressed us earlier. She sounded tired. Defeated.

"Hang on," said Jack. He swept out an arm to encompass the deserted buildings surrounding us. "If I understand you correctly, Miriam, more than two-thirds of the Earth's population came here to Terra Two through some combination of wormhole and space bubble, or whatever. They arrived here safely?"

"Yes."

"So where are they now?"

The box attempted to explain in simple terms that we might have some hope of understanding. How Bruder's technology allowed a portal to open directly into another planet with an atmosphere that would support human life; the downside was that his discovery could not pinpoint where that planet was situated. How the portal only worked one way: billions of people could pass through, but none could return. They would have to remain at the destination until the first portal had been closed and a new one could be opened. The portal that had brought people to Terra Two had been closed many centuries past and a new one had been created to allow the descendants of those original settlers to transit to Terra Three.

"Where is this new portal?" asked Jack.

"It is called a Bruder Gate," said Miriam. "You are standing on it."

I looked down at my feet, but all I could see were paving stones.

"Is the gate still open?" Jack wore a strange expression. One of longing.

"I may open it, though none has passed through for sixty-two years."

"Let me pass through."

"Hang on a minute…" I began.

"No," said Miriam. "It is only open to humans of this time and place."

"But I'm here right now. Let me pass through."

"No. It is not permitted."

"Let me anyway. You are an intelligent machine. You can make your own decisions."

"To a point. I am unable to override explicit instruction. It is not possible." Although the voice remained friendly, the note of finality was unmistakable.

Jack's shoulders sagged.

Miriam went on to explain how those who fled Earth in the weeks before Yellowstone's caldera erupted found themselves in a galaxy so far from The Milky Way that its whereabouts could only be estimated by extrapolating from the stars in the night sky; even then the estimates varied greatly because of the unfamiliarity of the visible constellations. All had one thing in common: Terra Two spun in space many thousands of light years from Earth.

"Where is Terra Three?" I asked.

"I do not know," said Miriam. "They may have been able to estimate its location by now."

"Why have they left here?"

"Terra Two is due to be annihilated."

"Huh. When you say 'due', when precisely do you mean?"

"In under three minutes."

Six

We had been so engrossed by what the box was telling us that we had not noticed how much brighter the air had become. The shadows cast by the nearest buildings had grown deeper and darker. Sharper. One glance at the sky and the reason became clear. The sun had lost its bloody tint; had turned the colour of a freshly sliced carrot. And bright. Too bright.

A breeze sprang up from nowhere, bringing hot air swirling between the buildings. The first beads of perspiration popped out on my brow.

"We need to go. *Now*," said Kim, authority returning to her voice.

"Yes." But there were still one or two things that I needed to know. I turned to the box. "What year is this?"

"PE 812," said Miriam. "By your reckoning, it is the year 3092."

"Why don't they return to Earth, I mean, to Terra One? It must be habitable by now."

"As I explained, they do not know how to dictate the destination of a Bruder Gate; the only non-variable is that it open to a world that supports human life. They will continue to transit from planet to planet until, perhaps, one day they find themselves back on Terra One." If the machine had possessed shoulders, it would have shrugged.

The breeze blustered; became a wind. A dry, uncomfortably hot one. Sweat ran down my back.

"What's happening?" asked Jack. "Is the sun about to explode?"

"It is expanding," said Miriam, "to a state sometimes known as a red giant. The same thing will happen to Sol, but not for an estimated five billion years. The atmosphere of Terra Two has been reinforced—thus the red colouration of the star that you perceived—but was compromised many weeks ago. In approximately two minutes, the damage will reach critical point and Terra Two will be consumed."

"*Matt.*" Kim's tone contained an edge of panic. "Let's go."

I glanced towards the lift. Tara stood with her hand held against the gap from which the door emerged. She noticed me looking and beckoned fiercely.

"Yep," I said. "Looks like the lift's ready to depart."

"Wait!" Jack looked imploringly at me. "Let's take Miriam with us."

A look of dismay passed across Kim's face. I opened my mouth to reply, but the box beat me to it.

"No," said Miriam. "The source that powers me is buried beneath the surface. I have no inbuilt power source, for it was not intended that I should be mobile."

"But we can't leave you here to be destroyed." I had never heard Jack's voice filled with so much passion.

"Get going, Kim." I waved her towards the lift. "I'll bring him."

Jack's face glistened in the bright light which filled the square and banished the shadows. I had to squint to see him clearly against the glare. The skin on my brow felt tight, like wearing a hat two sizes too small.

"*Come on!*" I grabbed his arm.

He resisted, pulling against me in a deadly game of tug-o'-war.

"Let me go. I can't just leave her here."

"Stay here and you'll die with her."

For the last time, the machine spoke.

"Farewell, Jack and Matt. I must transfer my data packets to Terra Three. You should depart Terra Two without further delay."

The lights went out. Miriam once more resembled a metallic box standing on its end.

"Hear that?" I said. "All its data is going to Terra Three. There's probably another box just like it at the other end waiting to receive the data. So Miriam will live on. Unlike us."

Something cleared in Jack's expression. He gave one last regretful glance at the box, then nodded.

"Let's go."

We didn't have far to walk to the lift. Just as well. The air had grown so hot that if my hair had burst into flame, it wouldn't have come as a complete surprise. Lungs burning, legs heavy, faces scrunched against the furnace glare, we stumbled across the paving stones; the same stones which doubled as a movie screen and, allegedly, as a gateway into another galaxy.

"To some people, the pursuit of AI is the top of a slippery slope to damnation," Jack muttered behind me, his voice hoarse. "But to any computer geek, it's the Holy Grail. And it—*she*—was there, right there, in front of me. Close enough to touch. I *did* touch her. And conversed with her. I bet she'd have passed the Turing test, no bother. If only—"

"Shut up." It was all I could manage. My throat felt as though the strongest whisky was being poured down it.

"Just saying, that's all…" But I had stopped listening.

"Aw, *no*!"

The lift shaft stood a few steps away.

Kim had disappeared inside. The door was sliding closed.

I watched the door shutting through a wavery heat haze, with a leaden lump where my stomach should be. Although mere feet away, we wouldn't make it in time. But with barely an inch to go before the door closed completely, two sets of fingertips appeared around its edge and it began to open.

"Oops," said Kim as her head and torso appeared. "Almost let it shut." She started to grin, but her expression sobered immediately on squinting past us. Her hand came up to shield her eyes. "Inside, *now*!"

We needed no second invitation. Sweating profusely, Jack and I stumbled into the lift, Kim stepping aside to usher us in. Tara waited for us in her accustomed position in one corner.

"Not before time," she remarked.

"Everyone back from the door." Kim's voice contained a note of panic which made me turn around.

Outside the lift, the world—Terra Two, or whatever the box had called it—had grown as bright as the hottest summer day, when sand and sea and sky are white and dazzling and almost indistinguishable from one another. The wind had become a squall, gusting scorching air into our faces.

The lift door stood wide open—those few moments of pregnant pause before it decided to attempt closing again. It wouldn't be the first time during this crazy morning that the door's closing had saved our skins, but if it didn't happen quickly we'd have no skins left. They would scorch and blister and split like the casings of overcooked sausages.

The squall strengthened, drying the sweat on my brow, tightening my cheeks and searing my lips.

A rushing noise filled my ears, as loud as a football crowd, rising in a shrieking crescendo like a revving jet engine. The light became blinding, brighter than a phosphorous flare. I would have sworn there wasn't enough room for all four of us to crouch simultaneously while being wary about obstructing the door, but somehow that is what we did, bowing our heads and wrapping our arms around them to shield our ears and eyes and faces from the noise and glare and heat.

The gale buffeted our huddled forms, the heat so intense that the hairs on the backs of our hands shrivelled and our clothes began to smoulder. The stench of sweat and terror and burning seared my nostrils. We must have cried out in anguish or fear, but any sound we made was lost beneath the din. The first crashes of tumbling masonry added to the pandemonium. The floor of the lift shook beneath my knees.

The brightness increased impossibly, registering through bowed and covered head, and tightly clenched eyelids. Brilliance like I had never before, or since, experienced; how I imagine it must be to fall into a star. Which, in a way, is what was happening.

Then—

Calm.

Moving like people awaking from a shared dream, we raised our heads and blinked at each other. The air in the lift had already begun to cool, but the interior remained stuffy and dry. It reminded me of my flat when I returned home from work on a fine summer's evening having forgotten to leave any windows open.

The door had, of course, closed and saved our bacon yet again. Or maybe saved us from becoming oversized rashers of the crisp variety. I stretched out an arm and touched the door with my hand, yanking it back with a hiss a moment later.

"That's hot."

"It must have taken a baking before it left that place," said Kim. "We *have* left that place, haven't we?"

Now that she came to mention it, I couldn't recall the judder of the lift jerking into motion or the sinking sensation as it descended. No sooner had the thought occurred than the familiar judder came, followed closely by the sensation of descent.

Kim grimaced. "Another lucky escape." She let out a heavy sigh. "Man, that was a close call." She glanced at Jack and shook her head.

I also looked at Jack. He stared at the door from his kneeling position.

"Hey," I said. "You asked that box if you could pass through the star gate it talked about. To end up goodness knows where. What were you thinking?"

Jack's lips drew tight and his shoulders moved in what might have been a shrug or a twitch of irritation.

"Come on," I insisted. "What if the box—okay, Miriam, if you'd prefer—what if she'd agreed you could step through the gate?"

He looked at me. The skin had drawn tight over his cheeks and shone in the lift lights.

"I'd have gone in a heartbeat."

"But if what Miriam said wasn't merely some mechanical fantasy, you'd have ended up on a planet in an unknown galaxy centuries into the future. You wouldn't have a clue about their technology or culture. You wouldn't know a soul. What sort of life would you have been able to make for yourself?"

Jack's top lip curled into a sneer. "Seriously? You think that it would be any worse than the life I've got now?" He looked away, dismissing me.

I could think of nothing intelligent to say that wouldn't have sounded patronising or trite, so I said nothing.

Part 4: First Floor and Basement

One

Existing in a state of fear and disconnection from reality brought on by repeated exposure to the unnatural and extraordinary, we grow hardened to the unnatural and extraordinary. Being constantly thrust into situations which would ordinarily have us rubbing our eyes in disbelief or regressing to a condition of gibbering infantility, instead our gaze might widen fractionally, our breaths draw deeper in resignation, but otherwise we give a Gallic shrug and soldier on. Wearied to the point of becoming blasé.

When the lift jolted to a halt, I only glanced at the display to confirm what I already knew.

1.

Maybe our pulses quickened a little during the pause before the door slid open, but nobody spoke. We merely stood and waited. We had become stoic.

A blasted land met our gazes. The horizon was formed by a ring of jagged hills, enclosing a featureless, desolate plain. A weak sun shone in a clear, pale sky. Into our faces blew a cool breeze, raising swirling eddies of dust in its passage.

Kim poked out a foot gingerly and made an imprint in the dust with the toe of her clunky shoe.

"I think it's ash," she remarked.

I sat down, my back to the side wall; I had no intention of setting foot outside the lift this time. The stinging sunburn to the back of my neck attested to how close we had come to disaster on the Second Floor.

The others followed my lead, taking up their usual places so that Tara and Jack occupied the rear wall, while Kim and I faced each other across the opening. It felt snug with all four of us sitting. Cosy.

We waited to find out what the First Floor held in store.

《 》

"Anyone know what time it is?" asked Tara. "My watch seems to have stopped."

"I don't think time has much meaning here," said Kim.

"I'm due to give a presentation at half past nine." Tara patted the document case, which sat on the floor by her feet. "It's in here, all ready to go." She frowned. "The slides are on a memory stick in the pocket of my jacket." She glanced at the shredded garment bundled into one corner. "Wonder if it's still there?"

Jack grunted. "Worrying over whether you've lost presentation slides probably shouldn't rank high on your current list of priorities."

Tara looked genuinely puzzled. "Why ever not? This dream can't last for ever. When it's over, I'll still have a career to advance."

"You don't happen to have anything useful in that case?" asked Kim. "Like a bottle of water?"

Tara gasped. "Why, yes. I do." She reached for the case. "I'd forgotten all about it."

Kim and I straightened, our tongues hanging down like pink roller blinds. One bottle, even split four ways, would be heavenly. More so than coffee, or even beer, I was that thirsty.

It should have been obvious from the way Jack avoided my gaze. While Tara rummaged in her case, I happened to glance at him. He quickly looked away, finding his fingernails suddenly fascinating. The first forebodings stirred in my empty stomach.

When Tara stiffened, a frown creasing her forehead, it didn't come as a surprise. She drew her hand from the case, clutching a plastic bottle. An *empty* plastic bottle.

"I don't understand…" she said slowly.

I did, all too well. "Was it full when you entered the lift this morning?"

She nodded.

"And you haven't touched it since?"

She shook her head.

"Bastard!" I glowered at Jack.

"What?" he said, at last daring to look in my direction, though not directly at my eyes.

"You drank it."

"Fuck off. I haven't done nothing."

"When the three of us were out in that desert. You drank it all and didn't leave us a drop."

He shook his head, just once. Emphatically. But he wasn't fooling me.

Nor, apparently, Kim. "It could only have been you, sweetie," she said. "You're the only one who's been in here alone while everyone else was outside."

"Actually," I said, "that's not true. Tara stayed in here while the three of us were talking to Miriam. But look—" I pointed at Tara's drawn face, at her white, cracked lips. "She's as parched as we are. She hasn't drunk anything."

Kim favoured Jack with her best glare, then turned away in disgust.

I wasn't ready to be so lenient.

"Of all the selfish…" I began, hoping that he would give me some lip or at least shrug in that insolent manner that seemed to come so naturally. It shames me a little to admit that I wanted him to give me an excuse to rough him up, but I'm glad now that didn't happen.

I never completed my sentence for Kim gave a gasp and jumped to her feet.

"Look!" she said.

I looked and all thoughts of retribution against Jack went clean out of my head.

The landscape had changed. The hill-enclosed, desolate plain remained the same roughly circular shape and composed of the same ash, puffing and eddying in the breeze, but its uniform flatness had been broken.

I joined Kim at the lip of the doorway. From behind me came rustling movement as Tara and Jack rose to peer past us.

There was no way to accurately judge the distance across the plain, but I'm guessing that it was a mile or so away, towards the centre of the circle, that something protruded from the ash. Rather, many things. They hadn't been there when we'd arrived.

I narrowed my eyes, trying to make out their precise shape. They were dark in colour, making it harder to differentiate their contours against the charcoal background, but appeared to be tall and slim, with narrower limbs extruding from the main body.

"They're trees," murmured eagle-eyed Jack from over my shoulder.

Of course, he was right. Trees, hundreds of them, a small forest, were materialising from the ground before our eyes. As they grew, so they became clearer and colours became apparent. Browns and reds, greens and yellows. Deciduous trees, evergreens and species I had never seen before sprang higher and broader, bloomed and matured like a series of stop-motion photographs taken over many seasons played back at crazy speed. Leaves sprouted, blossom flowered, fruit ripened.

"This is mad," I said, tearing my gaze away from the trees to glance at Kim.

She no longer watched the trees; she stared drop-jawed at the ground outside the lift.

The activity wasn't confined to the central area of the plain. If anything, the land nearby was busier. It had come alive with colour as ground shoots and shrubs and bushes erupted from the ash. Clouds of dust thickened the air like swarms of gnats.

A vine curled around the edge of the lift and began to climb. A goofy smile stole across my face; I was helpless to prevent it.

It grew wider as I watched the bunch of grapes form and grow plump.

《 》

My stomach growled and my dry throat contracted at the fragrant scents carried to us on the breeze. The bunch of grapes weighed heavy in my hand. I picked one and held it up between thumb and forefinger for closer inspection.

Beneath its fine dusting of powdered ash, it looked to be a perfectly ordinary grape: purple deepening to black, duskily sheened, almost as large as a plum and as fat as a coiled witchetty grub. It felt lightly cushioned when I squeezed, with an underlying firmness that suggested an optimum state of ripeness.

Saliva flooded my mouth, but still I hesitated.

All three of my companions watched me closely. Tara's breathing was so shallow she almost panted. Jack's tongue kept darting out to lick his lips. Kim's chest heaved like a regency heroine's.

I took a deep breath and popped the grape between my teeth.

And bit.

Imagine tasting for the first time your favourite chilled drink on the hottest of summer days after trekking five miles across baking asphalt without shade or refreshment. *That's* how good the grape tasted.

On occasion, I have been known to play practical jokes on work colleagues—inverting the screen of their monitor, sending spoof e-mails if they leave their computers unlocked and unattended, that sort of childish yet amusing prank—and it did cross my mind to allow the half-chewed grape to dribble down my chin while feigning a pained rictus and clutching at my neck, but the thought was driven away by the sweet explosion on my taste buds and the trickle of cool juice down my parched throat.

It was the most exquisitely delicious thing I have ever tasted. But I didn't eat another for something else caught my eye.

I handed the bunch to Kim. While she and the others fell on

the grapes like vultures on a corpse, I forgot all about my vow not to set foot outside and stepped onto the soft ash.

Three paces away, a straggly plant had spewed from the ground in a profusion of green leaves and hairy stems. Its fruit—the size of a bowling ball, dark green with yellow stripes, or yellow with dark green stripes—demanded my attention. I could almost see and taste the flesh beneath the rind: pink and sweet and nearly entirely water.

Ignoring the powdery ash that billowed under my steps, I crouched by the watermelon, grasped it and tugged. The stem was tough but thirst lent me strength. With a grunt of effort and satisfaction from me, accompanied by a faint tearing sound from the plant, the fruit came free and I rose to my feet triumphantly clutching my prize.

"Matt!" It was Kim's voice.

I turned, the smile dying on my lips when I saw her expression. Pale and thin-lipped, she pointed behind me.

"Come back inside," she said in a low voice.

"There could be more—" She didn't let me finish.

"Inside. Now." She looked at me and I read the fear in her eyes. "The hills are moving."

Two

If I had thought of Kim when I first saw her that morning as the stereotypical, cocksure American with a large appetite for food but little for knowledge of other cultures, that impression had been swept away along with my preconceptions of how well I believed I understood the world around me and the universe in which it floated.

Impressed by her courage and forthrightness, my faith in Kim had grown throughout that endless ride in the elevator. If she said I needed to step back inside immediately, I didn't need to waste time looking around to confirm she was correct.

Still clutching the watermelon—nothing was going to make me give up that prize—I strode to the lift and past her. Jack and Tara, still munching grapes, pressed back to let me in.

"Right. Everyone away from the door," said Kim, the worry in her voice unmissable. "We need it to close. Like, *now*."

Whatever Kim had seen, so had Tara and Jack judging by their sober expressions and apprehensive stares past me. It had not stopped them from continuing to enjoy the grapes, a sign that they, like me, had become to some extent immune to paralysis through exposure to strange and terrifying experiences.

No matter what was about to happen, my first concern was for the watermelon. I placed it carefully, reverentially, on the floor next to Tara's document case. That done, my attention could turn to whatever devilry came next.

What I saw when I followed the direction of the others' gazes made me suspect that Floor One was about to test our newfound resistance to fear to the limit.

Kim had said that the hills were moving. As usual, she wasn't wrong.

The line of jagged peaks which formed the horizon rippled and heaved as if at the epicentre of a localised, circular earthquake. Some rose into the air, revealing a broader, curiously marked area below, though the distance was too great to make it out clearly.

"What are those markings?" I murmured. "Jack, what can you see?"

"They look like…" He hesitated.

"Spit it out."

"They look like scales."

"Huh?" An image popped into my head of weighing scales like the old-fashioned set my grandmother used for baking, with cast iron weights which she'd carefully lower onto the pan on one side until they balanced the weight of the flour on the other. Then I realised what Jack meant. "Like fish scales?"

"Sort of."

"It's getting darker," said Tara. "Why is it getting darker?"

The pale sun had barely altered position and no clouds had appeared to mask it. Yet something…

"What's making that shadow?" asked Kim.

A dark shade crept across the plain from the hills towards the forest in the centre. I peered at the sky, trying to spot the cause.

Jack, with his 20:20 vision, had already seen it.

"What the…" he muttered.

Then I saw it, too. An enormous shape, moving across the sun like an unfurling sail. Ragged-edged, it resembled a gigantic bat. Or, at least, its wing.

The plain grew darker, masking the profusion of colour. The sun slipped behind a shroud, the crinkle-cut edge of which was outlined by a corona of pale light.

"I have a *really* bad feeling about this, guys," said Kim in a low voice.

She reached out a hand to the panel and started pressing the button with the close doors symbol.

"Careful," Jack said. "Don't go pressing any more floor buttons."

"Except maybe the Ground Floor," I added.

"We don't even have ground floors in the States," said Kim. She gave a nervous laugh. "Well, of course, we *have* them but we call them the First Floor."

"Like that matters now," said Jack. "Just press the fucking button."

She clicked the close doors button a few more times, moved her finger to the G button and pressed that. Nothing happened.

We stood back from the doorway. Watched and waited. There was little else we could do.

We didn't have to wait long. Gasps from the others signalled that something had changed. It took me a few moments to grasp what my eyes thought they were seeing.

It seems ludicrous to ascribe the word 'head' to something bigger than a department store, but it *was* undoubtedly a head. Reptilian, snouted, with spikes and horns and ridges. Vertically slitted eyes glowed like embers in a draught.

The head swung into view towards the centre of the plain. In the background the hills rose higher, exposing more of the scaled area below. A thin strip of twilit sky showed between scales and horizon.

"I know what that is." Tara's voice sounded distant, dreamy, as though she was determined to continue with her we're-only-hallucinating delusion. "It's a giant lizard."

Jack snorted. "A lizard with scales, horns, ridges and wings is usually called by another name."

"Nah," I said, still doubting the evidence of my eyes. "They're creatures of myth and legend."

"Aye," agreed Jack, "razor-toothed fairies and aquatic acid women don't exist either."

"Nor clawed yetis and giant floating eyes," added Kim.

"Nor—" began Jack, but I cut across him.

"Okay, okay. I get the point. Whatever it is, do you reckon—"

The plain lit up brighter than a flaring furnace and my words were drowned in the roar of white-hot flame.

If you've seen the film *Apocalypse Now*, you may recall the scene where American forces use helicopters to carpet bomb the jungles and village clearings of Vietnam with napalm. Leaves and wood and grass and vines erupt into flames; soon they are little more than smouldering, misshapen twists of charcoal or flakes of ash under the intensity of the inferno.

This was worse.

The head of what Tara had dreamily referred to as a lizard opened its jaws and let forth a stream of fire brighter and hotter than any oxyacetylene torch. Blue around the snout, the flame jet turned to white as it shot away from the creature, becoming yellow and then orange only at its farthest extent.

The trees and other vegetation were vital and fresh, still growing at an unnaturally rapid rate, but that did not prevent them disappearing in a flash under the onslaught. Whatever the flame touched incinerated like a firework exploding. Sap spat and sizzled, and evaporated. Plumes of black soot took to the skies on broiling draughts. Wafts of uncomfortably hot air and ash blew into the lift.

We cowered, huddled together like frightened children, our faces lighting up in flashes of brilliant light.

"The door will close." Kim had to raise her voice to be heard above the inferno. "It *always* closes." She glanced at me as if seeking affirmation.

"Well…" I shrugged. "It has so far."

It sounded weak, not the comfort she sought.

Tough titties.

She wasn't the only one worried that the lift would soon become the equivalent of a barbecue pit.

The small forest in the centre of the plain had been reduced to narrow stacks of charcoal and ash; many of them toppled, creating fresh clouds of dust. The breeze strengthened considerably in the atmospheric upheaval caused by streams of superheated air. The ash being blown into our faces, which had initially felt as insubstantial as snowflakes, began to sting as it became grittier. But these things were peripheral.

Peering between half-closed eyelids, our attention focused on the fire-breathing head.

Apparently satisfied that its destruction of the forested area was complete, the creature…

(Like I struggled to refer to the AI box as Miriam, so I'm hesitant to call the creature by the name we all know. Doing so somehow makes it more real. Perhaps by adopting Tara's approach of assuming it was all a dream—a realistic one, maybe, but fantasy nonetheless—that would put an end to lying awake through long, dark hours, afraid to close my eyes.

But I'm not Tara. I *know* that what happened to us was real. Pretending otherwise would be just that: pretending.

Time to man up…)

Apparently satisfied that its destruction of the forested area was complete, the *dragon* turned its attention to the bushes and other ground vegetation which had sprung up between the forest and the horizon. It lowered its head to bring its snout closer to the ground, parted its jaws and exhaled.

The jet of flame that came from its mouth was shorter than the streams which had obliterated the trees. Bluer and whiter, too, without the yellow and orange extremes. Even from our distance, we could hear the roar, as of a cataract, of pure, intense heat.

"It's like a blowtorch turned to eleven." The awe in Jack's tone was unmistakable. And the fear.

Maybe the beast had to be careful not to scald its scaly hide, if that were possible, but it approached this new stage of wreaking devastation in a more circumspect manner.

It seemed to be able to maintain the more controlled blast of flame for longer periods without drawing breath. And the pauses between the jet dying away and flaring anew were shorter, mere seconds at a time.

Bush and fruit and vine turned instantly to ash as the dragon swayed its ridged neck across the ground. The land rapidly returned to the blasted plain we had first seen on arrival.

Soon—a few minutes at most—the snout would point at us. There was nowhere we could run; nowhere to hide.

Three

It goes without saying that we were scared. Even Tara, with her dream world defence mechanism, regarded the fiery waste with grim-faced trepidation.

Yet we weren't paralysed with terror. We crouched together on the floor of the lift, not doing anything; there wasn't much we could usefully do.

The reason for the lack of bowel-liquefying horror wasn't only that we had grown accustomed to peril. We also anticipated that the lift door would slide shut and save us like it had on the previous floors. Kim had already mentioned that the door would close, but nobody spoke of it again—to do so might jinx it.

The head of the dragon drew nearer, leaving heat-crinkled air and billowing ash in its wake.

I have no idea how good a dragon's eyesight is supposed to be—there's a sentence I never thought I'd write—but I wasn't banking on the beast stopping in surprise when it noticed the lift shaft poking from the ground. If it were to see us, the dragon would probably think, if it thought at all in terms we can express, that the shaft was some unusually angular form of tree. I doubted it would hesitate in turning the lift and us to grey powder.

The door began to close.

Before it slid fully shut, the dragon's nostrils flared and its eyes narrowed, leaving a silvery slit visible. Silvery; not the ember-orange of moments before. Maybe my imagination is combining hindsight and the events that came later to construct an image that didn't actually exist, but I don't think so. I really don't think so. In my memory, the beast's eyes had turned the colour of mercury.

Its mouth opened wider to reveal a blue glow within as it prepared to flame.

Deep sighs of relief filled the lift as we rose to our feet behind the closed door. I grinned at Kim.

"Never in doubt," I said.

She started to return the smile, but it faded at Jack's words.

"We're not out of the woods yet," he said. "The dragon's breath could melt the door. Buckle it, at least. Strand us here. Or worse, leave us stuck between floors."

Four gazes turned to the door.

The temperature inside the lift rose. Sweat trickled down my brow. I stared at the door, waiting for a hole to appear like a patch of grass shows through a snowy lawn during a thaw. My imagination worked overtime for I am certain that a circle was materialising in the scratched metal surface: orange tinged, the size of a manhole cover.

Before I could confirm or dismiss the sight, the familiar judder came and we began to descend.

I slumped back against the side wall. That should be it. Ordeal over. We had visited all levels above Ground Floor. If the lift called at every floor in turn, it should now stop back where we started. Assuming that hadn't changed into some alien landscape, we would shoot out of the door the moment it opened onto the grotty lobby of Claridge House. All the gold in the Vatican wouldn't entice me back in.

"Anyone else notice a pattern?" Jack asked.

"What d'you mean?" said Kim with a frown.

"Well, the further we descend, the more fire seems to be the major theme of the places we visit."

Something in his voice, some undefined tone, gave me a sense of unease, dissipating my relief of moments before. A thought occurred to me. Not a particularly comforting one.

"Kim," I began, "when we stopped on Sixth and the door opened onto countryside instead of office, you panicked and pressed all the buttons on that panel. Right?"

"What if I did? I wasn't the only one freaking out."

"Did you press them *all*?"

"Huh?"

"The buttons. Did you press them all? As in, every single one?"

She glanced at the array of buttons on the panel. "I guess so."

Jack and I shared a look. He mouthed one word to me.

Fuck.

Kim hadn't missed the exchange.

"Guys? What?"

"I think," I said slowly, "that we probably won't be stopping at the Ground Floor next. I have a sneaky feeling we're on our way to the Basement."

All eyes turned to the display panel.

1.

Changed to:

G.

The lift juddered like it did when preparing to come to a halt and there was a general sharp intake of breath.

But it was messing with us. The sinking feeling in my stomach did not lessen. If anything, it increased as though the lift was hurrying to the depths.

The display on the panel changed again.

B.

Ordinarily the basement of Claridge House is a gloomy, echoing space. Each occupier of the floors above is allocated a storage area, cordoned off by wire meshing with a lockable gate, not surprisingly known informally as a 'cage'. I had been to our cage once or twice to hunt for cancelled policies among mouldering cardboard boxes which had been down there since before the office became paperless.

They hadn't been particularly pleasant visits. The few bare bulbs dangling from the concrete ceiling struggled to illuminate more than circles of dusty floor immediately below them; clumps of ancient, dirt-encrusted spider webs clung to every wall; the air was redolent with the sweetish odour of dry rot; ticks and clunks, gurgles and rattles came from the profusion of water and heating pipes and ducts that formed intricate patterns across the ceiling and walls.

Whatever view greeted us when the lift door slid open could only, in my opinion, be an improvement.

The lift shuddered, clanked and creaked to a stop. The usual pregnant pause followed while the door contemplated opening.

Then, once more, the world tilted.

The door hadn't finished sliding open when we pitched through the widening gap. I landed on something soft and rolled. For a few moments, my vision became a confused montage of greens and browns and blues, before I thudded to a halt.

I lay on my back, looking at a clear sky. I waited for a few moments to allow my head to stop spinning, then sat up. Tara lay next to me, uttering soft moans, Kim and Jack the other side of her. Shaken, but nobody seemed hurt. Rather, nobody's existing injuries seemed to have been made worse by the fall.

The watermelon had followed me. It lay a few feet away, appearing none the worse for its brief journey. Tara's document case, a little battered, lay on its side near her.

We had tumbled down a steep, grassy slope. The shaft had emerged at a right angle to the slope so that relative gravity meant that we had been standing almost perpendicular to the ground. As soon as gravity asserted itself, it had yanked us from the lift like greyhounds exiting traps.

I gazed up the slope, wondering how we could all manage to cling to the inside of the lift with it tilted at such a steep angle.

The door began to slide closed.

"No!"

I started up the slope on all fours, grabbing handfuls of grass to yank myself up. My shoes with their smooth soles didn't provide much purchase so I dug my knees into the grass, adding green stains to the blood and muck that already plastered my trousers.

Three yards… two.

I had almost reached the lift, could have stretched out an arm and touched the door with my fingertips, when my ears popped like they do in an aircraft when the cabin pressure changes. The shaft, elevator, door and all, disappeared.

Scrabbling desperately, tearing up clods in my haste, I arrived at the place where the shaft had been moments before.

Thick grass covered the area, like it did the rest of the slope. There wasn't any sign of disturbed earth, no indentations, not so much as a flattened blade of grass to suggest that a brick elevator shaft had arrived, and left again, at this spot.

I moved forward, feeling around like a blind man who has dropped something, then thumping the ground with the sides of my clenched fists like a madman.

The sound that escaped my lips can only be described as a wail.

I knelt on the hillside, forehead pressed to the grass like a fervent worshipper, in a fugue of despair. When at last I raised my head and looked down the slope, the others were watching me, Kim with an expression of concern, Tara and Jack more guarded, as if they wondered quite how crazy I had become.

Despondency making my movements sluggish, I made my way down to them in a half-crawl, half-slide.

Kim reached out and squeezed my forearm in a gesture that I found strangely comforting.

"What now?" she said.

My tongue came out to lick cracked lips. My throat felt as dry as sun-baked gravel. I picked up the watermelon and hefted it.

"Now we eat this."

Four

The grassed area at the foot of the hill gave way to coarser, brackeny ground which sloped gently to a sluggish, brown river. Within fifty yards or so of the bank, the river became obscured by a thick wall of milky fog. It swirled and shifted but did not draw nearer.

The sky looked as blue and clear as a summer's day, the air felt comfortably warm, yet no sun could be seen. If hidden behind the fogbank, it didn't seem to be having much success burning the fog away.

To either side, the land was hemmed in by dark, thick forests of fir trees. An area half the size of a football field immediately before the forest to our right was scattered with light-coloured objects which appeared jagged and broken. They would bear closer examination, but we needed to slake our thirsts before we did anything else.

Finding a rough boulder partly hidden in the grass, I brought the watermelon down onto it hard. The rind split and juice flew up. My stomach gave a low rumble like distant thunder.

"What about the river?" Jack looked doubtfully at the slow-moving water. "Think we can drink that?"

"Be my guest," I said. "Me, I'm sticking to watermelon."

"How do we know *that's* safe?" The petulant whine had returned to his voice. I could feel my hackles begin to rise and brought the fruit down again onto the boulder with such force that dark seeds and flecks of pink flesh spattered my cheeks.

"Well, the grapes were okay," said Kim, "and they were from the same place. Planet. Dimension. Whatever."

I handed her a chunk of melon. Then Tara, who took it without a smile or nod of acknowledgement.

Away with the fairies again.

Jack's petulant tone reminded me that he had guzzled Tara's bottle of water. I paused before holding out a chunk of melon towards him. Juice ran down my arm.

He noticed me hesitate and dropped his gaze from mine. He took the melon, though.

"Thanks," he muttered.

I held up my own chunk. The flesh looked like it had been formed from red ice crystals. Another low rumble came from my stomach.

Three pairs of eyes watched me closely, once more waiting for me to make the first move.

I raised the fruit to my lips and bit deeply.

The watermelon had over-ripened a little past its optimum crispness so that it had started to become mushy. Nevertheless, it tasted every bit as good as the grape I'd consumed on the First Floor. Judging from the others' blissful expressions as they tucked in, they felt the same.

I handed out more chunks and within minutes the ground around us had become littered with black seeds and leathery segments of rind stripped of flesh. We wiped the juice from our hands and faces with handfuls of grass.

The melon had served two timely purposes: it had slaked our raging thirsts and, for me at least, had softened the devastating blow of seeing the lift shaft disappear. It had also given me some moments for reflection.

"Lightning," I said.

Blank stares met me.

I continued, "When I was walking to work this morning, forked lightning struck the roof of Claridge House."

Jack sat straighter. "Yes, it did," he agreed. "I'd forgotten about that."

"So?" said Tara. "What of it?"

"Well," I said, "maybe, just maybe, that has something to do with what's been happening to us. Perhaps it somehow caused it."

She snorted; she was good at conveying contempt with her nostrils. "Yeah, right. I always experience nightmares after lightning strikes."

I wasn't too shabby at conveying contempt myself when I had a mind to. "Still persisting with the this-is-all-a-bad-dream delusion?" I said in my most withering tone.

Tara coloured and looked away.

"I doubt that lightning could *cause* something like this," said Jack. "It's only electrical energy, after all." He chewed his bottom lip for a moment before going on. "But maybe it *facilitated* it."

"What d'you mean? Like a catalyst?"

"Dunno. I mean like it provided the energy required to move us between dimensions." He shrugged. "Or whatever."

"Frankenstein's monster." I felt a surge of excitement, as if we were getting close to something. "The lightning provided the energy to spark life into a corpse."

Jack shrugged again; it was definitely his favourite gesture. "Dunno about that. Dunno much about anything, really." He resumed his former slouched pose, his interest in the discussion apparently exhausted.

My excitement waned. The sense of being close to an answer dissipated like smoke in the wind.

Kim hadn't taken any part in the conversation about lightning. Her fleeting look of joy on biting into the melon had been replaced by a brooding, sombre expression.

"Cheer up," I said, as much to take my mind off my failed theory as out of concern for the American. "It's bound to come back. The lift, I mean."

"You don't know that." She sighed. "Besides, that wasn't what I was thinking about."

Not being the sort to persuade someone to talk about something they'd rather keep to themselves, I said nothing. But Kim obviously wanted to get it off her chest.

She gave a deeper sigh. "It's Miriam. Or what Miriam showed us." I became aware from the corner of my eye of Jack, at the mention of Miriam, paying close attention. "You know,

Yellowstone erupting. Everyone ending up on that planet with the red sun. Moving from planet to planet, galaxy to galaxy, never knowing whether they'll ever return to Earth." She looked down at her juice-stained hands. "What sort of future is that?"

"The box—" I still could not refer to it as 'she' or by name "—said that Yellowstone doesn't erupt until more than two hundred years from now."

"I know." Kim's voice sounded small, shorn of its normal confidence. "But our descendants, our great-great-grandchildren or whatever… what's the point in us having kids?"

"Look," I said gently. "We all know that Earth will become uninhabitable one day through some cataclysmic event like nuclear war or the icecaps melting or, or… Want to help me out here, Jack?"

"Asteroid strikes," he supplied. "Terrorist strikes. Pandemics of superbugs resistant to antibiotics. Overpopulation. Bee extinction. Alien invasion. Solar flares. Electromagnetic pulses."

I looked at him. "Think about the end of the world a lot, do we?" I turned back to Kim. "The point is, what the box told us offers us hope. That Swiss guy—"

"Bruder," interrupted Jack.

"Yeah, Bruder. Well, he's going to discover a way for us to continue so our descendants won't be wiped out by Yellowstone. Humanity will survive. Our great-great-grandchildren will survive."

"Unless," added Jack, not so helpfully, "they're among the thirty-three percent who decide to stay behind."

I frowned at him.

But Kim seemed to be perking up. "Miriam said the possibility of people still being alive on Earth can't be discounted."

"Yes, er, she did," I said. "If what we saw and heard on the Second Floor is true, we should take comfort in the knowledge that the future of our species is assured for many, many centuries to come."

Kim sat straighter. "You know, Matt, I think you're right." She smiled; it became a mischievous grin. "Yep, maybe we should go ahead and have kids." She favoured me with a look that made me blush and Jack snigger.

I jumped to my feet. "I'm going to take a look around."

The water in the river looked dark and uninviting. The occasional whiff of an acrid, chemical odour reached my nostrils. From the water's edge, the fog bank appeared as dense and impenetrable as from farther back, and no more of the river was visible from this closer vantage point.

There *was* something that I hadn't noticed earlier: a small wooden jetty jutted from the bank a few inches above the water level. Next to the jetty floated a wooden raft, tethered by a thick chain made of a metal which had not corroded. The chain ran through a sturdy metal loop affixed to the centre of the front edge of the raft, across its deck and through an identical loop at the rear, before disappearing into the murky water.

The deck was rough-hewn and empty except for a pair of heavy-looking gloves made of some sort of hide. Maybe 'gauntlets' would be a better word to describe them—they were serious gloves. I was contemplating walking to the jetty to examine the raft up closer when a shout distracted me. It was Kim.

"Matt! You have to come and see this."

Kim and Jack stood at the edge of the area strewn with light-coloured, irregular objects. Kim beckoned to me.

Tara remained sitting where we'd ended up at the foot of the steep embankment. The document case lay ignored where it had fallen. As I walked past, I glanced down. Tara stared off into the distance, a strange half-smile on her face. It gave me the creeps and I hurried on.

The ground in front of Kim and Jack was scrubland, little more than packed dirt. The objects which covered it drew my eye.

Bones. Hundreds of them. Probably thousands. Various shapes and sizes, though none that looked bigger than a man's. I'm no human anatomist, but skulls and ribcages, pelvises and spines, and skeletal hands and feet are easily recognisable. All picked clean, whether by birds or beasts or bacteria it was impossible to say.

Among the bones, in varying states of decay, lay what appeared to be clothes. Fraying and torn materials; faded leathers; tarnished buckles and buttons.

Kim's face looked as pale as the bones littering the ground behind her.

"Whose do you think they are?" Some of the old vigour had returned to her voice, though she softened it in much the same way that people talk to each other inside libraries or cathedrals.

"Search me."

Jack peered closely at the ground. "I think I can see a sword."

I followed his gaze. Sure enough, there lay a sword. Corroded, buckled, but undeniably a sword. A few yards away lay another, with a curved blade like a cutlass, its handle still clutched by bony fingers.

"This is more than a graveyard," said Jack in a low voice. "It's a killing field."

"Guys," began Kim, "I have a bad feeling about this place. A *very* bad feeling."

"You're not the only one," I muttered.

"We need to get out of here."

"Tell me something I don't know."

Jack had taken a step or two into the bone-strewn area and poked at objects with his foot. "Wow. Most of this stuff is *old*."

He stooped and straightened, clutching a faded brown object. Kim and I stepped to his side, being careful not to tread on any bones. We peered down at the object as Jack examined it.

A book, small enough to slip into a pocket. On the rotting leather cover, the faded impression of a cross could be made out. As he opened the cover, it disintegrated and fell from his fingers. On the page revealed beneath lay an ink inscription. It had run a little with damp but it seemed that the cover had borne the brunt of decay and protected it. We could read the words written in a neat if childish hand:

B. Briggs, Wareham, Mass. April 24 1845.

Jack gave a low whistle. "Look at that date. This bible isn't old. It's practically prehistoric."

"'Mass'..." I murmured. "Massachusetts?"

"Yep," said Kim. "Hmm. 'B. Briggs'... that name's familiar. Something we did in a class project around fifth or sixth grade."

At that moment, Tara appeared. The away-with-fairies-look had been replaced with a sharper expression. An apprehensive one. She gazed towards the forest at the far side of the field of bones.

"Don't want to worry anyone," she said, "but we're being watched."

Five

A figure had stepped out from the line of trees and stood facing in our direction.

It wore a long robe with a baggy hood; a monk's robe complete with cowl, an image that seemed all too familiar.

Without speaking, we all took a few paces back.

The figure began to move forward.

It reached the area where the scattered bones began, but didn't pause. Crunching noises like breakfast cereal popping reached our ears. A sandalled foot, in the act of completing a step, struck a skull and sent it spinning to land grinning at the sky.

As one, we retreated another couple of paces, unnerved to near panic by the silent, cowled shape walking towards us.

The figure's arms swung by its sides in the loose sleeves of the robe and held no weapon that we could see. It didn't appear particularly tall, yet the way it strode without pause, contemptuous of the human remains it crushed in its passage, its bearing seeming to radiate determination and a confidence that said we were intruders in its domain and would do well to fear it… 'unnerved' might be putting it too mildly.

Of all the monstrosities we had faced that morning, strange that we should be brought to a state of near-paralytic fear by the figure of an unarmed monk.

It arrived at the closest edge of the bone field and stopped. We could now see what the robe contained and it wasn't, as I'd half-expected, a skeleton clutching a blue-edged scythe.

More Friar Tuck than Death. But a Friar Tuck who had not taken care of himself.

A plump man; if not human then in human form. Face florid, all chins and jowls. A fly crawled along the vein-tracked nose; he made no move to brush it away. Eyes made piggy by puffed cheeks gleamed silverly beneath the cowl like far distant stars in the night sky. Thin lips turned into a humourless smile. A calculating smile. Knowing. Sly.

More flies crawled on the hood and front of the robe, taking off with a faint *buzz* and completing a lazy circle of the wide girth before realighting. Maggots the colour of skin that forms on forgotten cream wriggled amidst the robe's folds.

Tara coughed; and again. It sounded like she was gagging. Kim gave a low moan of disgust. Then a waft hit me and I instinctively brought up a hand to cover my nose and mouth. He exuded an odour not exactly like suppurating mushrooms and rancid pork and choked ponds all rolled into one, but damned close.

Jack broke the silence.

"Who are you?"

The monk's smile widened, though still it contained no trace of humour. "I am the Quartermaster."

Tara tittered.

The Quartermaster looked at her. When he grinned—and he grinned a lot—he revealed blackening teeth supporting each other like drunken dominoes in beds of weeping, grey gums. A fresh, foetid wave washed over us.

"*Quartermaster?*" Tara managed to express a mixture of amusement and contempt in that one word; for a moment, I almost admired her. "Where's the army you're supplying, mate? Or the ship you're navigating?"

He did not reply, except to curl the corners of his mouth into a sneer. Or it might have been a snarl.

"Tara, I don't think 'quartermaster' means the same thing here as it does back home," I said.

"Huh!" The exclamation came from Kim. Her gaze was fixed on the Quartermaster with something approaching awe.

The monk's head had tilted to one side and his grin had grown wider. He flipped his head to the other side and uttered what might have been a snigger.

"Do you see?" said Kim. "He's telling us something."

"What?"

"That maybe the head we found ourselves inside on Floor Three was his."

"Don't be daft. That's crazy!"

"What, being inside *his* head is what makes it crazy?"

I opened my mouth, then shut it again. In the absence of anything half-intelligent to say, it's often best to say nothing.

"So, er, Quartermaster," said Kim. "Who did all those bones behind you belong to?"

"To those who chose unwisely." His voice contained no inflection or detectable accent or timbre. Monotonal. The box calling itself Miriam possessed more personality when it spoke.

But it wasn't his voice that bothered me. Rather, the words he used. Unease coiled inside me like a constricting serpent.

Kim had picked up on it, too. "What do you mean by 'chose'?"

"All existence consists of choices." The Quartermaster's stomach quivered, dislodging maggots which fell like chunky flakes of dandruff. It took me a moment to realise he was chuckling soundlessly.

"And what choice do we need to make?" I asked. "In order to leave this place and return to our own world?" The serpent in my gut squirmed. What with that and the stench coming from the figure standing before us, I wondered for how long I'd be able to retain the watermelon.

The Quartermaster's mound of stomach wobbled more vigorously. He brought his hands across to clutch it as though to stop his guts spilling out with mirth. Flies disturbed by the motion took off and circled like angry satellites. Still he made no noise. It took him a few moments to compose himself sufficiently to reply.

"Returning to your time and place is not an option. In any case, not for you all."

The four of us glanced at each other. I saw expressions of fear and bewilderment and anger, all of which I was also experiencing.

Jack, especially, looked annoyed. "I've had a titful of this," he said. "Everywhere we've been, things have tried to bite us or slash us or burn us. Now we've got some fat twat telling us we can't go home. Sod that."

He turned towards the Quartermaster, a reckless look in his eyes. Kim tried to snag his arm. He shook her off and stalked forward.

Less than a pace from the monkish figure, Jack stopped, hands planted on hips. "Where's the lift?" he demanded. "You know, the lift, the elevator, or whatever the fuck you'd call it. Where is it?"

The Quartermaster watched Jack's approach with an expression of smug merriment. He gazed steadily back at Jack, apparently unfazed by his aggressive attitude.

"Well?" Jack raised one hand and pointed a finger at the man's chest.

"Your conveyance cannot return. Not unless the Task is completed." Despite the lack of emphasis in his tone, the Quartermaster managed to intimate by the slightest of pauses that the word 'task' began with a capital T.

"*Task?* What are you talking about? This isn't Dungeons and Dragons. We're not on some frigging quest."

"All who come here must complete the Task. Or perish."

Jack said nothing for a moment. I saw him tense and knew he was going to do something stupid. Maybe I should have called out or tried to stop him, but I let him continue. If he wanted to get himself hurt or worse, why should I interfere? The little bastard had drunk all Tara's water.

He lunged at the Quartermaster.

Jack recoiled as if tethered to an elastic rope which had run out of slack. He turned aside and I caught a glimpse of his face: white as a fish's belly, contorted into a grimace of sheer revulsion. He sank to his knees, head bowed, and vomited a stream of pink, speckled liquid.

He climbed unsteadily to his feet and tottered back to where we waited, wiping weakly at his mouth with the back of a hand.

"What happened?" I hadn't seen the Quartermaster raise so

much as a finger and was curious to know what he had done to repel Jack so effectively.

"Aw, man, that was vile. I went to grab him and saw an image in my mind so clear, like it wasn't an image but was really happening. In the image I touched him and *became* him. Or like him. The waxy skin and ponging like runny cheese was bad enough. But the worst thing…" He drew a long, shuddering breath. "The worst thing was what my mind became as him. He—if he's even a he, not an it—is as mad as a jar of wasps. Not just a little bit crazy, but completely and utterly barking. And…"

"And what?" Kim had gone nearly as pale as Jack. She kept shooting nervous glances towards the Quartermaster, who hadn't moved from where he stood at the edge of the bone field.

Jack turned haunted eyes to her. "He's evil. Filled with spite and poison. More black-hearted than the cruellest Nazi running a Polish death camp." He grimaced. "I'd rather die horribly than become like him."

The Quartermaster continued to watch us with a look of amusement on his glistening face. From what little I could see of his silvery eyes beneath the cowl, they seemed to dance with the dead lights of insanity.

"You should perhaps consider yourself fortunate," said the Quartermaster in his tuneless voice, "that I am not one readily given to taking umbrage at verbal slights." He flicked out a hand impatiently, making the baggy sleeve of the robe flap, disturbing more flies and maggots. "You are wasting… *time*." He spoke the last word as if it represented a concept that was unfamiliar or, perhaps, repugnant.

"This task," I said. "Please would you explain exactly what it entails?"

The Quartermaster looked past me towards the river. "No fewer than one of your number must cross to the farther shore."

"What the hell?" Jack had recovered his poise somewhat. "What are we supposed to do—swim?"

I shook my head. "There's a raft. It's attached to a chain and there are heavy-duty gloves… ah. Of course. The chain runs out into the water. We'll have to pull ourselves along hand over hand. That's what the gloves are for."

"*We?*" said Tara. "I'm not going anywhere."

"No," said Kim, pursing her lips. "You can't risk being away from the office too long, can you? I wonder quite how the false leg industry is managing without you."

Tara shot the American a dark look. "Well, dearie, I imagine the world of loss adjusting is coping perfectly well without *you*."

Kim bristled.

I looked at them both. "*Really?* You want to take pops at each other now? Time and place, ladies, time and place." I turned to the Quartermaster. "Let's be sure I've got this straight. All of us, or three of us, or two of us, but at least one of us, must cross the river on that raft. If we do, the lift will return and whoever remains may go home. Is that it?"

"You have summarised the Task succinctly."

"How wide is the river?"

"You see the mist. Where it begins is mid-stream."

"And what's on the other side?"

"Those who make the crossing shall know, but they alone shall know."

"If we cross, can we come back the same way?"

The Quartermaster's knowing smirk grew wider. "Those who cross can never return."

"What if we refuse, all of us, to get onto the raft?"

"Then the creatures of the forest shall feast well this night."

At first, I didn't know what he was talking about. Then, at the same time as someone drew in a sharp breath, I saw movement.

Something emerged from the forest behind the Quartermaster.

Not one, but lots of things.

Six

As phobias go, mine is not uncommon. Ophidiophobia: the abnormal fear of snakes. I blame my mother. She can't even look at a picture of a snake in a book. If one should appear on the television screen, she has to leave the room.

I'm not quite as bad as her. I'll sit and watch a documentary about our slithery friends, although I have to pick my feet off the floor and curl them under me where I know they're safe from sneak attack, and will experience dark dreams that night involving hot jungle smells and the papery sounds of sinuous, scaly skin.

It's one thing to watch a programme on television; quite another to be standing in the path of hundreds of approaching serpents. That's no exaggeration. There *were* hundreds of them, probably in excess of three hundred, getting in each other's way so that they slinked and slid over one another like tangled vines.

Assorted colours, sizes and species, some of which I could identify from those documentaries: cobras, black mambas, rattlers, pythons, puff adders. Some were multi-coloured and as thin as shoelaces; others thicker than my arm. A few specimens looked to be long enough to swallow me whole if they could unhinge their jaws wide enough.

The snakes had emerged from the tree line and were making their way slowly but steadily towards us. In moments, they would reach the edge of the bone field.

Each snake, on its own, would have caused me extreme fright and revulsion. To see so many slithering my way was too much to take in. I turned my head away, towards my companions.

It took a glance to confirm that they, too, were watching the approach of a nightmare.

Kim and Tara clutched each other, their spat of moments ago evidently forgotten. Tears rolled down Kim's cheeks, cutting through the accumulated sweat and grime of the worlds we had visited. Tara didn't cry, but her face had gone as pale as moonlight.

Jack stared towards the forest, slack-jawed with repugnance and disbelief.

"Jack!" I hissed. "We need weapons."

He looked at me as if he had never seen me before.

"Huh? What use are weapons against *them*? Not unless you can rustle up some machine guns."

"Yeah, there are a lot of them, but if we each grabbed a sword…" I floundered as his look of incredulity deepened.

"Are you nuts? A rusty sword won't do any good. Can't you see what they have in place of teeth?"

A suspicion rose in my mind. "What do you see, Jack?"

"Clowns," he said and shivered.

If I hadn't been quietly freaking out about the mass of serpents heading my way, I might have laughed.

"*Clowns?*"

He nodded miserably. "Don't you see them?"

"I see snakes. Hundreds of snakes."

He looked towards the forest and his lips moved silently as he did a rough count. "There are around fifty of them. And they're not circus clowns. These are the ones from my nightmares. Razor blades instead of teeth. Tongues and gums shredded to stumps. They'll smell worse than the fat monk. What's left of their lips split open when they grin."

The snakes had reached the field of bones. I expected them to continue advancing, to wriggle through eye sockets of skulls and thread between rib cages, but they slid to a halt as though obeying some unheard command. Many raised their heads and swayed to a silent tune. Cobra hoods inflated. Rattled tails oscillated; the sound reached me like a distant game of dice.

I looked at the women. They had stopped clutching each other. Kim wrapped her arms tightly around herself, her stricken gaze transfixed by what had appeared from the forest. Tara seemed slightly the better of the two so I addressed her.

"What do you see coming out of the trees?"

She replied without hesitation. "Dogs. Not the yappy kind, but Dobermans and Rottweilers and pit bulls. I've been terrified of them since I was a kid. Their snarling is so loud, you wouldn't be able to hear me talking if…" Her voice tailed away dreamily.

"If this were real," I finished for her. "Kim, what about you?" She didn't make any move to show that she'd heard me. "Kim?"

I took a step closer and laid a hand gently on her arm. She jumped and I moved my arm around her; she trembled like someone in the grip of a fever.

"It's okay." I tried to make my tone soothing, but I'm not good at that sort of thing. "It's me. Matt."

At last, she seemed able to tear her gaze away from the forest.

"What do you see?" I repeated.

She let out a deep breath. "Dolphins." Before I could react, she continued, "Yeah, I know how that sounds, but I've always had a phobia about them. Those bulging domed brows and holes in the top of their heads, they're like mutant babies. And what's with those beaks? Are they supposed to be a fish or a freaking bird? Yeah, I know they're mammals and they normally live in water, but they're over there, waddling across the ground, a goddamn lot of them. They totally bug me out."

"Huh." I didn't know what else to say.

"And I've remembered where I know the name B. Briggs. Benjamin Briggs. He was the captain of the *Mary Celeste*."

"The what?"

Kim rolled her eyes at my display of ignorance. "If we ever get back, Google it."

"Our worst nightmares," murmured Jack. He nodded in the direction of the Quartermaster who hadn't moved and continued to watch us with a sardonic smile playing on his chubby face. "He's reflecting back what we fear most."

"So," I said slowly, "for once Tara's right." I ignored her smug snort. "Those snakes, clowns, whatever, aren't real."

"Oh," said Jack, "we're not seeing them in their true form, but I think they're real enough." He indicated the piles of bones and rotting clothes. "There lies the proof. Their swords did them no good and they must have been sharp then." He sighed. "There's only one way out of this. One of us will have to perform the task."

Much as I'd like to say I stepped forward and volunteered to save my companions, I'd be lying. Instead of unselfish deeds of valour, what popped into my head was an image of my parents trying to rebuild the bonds between us which I had largely been instrumental in breaking.

We all looked at each other and, before I dropped my gaze, I saw similar thoughts on the faces of Tara and Kim. No doubt Jack saw them, too. To cover my shame, I turned to the Quartermaster.

"Hey!" He turned his lazy gaze to me. "What are you, then? The Glimmer Man? All smoke and mirrors, but no substance?"

I wasn't trying to rile him, but embarrassment at my inability to sacrifice myself to save others made me reckless.

For the briefest moment, the Quartermaster's mask slipped. I'm sure that he did it on purpose and for my benefit only so that I alone saw what lay behind the sweaty monk façade.

Forget snakes. Forget vampires and zombies and werewolves. Forget the real-life horrors in our world. They all pale into insignificance next to the Quartermaster's true face. It will haunt my dreams to the day I die.

Jack had gained some idea of the Quartermaster's nature when he tried to attack him. Now I, too, saw it clearly laid bare. All too clearly. All too bare.

Despair. Chaos. Desolation. Intelligence so vivid it blinded me. Eyes like bottomless pools of utter bleakness, yet also alive and dancing with infinite depths of depravity, derangement and vast knowledge. And, perversely, joy, a constant rejoicing in the sheer immensity of his insanity.

Mere words. They cannot adequately describe what I glimpsed, yet are all I have.

He called himself the Quartermaster and I do not know who

or what he really was. But I shall always think of him, when I cannot avoid doing so—which will be often, I suspect, in the dark, sleepless hours—by one title. There are other possibilities, but this one fits so perfectly the creature whose inner being I glimpsed.

The Lord of the Dance.

"Matt! Matt! Snap out of it!"

"Huh?" I was being shaken. Kim's face swam into focus. "What's wrong?"

"It's Jack. He's made off towards the river. And…"

"What?"

She took a sideways glance in the opposite direction. "I know you don't believe me about the dolphins—" she held up a hand to quell my objection "—but they're coming for me."

"So are the dogs," said Tara in a breathless voice.

My head turned towards the forest. The snakes were on the go again, slithering across and through the bone field, moving together, as one. The fastest, like the black mambas, the sprinters of the anguine world, weren't forging ahead as would be expected. More confirmation that what I saw was a projection and not in fact a multitude of serpents.

I spared one last glance at the Quartermaster. He nodded as if we had shared a confidence. My skin crawled and I almost, once more, gave up the watermelon. But I swallowed hard and set off for the river, Kim at my heels, Tara hobbling along behind on her sprained ankle.

Jack had already reached the raft and stood on its surface—it barely rocked—pulling on the gauntlets. In the few moments it took for me to run to the jetty, he had lifted the chain dripping from the water and heaved the raft a few yards from the water's edge.

"Jack, wait!"

Kim arrived by my side. "No!" she hissed.

"What?"

"Let him go."

Tara also reached us and nodded in agreement.

"We can't," I protested.

"Yes, Matt, you can." Jack had pulled a few yards farther out, but his voice carried to us easily.

"I saw him, too, Jack," I called. "Stay away from him. He's the Lord of the Dance." It sounded silly to my ears and I expected Jack to say something sarcastic in mockery, but he nodded grimly.

"That's as good a name as any." He glanced back. "Better make your way to where the lift's going to appear. Those razor-mouthed bastards are getting closer."

I looked up the slope in the direction of the bone field, but could not see the Quartermaster or any snakes. Not yet, at any rate.

When I turned back to the river, Jack had reached the bank of fog. He looked back for the last time.

I raised my hand in a wave-cum-salute. He grinned and flipped me the finger.

Within moments, he was lost to sight in swirling mist.

Seven

Tara was the first to turn away.

"Right, then," she said. "Let's split this joint."

"The elevator won't be here yet," said Kim. "Didn't that Quartermaster guy say it can't return until Jack reaches the far shore?"

"Oh, balls!" I thought back. "Even if he didn't come right out and say that, he certainly implied it. And talk of the devil…"

The Quartermaster walked along the narrow embankment towards us. I say 'walked', but it more resembled a short-strided waddle. Snakes slithered by his feet, forced by the narrowness of the embankment into a line that stretched back for many yards behind the cowled figure. They were close enough that I could see their tongues darting out to taste us and hear their sibilant whispers.

Much as I feared them, I would rather have stepped into the line of serpents, clambered bare-footed over their backs while they coiled and thrashed and lashed at me with dripping fangs, than look once more upon the Lord of the Dance.

The Quartermaster came to a halt a few paces from the jetty. The stench of corruption wafted over us. I barely dared to glance at him for fear that he would once more allow me to glimpse behind the mask, but to my great relief he kept it firmly in place.

"You are favoured," he said in that uninflected tone. "Many who come here refuse to complete the Task. They did not include any among their number possessed of as stout a heart as your companion."

"How did the others come?" asked Kim. The question had also occurred to me.

"Oh," he said, "in a variety of conveyances. Machines that float in air or on water. Or even beneath water." He chuckled as though at a comical notion, causing a mini-shower of maggots. "Carriages drawn by beasts; others that move of their own volition. And others that run along predetermined tracks. Yet no form of conveyance has been so curious as that which delivered you. Tell me, is your vehicle designed to move within artificial structures?"

"Yes," said Kim. "I suppose it is."

"It has returned."

"Jack must have reached the other shore," I murmured.

"So it would seem," said the Quartermaster. "The other clue to your companion's success in completing the Task is that the creatures of the forest are not feasting on your flesh."

There was a moment's awkward silence while we stared at the snakes (or dogs, or—I still find it difficult to believe—dolphins).

"Before you depart," said the Quartermaster, "as I am sure you must be anxious to do, be aware of one rule that will apply without exception should any of you venture back. On the next occasion, all of you must complete the Task. None may leave by the way they came more than once."

"Jolly good," said Tara. "So are we all done here?" She grabbed my arm and Kim's. "Come on," she said brusquely. "Let's get the hell out of Dodge."

The lift shaft had reappeared in the same spot from which it had blinked out of existence. We reached it by grabbing handfuls of grass and hauling ourselves up the steep slope, much as I had done in desperation when the door slid closed with us on the outside.

We approached from a different direction because none of us wanted to stray too near to the Quartermaster or the 'creatures of the forest' who still milled about his feet. I made it to the shaft first and grabbed hold of the dusty brickwork as though it were a long-lost lover. I'm not ashamed to admit that when I manoeuvred myself around to the door and found it standing open that I shed an involuntary tear.

Clambering into the lift wasn't easy what with the angle at which the floor of the car stood, but nothing was going to prevent us getting, and staying, inside. With a series of grunts and contortions and entanglements, during which we became far too intimately acquainted for three people badly in need of perfumed baths and clean clothes, we managed to wedge ourselves in with no parts protruding that may prevent the door from sliding closed.

My last sight of the place which had replaced the Basement of Claridge House was of the Quartermaster regarding us from the foot of the slope. Before the door slid fully shut, he winked at me in a flash of silver from beneath the cowl, as if to say *See you again someday.*

I didn't have time to ponder that wink—though I've had nothing but time since—for gravity reorientated itself and we fell in a groaning heap to the lift floor.

By the time we'd untangled ourselves and gained our feet, the lift had juddered into ascent. We all watched the floor display and held our breaths.

B changed to G.

The lift shuddered to a halt.

Probably because we were so anxious for the door to open that the customary delay seemed longer than normal, but slide open it eventually did. I have never been so glad to see the dingy foyer of Claridge House. Bumping into each other in our haste, we stumbled out.

The employees waiting for the lift to arrive jumped back in astonishment. We could not have presented a pleasant sight.

Judging by the wrinkled noses and expressions of dismay, neither did we give off a pleasing odour.

We were all three of us arrested, of course. Four people had been filmed on Claridge House's CCTV entering the elevator, only three of us coming out. They found traces of Jack's blood on our clothes and skin—he, too, must have been cut by the wings of the flying creatures on Floor Six—amidst a fair amount of our own and each other's.

Kim and I told them the truth.

We were wasting our breath. It must have irritated the crap out of them: that our stories were so obviously concocted, so obviously fake, yet tallied in every particular.

They examined every inch of the lift shaft, every cable, winch and pulley wheel. They removed the elevator car and tore it apart. Except for the interior, where they found blood that had belonged to all four of us, not to mention other fluids—Jack *did* piss in the corner, and if they made any sense of the smeared remains of flying pixies, they didn't share it with us—they could not find the slightest trace of any misdeeds. They scoured the other floors of Claridge House, lifting carpets and floor tiles, removing ceiling tiles and coffee machines for examination. They could find no forensic evidence that any one of us had exited that lift between getting in on the ground floor at 08:51 that morning and it spitting out me, Kim and Tara, blood-drenched and gibbering, at 08:54.

How that hard-nosed detective wanted to lean across the interview desk and smash my face into it. I could read it in his flinty eyes. Don't suppose I can blame him. He thought I had been complicit in murder; I was probably the most likely candidate for having delivered the killing blow or whatever method he theorised as having dispatched Jack. In his view of the world, there was no explanation other than Kim, Tara and I had murdered Jack and disposed of his body somewhere between the Basement and Sixth Floor.

After my third interview, he reached over to the digital recording machine and switched it off. He leaned in and spoke in too low a voice for the plod standing by the door to hear.

"Look, Matthew, off the record. Just so's I can get to sleep tonight. Tell me how you did it. How you got rid of the corpse without leaving a single trace outside that fucking lift."

His expression was so pleading that if I had performed some bloody version of a magician's disappearing trick I'd have spilled the secret, if only to turn off that beseeching gaze.

"If I knew how to do something like that," I said in a voice as low as his, "don't you think I'd put it to better use than topping someone I barely knew for no financial gain?"

And that was their real problem. Even without the body or any explanation as to how we'd disposed of it, I suspect they might have charged us anyway to see if any mud thrown at the eventual trial stuck. Or if Jack had a family who cared about him enough to make a fuss and demand that we face a jury. But the police did not possess one fundamental part of most successful prosecutions: we lacked a motive. Never mind a strong or compelling motive—we had none at all. No matter how they tried to unearth one, harassing family and friends and work colleagues, they could find no common thread, nothing to link us to Jack, except that we all worked in the same building.

With the greatest of reluctance and with 'quiet aside' warnings ringing in our ears that they would be keeping a close watch on us in future, they had no choice but to let us go.

We never discovered what Tara told the police. I imagine that it was either nothing, or something that at least broadly corroborated mine and Kim's tales. If she had said anything that contradicted our version of events, the police would surely have used the conflicting evidence as a peg on which to hang the prosecutor's horsehair wig.

They naturally kept the three of us apart inside the police station and there was no sign of Tara when I left the station late on a rainy spring evening, but I have seen her once since.

It happened a couple of weeks after the events in the lift took place, when the cuts on my arm and ankle and hands and nose had faded to pink scars, reminders if ever I needed them of what had happened to us that morning. The other reminders were the nightmares.

Tara was coming along the pavement towards me one sunny morning. I slowed as she drew nearer, intending to stop and ask how she was.

She looked the other way and kept going.

I stopped anyway and turned to watch her, shaking my head. If pretending that she didn't know me helped her to pretend that we hadn't taken a trip to strange and dangerous dimensions in an ordinary elevator, who was I to spoil her delusions?

Tara retreated from me without once looking back. As she walked, one shoulder dipped slightly, a symptom of her uneven gait due to the pronounced limp from the sprained ankle she had suffered when the lift tipped her back inside with me desperately clutching her wrist.

Wondering for a moment how she squared acquiring that sprain with denial of all that had happened, I continued on my way. I've barely spared her a thought since.

Unable to face going back into Claridge House, I changed jobs. Always hated cold-calling, anyway. I now wait tables on a permanently moored boat on the river and serve overpriced drinks and snacks to tourists. It pays the rent.

And Kim? You might think that we were thrown together in highly unusual circumstances and would be unlikely to become friends when the ordeal was over. If so, you couldn't be more wrong. We've stayed in touch, met up often, discovered that when no strange creatures are trying to eat us or rip us apart that we enjoy each other's company.

She came with me to visit my parents. My mum gets on easily with anyone, but my dad surprised me by taking an instant liking to Kim. He seems to think that she is a calming influence on me, the sort of person who will make me more responsible. I'm not so sure, but I'm happy for him to go on thinking it.

Once or twice, when we're sure no one's within earshot, we've spoken about Jack. We've wondered what he discovered on that concealed shore, if he's still alive and where he is now. We have no answers, merely questions and pointless speculation.

I've never teased Kim about her terror of dolphins. It's more common than I imagined and even has a name: delfiniphobia.

As I'd thought, she didn't see the real face of the Quartermaster.

"You're lucky," I told her in hushed tones. Even with no one else listening, it wasn't something I felt should be discussed openly. "If we ever find ourselves back in that place, it won't be snakes I'll see coming for me from the forest. He only needs to reveal his true self and I'll piss myself with fright." I took a deep breath. "I call him by another name now. The Lord of the Dance."

"I heard you tell Jack. I assume it has nothing to do with clog-dancing Irish people?"

I glanced at her sharply, sure she must be taking the mickey, but she looked deadly serious.

"No," I said. "It's to do with life. Or, perhaps, death. Randomness and predestination, too. They're all connected, like one big dance. And he's the choreographer."

Kim looked at me intently, then shuddered.

"Let us hope," she said, "that we never run into him again."

There's nothing more to tell. Thanks for reading. Believe what I've written or not, I feel lighter for the telling.

Now I must be on my way; I'm already running a little late.

I'm meeting Kim for a drink at the new rooftop bar that's opened the other side of town.

Of course, late or not, I'll be taking the stairs.

Jack's Tale

Part 1: The Far Shore

One

The river slipped by like spilled syrup. Water didn't so much drip from the chain as dangle. A faint chemical odour drifted from the brown surface, suggesting that contact with human skin might not be advisable.

Jack's hands were protected by hide gauntlets, which covered his forearms nearly to the elbows. He was glad of their protection: the pads of his fingers bore shallow cuts that no longer bled but occasionally caused him a twinge of discomfort. The gauntlets also enabled a firm grasp on the chain, which he pulled hand over hand as effortlessly as if he had been a ferryman for most of his twenty years. By these means, the raft moved easily across the sluggish water.

The bank of fog rose ahead like a wall of cloud. Jack looked back to the shore he was leaving behind.

Three people—two women and a man—stood on the jetty watching his progress. The man raised his hand in a funny half-wave which made Jack grin. He held out a fist and raised his middle finger.

Farther back and to one side of the watching people, a party of razor-toothed clowns, led by a fat, silvery eyed figure in a monk's robe and cowl, moved towards the river bank. Jack repressed a shudder and returned his attention to the chain. A few more tugs and he had reached the fog bank. With the slightest hesitation and a deep breath, he yanked on the chain again.

The mist swallowed man and raft like a ravening beast.

Dank silence. Even the faint gurgle of the river was deadened by the fog. Jack stopped hauling on the chain so he could strain his ears for any sound, but none came.

He sighed. The whisper of exhalation died before it could leave his lips. He began pulling the chain through his gloved hands once more.

Despite his current situation, or perhaps because of it, his mind, with nothing to occupy it but the swirling patterns of fog and rhythmic tugging on chain, wandered a little. He thought, randomly, of his name. More specifically, his surname.

He despised it and only used it when he had no choice on opening a bank account and applying for a provisional driving licence, or when completing formal documents like job applications. It was *her* name. She who had brought him into the world, raised him in an atmosphere of bitterness and neglect, before abandoning him on his sixteenth birthday.

He didn't know what awaited him when he arrived at the far shore, but some things were certain: there would be no more call for bank accounts or driving licences, no more formal documents to complete. He no longer needed a surname so he would discard it along with the life on which he had turned his back.

Willingly turned his back. Jack—just plain Jack, thank you very much—wondered if the three people standing on the jetty imagined he was doing something noble, something heroic. If they believed he was performing a selfless deed in order to save their miserable existences at the expense of his own, they were bigger fools than he'd thought.

Something made him blink, breaking his reverie.

Bright light and warmth on his face. Sunlight.

He emerged from the mist.

The chain ended at a wooden jetty similar to the one from which he'd set off. Beyond lay green plains and undulating hills, darkly wooded slopes and, striding away in the clear distance, purple-tinged mountains.

Jack hesitated, eyes narrowing as he scanned the shoreline for signs of a welcoming committee. If clowns with stumps for tongues and razor blades instead of teeth awaited him here, he didn't know what he would do. If he didn't reach the shore, he wouldn't complete the Task and the others would be set upon by their versions of the clowns—Matt had said he saw them as snakes and hadn't one of the women, the brash Yank, been confronted by, of all things, dolphins?—but Jack could no more advance to meet his worst nightmare than he could choose to thrust his arm into a cauldron of boiling water, no matter the consequences if he failed.

The grassed slopes leading to the water's edge looked clear of life. He could see no evidence of the presence of clowns or a waxy skinned bloke in a robe. And, Jack suspected, seeing the monk here—the Quartermaster, he'd called himself, but Jack preferred the title Matt had given him—would be worse, a great deal worse, than even the clowns. Jack had been shown a glimpse of the monk's true nature when he had tried to grab the cowled figure; his greatest wish, more fervently held than his desire to avoid murderous clowns, was never again to enter the presence of the Lord of the Dance.

Now that he was clear of the mist, the air had turned warm and fresh, despite the chemical odour rising from the water being stronger, sharper here. Jack filled his lungs, grimaced at the bitter taste and cast aside his doubts.

After a few more minutes of tugging on the chain, the raft bumped gently against the jetty and came to rest.

Jack removed the gauntlets, dropped them to the deck and stepped ashore.

He stood on the jetty, poised to leap back onto the raft at the first sign of danger. The noise—more the sensation of movement rather than an actual sound—came from behind him. Jack whirled around.

The raft was ten yards from the jetty, moving steadily towards the fog bank. The chain trailed slackly behind it, disappearing into the murky water. The deck of the raft was empty except for the gauntlets lying where he'd left them.

"Oh, fuck," he muttered.

Even if the river hadn't been giving off an acrid smell of chemicals, Jack knew he would never be able to swim to the other shore. He wasn't the strongest swimmer and the water moved listlessly, as if too heavy to hurry, giving the impression that to attempt to swim it would be like trying to negotiate thin treacle. He doubted he could even make it as far as the fog.

He watched the raft until it slipped into the dense mist and was hidden from view.

Whatever awaited him on this shore, he no longer had an alternative but to face it.

He turned inland.

A path, worn into bare earth, led from the jetty through grassland. In many places tufts of young grass poked through, suggesting that the path was not used frequently. The mature grass to either side grew thickly and free of weeds, as luxuriant as an oriental rug.

Jack proceeded cautiously, senses on full alert, feeling exposed and alone. The latter sensation was a familiar one. Also, in a way, a comforting one.

When loneliness has become your natural state of existence, finding it again after a period in the company of others can provide solace.

Jack came to a stop. The newfound solitude looked like it might be short-lived. A few hundred yards ahead, to the side of the path, stood a ramshackle wooden hut. Sitting on a wooden chair in front of it was a girl.

It was too late to make a stealthy approach since he had clearly been spotted—the girl's bearing had stiffened from casual slouch to ramrod straight. He could not see anyone else, but there could be someone in the hut. It wasn't huge, not much bigger than a child's playhouse, but that didn't mean it wasn't concealing another person.

Jack dithered. He contemplated retracing his steps, finding another path, but dismissed the idea. The next path could lead him to a gang of men, or worse. At least this looked to be a girl on her own. After the Lord of the Dance and the clowns, not to mention some of the other sights he had witnessed during this endless day, the current situation, whilst warranting caution, did not demand evasion.

He stepped forward.

He continued to scan both sides of the path ahead for danger, although a covert approach to either of his flanks would be nigh-on impossible to pull off here. In the near distance beyond the hut, trees spread across the landscape like a rash, the path disappearing into dark forested tunnels, but here the path was open to gentle, grassed slopes to either side, providing no cover behind which a potential assailant could advance in concealment.

The girl stood as he drew nearer and stepped behind the chair, gripping its back as though ready to wield it like a lion tamer should the need arise.

Jack drew to within five paces before coming to a halt.

"Er, hello," he said.

She was slight, dressed in a shapeless woollen garment which Jack would have hesitated to describe as a 'dress'. Dark eyes watched him carefully from a face of sharp, sparrow-like features. He guessed she was aged sixteen or thereabouts.

"Hello?" he repeated.

Without taking her eyes off him, she removed one hand from the back of the chair and pointed inland at the path.

Jack took a step closer. She tensed like a nervous cat.

"My name is Jack. *Ja-ck*." He found himself speaking slowly and loudly, like addressing someone hard of hearing. "Do you have a name?" He tried a smile. It felt fake and unconvincing.

She pointed again, jerking her hand for emphasis.

"I get it," Jack said. "You want me to continue along the path. And I will. But I need to eat and drink before I do." He patted the pockets of his trousers and then pointed at his mouth. "Hungry. Thirsty."

To underline the point, his stomach gave a low grumble. The last nourishment he'd consumed had been a few chunks of watermelon shortly after the Elevator had disgorged them on the opposite side of the river several hours ago. (Not that, Jack suspected, based on all he had experienced since stepping into the Elevator that morning, concepts like 'hours' and 'minutes' held much meaning in this place.) He had vomited most of the watermelon when the Lord of the Dance had shown him what true madness looked like.

The girl bit her lip.

"Wait there," she said.

"Ah. So you can speak."

She turned towards the hut. For the first time Jack noticed two or three bushes that grew next to it, and heard the tinkling chatter of a stream that ran behind it before disappearing across the meadow towards the river. The branches of the bushes hung heavy with some sort of fruit. Jack's stomach rumbled again like distant thunder.

He took a step from the path, meaning to follow her to make it easier to bring him fruit and water, assuming that was her intention. But she immediately turned around as though sensing his tread on the grass.

"No!" Her sharp gaze darted fearfully towards the dark line of trees in the near distance. "You must remain on the trail." She spoke with a hint of inflection. Jack was not good at placing accents, but thought that it might be Eastern European.

The last thing Jack wanted, with sustenance beckoning, was to spook this girl into intractability or flight or worse. The thought crossed his mind that he could simply walk up to the bushes and help himself, with or without her blessing, but he was not yet ready to take such a risk without knowing anything about the world in which he found himself.

"Why?" He tried to keep his tone even. "Why must I remain on the trail?"

Her head darted and ducked to facilitate her flitting gaze, making her appear even more like a sparrow. She lowered her voice to a whisper. "If you stray from the trail, the Scourgers will come."

Two

A sound came, like the crackling of a raging fire heard from afar. Or of dense undergrowth being trampled. An echoing *crack*, like a pistol being discharged.

The girl's head jerked so violently at each noise that Jack was afraid her neck would snap. Her eyelids stretched so wide it was a wonder her eyeballs didn't pop out like the sprung eyes on joke spectacles.

"They come," she whispered, and thrust her hands to her mouth.

Jack was more unnerved by the girl's reaction than by the distant noises. He hurriedly moved back so that his feet once more stood on the path.

While continuing to watch the girl's silent distress, he considered his options.

There was no point retracing his steps: once he reached the jetty, there would be nowhere else to go. He was too hungry and thirsty to continue on his way, wherever 'his way' might lie. It seemed inadvisable to leave the path again, at least until he knew more about this place, and he didn't want to upset the girl any further and remove what appeared for now to be his only chance of obtaining sustenance.

He stood and waited.

The distant cracks and snaps sounded a few times more, but fainter, like applause tailing away. Silence fell.

Jack let his breath out in a long sigh. The girl lowered her hands and looked to the forests, before glancing at him.

"You *must* remain on the trail." She sounded like someone so filled with relief they find it impossible to be stern, though they feel they ought to be.

Jack nodded. "*Please*, I need water. And food."

The girl turned and disappeared into the hut. Jack stiffened, but forced himself to relax; if there was someone inside wanting to do him harm, they surely would have made themselves known by now, especially when he'd apparently endangered not only himself but the girl by stepping from the path.

She emerged within moments, alone, carrying some small items. After busying herself by the stream and bushes, she returned to where he waited.

"Fill this only where the stream meets the trail." She handed him a sloshing container made of hide, with a cork stopper. Judging by the weight, Jack estimated that it held around a pint. He resisted the urge to yank off the stopper and glug the lot.

"Tell me," he said, "what is your name?"

Her only reply was a brief shake of the head. She handed him a small bundle roughly the same weight as the liquid container and made of a similar woollen material to her dress. Jack pulled back a corner to reveal berries as red as currants, large as grapes, round and plump as ripe blueberries. "You will find bushes growing alongside the trail. Berries like these are good, but do not eat any other fruit you might see." She pulled a face. "Not good."

"What are these called?" Jack nodded at the fruit in the cloth.

The girl shrugged. "Berries." She handed him the last item she was carrying: something else wrapped in cloth. Much lighter than the fruit.

Jack partly unwrapped it to find around half a dozen thin strips of dried flesh. "Let me guess," he said. "You call this 'meat'?"

"Yes." She did not smile.

"What type of meat?"

"I do not know. Some mornings when I awake it is there. Eat no more than one each day. It should last until you reach Tumble Down."

"Tumble Down? What's that?"

"It is where the trail leads."

"And ends?"

She shrugged again. "I have never been there. Now you must leave."

"Wait. At least tell me your name. Mine's Jack."

The girl sighed. "I suppose it cannot hurt that you know my name. It is Anna."

"Where are you from? I'm from Britain."

She shook her head. "I am permitted to give you food, but otherwise I can only point the way. Not chit-chat." She held up a finger. "One other thing. Wait here." She walked back to the hut and returned moments later with a larger piece of woollen cloth. She folded it to form a pouch big enough for the food and drink, and which Jack could tie around his waist.

"I suppose I ought to thank you, Anna."

The girl nodded, then raised her arm and pointed once more along the path. "Do not forget: no matter what happens, stick to the trail. Or the Scourgers will come." She grimaced. "Not good."

Despite Jack's efforts to elicit more information from Anna, she refused to say another word. He pressed her until she grew agitated and began to twitch, sparrow-like, once more.

"Okay," he said, letting out a deep sigh. "I'll go." He took a step along the path, but stopped and turned back to her. "Last question. Am I—are we both—dead?"

Anna shook her head. "But perhaps you may come to wish that you were. Now, *go*."

Jack stared intently at her for a moment, but she lowered her gaze. Clearly he had pushed his luck far enough.

Besides he thought as he turned away *what use would food be if I was some sort of ghost?*

He looked back after he had trudged about fifty yards. Anna had returned to sitting in the chair in front of the hut. She faced away from him, towards the jetty.

His stomach growled.

The girl's admonitions to remain on the trail and the distant crackling noises fresh on his mind, Jack made sure his feet didn't leave the beaten earth path, but couldn't resist setting his backside on the lush grass that grew alongside. For a few moments he held his breath, straining to hear for any sound of undergrowth being disturbed. When none came—he heard not so much as a bird call—he relaxed and opened the cloth pouch.

The berries tasted as good as they looked, fresh and bursting with sweetness. The water was cool with only the mildest tang from its hide canteen. He made himself stop swigging once the canteen was half empty.

The meat made him hesitate. He extracted a slice and held it up for inspection. Pink with darker edges, it smelled like cold bacon. When he took a tentative nibble, it tasted a little like bacon, too, or in any event as salty. And chewy, like beef jerky. *Or old leather* the less charitable part of him insisted.

He finished one slice and found, to his surprise, that he no longer felt hungry. Allowing himself one last swig from the canteen to rinse the salt from his mouth, Jack repacked the pouch and attached it to his waist.

There was one more thing he needed to do before he set off. He hadn't emptied his bladder since his three companions in the Elevator had stepped out for a reckless, and near fatal, trek across a desert landscape which once had been the drab office space known as Floor Four of Claridge House. Jack's brow furrowed as he spent a moment contemplating the fact that he would never set eyes on his former place of employment again.

Nope, he wouldn't miss it. Or his up-their-own-arses colleagues. Or the wankers he shared a flat with. Or the town.

Place was a fucking dump.

He stood and unzipped his flies, mouth twisted into a bitter smile. As if enacting a metaphor of dismissal of his past life, Jack let go a steady stream of orangey-yellow urine onto the thick grass.

Zipping himself back up, he stepped along the path without another backward glance.

In places grass had encroached, nearly obscuring his route. The path curved on occasion—on one steeper incline it was worn into short terraces which acted like steps—but on the whole followed a line directly inland. Towards the sun. It shone above the distant mountains, strong enough to warm the air pleasantly, not so much that it caused a nuisance shining into his eyes; provided he didn't gaze directly at it, Jack found that he could proceed without squinting.

The sun rode a little lower in the sky than when he'd first seen it from the raft, dipping a little towards the mountain tops as though preparing to set.

West. I must be heading west.

He examined that thought for a moment and concluded that it did not constitute a safe assumption. If he was fairly certain that time did not operate in this place as it did back home, or at all, then he ought to be at best suspicious of concepts like direction. Still, he saw no harm in sticking with conventions, at least until they were disproved.

West it is, then.

Buoyed by a full stomach and slaked thirst, he settled into a steady stride. Outdoor exercise wasn't something with which Jack was on more than nodding acquaintance. He possessed the pasty complexion often sported by those whose preferred occupation and recreational pastimes involve sitting for hours in front of a computer screen.

The impression of unhealthiness wasn't helped by the clusters of red rash-like spots smattering his cheeks, nose and forehead, a leftover not of teenage acne but of his drug-taking days and consequent fall in standards of personal hygiene. Difficult to be overly concerned about keeping your skin clean when your mind is soaring across jasmine-scented skies of silver, light-sabre fencing with naked film stars and skipping over bottomless canyons with rainbow ropes.

Maybe the sun would help clear up his skin. He turned his face towards it as he walked.

The forest was only a few hundred yards ahead when Jack noticed that the air had grown considerably dimmer. The sun touched the mountains and began to slip behind them. He had wondered vaguely whether this might be a land of perpetual sunlight, but this settled that fanciful notion.

Strangely, the air had not grown cooler as it darkened. Just as well: he was dressed in only the chinos and fraying shirt that he always wore to the office. The light jacket he'd been wearing on entering the Elevator that morning had been lost, flung from the corner where he'd discarded it when the lift tipped on the Third Floor, or maybe the Basement, in which latter case it lay on a grassy hillside on the other side of the river.

At least he wouldn't freeze when it grew fully dark.

The other, and perhaps even stranger, thing he noticed was the complete absence of wildlife. No birds wheeled and called, preparing to roost. No small animals snuffled across the path or made trails of their own through the lush grass.

Maybe the local fauna were all nocturnal. Maybe they preyed on travellers.

Jack shivered despite the warmth. He eyed the forest and shivered again. The path led directly into its heart no more than fifty paces ahead.

He stopped, reluctant to take one more step with night approaching.

The path here was overgrown. Jack lowered himself onto the grass and sat with knees raised, arms hooked around them. The last of the sun's rays glinted off the mountain tips and the land was cast in dusk.

He yawned, but the thought of nocturnal beasts of prey had unsettled the equilibrium gained from walking in clear, sunny air.

Jack decided to sit up all night.

Three

Light in front of his eyelids; he must have forgotten to close the faded curtains. Jack fidgeted, trying to find a comfortable spot. His bed had become unaccountably firm and lumpy. And the sheet under his hand felt like grass.

He opened his eyes and sat bolt upright.

The sun had risen behind him. Its clean light picked out the variegated shades of greens and browns of the trees before him, while making the shadows between deeper and more sinister.

Jack could not remember it becoming completely dark last night. Or lying down on the thick grass. No sooner had he avowed to remain awake than he must have fallen soundly asleep.

Silence reigned.

He glanced around. Nothing appeared to have changed. Except…

A trail of flattened grass, no wider than one person might make, led across the meadow to the point where he had been sleeping. Only one trail, so the person must presumably have retraced his or her steps.

Or flown away.

He didn't crack a smile. The thought had occurred jokingly, but for all he knew it could be true. He really needed to get a handle on what was and wasn't possible in this place.

Jack stood to try to see where the trail of flattened grass originated. It led directly away at right angles to the path, parallel with the forest, but faded from view before he could tell where it had started.

Maybe the trail-maker had been curious, or hungry. Jack checked the cloth pouch. The hide canteen sloshed when he shook it, and what remained of the berries and meat was intact. Whoever, or whatever, had come upon him in the night clearly hadn't been intent on pilfering his meagre provisions.

Something more sinister, then? As far as he could tell, and he felt safe to assume that he *would* be aware of it had it happened, he remained unmolested; he could not see or feel anything to suggest he had been interfered with while he slept.

Jack sat back down. He breakfasted on berries, his gaze flickering apprehensively to the dark trees crowding the path ahead.

The sunlight was warm, but not uncomfortably so. It felt pleasant on his back as he neared the tangle of boughs and leaves beneath which the path led. His pace slowed until he came to a stop, reluctant to step into the shade; it looked dank and creepy in there.

A shiver ran down his spine and he turned sharply, sure that someone was standing behind him. The path stretched away, empty. He had not seen any more newly-laid trails in the grass to either side.

"Man up," he muttered.

Still he didn't advance into the forest. He knew that he must; he had drunk the last of his water to wash down his breakfast. Anna had said he could refill his canteen where the stream met the path. He needed to keep moving and find the intersection point. The alternative was to die of thirst because he was afraid of a few trees and shadows.

Really? I'm actually contemplating dying rather than step in there?

Glancing around once more to ensure he was alone—the sensation of being watched hadn't disappeared entirely—Jack took a deep breath and walked into the forest.

Trees grew thickly to both sides of the path. Boughs slim and sinuous, or thick and thrusting, intertwined in a profusion of leaves, creating an arboreal tunnel. The little sunlight that was able to pass through the foliage dappled the ground to resemble the hide of a sparsely marked leopard.

Having been raised—if 'raised' is the correct word to describe his haphazard upbringing—in an urban setting, Jack considered himself to be a town rather than a country boy. As such, he knew next to nothing about tree varieties; for all he knew, the flora species he was passing between and under might not even exist at home.

He had been wrong about the forest being dank. Maybe it *was* damp and dripping in the thickets to either side where brush filled the gaps between trees, but along the path a breeze blew into his face, strong enough to lift the strands of hair that fell across his brow, but not enough to make the going arduous, and the ground underfoot remained firm and dry.

As his sight adjusted to the relative gloom and his ears grew accustomed to the rustling of breeze-blown leaves, he relaxed into a less hesitant stride. His gaze stopped darting from side to side looking for furtive movement, his imagination ceased conjuring visions of dark faces watching him from the shadows—his imagination would, in any event, struggle to match the actual sights he had seen during his prolonged jaunt in the lift of Claridge House—and he began to take stock of his situation.

Aim: keep going until he came across Tumble Down, whatever or wherever that was. In the absence of something more attractive suggesting itself, there was nothing better he could think of to do.

Food: a child's handful of berries remained and five strips of dried meat. Obtaining more berries would be sensible, though not yet pressing.

Water: none left. Finding more was a top priority.

Danger to person: unknown. Not straying from the path would be advisable until more information was to hand. Jack tried not to think too much about the distant noises he had heard the previous day when he had taken a couple of paces off the path: the noises of something heavy pushing through undergrowth, apparently unconcerned about being heard.

Or perhaps the whole point was *to be heard. Like the old bald git hiding behind a curtain pretending to be a powerful wizard in that old film.*

That thought led to an image of winged monkeys, the subjects of a recurring childhood nightmare. They had been supplanted by a deep fear of clowns. But he didn't think either would haunt his dreams in future.

He suspected that the chubby monk had cured his clown-phobia for good by showing him a glimpse of something so scary that Jack had, for the first time in years, pissed his pants. Just a little. Just enough to remind him that maybe there were other things more deserving of his terror than a bloke wearing face-paint and an orange wig.

Everything is relative. Even fear.

Occasionally the trees thinned, allowing Jack brief glimpses of the sun. It rode higher in the sky and had begun to circle to his left; in a few more hours he would be walking directly towards it.

Still heading west, then.

Except for the papery whispering of leaves, he made his way through woods as quiet as a tomb. No birds twittered or darted between branches; no animals disturbed the undergrowth; no insects chirped or buzzed.

He stopped once to finish his berries and eat a slice of meat. Almost immediately he regretted it. The meat assuaged his hunger, but increased his thirst. The need to find more water was becoming urgent.

To take his mind off his dry mouth, he thought about the floors he and the others had visited after stepping into the lift in the foyer of Claridge House. Six floors the lift had stopped at, then the Basement. In a sense, that is where Jack still was—in the Basement of Claridge House, except it was no longer a concrete cave of spider webs, gurgling pipes and mouldering boxes, but this place of chemical-smelling rivers, strange food-giving girls and dense woods containing some as yet unseen menace.

Jack spent a moment wondering whether the lift had returned for the others and whether its next stop had been the Ground Floor, then found that he didn't much care. He had done all he could to enable them to return to their own time and place; his only concerns now were ones of self-interest, as they had been since the woman calling herself his mother had kicked him out.

Besides, the others had, by and large, irritated the crap out of him. Matt with his mock sincerity and cavalier attitude which had placed them all in danger; Kim, the Yank, with her fake forthrightness masking a scared little girl; and that career-driven bitch Tara with her insistence, in the face of overwhelming evidence to the contrary, that they were all experiencing the same nightmare. And hadn't each of them, when faced with the stark realisation that one of their number must sacrifice themselves to save the others, demonstrated a more ruthless streak of self-absorption than he considered himself capable of?

"Selfish twats," muttered Jack, and turned his thoughts back to the floors.

Or, rather, what had replaced them. For it wasn't the tired office spaces of Claridge House which had greeted them each time the lift door jerked open, but exotic lands of deadly creatures and hazardous environs. And all run through with a common thread.

For, Jack was certain, the Lord of the Dance had played a part in each land they had visited. Whether in the silvery core of the red sun and the pupils of dragon eyes, or in the cowled forms taken by the acid-sea woman and swarm of pixies, or by hosting them inside his very skull, the monk's influence appeared as clear to Jack as his former companions' selfishness.

Except for one place.

Jack exhaled softly.

Miriam.

The dead city of Ultimus, inhabited only by a sapient machine on a planet she'd called Terra Two, had been the one place they had visited in their jaunt between floors where the hand of the Lord of the Dance was not evident.

"Miriam," he murmured.

A sound intruded on his thoughts. A new sound—not the rustle of leaves, but faint, musical notes. The tinkle of water.

Jack increased his pace, tongue coming out to lick at dry lips. A glint through the trees ahead. The tinkling grew louder. The path rounded a bend and there, gurgling merrily along a bed of smooth pebbles, ran a stream.

It crossed the path ten yards ahead. Jack covered them at a trot and sank to his knees at the stream's edge. The water looked as clear as glass. He plunged his arms in to his elbows and gasped at the cold.

He cupped his hands and scooped. The water tasted as good as it looked.

Could bottle this and make a fortune.

If there was a way to transport it back to his own time and place, he added, with a rueful smile.

He drank until he felt he might burst, then filled the hide canteen. Shaking his hands in the air to dry them, he took better note of his surroundings.

The stream was in excess of two yards across; he would need to get his feet wet to ford it. Where it ran through the woods, the trees had drawn back to form an avenue which allowed the sun to hit the surface of the water and make it glitter. As Jack's gaze followed the stream to one side, it alit on a bush heavy with fruit; it looked like the same fruit which Anna had given him.

He stood and took a tentative step off the path towards the bush.

"Wouldn't do that if I was you, gov," said a voice.

Four

The voice had come from behind him. Jack turned, pulse racing. He couldn't see anyone. Then a darker patch of shade beneath a tree the other side of the path detached itself and a figure stepped forward.

Jack inhaled sharply and tensed like a deer about to take flight. The figure took another step, bringing itself into the sunlight alongside the stream.

At first Jack thought the figure was of a boy, but looked closer and realised that it was a man around his own age, though slight in stature, making him appear younger. He was curiously dressed in a torn and frayed waistcoat, and trousers made from a rough-looking material, threadbare at the knees.

Jack unglued his tongue from the roof of his mouth. "Who are you?"

"You're new," said the stranger. "Or you wouldn't have tried to leave the trail." His accent was coarse but recognisable: London or somewhere nearby. Yet there was something about it that didn't quite ring true to Jack's ears, as though the man had learnt Cockney by watching Dick Van Dyke's chimney sweep in *Mary Poppins*.

"Who are you?" Jack repeated, reluctant to divulge anything about himself until he knew more.

A smile touched the man's face, lighting it up like a cheeky child's. "Francis Brown at your service." He swept one arm out and bent at the waist in an elaborate bow. "But call me Frankie," he added as he straightened. "Everybody does."

"Um…" As he could usually rely on it to do, Jack's social awkwardness came to the fore.

"Now you have me at a disadvantage and right enough."

"Huh?"

"Your name, gov. I assume you bear one."

"Oh. Right. Er, it's Jack."

"Welcome, Jack," said Frankie, the cheeky grin never leaving his face. "A word to the wise. Do not stray from the trail. There are fruit bushes within reach beyond where the trail bends."

"But… how are you allowed to leave the path?"

"Allowed?" The grin grew so wide it threatened to split the man's face apart like the melon Jack and his companions had shared on the other shore. "Not me, gov. The Scourgers will cotton on soon enough. Then I'll be off with not so much as a by your leave."

"Wait. Who are the Scourgers? Where are we? What is the name of this place?"

"My, my, aren't we an inquisitive fellow? As for who, the better question might be 'what'. As for where, we are nowhere. The name of this place? I've already told you."

"Huh?" Jack frowned, trying to keep his irritation in check. "You're talking in riddles." A notion occurred to him. "Was it you who crept up on me in the night?"

"Ho, ho, so you *do* pay some attention to your surroundings. But it was after daybreak. Nothing moves here at night."

"What the fuck? Why would you do that?" Jack took a step closer. Frankie's grin didn't falter. "Look, all I want to know—"

Jack broke off as a resounding crash came from deeper in the forest behind Frankie. It was the sort of noise that would have birds taking to the air on startled wing if they existed here. It was followed by a series of smaller crashes and rustlings, drawing nearer and louder.

"There's my cue," said Frankie. "Be seeing you, gov."

"Hold on…" But Jack was addressing thin air. The man had melted into the woods as quickly and completely as a shadow disappears when the sun slides behind a raincloud.

The crackling of undergrowth being disturbed—violently disturbed, by the sound of it—drew nearer. Jack took a couple of paces back, glancing down to make sure his feet stayed on the path.

From the direction in which Frankie had appeared, and

disappeared, Jack saw movement. Leaves quivered, branches swayed, bushes trembled. An impression of a large creature, the size of a small elephant, passing; then another; and yet another. Wet snuffling, snorting noises, as might be made by a team of wild hogs, came from the undergrowth. Another *crack!* like a pistol shot made Jack duck. He crouched.

The movement caused a twinge in his bladder. After all the water he had drunk, he needed to relieve himself. If the things making the noises in the undergrowth came any closer, he feared his bladder would let go in a hot gush where he crouched.

The noises and motion of disturbed vegetation faded.

Jack waited until they had completely died away. With a deep sigh, he stood and fumbled for the flies of his trousers.

Jack might not have understood everything he'd said, but in one aspect at least Frankie had spoken truly. He rounded a sharp bend, his shoes squelching from fording the stream, and there alongside the path grew half a dozen fruit bushes that he could reach without straying into the forest.

He hurriedly filled his stomach and his pouch. His encounter with Frankie and, more particularly, the noises of the unseen creatures pushing through the undergrowth had left him feeling uneasy. Vulnerable. He needed to get out of these woods.

Ignoring the sloshing of a stomach replete with fruit and water, he stepped up his pace.

Despite the twisting nature of the path, it still led in what he thought of as a general westerly direction, judging by the occasional glint of sun in his eyes when gaps between the trees allowed.

The breeze which had cooled his brow dropped. The trees drew closer together, making glimpses of the sun rarer. The spaces between trunks narrowed, the shade growing deeper and darker. A stroll in the woods became a trudge through a shadowy tunnel. Perspiration dampened his brow and trickled down his back.

Without the rustling of wind-blown leaves, all Jack could hear was the dull thud of his footsteps. And sometimes the rhythm of his pulse. He increased his pace to match it.

The oppressive atmosphere did nothing to settle his mood.

The path continued to twist and meander between tightly crowded trees, making it impossible to see farther ahead than the next bend. As what Jack optimistically continued to think of as afternoon wore on, his lack of physical conditioning began to tell and his pace dropped.

Not knowing for how much further the woods extended and reluctant to pause in the gloom cast by the stilled leaves, Jack munched the occasional berry and took swigs of water as he walked.

Only once did any noise make itself heard above his thudding footsteps and panting breaths: the now familiar crackle of wood snapping and undergrowth being forced aside. The sounds echoed in the hushed air, but came from such a distance that Jack barely broke stride. The last thing he wanted to do was spend a night in this forest.

This accursed forest.

The absurdity of the thought, as if he was starring in some sort of fairy tale, made him laugh. This sound, too, echoed, rolling off the tree canopy and back to his ears as if the woods mocked him.

The afternoon remained warm, but Jack shivered and once more picked up his pace.

Fatigue made him drag his feet. Determination had never been one of his strong traits—except during his addict days, when he would move heaven and earth to obtain his next fix—but resolve to get out of the silence of the woods before darkness fell drove him on.

Occasionally his glance turned to the impenetrable-looking gloom which lay either side of the path. The trees grew so closely together that their interlocking boughs formed a suspended ceiling of leaves, blocking out the sun. The gaps between trunks appeared barely wide enough to allow a man to pass through.

Though he was a slip of a thing.

At the same time that Jack wondered whether, and how, Frankie had managed to evade his pursuers—for there was no doubt in his mind that the bulky creatures who had made all the noise crashing through the forest *were* in pursuit of Frankie—he tried to avoid considering what those creatures might be or what they looked like.

Scourgers.

That's what both Frankie and Anna had called them.

He couldn't afford to speculate about the Scourgers. The unnatural silence of the woods and the growing darkness were already spooking him to a state of tension like a tightly strung wire. It wouldn't take much to send him bolting into the shadows, sprinting mindlessly until he brained himself against a trunk or they came for him.

Frankie and Anna; the only people he had met this side of the river. He concentrated on thinking about them, trying to put his finger on what they had in common.

It clearly wasn't their speech. Anna's accent might not have been Eastern European, but it most definitely wasn't British. Frankie, on the other hand, spoke like a character from *Eastenders*, if perhaps a slightly off-key version. And the same with the way he looked. More like someone from that old musical, the one about the workhouse boy who wanted more gruel, than a modern-day Londoner. Old-fashioned.

Old-fashioned…

There it was. The similarity between Anna and Frankie lay not in how they spoke but in how they dressed. Her in her shapeless, woollen garment that a peasant in a pre-industrial age might have worn; he in his coarse waistcoat and trousers like an extra in a Dickensian period drama.

But so what?

Jack shrugged and continued to trudge as afternoon turned to evening.

Dusk fell. Shadows deepened and the air turned grey. His stride became heavy, more stumble than stroll. The calf muscle in his right leg felt tight, as if it might snap at any moment like an overstretched elastic band. Weariness seeped through his legs; it felt as if the blood in his veins had been replaced by slow-drying mortar.

Can't stop here.

Jack gritted his teeth.

And stuttered to a halt.

He blinked sweat from his eyes. He could no longer distinguish the path ahead from the trees crowding to either side or the shade that lay around them. A sensation of claustrophobia threatened to overwhelm him. His breath came in short, sharp gasps. His hands rose to his throat and clutched at the open collar of his shirt, though it was too loose to constrict his breathing.

The final dregs of strength drained from his legs and he staggered like a drunk. Feet feeling like they belonged to someone else, Jack stumbled from the path, struggling to maintain his balance. Bereft of energy, it was a struggle he couldn't win.

When he hit the ground, soft with fallen leaves, it felt good. Perhaps he could lie there for a few minutes and regain some strength.

And then be on my way. Can't spend the night in here...

The noises brought him back to his senses. The snapping-creaking-crackling of bulky, snorting creatures approaching.

Jack gave a low groan and pulled himself to his knees. Panic drove away the last of his lethargy.

The sounds grew louder as the creatures drew closer. He doubted he could make it to his feet; he didn't waste time trying. Like a toddler making for chocolate, he crawled to where he estimated the path to be. When he felt the ground grow firmer beneath him, he paused and listened. Not even the *rat-ta-tat* thumping of his heartbeat could drown out the noise of bushes and branches being thrust aside. It sounded so close that any second he would see approaching movement through the gloom.

The path… maybe I'm not…

Jack scrabbled to either side with his hands. The ground on which he knelt *felt* like compressed earth; it *looked* a little lighter than the ground to either side, the paler section leading off like a ribbon into the gloom.

Another pistol shot *crack!* sounded and Jack jumped, his bladder, which he hadn't even realised was full, almost letting go. He sank onto his forearms, his brow touching the earth so that he resembled a devout man at prayer.

He clenched his eyes tightly shut and waited for whatever approached to arrive.

Five

At some point during the night he must have rolled onto his back, for when he opened his eyes he found himself lying spread-eagled, gazing up at the canopy of criss-crossing branches which shafts of sunlight struggled to penetrate.

He must also have relieved himself, for the pressure in his bladder had gone. He sat up, bringing his hands down to his crotch. Dry. At least he had been spared the ignominy of wetting himself. Not that there was anyone to be embarrassed in front of, but still.

Jack glanced down at the path; he had crawled onto it in the darkness last night and now sat squarely in its centre. Perhaps this explained why he remained unmolested by whatever had been working its way through the trees towards him.

For a moment he felt a sense of displacement, of disorientation. He wasn't sure which way he'd come. The path and the trees through which it wound looked the same to him in each direction.

Then he remembered how he had worked out in which direction he'd been heading. He craned his neck to peer through the canopy. So dense was the cover of intertwining leafy boughs that it wasn't easy to make out the position of the sun, but when he peered in one direction he needed to squint slightly against the increased intensity of the light that did make it through.

That's east. I need to go the other way.

Wincing against the stiffness that he anticipated would inhibit his movements, Jack rose to his feet. His brow creased in puzzlement; he felt as good as new, like someone who had taken it easy the previous day, not walked further than he had ever walked before. He flexed his right leg, expecting the tightness which had cramped his calf muscle to still be evident, but there was no trace of it. The right calf, like the rest of him, appeared to have been completely renewed by a night's sleep.

Odd.

Jack made one of his favourite gestures, a full-shouldered shrug. There were many things he couldn't explain; no point wasting time pondering them.

Extracting a slice of salty meat to chew as he walked, Jack turned away from the sun and stepped along the path.

The trees continued to press close, showing no signs of thinning, but the path itself remained clear and continued to lead him westwards. It took a little while, but soon he stopped darting glances to either side, dreading seeing broken branches or torn up undergrowth, evidence that he had not imagined the Scourgers coming for him when he'd strayed from the path in the dying light of yesterday. There was nothing to see except tangled boughs and dense bushes and endless shadows.

Expecting the effects of the previous day's exertions to make themselves felt at any moment, Jack's stride was hesitant at first. But a gentle breeze cooled his face and after an hour or more of steady walking without his legs feeling leaden or his feet sore, he increased his pace and the morning passed without incident.

The stream appeared close to the path, without crossing it this time. There were no berry bushes that he could see within reach, but that was okay; he still had a couple of big handfuls remaining. He stopped alongside the stream and refilled the canteen without having to step off the path. He paused only long enough to eat a mouthful of berries and wash them down with fresh water before resuming his trek. Although the panic of the night before was merely a bad memory, he remained anxious to leave the forest. The sense of confined oppression had receded, but not left him entirely. It lurked beneath the surface, dormant yet ready to spring to overwhelming awareness at a moment's notice.

Like a computer in sleep mode. It only takes a nudge to wake up…

Jack pushed the thought away. He never wanted to again experience the helplessness and loss of control brought on by the state of extreme fatigue and terror he had worked himself into last night.

The sun moved around the sky so that its glare, such as was able to penetrate the leaf canopy, faced Jack. The breeze faded and the air grew still. Drops of sweat broke out on his brow and the small of his back.

His pace slowed as fresh tiredness pervaded his legs and his stride grew sluggish. The prospect of having to spend another night beneath the leaves began to loom.

No! There must be hours of daylight remaining. I can walk miles yet before it gets dark. How big is this fucking forest?

Without breaking stride, he extracted another slice of meat from the pouch, leaving only one in there, and crammed it into his mouth, hoping that would fill him with a fresh burst of energy.

Maybe it worked, or perhaps it was the sense of fear preparing to bubble to the surface like a pan of water coming to the boil which drove him on, but he managed to pick up his pace again.

The sunlight grew stronger, the air warmer.

Wait. It's getting towards evening; the sun should be cooling, not getting hotter…

He peered closely at the path ahead, squinting when his gaze moved upwards to the leaf canopy. It wasn't his imagination: more sunlight was reaching him. The trees were beginning to thin.

No matter how weary in spirit and body, fresh hope brings an injection of energy that lifts both step and mood. The sudden promise of not having to spend another night in the forest infused Jack with waves of vigour and enthusiasm.

Shoulders thrust back, arms swinging freely by his sides, he marched in quick time, humming a tuneless beat beneath his breath. Sweat ran freely from his brow and he blinked it away, reluctant to raise his hand to wipe it for fear of spoiling his newfound rhythm.

When an outbreak of splintering wood and thrashing underbrush noises sounded a little way ahead, he almost didn't notice, so intent was he on maintaining his stride pattern. It was only when something burst onto the path that he started, drew in breath sharply and came to an abrupt halt.

The figure which had emerged from the cover of the trees shot him a familiar, cheeky grin.

"Watcher, gov."

"Frankie?"

The man, who looked like a boy in Oliver Twist clothing and spoke like an American actor hamming it up as a Cockney, glanced back in the direction from which he'd come. The noise of violent woodland disturbance grew louder. Branches swayed.

"Can't hang about, gov. Those Scourgers are relentless devils."

"But, where…"

Jack was already addressing an empty path. Frankie had faded into the bushes the other side, leaving in Jack's mind an imprinted image of his grin, like the Cheshire Cat's.

The thought occurred to move forward to the point where Frankie had disappeared to see if he could catch sight of him in the shadows, but there was no time to act upon it. The cracking of wood grew deafening. The trees growing close to the path rocked in an unfelt gale and leaves showered from the canopy.

More leaves and splinters of wood exploded across the path as though a shotgun had been loosed in the undergrowth. The sight of what emerged in the eruption's wake made the last of the strength run from Jack's legs.

It is difficult to accurately judge the height of a man when he rides a beast larger than a Shire horse, but Jack reckoned the figure which had appeared from the undergrowth to be at least seven feet tall. Its body was clad in mail, the sort made of interlocking rings or chains, like a Saxon knight, and a full helmet covered the head. He—at least, Jack assumed it was a man—clutched leather reins in one gauntleted fist; the other held a furled whip by his side, looking ready to use it should the chance arise. But this was no ordinary whip of the sort favoured by Indiana Jones. Metal barbs protruded at intervals and the whip ended in a spiked ball like the tip of a morning star mace.

The knight sat astride a charger which resembled a horse much as a rabid Alsatian resembles a poodle. The huge beast paused on the path and stamped a hoof. Jack could feel the vibration in his shoes. It reminded him of the rumbling sensation he had felt in his feet on Floor Four of Claridge House when he and his companions had been assailed by a furry creature resembling a character in *Monsters Inc*. That had been two or three days ago; it felt like half a lifetime.

He stood stock still, afraid to move and draw attention to himself. Besides, he wasn't sure that he was capable of moving even if he wanted to.

The knight's legs twitched, giving a nudge from steel boots to the horse's flank. The beast strode forward and the fresh crackling of snapping wood came as the knight was borne in the direction in which Frankie had disappeared.

Jack let his breath escape in a soft sigh, but gasped again as another whip-wielding knight appeared. This one didn't pause but followed the first into the forest the other side of the path.

No sooner had that one moved out of sight than a third appeared. There was nothing about the second or third figures, or the beasts on which they rode, to distinguish them from the first or from each other. This last one also paused. The helmeted head turned in Jack's direction.

It was as much as he could do not to whimper. The helmet contained two narrow eye slits and Jack caught a flash of silver. A phrase popped into his mind with clarity honed by terror.

The Lord of the Dance.

Jack was in no doubt that the silvery eyes of the figure before him was no coincidence. And it came as no surprise that the monk who had sent him to this place continued to play a part in events.

Be gone be gone be gone…

Jack's mind raced under the regard of the knight; its stare seemed to stretch into minutes.

Then the head turned, the legs twitched and the horse followed the first two into the forest.

It wasn't until the cracks and rustles had faded into the distance that Jack felt capable of walking.

If the trees hadn't shown signs of thinning out, he doubted he would have found the will to continue. But in a shambling manner, more stumbling than walking, continue he did. As he drew level with the point of the path at which Frankie and the mounted knights had appeared, and disappeared, he glanced quickly to either side merely to confirm that he hadn't imagined them—no, the evidence in the form of trampled undergrowth and broken branches was incontrovertible—before hurrying on.

He was unable to replicate the steady rhythm of earlier, but his stride grew more confident as he put distance between him and what he could only assume had been the Scourgers.

So-called because of those vicious-looking whips, I assume.

The barbs on the whips and the spiked ends had looked like they could flay the skin off a person, clothes and all, though perhaps weren't the most practical weapon for use in a forest. A thought struck Jack so abruptly that he almost stopped.

Of course, that's why Frankie stays in here amongst the trees where the whips won't be as effective. Smart man.

He didn't know why, but the thought encouraged him. With a new spring in his step, he marched towards the brightening sun.

Six

The trees continued to thin until, with a grin of relief, Jack stepped past the last of them. The sun had almost reached the tips of the mountains, but for now shone full in his face. He didn't mind having to scrunch his eyes a little against the unaccustomed glare.

The beaten-earth path continued, wending into the distance in a gentle downwards gradient. After the browns and shades of the forest, the meadow through which the path ran seemed uncommonly green, like the colour of grass as painted by a child. It stretched away towards the mountains, unbroken except for the occasional bush growing alongside the path.

Jack's stomach growled. He still had one slice of meat in his pouch, but had consumed what remained of the berries during the last leg of his yomp through the trees. The endless trees. Even if the bushes ahead were not fruit-bearing, he doubted that such a minor setback would put much of a dent into his good humour.

With one last glance back at the forest, Jack set out across the grassy plain.

The nearest bush was farther away than he'd thought. By the time he reached it, the sun had begun to dip below the shark-tooth mountain tops.

The bush hung heavy with the familiar fruit. Jack ate his fill and refilled his pouch. He yawned.

For the first time since he's been in this strange land, he did not feel the need to try to stay awake. Although out in the open, no longer surrounded by dense, pressing vegetation, he perversely felt less vulnerable.

He lay back on the path, resting his head on the luxuriant grass growing thickly alongside.

His last thought before sleep claimed him was to wonder whether the next day he would reach the place Anna had mentioned. Tumble Down, she'd called it.

Peculiar name for a place…

He awoke to a day much like the ones that had passed: a warm, full sun behind and a gentle breeze in his face. There appeared to be very little variation in the weather here. Once more he felt refreshed, as though he hadn't spent the previous day tramping through forested terrain. He'd possibly walked more in the last few days than he'd walked in the past few years, yet one unbroken sleep in open air and he felt as good as new.

Jack breakfasted on berries and the last slice of meat. He was down to his final few swallows of water, but wasn't overly concerned. If there was one thing he had learned about this place, it was that it seemed to provide when his need was great. Even if he ran out of water, he had confidence he would come across a stream before his thirst grew too uncomfortable.

A glance in the direction from which he'd come showed the forest as a long, black smudge on the horizon. Setting his back to it, Jack began walking, his pace once more enthusiastic, his arms swinging almost jauntily to the rhythm of his stride.

By the time the sun had swung around to shine into his face, he could no longer catch sight of the forest when he looked back. He lunched on berries and the final drops of water. They weren't enough to fully quench his thirst, but he fancied he could hear the tinkle of a stream ahead.

Sure enough, he was soon crouching to fill the canteen in water as clear as purest ice and almost as cold. More bushes grew alongside the stream, but the fruit they bore was not that to which he had grown accustomed. These berries were smaller and a mustardy brown in colour. Remembering Anna's warning only to eat berries like the ones she had given him, Jack ignored them. He still had sufficient stores to last him well into the next day.

Fully loaded with liquid sustenance, Jack continued towards the sunset.

《 》

A dark line appeared in the distance. With the sinking sun casting its light directly into his face, Jack struggled to make out what it was. He drew nearer and, with a sinking heart, knew what the dark line represented: more trees.

No. I'm not spending another night in a bloody forest.

Although enough daylight remained for him to cover another few hundred yards, Jack came to a halt. This was close enough to the trees for now. He would be able to gain a clearer idea of the extent of the wooded area in the fresh light of a new day.

He was about to lower himself to the ground, to wriggle about on the path until he found a comfortable spot for the night, when it happened.

The *crack!* followed by a commotion made him jerk his head towards the line of trees. In the fading light, a figure burst into the meadow. A woman, running as if pursued by the hounds of hell.

Jack watched the woman run closer to where he stood rooted to the spot. She wore a plain grey dress, the skirts of which she held up as she ran. Her shoulders were covered by a dark shawl, knotted over the breasts. He could not tell in the gloom how old she was or what colour hair she had—it was concealed beneath a white mob cap.

More sounds of disturbance came from the line of trees and two more figures emerged into the meadow: figures in medieval mail astride gigantic chargers. Their beasts moved at an easy canter. They didn't need to gallop; they would overtake the woman easily.

The woman glanced behind her at the sound, lost her footing and fell headlong, throwing out her arms to try to cushion her fall. Jack gasped and took a pace forward, his leading foot stepping off the path and onto the grass.

She was back on her feet in moments, lifting her grass-stained dress to free her legs and running towards him. He could reach her in seconds.

But he didn't move.

There's nothing you can do, he told himself. *There are two of them, they have those awful whips and I have nothing to defend her with.*

One of the Scourgers urged his mount faster so that it wheeled in front of the woman. She uttered a shriek and skidded to a stop, barely yards from Jack; if he stretched out an arm, he might have been able to touch the flank of the mount. An earthy scent, not exactly like a horse's but close, reached him.

"Hey…" he began, not knowing what to say but feeling he had to say something. His voice came out in a rasping whisper and not one head turned his way.

The woman's eyes darted from the mounted figure in front of her to either side as if looking for an escape route. She didn't see the figure behind her unfurl its whip.

"Look ou—" Jack's voice was louder, but it cut off as the whip snaked out and he realised that his warning was too late.

He had encountered death before. When five years old, his mother had taken him to a white room which smelt of urine, where her father was gasping his last breaths. Jack had stood at the end of the bed, watching the old man splutter and groan and snore, while his mother sat tight-lipped at the bedside, until his grandfather gave a last sigh and fell silent. Jack stared at the shrunken figure, waiting in vain for the thin chest to rise again. His mother, tighter-lipped and dry-eyed, took him roughly by the hand and stalked away, ignoring Jack's questions.

Later, much later, he had seen acquaintances—'friends', suggestive of mutual fondness or, at least, respect, would be far too strong a descriptor of the people with whom he hung about in pursuit of chemical stimulation—overdo the dosages or overestimate their tolerance levels and sleep or fit their way into a state of permanent lifelessness.

His own heart had stopped beating after he'd injected himself with a cut of heroin which turned out to be purer, and more potent, than the usual junk to which he was accustomed. Jack had the haziest memory of his heart beat racing like a drum roll and then nothing until he had awoken in a room much like the one in which he'd watched his grandfather expire. He had, so he was told by a grim-faced policeman, stumbled from the squat down an alleyway and onto a busy street before collapsing. The quick actions of a passer-by, trained in first aid, saved his life.

"If you'd like to write a thank you note," said the policeman, "I'll make sure it gets to your saviour."

Jack had mumbled something. He never wrote the note.

The brush with death had left him with a heart weakness which, the brusque hospital doctor informed him, would probably foreshorten his life.

"Or continue injecting yourself with chemicals," the doctor said, no trace of pity in his gaze, "and finish yourself off before the year's out."

When the doctor had left to continue his rounds, Jack tugged the drip from his arm, dressed and left the hospital without challenge—it was severely understaffed, lacking both manpower and inclination to try to persuade unwilling patients to remain in beds sorely needed by others. He had since steered clear of drugs, trying to substitute a craving for knowledge of computers and programming for the craving for chemical stimulation. A poor substitute, but one he had thus far been successful in maintaining.

The deaths he had witnessed had been unspectacular, as would his own have been had he not made it to a densely populated area before his heart gave out. People slipping into comas and failing to wake up. Undramatic deaths. Bordering on sedate.

The polar opposite to the death of the woman in the mob cap.

The whip had been expertly aimed. The morning star tip could only have narrowly missed striking the woman in the nape of the neck. It streaked past her cheek, causing her to instinctively jerk her head away. The whip drew taut as it reached its fullest extent and the vicious-looking tip curved back towards the woman's face. She gave a shriek and pulled her head back sharply, ensuring her neck to be centred within the rapidly decreasing circle created by the thong and the spiralling trajectory of the tip.

Recognising her danger, the woman raised her hands and cupped them beneath her chin, grasping the leather thong as it tightened around her throat. A metal barb bit into her hand, bringing a gasp which Jack heard as clearly as though he was standing next to her rather than a few yards away. Blood bubbled from between her fingers like an underground spring and ran down the backs of her hands. In the failing light, it looked like ink.

She fought against the tightening noose, straining against it with her fingers and forcing it upwards. She might have possessed sufficient strength and determination, probably buttressed by fear, to succeed in freeing herself if the second Scourger hadn't chosen that moment to act.

The mounted figure nearest Jack drew back its arm and flicked out the whip. The spiked tip *thrummed* through the air towards the struggling woman. Like the first, the accuracy with which the lash was directed was faultless. The tip flashed past the woman's cheek, drawing a startled yelp from her. A short tug on the whip's handle by the armoured rider and the tip began its spiralling return journey, wrapping the thong around the woman's neck.

She had succeeded in lifting the coils of the first whip over her nose; it would have been a relatively simple matter from there to duck so that her head slipped clear of the loops. But the second whip had coiled around her forearms. As the loops drew smaller under the pressure exerted by the rider, barbs cut into the woman's arms, drawing fresh inky blood.

The woman gave a moan of such despair that Jack almost ran to her aid, such as he could offer. But he caught himself in time and remained on the path.

The sun had fully disappeared behind the mountains and only its residual glow illuminated the scene. Soon that, too, would fade to blackness, but not soon enough to spare Jack sight of the woman's end.

Both riders leaned back in the saddle, drawing their leashes tighter as they might if trying to quell an agitated dog. With a twitch of their legs, they urged their mounts backwards.

The nooses tightened around the woman's neck. Her shoulders slumped in resignation and she yanked her hands free, perhaps instinctively since Jack doubted her thought processes were operating normally, before her fingers could be severed by the barbed thongs.

She looked at Jack, jutted out her chin defiantly and with her final breath uttered her first, and last, words.

"*Vive la France!*"

The beasts continued to slowly back away from the woman and the nooses tightened further, cutting into the soft, pale skin of her neck. Rivulets of blood ran down her chest to stain the shawl darker.

Jack forced his gaze away, but could not block out the thump of her mob-capped head landing on the grass.

Seven

How he'd managed to sleep, he didn't know. His last coherent memory of the night before was of stumbling along the path, not caring in which direction, desperate to put some distance between himself and the Scourgers.

The sun slanted across his face. He lay on the path, curled foetus-like, facing up the mild slope in the direction from which he'd come.

Jack lay still, enjoying the warmth of the sun on his cheek, reluctant to raise his head for fear of what he might see. The seeping damp sensation in his groin made him sit up.

To put off looking around, he examined his nether regions. The brown cotton of his chinos and the fading grey shirt bore a reddish stain around the hip and groin area. He peeled away the pouch and grimaced at the gooey mass of squashed berries it now held.

"Yum, yum. Redcurrant jam," he muttered.

He scooped some of the mess onto his fingers and raised them to his mouth. Squashed or not, the berries still tasted good. Then he remembered the *thud* of something heavy landing on grass and his appetite disappeared.

Maybe there was some other explanation for that sound. Only one way to find out.

Jack raised himself to his feet and turned to look down the path.

The lush grass to either side at this point of the path had not been disturbed, but ahead—perhaps twenty yards or so—lay darker, uneven areas to one side, with trails of trampled grass leading to the black line of trees in the distance. Otherwise, the smoothness of the meadow was unbroken. No gigantic horse-like beasts or whip-wielding, armoured figures in sight.

Jack swallowed hard. He began to walk, not wanting to see the aftermath of the previous night's events, yet needing to if only to confirm that they had actually occurred and he wasn't stumbling through some elaborate dream.

No, I'm not bloody Tara and this is no dream.

He drew level with the disturbed areas of grass. They had been flattened. Apart from dark patches of what might be blood, there was no sign of a body. Or a head.

Jack stopped and peered closer. What at first glance he had taken to be dried blood was in fact brown earth, showing through where the grass had been churned beyond recovery. There was no blood, dried or otherwise, to be seen anywhere.

His brow crumpled in a frown of puzzlement. Didn't the human body contain a lot of blood, pints and pints of the stuff? Even in the unlikely event that the Scourgers had released the pressure on the women's neck the instant he had looked away, she had already been bleeding profusely and he had heard her body hit the ground a moment after the *thud* that something the size and weight of a disembodied head would have made. Surely, then, some of her blood should be evident.

But, nothing. Not so much as a single drop of blood on a single blade of grass.

In keeping with his manner of reacting to the curious or inexplicable, Jack shrugged.

Turning his back to the sun, he walked on.

Once again he felt no ill effects from his physical exertions of the day before. His energy seemed fully replenished, he couldn't detect any niggling aches or twinges, yet he did not stride forth with the jaunty confidence of the previous morning. Not a complete stranger to death, habitually shrugging off the uncanny or the unsettling, nevertheless the violent demise of the French woman—he assumed from her last words she had been French and that, despite the lack of blood amidst the trampled grass, she had died—had left him more unnerved than he cared to admit.

Putting some distance between himself and the spot where the killing had taken place might have made him feel better, if it wasn't for the line of trees ahead.

The path continued to slope gently downwards so that when drawing to within a couple of hundred yards of the trees, he could still see over them. Jack paused and narrowed his eyes, trying to gauge how far the wooded area extended and what lay beyond.

His heart might have been damaged from the chemical abuse to which he'd subjected his body, but his eyesight hadn't been affected. In the bright sunlight he could see where the trees ended. A mile, maybe two at most. If the path wasn't obstructed and led more or less in a straight line, he should comfortably make it through to the other side with hours of daylight remaining.

"No sleeping under bloody trees tonight," he murmured.

He narrowed his gaze further, squinting to see beyond the trees. The land seemed to widen out into something like a bowl with the saw-toothed mountains forming the backdrop. The distance was too great for Jack to make out clearly what lay in the bowl, but he gained a fuzzy impression of dark, indistinct shapes all melding together into a higgledy-piggledy mass.

Maybe that's Tumble Down...

He scooped more squashed berries from his pouch and washed them down with a few swigs of water, before setting off once more.

The wood might only have been a mile or two wide, but the trees grew thickly together, forcing the path into wide, meandering loops. Branches thrust across in places, forcing him to duck beneath them. Any breeze was lost amidst the densely packed trunks and whispering leaves. Jack had not gone more than a hundred yards before he felt stillness and jungle-like heat pressing in on him. Silence, too, apart from the occasional flurry of rustling leaves—there must be a breeze somewhere—and creak of a branch. He wasn't by any means a nature lover, but how he would have welcomed the chirp of a bird, croak of a frog or zither of an insect.

The only other noise he heard was the chatter of a stream, but even that seemed subdued in the oppressive atmosphere. So subdued that he almost walked past the point where the stream ran alongside the path. He first noticed the berry bushes growing along the stream's bank. 'His' berries, as he now thought of them.

His supply of water and berries replenished, he began to whistle as he picked his way along the winding path. The notes hit the air and died as they would on encountering a vacuum. Jack stopped whistling and his sense of melancholy deepened.

The trees grew more closely packed, forming such a dense canopy of foliage that sunlight failed to penetrate and the air grew thick with moist heat trapped as though by a Perspex roof.

Jack's pace slowed and he began to pant in the stifling atmosphere. He had to duck beneath and step over trailing branches with increasing frequency. So winding became the path in order to find a way through the thickets that he began to fear that he might once more be forced to spend a night under cover.

To quell a subtle but unsettling sense of creeping panic, he thought about the people he had met since stepping from the raft onto this side of the river. The girl in the hut, Anna, with her suggestion of Eastern European accent and sparrow-like nervousness. The youthful-looking Cockney, Frankie, who seemed to be leading the Scourgers a merry dance through the forest. But there was only one station to which such a train of thought could lead: to the French woman and her violent apparent demise.

Jack repressed a shudder and sought happier musings. And, as so often happened since he had encountered her in the dying planet she had called Terra Two, his thoughts turned to Miriam.

An oblong, metallic box, resembling an upended aluminium suitcase—hardly something to grow misty-eyed over. And yet…

Jack did not consider himself, and would not be objectively judged, an expert in information technology or computing hardware—far from it; compared to his fellow trainees at work, he felt like an English-speaking immigrant in a class of Spanish students. Yet he knew enough to recognise Miriam for what he was sure she was: a highly developed form of artificial intelligence. AI—the ultimate wet dream for any computer geek.

The letters making up her name had stood for a phrase. An anachronism, it was called.

Jack frowned.

No... an acronym, that's it.

He couldn't remember what all the letters stood for. Migration something something Activation Module. It didn't matter.

Unlike Matt, his erstwhile travelling companion between the floors of Claridge House, Jack had no problem thinking of Miriam as a real person. A person who had triggered deep inside him a longing that he hadn't been aware existed. More than that, a *yearning*. But for what...?

To talk with her again, certainly. To learn more about her processing abilities, absolutely.

He shook his head: not enough.

To travel to the place where a newer model of her awaited; to where she said she was transmitting her data packets in the moments before Terra Two conflagrated beneath an expanding, dying sun. To where the survivors of the human race now made their home in an unknown galaxy on a planet Miriam had called Terra Three.

To pass through a Bruder Gate.

His brow creased in thought as he followed the winding path; he stepped over and ducked under straggling boughs without being aware of them, no longer bothered by the oppressive jungle atmosphere. In this way, he reached the edge of the woods.

A fresh breeze struck his face, bringing him out of the contemplative daze. The sun rode high; it had taken him the entire morning to traverse the wooded area. He came to a halt, enjoying the cooling sensation on his brow, and surveyed what lay ahead.

His earlier impression of jagged mountains forming a rough semi-circle around a depression had been correct. From where he stood, the path continued on a gentle downward gradient, passing through lush meadowland for another five hundred yards, before opening out into a shallow circular bowl perhaps half a mile or so across.

This much nearer, he could make out clearly what filled the bowl and it was this that drew his attention.

A motley collection of ramshackle wooden structures stretched drunkenly from one side of the dip to the other. They resembled at distance an assortment of crates and tea chests thrown together by a gale.

"I guess that must be Tumble Down," he murmured. "Well named by the looks of it."

Jack took a moment to eat some berries and consider his options. It didn't take long. Retracing his steps wasn't a serious candidate—stepping towards the unknown appealed infinitely more than going back into the stifling gloom of the woods. He could remain where he was until his supplies ran out and then face the same choices. Or he could proceed.

Holding his head high to allow his face to catch the full benefit of the cool breeze, Jack set off across the meadow.

Part 2: Tumble Down

One

The sun had begun to sink towards the ring of mountains by the time he reached the wooden structures. As he drew closer he could see they were buildings, of a sort. He caught glimpses of unhurried activity, impressions of people moving about as they would in any town or village.

While the buildings were indeed higgledy-piggledy, as if constructed to fit the raw materials at hand rather than in accordance with a blueprint, there looked to have been some attempt made to order the way they were laid out. They had been built in a series of three concentric circles, with a clear space at the centre of the smallest like the enlarged bullseye of a shooting target. But the nearer the settlement loomed, the more that sense of order became lost in a jumble of rudely assembled logs on which not even the most rudimentary effort seemed to have been made to give plank-like form.

The path levelled out and, for the first time since Jack had stepped onto it from the jetty, split in two. He could now see that his impression of the settlement nestling in a bowl hadn't been quite accurate: it was more dinner plate than bowl, with a flat base and an upraised lip around which the path ran. To either side of the path, thick grass led away to the semi-ring of mountains.

He had no clear idea of what to do next. Entering the village—it was too small to qualify as a town—would mean leaving the path, unless the pressed dirt between the structures was considered by whoever made the rules here as forming part of the path. Maybe it would be wise to exercise caution and circle around to try to gain some idea of how the land lay before revealing himself.

"Oh, fuck!" he muttered beneath his breath.

The choice had been taken away; a man was approaching from the village.

《 》

Jack tensed and glanced to either side. If he needed to take flight, the path was clear in both directions. He took a step back, turning his head to check behind. Clear there, too. He breathed deeply to calm his nerves and focused on the approaching person.

Anyone over the age of forty looked old to Jack. The man limping towards him appeared positively ancient. The hair which clung to the sides of the bald head, and which formed coarse-looking whiskers on his cheeks and top lip, was grey fading to white. The impression of age wasn't helped by the man's attire: a dark 3-piece suit over a white shirt and charcoal tie. An old-fashioned suit to Jack's eye, though perhaps 'classic' might also be a fair description.

The man's right leg remained stiff as he walked, giving him a lopsided gait. He leaned heavily on a stout wooden cane clutched in one hand.

He drew within five yards of where Jack stood, taut as a violin string, and came to a halt. The skin around the man's eyes crinkled like scrunched-up paper as he smiled.

"Greetings," he said. "You must be Jack."

Jack had resigned himself to having to come to Tumble Down, but quite what would happen when he arrived he had little idea. One thing was certain: being addressed by name hadn't featured highly on his what-to-expect list. He blinked.

"How do you know my name?"

"Let me first introduce myself," the man said. "My name is George Morgan. George Morgan Junior, to be precise, though such niceties of custom and manners rather lose their lustre in these strained circumstances in which we find ourselves. Do they not?" The eyes crinkled again, though the smile this time was wry.

The man's accent reminded Jack of Kim's, the American girl with whom he had shared the peculiar trip in the lift—or elevator, as she had been persistent in calling it—though hers had been a little less refined and had contained a twang, perhaps caused by her residence in the UK for several years. He detected no such twang in the speech of the man before him.

"Um, you're American?"

"Yes, sir," replied George. "Boston, Massachusetts, born and bred, and a resident of New York City these twenty years past." A frown appeared on the man's brow like a cloud eclipsing the sun, as though the mention of time had temporarily discomfited him, but his expression quickly cleared. His bushy eyebrows raised in enquiry. "So, Jack, do you have a second name?"

Jack opened his mouth to reply, then paused. He had been about to blurt out his surname automatically, but just in time remembered the vow he had made to himself to abandon *her* name.

He shrugged. "Just Jack."

George favoured him with a considering look before saying slowly, "I guess a man's name is his business." He took a step forward and held out his right hand, the one not holding the cane. "I welcome you to Tumble Down, Jack."

Jack hesitated and glanced once more each way—the path remained clear.

"It is sensible to exercise caution," said the American. "But you have nothing to fear here. Of course, I would say that if I intended you harm, would I not?" He chuckled, still holding out his hand. "How else to lure a young fly like you into my dusty old web?" His expression grew sombre. "I am a man of my word, and my word is that you are in no danger. At least, not from me or anyone here."

This time Jack's hesitation had nothing to do with apprehension about shaking the old man's hand; he sensed no threat from the American and, in any event, hadn't come this far only to balk when possible answers to the umpteen questions cluttering his mind might be at hand.

He would need to take a few paces forward to shake hands and it was the prospect of stepping from the path that made him pause. He had no wish to hear the crackling of underbrush or feel the ground tremor or look once more upon those mounted, whip-wielding giants.

Yet George wasn't standing on the path and there was no sign of the Scourgers.

Stop being such a frigging pansy…

Taking a deep breath, Jack stepped forward.

Nothing happened. He was standing completely off the path for the first time since he'd started to follow Anna towards her cabin. Jack glanced around once more and strained for any unusual noises, before taking another step and grasping the man's outstretched hand.

George's palm was warm and dry, his grip firm.

"I'm guessing," he said, "from the way you keep shooting glances every which way that you've encountered the Scourgers during your journey to Tumble Down. Am I wrong?"

Jack released his hand. "I saw them chasing a man. He said his name was Frankie."

The American smiled. "You asked how I knew your name…"

"Frankie told you?"

"He calls back here from time to time. Tarries a short while before his itchy feet get the better of him." George chuckled. "He likes to lead those Scourgers a merry chase."

"I…" Jack drew a deep breath. "I think I saw them kill someone. A woman."

The older man's expression sharpened. "Grey dress? Mob cap?"

Jack nodded. "She said something in French."

George let out a deep sigh and his shoulders sagged. "It was Camille. I feared the worst when she failed to return before it grew dark last night. You said that you 'think' they killed her…?"

"They…" Jack swallowed hard. "I looked away at the last moment, but I'm pretty sure they tore her head off. Only—this makes no sense—when I woke up the next day, she had gone. There was no body, no…" He swallowed again. "No head. Not even any blood. And there'd been a *lot* of blood. It was as if I'd dreamt it. Yet…"

"Let me guess. There were signs that *they* had been there. Broken branches, hoofprints in mud, that sort of thing?"

"Yes, the grass was trampled, but how did you—"

George held up a hand in a shushing gesture. "We'll share all that we know, which doesn't really amount to a hill of beans, but let's go and sit down." He winced. "This leg aches something fierce if I stand on it too long. And don't pay no mind to the Scourgers. You can go anywhere within the circle created by the trail without drawing them."

The circular plate onto which Tumble Down had been built consisted of compressed dirt, which remained firm underfoot. Whatever rain fell in these lands to feed the streams, it must be confined to the mountains, Jack thought, because the only mud he had trodden in during the entire journey had been when he'd had to ford the stream where it crossed the path in the forest beyond Anna's hut.

He followed the hobbling American between ramshackle buildings, describing a gentle spiral towards the centre of the village. They passed other people, who all stopped what they were doing, such as it was, and subjected Jack to frank scrutiny. The people seemed to be of varying ages, a mix of men and women. They shared one similarity, something that seemed a common thread in this world: they all wore attire that looked old-fashioned to Jack. And the same could be said for most of their hairstyles. They resembled the subjects of crinkled, grainy photographs.

Jack's cheeks grew warm—he hated being the centre of attention—but he didn't lower his gaze. There was too much he needed to see to try to make sense of this place to give in to shyness.

The buildings had been crudely erected. Minimal attempts, if any, had been made to shape the wood from which the lean-to structures were formed. Logs were lashed together with what looked like a thin, vine-like plant to form walls and roofs with gaping holes, which must surely allow rain and wind to enter—more evidence suggestive of the absence of inclement weather conditions. Ill-fitting doors had been attached to crude frames with the same vine-like material. No glass filled the window frames. Instead, rudimentary shutters formed from knobbly sticks covered the gaps where windows would normally be, or stood propped open to, presumably, allow more light in than already entered through the gaps.

They arrived at the smallest ring of buildings, which opened up into a broad, circular space. People milled about the circle, stopping to appraise Jack with candid stares. George paused to hold a whispered conversation with a middle-aged woman, who shot Jack a troubled glance.

"Spreading the word about Camille," the American explained with a grimace.

Most of the buildings which formed the circle had chairs and tables, constructed in the same roughshod manner, outside. Many of the chairs were occupied by people who broke off their conversations or the tasks to which they had been bent to stare at the newcomer.

George, limping heavily, led Jack to one of the few tables flanked by empty chairs. He sank into one with a deep sigh, making the chair creak alarmingly, though he seemed unconcerned. Sweat ran freely down his brow and he fumbled for a handkerchief in the pocket of his suit jacket with which to mop it.

"Please," he said, indicating a chair. "Take a seat."

Jack sat down, trying to ignore the gazes directed his way. His chair, too, groaned but felt sturdy enough.

"That's a nasty limp you have," he remarked, more for something to say than out of any concern for the older man.

George nodded. "Snapped it in two places when it was struck

by flying debris in the explosion."

"Oh? What explosion was this?"

"A bomb was detonated in Manhattan's financial district in New York City. I work, or should more accurately say *worked*, at J.P. Morgan and Co. at number twenty-three Wall Street." He uttered a short, barking laugh. "My name's Morgan but I have no blood ties to the bank's owners. More's the pity."

"A bomb in Wall Street?" Jack frowned. "Can't say I heard about that."

"Well, judging from your dress and mode of speech, I'm guessing that, one, you're British and, two, the explosion happened some years before your time."

"Yeah, I'm British," Jack muttered. That didn't seem important. "So when did the explosion take place?"

It was the American's turn to speak as if the subject was of little import. "September sixteen, 1920," he said.

Two

Despite all he had experienced in the past few days, since leaving his crappy flat to spend, so he'd thought, another head-scratching day in the office trying to catch up with programmers so more advanced than he that it seemed they spoke a different language, Jack nevertheless felt a curious sense of disconnection at the American's words. "*1920?* That's almost a century ago."

"Ah," said George, regarding Jack with new interest. "So you've come from the early twenty-first century? I was wondering. There is much I would like to learn about your time."

Jack said nothing while his mind whirled. How could he be sitting talking to a man who claimed to come from the early twentieth century? And yet, after all he'd been through, was it really that inconceivable?

He thought of the lands he had visited during his trip in the lift, though he was coming to think of it more and more frequently by the Americanisation, Elevator, capital letter and all. He thought of the flying pixies bearing an uncanny resemblance to Freddy Krueger, of the dragon large enough to encircle an entire planet, of the living brain he had watched flash with eerie light when they'd fetched up inside a head.

Inside a head! If I can swallow that, I can swallow anything.

Most of all he thought of Miriam. He hadn't for one moment doubted her when she said that the city of Ultimus was on a planet in a galaxy many light years removed from Earth in the year 3092. He'd accepted without question what she said about people escaping a threatened world via Bruder Gates and planet-hopping between galaxies to ensure humanity's continuation.

Not such a stretch, then, to accept that the American sitting in front of him was from a mere hundred years in the past.

And it helped to explain something else that Jack found puzzling.

"The clothes," he murmured.

"What's that?" asked George.

Jack nodded at the people milling about the circular area. "Everyone I've seen here—and on the way here—has been wearing old-fashioned clothes. Old-fashioned hairstyles, too."

George nodded. "Though you're not the first person to arrive from the Third Millennium."

Jack glanced around, but could see nobody wearing more modern dress. "There's someone else… Who?"

"Oh, no doubt you'll get to meet her."

"And everyone else is from the twentieth century?"

"No, sir. Some are from earlier. One or two from *much* earlier."

Jack whistled.

"It seems," said George, wincing as he struggled to his feet, "that we have much to learn from each other. But, first, let us repair to my humble abode. And when I say 'humble', I mean 'hovel'. Darkness is falling, my leg is recovered sufficiently to bear my weight and the need for victuals is making itself keenly felt."

Jack blinked. "Huh?"

George smiled. "You must excuse my pompous mode of speech, young man. That is what thirty years of high finance does to a man. I merely said that I am hungry and thirsty. Let us eat."

The elderly American hobbled out of the inner circle of huts, leaning heavily on his stick, Jack following closely. People again stopped whatever they were doing to stare at him as he passed. He grew increasingly uncomfortable under their scrutiny and avoided the gazes by keeping his head turned to the front to focus on the back of George's old-fashioned suit jacket.

Dusk settled and the air dimmed; only a reddish smudge above the jagged mountain tops showed where the sun had slipped behind them.

George led him to a lean-to in the middle circle of buildings.

"We don't really need shelters," he said. "As you might have noted, the weather here remains dry, mild and constant to the point of tedium. But old habits die hard, I guess."

"Maybe it helps you to sleep," said Jack, thinking of how vulnerable he'd felt in the forests when it grew dark. "You know, more secure, that sort of thing."

George paused with his free hand on the door and glanced at Jack with the facial equivalent of a snort of derision. "Oh, no one has trouble sleeping in Tumble Down." He shoved at the door, which opened jerkily on its vine hinges. "Here we are. Come on in, young sir. Come on in."

The interior of the hut was so dark that Jack stopped inside the doorway, fearful of walking into something. George disappeared into the gloom and there came a rustling sound, followed by the flare of a match. A flickering glow illuminated the space.

Jack blinked, his sight adjusting to the shifting light. He could make out a wooden table and a couple of chairs, similar to the ones outside, and shelves made from logs, to which some effort had been made to form them into planks, protruding from the back wall, but nothing much else. The room—and he could see no doors or other apertures suggesting other rooms leading off it— was as sparsely furnished as it was crudely assembled.

The light came from a flame burning in a bowl of liquid placed on the table.

"Come, sit down." George motioned to a chair. "You hungry?"

Jack nodded and patted his pouch. "I have some berries left, but I ran out of meat this morning." He stepped into the room, shoving the door closed behind him, and sat in the nearest chair.

"Ah. So you met Anna."

"She gave me this pouch and canteen, and told me not to stray from the path. That's what makes the Scourgers come, I'm guessing, though I can't see how they can possibly know if I take a step or two off the path."

"Oh, they know." George was doing something with objects on the shelves, but he turned to favour Jack with a shrewd look.

"You're wondering why Anna was able to move about off the trail without drawing them to her?"

"It did cross my mind."

"We believe that she was the first one to cross the river and assigned the role she performs today, to point newcomers in this direction and provision them for their trek."

"Assigned? Who by?"

George turned back to the shelves and busied himself as though he hadn't heard Jack's question. When he turned his way once more, he held two wooden bowls filled with food. Jack's stomach rumbled.

The meat in the bowls was a chunkier version of the salty strips which Anna had given him; the fruit a larger, sweeter version of the berries he was used to.

"No utensils, I'm afraid," said George. "These bowls were here already, like the huts, but otherwise we only have the items we arrived with." He reached into the pocket of his jacket and withdrew an object. "I have this clasp knife." He unfolded the blade. It glinted orange.

"These huts were already here? Who built them?"

George shrugged. He placed the knife on the table beside his bowl and bent to his food.

While he ate, Jack examined the source of the light: it appeared to be a wick floating in a small wooden bowl of liquid.

"There are trees growing at the trail's edge mountainward whose sap you see in the bowl," said George, noticing the direction of Jack's gaze. "More like lamp oil than sap. The wick is formed by plaiting strips of the trees' bark."

"This meat…" began Jack.

"If you're asking me what it is, I can't tell you," said George. "Not because I *won't* tell you, you understand, but because I don't know what it is. No one does, but…" He sighed. "We eat it anyway."

"So tell me what you *do* know."

"I assume you mean about this place and not what I know about banking in twentieth century Manhattan?" George smiled.

Jack didn't return it. He had been in this man's company for what must be getting on for an hour and had learned next to nothing. He nodded, making no attempt to keep impatience from his expression.

"Okay." George pushed his bowl away and leaned back. He extracted a thin cigar from the breast pocket of his jacket and lit it from the box of matches he'd presumably used to light the floating wick. The match looked to be made of sturdy wood, compared to the flimsy matches Jack was used to, and flared with a glare almost as bright as a phosphorous flare. The hut filled with the harsh aroma of tobacco smoke, though not as harsh as some of the substances Jack used to smoke. The walls and ceiling were so riddled with gaps that the smoke had ready means of egress. "I'll tell you what I can, but it's a tale which will have to be completed tomorrow for I fear there is insufficient time remaining of this evening."

"I'm not tired," said Jack, stifling a yawn. "At least, I can stay awake long enough to hear everything you can tell me."

George gave a humourless smile. "I will fall asleep in a little under thirty minutes by the way we reckoned time in my era, and I assume still do in yours, and am powerless to prevent it." He held up a hand to forestall the question which sprang to Jack's lips. "Let me begin my tale."

"I've already told you," said George, "that I was a banker on Wall Street. Not one of the top players, you understand, but I had built myself a sound portfolio of corporate clients and was achieving some pretty remarkable yields for most of them. I had grown adept at restructuring capital—"

Jack didn't bother trying to stifle this yawn.

"Ah. Sorry. My wife is always telling me that I can become a little enthusiastic when talking about the investment business." A look of profound sadness passed across his face like a shadow, then was gone. "Anyhow, I was hankering after a promotion, perhaps not a full equity partnership but salaried at least, when the bomb went off. Nearly three months I was laid up with my leg in plaster cast from toe to hip. But I was luckier than some…" He broke off and gazed into the distance.

Jack pointedly cleared his throat.

"Huh?" George blinked. "Yes. Okay. I was due to return to work on February 21st. That was the Monday."

"In 1920," interrupted Jack, still trying to get his head around the fact that he was having a conversation with a man substantially more than a century old.

"1921 by then. On the afternoon before, the Sunday, I met with some colleagues on Long Island where we lived. It wasn't a full-on business discussion; more an early dinner and an opportunity for me to catch up with all I'd missed while laid up. The idea was for me to feel more relaxed about returning to the office the following morning. And it worked. I felt ready to face anything. Ha! Almost anything.

"After a very pleasant dinner I decided to walk back to our apartment. It was a bitter night with a strong easterly gusting off the Atlantic. My colleagues tried to persuade me to call a cab, but there's no fool like an old fool. It was only four blocks and my leg had stiffened considerably during dinner. I thought it would do it good to stretch the tendons and exercise the wasted muscles." He paused. "I reckoned without the blizzard that blew up before I had limped a block."

George pulled hard on the cigar, making the end smoulder like the coals in the fireplace Jack's mother had kept almost constantly lit in the draughty cottage in which they'd lived when he was a toddler. One of his earliest memories was of sitting on her lap in front of that fire, mesmerised by the flames while she sang softly to lull him to sleep. One of the few happy memories.

"We have minutes remaining at most," said the American, smoke billowing around his head in a cloud. "And then, like it or not, we shall sleep. So there I was, struggling to maintain my footing on sidewalks turned white and treacherous. The wind blew harder and the snow fell heavier until I could see nothing and my face had grown numb with cold. In that biting darkness I must have stumbled into a vacant lot—there's plenty of land being developed in and around our neighbourhood. Next thing I know I'm falling, tumbling head over feet. Funny thing, but I kept tight hold of my cane as if somehow that would save me getting squashed like a bug when I hit the bottom of the foundation pit or whatever hole I'd strayed into. Then I wasn't falling any more. I opened my eyes—I hadn't even realised they were clenched tightly shut—and found myself lying at the foot of a green hill near a muddy river."

"The Lord of the Dance," Jack murmured.

"What's that?"

"The monk. Was he there?"

"Oh, yes. The Master he called himself. He presented me with a stark choice: cross the river or perish at the fangs of the spiders with which he surrounded himself. Spiders the size of puppies." George shuddered. "Even if we had time, I'd prefer to discuss that fellow in daylight." He held up what remained of the cigar. "Kept this back from the restaurant to smoke the next day over a mid-morning coffee to mark my return. To celebrate being alive, and to commemorate those who hadn't survived the blast."

"Surprised you haven't smoked that before now," remarked Jack.

George smiled, but without warmth. "I've been here for nigh on six months, as far as I can reckon it. I've smoked this cigar on every night of those six months."

Jack's mind reeled. "Yeah, right," he managed to get out.

The American regarded him thoughtfully. "There's no time remaining to convince you. Better to show you."

Before Jack could react, George flicked the butt of the cigar away, reached out and clamped Jack's right wrist in a grip which belied the man's apparent frailty. With his other hand, the American grabbed the clasp knife from the table.

Jack tried to tear his arm free but to no avail. As the glinting blade approached, he began to whimper.

Three

He came to lying on hard-packed dirt alongside the path, back pressed against the rear wall of a hut, face turned towards the mountains. Their tips appeared to give off a violet glow in the sunlight. Someone was standing on the path, watching him.

After sparing a glance at the stranger—a girl—to check she presented no immediate danger, he turned his attention to the matter most clamouring for his attention.

The blade had been as keen as a scalpel and wielded with the precision of a surgeon. It had sliced through his shirt and into the top of his forearm, parting both layers of skin and a millimetre or two of the flesh beneath. Enough for blood to well like water overflowing a flooded ditch.

George had released his wrist and sat back, saying something about it being a superficial wound and that he would be fine, but Jack had no longer been interested in anything the American had to say.

Shock and disbelief threatened to paralyse him, but the urge to flee was stronger. He staggered to his feet, tipping the chair with a clatter, and yanked at the door with his right hand while he used his left to clasp his forearm to staunch the bleeding. As soon as he'd managed to jerk the door open, he was through it and lurching into darkness. Through a gap between two huts and he was in the outer circle. Between two more and he found himself outside the last ring of huts, near the path. That's where he'd sunk to the ground, overcome with sudden weariness. He'd fallen into unconsciousness still clutching his sliced shirt sleeve and bleeding forearm.

Jack sat up and raised his arm to examine it.

"What the…?"

He hadn't imagined the ache in his right wrist where the American had gripped it or the stinging pain of the incision or the blood which soaked his sleeve and caked his left hand. The left hand which now bore no trace of blood; the sleeve which was as whole and clean as when he'd crossed the river on the raft.

Jack unbuttoned the cuff and drew the sleeve back to expose his forearm. The skin was freckled, covered in downy hair, but with not so much as a faint scar to show where the knife had sliced into it.

The girl watched him, her head tilted a little to one side like a curious dog. She looked to be around his age, perhaps a year or two younger, in her late teens. Unlike everyone else he had encountered so far, her attire didn't appear old-fashioned to Jack's eyes, though he didn't recognise the material from which her simple sweatpants and tee-shirt were fashioned. Still shaken up by last night's assault and the absence of any evidence of it this morning, he was in no mood to exchange pleasantries with some girl.

"What you gawking at?"

"Gawking? What a curious word. It is not one I have heard before." Her accent, such as it was, sounded flat and uninflected, like someone whose first language isn't English and who has learned it carefully and correctly and comprehensively, and who now speaks it in the same colourless manner in which they repeated words and phrases and sentences during instruction.

Jack felt at a disadvantage with her looking down on him. He clambered to his feet, rebuttoning the cuff of his shirt as he rose. It was a little grubby and sweat-stained, but otherwise none the worse for wear. "It means being nosy," he said. "You know, rubbernecking, sticking your oar in where it's not wanted."

"Ah," said the girl, apparently unruffled by his choice of words. "Nosy. That's one I know. Like Nosy Parker, yes?"

"Yeah." Jack glanced around. Beyond where the girl stood on the path, grassland ran away towards the mountains. He judged their foothills began no more than half a mile away. "If we step off the path onto that grass, what will happen?"

"They will come."

"The Scourgers?"

"Yes. But I think you already know this."

"I didn't know that it happens here, in Tumble Down. Are you sure?"

The girl nodded. "Only those with a death wish step beyond the trail."

"You can die in this place?"

"Oh, yes. But this also you already know. You saw Camille die."

"The French girl? I was there when the Scourgers got her but I don't know for sure…" He tailed off. Who was he trying to kid? "Yes," he added simply. "I saw her die."

"She was my friend." Her expression grew hard as she regarded Jack. "Did you try to save her?"

The question took him aback and he dropped his gaze from hers, but not before noticing her lip curl into a sneer of contempt. He thought of when he'd stood on the path watching the woman trying to escape the approaching riders, of the moment when she'd regained her feet after falling. He had almost stepped off the path to go to her aid. Almost.

He felt colour warm his cheeks and kept his gaze down.

By the time he'd mustered the courage to look back up, the girl had gone.

While standing with bowed head, Jack had noticed another change from the previous night: the purplish-red stain on his shirt and trousers from the berry juice was no longer evident. He checked the pouch, which still contained remnants of squashed berries and extensive staining, but his shirt and trousers looked like they had never been affected.

"Weird," he muttered.

Despite having spent the night lying on packed dirt against a wall made from rough-hewn logs, Jack felt fully rested. He decided to expend some of that renewed energy by taking a stroll along the path encircling the settlement. He turned to his right where he would pass around the back of Tumble Down.

The weather did what it seemed to do every day: the sun shone brightly and a light breeze lifted the hair on his brow, keeping him cool. The breeze blew from the direction of the mountains and carried upon it a sweet fragrance that reminded him of the berries which seemed to form the staple foodstuff here.

He hadn't gone far when he came across a cluster of bushes growing alongside the path. A few people knelt before them, filling wooden bowls with fruit. He stopped and watched them, receiving one or two curious glances in return. When a woman stood and walked away with her container full, Jack took her place by the bush. The berries were like the ones George had fed him the night before: larger—the size of plums—and sweeter than those he had found on the trail. He filled his pouch, making a mental note to remove it before falling asleep that night.

A few hundred yards farther on another line of people crouched at the edge of the path. They were filling wooden jugs from a stream that flowed from the direction of the mountains and chattered alongside the path for ten yards or so before meandering away into the meadowland.

Jack stooped and filled his canteen. When he straightened, he noticed a man watching him. A slight man with wild hair and pinched features.

"Help you?" Jack asked brusquely.

"G-got a me-message from Mr M-Morgan." The man's stutter was pronounced, making it difficult to detect an accent.

"Mr Morgan?" For a moment Jack was perplexed. Then he twigged. "Oh, you mean George, the knife-wielding psychopath. What the fuck does he want?"

The man's eyes widened and he took a step back. "He s-said he will me-meet you in the village centre if you wish to learn m-more."

Jack glared at the man, who took another step back. He looked ready to turn tail and flee, but Jack was in no mood to be conciliatory.

"Tell him he can kiss my pimply arse."

The man's eyes opened a fraction wider, before he turned and scurried away.

A moment of doubt crossed Jack's mind. Maybe it wasn't the smartest move to antagonise the maniac who'd taken a blade to his arm, but he pushed the uncertainty aside. He sensed a change beginning to take place inside himself, in the deep places where attitudes are forged.

Since the door of the Elevator had opened onto what should have been the Sixth Floor of Claridge House, but which had instead been a fragrance-filled, sun-drenched country vista, Jack had existed in varying states of terror.

The look of reproachful contempt he'd seen earlier in the face of the girl wasn't the first time he'd been subjected to such regard of late. He'd noticed the same look in the expressions of his recent travelling companions, especially Kim and Matt. Not so much Tara, but that was because she'd usually been away with the fairies, convincing herself that she was experiencing an unusually lucid dream.

It was a look with which Jack had grown accustomed, if not comfortable, over the last few years. He'd seen it in the faces of passers-by when he'd staggered past them during the comedown from whatever had been his most recent high, or when he'd begged for spare cash while huddled against the wind on a park bench, or in the faces of medical staff while they saved his life.

At other times he had been subjected to looks of pity, usually from council homelessness officers or hostel workers. And hatred—at least, that was how he'd interpreted it—from his mother and her constant supply of boyfriends.

Pity, hatred or contempt, he was fed up of seeing such expressions directed his way.

Most of all, he was fed up of being afraid.

Setting his jaw into what he hoped was a resolute line, Jack resumed his walk along the path. When he encountered anyone who stared at him, he returned their gaze, with interest. To his satisfaction, many looked away.

The path led him in a roughly circular pattern, never drawing any nearer to the mountains. The grassland appeared to stretch away to the foothills in an unbroken swathe. He passed a small stand of trees growing next to the path. Diagonal incisions had been scored in the bark near the foot of the trunks from which oily sap dripped into bowls placed on the ground. Strips of bark had been removed in places; the exposed wood beneath glistened orange in the sunlight.

Soon he came back to where the path had split in two, to the point where he'd approached Tumble Down and met George Morgan.

For a moment he stood and stared up the gentle incline leading back towards the forests and, ultimately, the jetty where his journey on this side of the river had begun. But there could be no question of retracing his steps. There remained too much to find out.

He turned away from the path and headed back into the centre of Tumble Down.

He didn't need to squeeze through narrow spaces between huts to work his way back to the inner ring. Although most buildings had been constructed close to or against their neighbours, wider spaces which would allow three or four people to walk abreast had been left at regular intervals in each of the three rings of buildings. It was therefore a simple matter in the golden sunlight of another splendid day to find his way back to the centre.

Most of the people he passed seemed to be mooching about with nothing particular to do except to stare at him with frank curiosity. He saw one woman carrying out rudimentary repairs to a door which had broken free of its vine hinges and a few people making their way from the back of the village—from the bushes and stream he had seen earlier—laden with containers of fruit and water, but that appeared to be the extent of the daily chores as far as he could make out.

He wondered idly where they went to relieve themselves, for it was business he would need to take care of soon, though the need was not yet pressing.

Then he was stepping through one of the wide gaps between two huts in the innermost ring and found himself back in the centre circle. At one of the tables, looking at Jack as though expecting him, sat George.

Four

Jack's resolve to learn more about the land began to drain away like water from an unplugged sink. His knees locked and for a moment he could go no further. Taking a deep breath to steel himself, he willed his legs to work again and stepped forward.

George offered a tentative smile as he approached. Jack did not return it. He walked up to the table where the American sat and came to a halt. On the table stood a wooden jug and two beakers.

"Good morning, young Jack," said George. His smile grew broader. "I trust the arm is as good as new?"

Jack didn't respond. He wanted to yell at the American or summon up the courage to strike him, but part of him also wanted to make off rapidly in any direction so long as it took him away from the man who had cut him.

"It was necessary, you know," added George quietly. "Sure, I could have *explained* how this place works, but there wasn't time to convince you. Far more effective to show you." He grunted. "And now you know. Now you believe."

Jack held up his right forearm. "You cut me. It's healed overnight. What is that supposed to make me believe? That I've suddenly developed superpowers?"

"I don't know what you mean." He motioned to the empty chair next to his. "Won't you sit down? Please?"

Still Jack hesitated, battling the fight or flight impulse.

Punch him and this time he could kill you. He has a knife, remember. A sharp one. On the other hand, run away and you'll never get to hear more about this place.

His anger and fear begin to dissipate. He allowed his shoulders to sag and let out a great sigh before sitting down.

George poured a purplish liquid from the jug into the two beakers and slid one of them across the table. Jack eyed it doubtfully.

"Relax. I'm not going to poison you," said the American with a wry smile. He drank from his beaker, bruising the edges of his moustache. "It's merely squished berries mixed with water. Our opportunities for culinary experiments are extremely limited, as you might have noticed. We have tried making wine, but not with any measure of success. Whatever sweetens these berries, it's not sugar as we know it. They *did* ferment, but the result…" He grimaced. "Tastes like horse's piss. Mind, that doesn't stop some from drinking it. Takes the edge off the tedium, I suppose."

Jack picked up his beaker, sniffed it and raised it to his lips. The liquid tasted as George had described: a watery version of the berries. Refreshing enough, he supposed, but not exactly what he'd call enticing.

George chuckled.

"What?" asked Jack.

"Pimply ass, eh?"

Jack felt the start of a blush, but jutted out his chin and hoped that he'd stopped it spreading.

"My arm," he said. "My shirt. I know I didn't imagine that you'd cut them."

George shook his head and his expression grew serious. "Nope. It happened. I cut them."

"Then how…?"

"You might have noticed that it's impossible not to fall asleep after dark."

Jack nodded.

"It happens to everyone every night," continued George. "No matter how hard we try to stay awake—and we've all tried to, believe me—everyone falls asleep at the same time. It's like a switch is thrown and we all shut down. Like we're machines, not people."

"Robots."

"Robots… Isn't that word from some European play? Not sure what it means, though."

"Doesn't matter. Is everyone being drugged or something?"

"We've speculated that there's something in the food or water.

People have tried fasting and not drinking, but they fall asleep anyway. Perhaps there's some sort of opiate in the very air we breathe. The truth is, no one knows." He paused for a sip of his drink. "It's weird, but not half as weird as what happens to us while we sleep."

"What you're saying," said Jack slowly, "is that every morning we wake up in precisely the same condition as when we arrived on this side of the river."

"Precisely the same *physical* condition," said George. "And so I'm stuck with this game leg. On the other hand, any fresh injuries that we suffered the previous day have not only healed, any trace of them has completely disappeared. Like with your arm. Any changes wrought to our clothes or any other objects we brought with us are undone like they never happened. It's how I possess an endless supply of matches in the box I had in my pocket and get to smoke the same cigar night after night. Ha! If only I'd said 'Blast the Eighteenth Amendment!' and been carrying a pint of bourbon."

Jack thought for a moment. "That's why the juice stain on my clothes disappeared and I never felt the effects of hard exercise the next day." He let out a low whistle. "Man, that's crazy."

George fixed him with a piercing gaze. "Yet you *remember* that physical exertion, and the stain, and me cutting your arm?"

"Of course I do."

"Well, given that no physical evidence remains, does anything about that strike you as peculiar?"

"Um… Do you mean that our bodies and clothes or whatever change back to their original condition, but our minds don't?"

George rapped the table with his fist, making Jack jump. "Exactly! It's the most peculiar thing of all."

Jack was finding his excitement infectious. "It's as if our bodies reboot overnight to their default state, that being the state in which they came to this place, but our minds retain new information. Like a hard drive remaining updated while the programs which run off it reset to default."

The American blinked. "I understood less than half of what you just said, but I think I got the sense of it and, yes, you're right."

"It was computer stuff," said Jack, "but I guess you come from a time *way* before they were even thought of."

"Ah. Thinking machines. There's someone here from the early 1990s who was trying to tell me about them, but she's from China and struggles a little with English, while my Mandarin is non-existent. I caught a flavour, but would like to learn more. I was going to ask Nadine—she's the girl from Third Millennium Switzerland, the one I mentioned to you yesterday. To be precise, which is always essential to a man of finance, she came here from the year 2176. Her English is excellent, but you'll do just as well."

"If she's from that far in the future, I can learn a lot of stuff from her, too." *Like how far they've progressed with AI. Nowhere near Miriam-level, I expect.*

Jack felt a small shiver of excitement at the prospect of discussing technological advances with a person from more than one hundred and fifty years in his future. He examined that feeling for a moment and found, to his surprise, that he had already grown accustomed to the concept of mixing with people from different time periods. Another relatively palatable concept after all the bizarre encounters he'd had since stepping into the Elevator.

George drained his beaker and stood, wincing a little, cane gripped in his left hand. "The trouble with our bodies resetting or… um, what did you call it?"

"Rebooting."

"Rebooting. A curious expression. Well, it means that I'm permanently stuck with this game leg. I've found that stretching out on a patch of thick grass in the sun helps to ease the stiffness a little. I shall see you this afternoon for the Bout."

"Bout? What's that?"

"You'll see. You arrived too late to witness yesterday's Bout, but today you can watch the return match. We can talk some more later as I appreciate there's more you'd like to know. And I'm keen to hear the story of how you came here." He glanced around. "I've asked Simone to give you the guided tour, which won't take long, and sort you out with your own shack. That basically means finding an empty one and moving in. Ah, here she comes. I shall take your leave, young man, and hope that no hard feelings remain from last night's, er, demonstration of how things work around here." He held out his right hand.

Jack hesitated for half a heartbeat before gripping it.

Simone turned out to be a middle-aged Canadian with a permanently forlorn expression. She nodded at George, who limped away, and offered Jack a brief smile, which momentarily lifted her hangdog look.

She led him to a building on the other side of the inner circle, as crudely constructed as its neighbours, but slightly larger.

"This is the Stores," she said.

The 'window'—a hinged section of lashed-together logs—which took up most of the front wall had been propped open with a stick, allowing daylight to enter the interior. Simone left the door wide as she stepped inside, allowing more light to enter.

Jack followed her and wrinkled his nose.

The air was filled with the fragrant scent of berries and a salty tang, a little like the smell of a breeze off an ocean, which he assumed was the meat. As his eyes adjusted to the relative dimness, he could make out shelves lining the rear wall and imagined he could hear them groan under the weight of the wooden jugs and bowls which sat on them.

"Our fruit and water supplies," said Simone, noticing the direction of his gaze. "Also oil and wicks for light. Anyone can help themselves to as much as they need or want. Each morning we take it in turns to gather more from the trees, bushes and stream behind the village."

Jack nodded. "I saw. Don't the bushes take time to replenish after they've been stripped?"

The woman gave a small laugh. "You'd think. But no matter how much we take one day, the next morning the bushes are laden with fresh berries."

"That's handy. And the meat—where does that come from?"

Jack's gaze shifted to a long table which filled one side of the shack. On it, in row upon row of wooden plates, was the source of the salty smell. The plates were piled high with chunks and strips and hunks of the meat which had helped sustain him in his journey from the ferry. No bones, though, not that he could see.

Simone laughed again, but this time Jack wondered whether he could detect a note of hysteria in the sound. "No one knows where it comes from. We eat it all day. We fall asleep. Poof! When we wake up, the meat's been restocked. Like magic."

The woman's eyes had grown wide and Jack had an abrupt insight: she was struggling to cling on to her sanity.

"Simone? How long have you been here?"

"Four months. Five months. Six months. Too long."

"How did you get here?"

She let out her breath in a long sigh and took so long to reply that Jack had begun to think she wouldn't. "I have a son. He's been doing okay for himself. Got him a little sail boat. Not much more than a skiff but, boy, was he ever proud of it. Insisted on taking his mother out on the lake. A storm whipped up from nowhere. Wind so strong we struggled to take down the sail. Lightning so fierce we was afraid it would turn the mast to cinders. I remember praying as waves thrown up by the wind threatened to capsize us. Next thing I know, we're both sitting in the skiff at the foot of a grassy hillside with no lake to be seen."

"The Lord of the Dance. Was he there?"

Simone frowned and shook her head.

"He would have appeared as a monk," said Jack. "The Quartermaster, he called himself."

"Oh, the monk. Hell, yeah. Talk to anyone; they all met the monk. 'Cept he called himself the Halfmaster."

It was Jack's turn to frown in puzzlement.

"To some," continued Simone, "he called himself the Master. Or the Thirdmaster." She shrugged. "George reckons it's all random what he decides his name is. But whatever he says determines how many have to cross the river."

"Huh. That makes sense. There were four of us and he said at least one must complete the quest, as he called it."

"Yep. Quartermaster. Just me and my son—one of us had to cross, so Halfmaster. When he calls himself the Master, everyone must cross. Or perish fighting his pets." She shivered.

"Clowns with razorblades in place of teeth." Jack also shivered.

"Figures of men in white hoods and sheets, carrying smoking torches and flaming crosses." She clutched her arms about herself. "My great-grandparents escaped the south and kept going, not stopping till they hit Toronto. Their stories were passed down."

"You crossed on the raft to save your son?"

"Yep. He wanted to fight—always had more than a touch of hellraiser about him—but I could see which way the wind was blowin' and there would be no way of winning a fight against that monster and his minions. So I ran for the raft and pulled away from the bank before my boy could stop me." Her eyes glistened with memory. "Before I disappeared into that wall of fog, I called back to him to go live his life." She looked at Jack, her eyes white in the gloom. "Not knowing whether he's safe is driving me crazy."

Jack nodded, but he had stopped listening. He had been distracted by the sight of something incongruous in this place of wood. Something shiny and metallic. Something that reminded him a little of Miriam.

Five

It sat alone on the floor of the shack in a pool of light entering the propped-open window. A little smaller in height and width than an attaché case, but plumper, with rounded corners. It was constructed—and this is what made him think of Miriam—from a silvery, metallic material.

He walked over to it, curious to see it closer. A handle protruded from its top, made of the same silvery metal, but otherwise unremarkable: a simple carrying handle. The surfaces of the object looked smooth and unbroken by logo or other markings. No hinges or latches were evident, casting doubt on his initial impression that it was some sort of container.

Jack bent and took hold of the handle. It felt cool to the touch. He hefted the object—it weighed little more than an empty shoe box—and turned it, looking for seams or other evidence that it might open like a case. But nothing marred the uniform smoothness.

He looked up when he heard Simone clear her throat. He had forgotten she was with him. She stared at him, an intent but unreadable—expectant, maybe—expression on her doleful face.

"Your name?" she said.

"My name? I thought you knew. It's Jack."

"Your *full* name."

Jack returned her stare, wondering at the sudden air of tension about his companion. Then he replied, "Just Jack. Plain old Jack."

Simone's shoulders sagged a little as her bearing relaxed. She sighed and stepped to his side. Taking the object from him gently, but in a way that suggested she could be firmer if necessary, she returned it to its place on the dusty floor of the shack.

"Then, Plain Old Jack," she said, "this isn't for you."

Simone led him to the outer ring of buildings. One of the huts had been half-demolished; broken timbers poked at the sky like snapped ribs. She did not pass comment and strode with such purpose that Jack didn't like to interrupt her to ask about it.

"Most all the huts in the two inner circles are taken," she said, coming to a stop. "But there's plenty empty on the outside." She glanced at Jack, her features suddenly sharp. "That suit you, Plain Old Jack? Living on the outside?"

Jack's brow creased. "What do you mean?"

"Oh, nothing." The woman's face resumed its doleful expression. "Here we are. This one should do you well enough, though there's a whole lot more to choose from." She uttered a short laugh. "There ain't much to tell 'em apart, in truth, so this one's as good or as bad as any of the others."

She led him towards a shack which looked much like its neighbours. It stood at the rear of the settlement, backing on to the mountains and, from what Jack could remember of his walk along the path which circled Tumble Down, close to the bushes and stream where he had watched people foraging.

After a brief struggle with the door, Simone yanked it open, took a peek in and stepped to one side.

"They all come equipped with wooden bowls and beakers," she said. "You can stock up from the Stores." She pointed to the area behind the shack. "Or you can collect your own fruit fresh from the bush."

"Do they have beds?"

Simone made what seemed to Jack the first genuinely amused sound she had uttered since he'd met her. "No need for beds, sugar. When it's time to sleep, you'll sleep, bed or not."

She made to turn away.

"Wait!" Jack felt a flutter of panic. "What should I do?"

Simone waved a hand vaguely towards the shack. "Make yourself at home."

"And then?"

"Do whatever you want. Other than taking turns to restock the Stores with fruit and water, that's all anyone does." She made to turn away again, but hesitated as if remembering something.

"There's the Bout later. It takes place in the centre."

"What *is* the Bout?"

Simone's expression grew more forlorn. "It's what passes for entertainment 'round here."

The interior of the shack looked like the inside of George's: a couple of shelves containing pitchers, beakers and bowls, all empty; a small table and two rough-and-ready chairs; an empty space on the pressed-dirt floor large enough for him to lie down; and not much else.

Jack surveyed his new home. "No worse than that shithole of a flat," he muttered. "Better in some ways. No rent or bills to pay."

And I don't have to share it with those wankers I had to pretend were my friends.

A rare smile curled his lips.

He made a couple of trips to the Stores, trying to ignore stares from the crowd gathering in the centre, and stocked up on berries, meat and water. The silvery case drew his glance, but he resisted the urge to pick it up again. The Canadian had made it clear it was out of bounds. Nevertheless, his gaze kept returning to it and he couldn't shake the sensation that somehow the case was paying him the same degree of attention.

"Don't be such a moron," he said, trying to add a laugh at his own expense. But the sound died in his throat. The notion of the case observing him, though absurd, held no humour.

Back in his shack, he added the remaining berries from his pouch to one of the bowls, leaving both pouch and canteen on a shelf. His waist felt strangely naked without them.

For want of anything better to do, he sat for a while and filled his stomach with salty meat and berries. Having washed them down with cool water, his bladder needed emptying. That's when he realised he hadn't asked Simone where locals attended to such basic needs. That led to another realisation: he hadn't moved his bowels, or needed to, since arriving in these lands.

Jack was a once-a-day man, but had attended to business in his flat before leaving for work and stepping into the Elevator. That had been—what?—three or four days ago, yet he hadn't felt the need to go again. He glanced at the meat and berries. Perhaps they provided such perfect nutrition that they didn't produce any waste.

Now you really are being a moron. It's because we reset overnight. As long as I'm here, I'll never need to take another dump.

The thought cheered him.

He stepped into the darkest corner of the shack, unzipped and relieved himself—the dirt floor was so dry it absorbed the liquid where it fell. Besides, Jack told himself, it will have disappeared by the morning after the reboot.

Now what? His brow crinkled in thought. *I suppose…*

"… I could go and see what this Bout is about."

He left the shack and made for the village centre, chuckling at his own wit.

The innermost ring of the village had filled with people. Perhaps as many as a hundred, all told. They stood in small groups, speaking in hushed tones. More stares greeted Jack as he walked in, but he ignored them. The tables around the circle were fully occupied. George Morgan broke off a conversation to nod at him, but made no motion for Jack to join him.

A sense of expectancy infused the atmosphere; a muted tension, like the calm before a storm.

Jack stepped back to the alley between two buildings through which he had entered the circle, stood to one side so that he could lean his shoulder against the nearest shack and watched.

For a while nothing happened. Knots of people continued their muttered discussions and the air of tension grew tauter, but Jack could see no obvious cause of excitement and began to wonder what else he could be doing. Finding out more about this place, and why he and all these people were here, would be a good start, but Jack wasn't the type to easily approach strangers and engage them in conversation; besides, everyone present seemed particularly unapproachable right now.

He had begun to consider wandering over to the table at which George was sitting, when two new people entered the circle and the bumble of conversation died.

The newcomers were both male: one was dark with thinning hair, heavyset and perhaps in his early forties; the other blond, slighter and younger. They each seemed to have stripped down to the bare minimum of clothing to preserve decency, leaving just rough-looking trousers and woollen vests. The bulge of the older man's biceps stood out in stark contrast to the younger's stick-like arms.

The groups which had been occupying the central circle broke up as people pressed back to create a space into which the two men stepped.

With no chatter of bird or insect to intrude, and no breeze to speak of, the two men regarded each other in silence. The darker man's face was fixed in a glower; the blond looked more circumspect, perhaps apprehensive, and his tongue darted out to lick at his lips.

The tension in the air increased. The onlookers seemed to be holding their breaths; many leaned forward, faces twisted into expectant, hungry expressions. Wolfish.

Jack straightened, the anticipation surrounding him palpable. He watched as the older man strode towards the younger.

The blond man was lighter on his feet, quicker than the other, but not quick enough to duck the swinging fist. It struck him on the nose with a crunching sound and blood spurted. A collective gasp rose from the spectators.

The blond staggered and shook his head, spraying droplets of blood onto the watching people nearest him. They didn't appear to mind; on the contrary, it seemed to drive their excitement up a notch.

Another punch caught the younger man in the stomach, driving air from his lungs. He staggered again and sank to the ground on his backside. He lowered his head in a daze.

A triumphant grin split the older man's features and he surged forward. He reached the stricken blond and straddled him. He pressed his hands to the younger man's shoulders in readiness to press him to the ground and trap him beneath his body, then paused to savour the moment. A sigh came from the spectators. Jack glanced at them and saw expressions of disappointment as if they didn't want the fight to be over so soon.

Their wish was granted. As the heavier man lunged forwards, pressing Blondie back by the shoulders, the latter brought his knee up to connect with a meaty thud in his attacker's groin. Jack winced; the crowd moaned.

The older man let out a shriek and collapsed to the ground on his side, curled up like a foetus and clutching at his groin. Blondie had already wriggled free and bounded to his feet with purpose and energy that gave lie to his apparent stupefaction of moments before.

He brought a hand up to his nose and examined the blood on his fingers.

A voice called from the onlookers, "Get him, Larry! Pay the bastard back for yesterday."

The blond—Larry, presumably—glanced around and grinned. It made his face, blood-caked and swollen, appear grotesque. Then he turned back to the man lying stricken on the ground and went to work.

Six

Jack was no stranger to violence. Thanks to his mother's string of dysfunctional boyfriends, he had grown up thinking it was normal for the senior male of the household to make liberal use of his fists on every other member. And it would be highly improbable to occupy the murky sub-strata of society in which he had existed for two years without witnessing violence on a frequent basis. From random acts of casual cruelty to attempted murder, he had seen more than many young men.

But, except on occasions when he had been the victim—regularly during his home life; less often while living on the streets when his wits and instincts for self-preservation, which the less charitable might ascribe to cowardice, had enabled him to avoid the worst confrontations—Jack had not actively participated in the assaults. He thought of himself as a runner not a fighter, though also told himself that he would stand toe-to-toe with anyone should the occasion demand. As luck would have it, he had yet to come across such a situation.

Unless he counted… the image of the mob-capped woman swam to the forefront of his mind, but he pushed it away. There had been nothing he could have done for her. Nothing.

Jack *was* a stranger to guilt and it wasn't a feeling he welcomed. To take his mind off the French woman, he cast his gaze beyond the fight, in which he had already lost interest. Larry, the blond guy, was raining kicks onto the body of his prone opponent, who was offering little resistance except to try to curl himself into the tightest ball he could, like an overweight hedgehog.

He could see George Morgan watching the Bout—it had become too one-sided to describe as a 'fight'. Like most of the faces of the people around him, George's looked flushed with blood lust. A little way along he could see the Canadian, Simone, who had showed him around the village. By contrast, her expression was one of disinterest, as though the scene bored her.

Near her stood someone else Jack recognised and thus far the only person whose expression suggested they were neither excited by nor indifferent to the violent spectacle. It was the girl who had been standing watching him when he'd awoken that morning. Jack now believed he knew her name. He started to work his way around the edge of the crowd towards her.

Below the animal moans and cries of the crowd came a steady noise, like someone repeatedly hitting a thick-cut steak with a mallet. A glance towards the centre of the circle showed Jack that the sound came from Larry aiming kicks at every exposed inch of his opponent's flesh with his bare feet. Feet that looked like they'd been thrust into an abattoir trough, so thick were they covered with blood from both men. Occasionally the supine man would move his arms from his head to try to protect another part of his body, whereupon Larry would aim a hefty kick at the exposed head.

Although the blond attacker had been keeping up this assault for minutes, he showed no signs of flagging, which is more than could be said for the thick-set man. His attempts at covering up were growing feeble, leaving more and more areas for the blond to attack, which the latter did with renewed vigour. This could not last much longer without, Jack guessed, a potentially fatal blow being landed.

In a rare moment of self-contemplation, Jack examined his feelings and found that the thought of the blond man kicking the darker man to death didn't sicken him as much as it ought. Perhaps his experiences since leaving home had made him unsympathetic to the suffering of others. Or maybe it was an effect that Nowhere was having—it certainly seemed that the great majority of locals were, at best, indifferent to the plight of the combatants.

He squeezed past the final clutch of spectators and reached the girl's side.

"Hello," he said. To his own ears, his voice sounded as tentative as a nervous child's.

The girl turned her head towards him. Jack hadn't noticed that morning how big her eyes were, or how deep a shade of brown, like buffed walnut.

"It's, um… your name." Now he sounded like a tongue-tied teenager; he mentally shook himself. "It's Nadine, isn't it?"

She nodded. "And you are Jack."

"Yep." *Word's obviously got around.*

She turned her attention back to the Bout, as if their conversation, as far as she was concerned, was over. Her expression suggested she found the scene distasteful.

Not good with small talk at the best of times, Jack struggled for something to say.

"Er, this fight. Does this sort of thing happen every day?"

Nadine shrugged. "Most days."

"How does it end?"

"They will pull Larry away before he kills Daniel. Yesterday they pulled Daniel away before he killed Larry."

"Yesterday? How…? Ah. Of course. Their injuries healed overnight. Do they fight each other every day?"

"No. Though it is beginning to feel like it." She sighed. "Tomorrow it will be two or three or four different ones. But always there must be someone fighting. To feed the bloodlust."

"I'm not that keen on it."

Her head turned to look at him again. Jack gained the impression she was appraising him and tried not to squirm under her silent regard.

"Um," he tried, coming over all tongue-tied again. "Er, do you fancy, uh, that is to say, would you take a walk with me? Um, just along the path around the village?"

She glanced away. "They are pulling Larry off Daniel."

Jack looked to the central space. People had indeed moved forward and were dragging the blond away from the dark-haired man. Not before time—the ground around the prone figure was stained black with blood. When he looked back at Nadine, she had started to move away. She glanced over her shoulder.

"Are you coming?"

The path was deserted. Whatever people did between the end of a Bout and sundown, it clearly didn't involve foraging or collecting water from the stream.

The sun had begun its lazy descent towards the mountain peaks, but the breeze had dropped and the afternoon had turned balmy. Jack walked slightly behind the girl. Whenever he tried to increase his stride to draw level, she did too so that she stayed a couple of steps ahead of him.

Jack didn't mind; he could think of nothing to say. That is, there were plenty of questions he wanted to ask about Tumble Down and how she had arrived here and what the real world was like in the time she had come from, but the death of the French woman and Jack's inability to save her or even make the attempt stood as an impenetrable barrier to his being able to behave normally, or as normally as it was possible to behave in the circumstances in which he found himself.

They arrived at the clutch of bushes growing alongside the path and the girl came to a stop. She sat on the path and began picking at fruit from the nearest bush, popping berries into her mouth.

Jack stood shuffling his feet in the dust, uncertain whether to join her, still not knowing what words might be suitable.

His feeling of awkwardness increased until he began to wonder whether he should leave. Then the girl stopped picking at the bush, leaned back and glanced up at him. She patted the ground next to her.

"Come. Sit."

"So, you are Jack. Just Jack."

He nodded, trying not to show his irritation. *What's all this fascination with my surname?*

"Tell me, Just Jack, how you came here."

"Uh, well, I'm from Great Britain in the early part of the

twenty-first century, difficult though that is to believe."

Nadine offered him a cool stare. "How so? There are people here from all times, all places." She gave a light laugh. "We look the same age, yet you are two centuries my elder, give or take a few decades."

Jack smiled, beginning to relax for the first time since coming into the girl's presence. "Old enough to be your great-grandfather."

"I think we can add a few more greats to that. How came you here from Britain? Oh, and speaking of 'great', no one uses that prefix before Britain any more."

"I never thought it was particularly great when I was there." A thought struck him. "Is it still also called the United Kingdom?"

"My history isn't the best, but Britain hasn't been called that for fifty years, perhaps longer. Its people squabble with each other and the rest of the world." She shrugged. "Apart from the financial centre of the city state of Metropolitan London, it is thought of, if at all, as an island of isolation, largely irrelevant in world affairs. Sorry to speak ill of your home."

"I don't have a home."

"That is a sad thing to say, Just Jack. Everyone must have a home."

"If I do, then it's here."

"But this is Nowhere."

"You're not the first person to say that. Is that what you all call this place: Nowhere?"

"Yes." She shrugged again. "It is not in any place. It is not in any time. It is nowhere and no-when."

Jack grunted. "Sounds the perfect place for me."

"Is someone feeling sorry for himself? But I wait for you to tell me how you came here."

He was about to take umbrage at her suggestion he was being self-pitying, but then decided to tell her about the Elevator instead.

He told it all, haltingly at first, from when he stepped into the lift with that smug git Matt, expecting to start another embittering day of playing catch-up with the other trainee programmers, to when he pulled the raft hand over hand from the bank of the brown river leaving Matt, Kim and Tara behind.

Nadine proved to be an attentive audience. She didn't interrupt but listened with rapt attention, her eyes widening now and again, her breath drawing in sharply on occasion. The more Jack talked, the more he relaxed in her company in spite of the dark tale he was relating.

"And that's it," he finished. "I met that girl Anna who gave me food and water, and followed the path until it brought me here. I expect that's similar to how you got here."

Jack glanced at the sky and was surprised to find that darkness was beginning to close in. The last sliver of sun was shrinking behind the mountains.

"Similar. Yet not," said the girl. "I was hiking in the Italian Alps with a friend when we were caught by a blizzard. No panic. We had brought a tent against such a hazard—lightweight but durable—and we huddled inside to wait out the storm. But the noise dropped, the quality of light outside changed and it grew unaccountably warm. We opened the tent flap to find not the snow-covered valley we had been scaling, but a grassy hillside and a muddy river."

"A friend, you say? A boy friend?"

She shook her head. "Annelise. Very much a girl."

Unaware that he had tensed, Jack felt tension drain from him. "And the monk?"

"Yes. The Halfmaster he called himself, though I think the word 'he' is not quite appropriate. 'It' is perhaps more accurate. He told us that one of us must cross the river or both would perish. Annelise has a fiancé, I do not." She shrugged. "So I crossed and, I hope, Annelise returned to Italy." She looked closely at Jack. "Do you see the difference between our tales? You travelled in this elevator to strange and marvellous lands; we entered our tent in one world and came out in this without visiting anywhere in between."

"Hmm. So did George. He said he fell into an excavation ditch, also in a blizzard, and came to near the river. And Simone came during a storm on a lake."

"Everyone I have spoken to here—and I have heard many, many tales—had the same experience: some intervening event like a blizzard or a fog or some sort of accident and they find themselves on the other side of the river. You are the first to tell of visiting other worlds."

"But what does that mean?"

"I do not know, Just Jack. What I do know is that soon we will sleep." She yawned. "I think I shall remain here and awake to breakfast on these bushes."

Jack considered for a moment and found that he didn't much like the idea of returning to his empty shack. "Can… um, I mean, would it be all right if I stayed, too? Not like, you know, I'm trying it on with you or anything. Oh shit, that sounds lame." He felt his face colour and was suddenly glad of the dark.

Nadine chuckled. It was a throaty sound that make his blush deepen. "Of course you may stay. We shall break our fast together."

"Great." There was one last thing he needed to say, to clear the air between them completely. "That woman, the French one…"

"Camille."

"Yes, Camille. I don't think I could have saved her. I mean, even if I'd tried. They would have killed me as well."

He heard her sigh beside him. Then he jumped and almost cried out until he realised that what had brushed his arm were her fingers. "It's okay, Just Jack," she murmured. "I know."

Seven

If someone had told Jack that he would spend nights sleeping on pressed dirt in open air and awake each morning feeling like he'd slept for ten hours cocooned in a luxurious bed, he would have scoffed. Yet refreshed—or, in any event, he reminded himself, rebooted—is exactly how he felt as he stretched, leaving his eyes closed while, like a lounging cat, he savoured the warmth falling across his face.

When at last he opened them, he blinked to adjust to the sunlight and moved his head to face Nadine. Except she wasn't there.

He sat up and glanced around. There was no sign of the girl; the path was empty in both directions. So much for breakfasting together. He pushed away a flicker of regret.

"Never expect, never be disappointed," he muttered.

He began to pluck fruit from the nearest bush, which hung full with plump berries of optimum ripeness. If this was the same bush from which Nadine had eaten the previous evening, it had replenished itself overnight.

A shadow fell across him and he glanced up, expecting to see her; she must have moved away to relieve herself.

The person blocking out the sun was someone he recognised, but it wasn't Nadine.

"We meet again, gov," said Frankie.

Jack grunted and began to scramble to his feet.

"If it's all the same to you, gov, I'll join you down there," said Frankie. He was dressed as Jack remembered seeing him in the forests, in old-fashioned waistcoat and trousers, though they looked to be in slightly better condition than on their previous meetings; still threadbare, but not so torn and grubby. They'd returned to their original condition after a reboot, Jack supposed.

Frankie sat next to him.

"The Scourgers aren't chasing you just now, then."

"Oh, no, gov. They only takes an interest in me, and in anyone, who strays. Stick to the trail, or to the confines of the village, and you'll be as safe as the Bank of England, like my old ma was fond of saying."

Once more Jack was struck by a note of discord in the man's accent, as if he had nearly mastered the art of speaking like a Victorian Londoner, but not quite.

Frankie nodded to the open grassland beyond the bushes, stretching away to the mountains in the near distance. "Those are the places you'll want to avoid, gov, if you want to keep yourself safe and sound. Those are the places you'll want to tread if you want to bring those mounted terrors upon you."

Jack frowned. "Why, then, do you stray from the path? I noticed you only do so in the forest, where they can't easily use their whips, but why stray at all?"

Frankie's face split into the same cheeky grin Jack recalled from their first encounter. "Why, gov, for the thrill of the chase, of course. I can't stay around here, resting on my haunches where the only relief from the humdrum of existence is watching people scrap like alley cats." The grin faded. "Or seeing them lose their minds, crumb by crumb, until all that remains is an empty crust."

"Is that what happens to people here? They go mad?"

"Not all. Not yet."

Jack pondered. "Our minds… George said that's the only part of us that doesn't reset during the night. So while our bodies remain the same, never ageing, we remember what we did the previous day. And week. And month." He glanced at Frankie, who was gazing at him with a faint smile playing about his lips. Jack didn't know if the smile was approving or mocking.

"Go on, gov. You're beginning to understand what Nowhere is about, if it's about anything."

"Okay. Our minds remember, but what do they remember? The same surroundings, food, people. The same aches and pains we came here with. Even the weather seems to be the same every day. It would be better if our minds reset, too, so we didn't remember that each day here is the same as the last."

"A bit of a design fault, that."

Jack glanced sharply at Frankie. For a moment there the faux Cockney accent had slipped entirely.

Frankie cleared his throat. Was that the faintest of blushes colouring his cheeks? "Yes, gov, you're right, by Jiminy. The sameness is what drives some fit for Bedlam."

Jack continued to regard Frankie through narrowed eyes.

"So, er," continued Frankie, as though in a hurry to move past Jack's suspicion, "what do some folk do who see no future, whose minds are turned to despair?"

"Try to commit suicide?"

"Cor blimey, gov, you've got it!"

Jack wasn't buying what he was now sure was a second-rate act, but decided to let it go. "What you're saying is that Nowhere is about making people want to kill themselves?"

"Not exactly. But the suicidal urge is a natural by-product of the monotony of existence in Nowhere."

Again, the choice of words didn't ring true to Jack's ears as being in character, but he was more interested for now in pursuing the train of thought sparked by the conversation than in exposing this man as a fraud.

"That French woman. Camille. She knew that by straying from the path she'd bring the Scourgers down upon her. There was no reason for her to stray unless that is what she wanted."

Frankie nodded. "Traditional methods like hanging or slitting wrists can fail. If the body has not expired by nightfall, the wounds will heal. Venturing from the trail into open land is the most certain way to end existence in Nowhere. The Scourgers are remorseless and merciless."

"Yet Camille was trying to get away from them."

"Ah, even the most resolute suicide attempt may falter at the critical moment." He nodded once more in the direction of the mountains. "There is another lost soul intent on ending her existence."

Jack followed his gaze. Around ten paces beyond the bushes, her back to them and walking slowly away, was Nadine.

"What the… ?" Jack was on his feet in an instant. "Nadine!"

Her step faltered at the sound of his shout, but she continued walking.

"What the hell's she doing?" he demanded of Frankie. "I was talking to her last night. She has no death wish."

Frankie remained seated, his posture relaxed. He nodded in Nadine's direction. "The available evidence does not support your statement."

Jack felt a sudden urge to kick him. "Don't just sit there, man. Do something!"

Frankie spread his hands as though to express helplessness, while the faintest of smiles danced around his eyes. "I cannot leave the trail here, where there is no cover. Long have I led the Scourgers a merry chase. If they catch me in the open, I will cease to exist here, for sure, and *I* certainly have no death wish."

Jack glared at him before turning away. A clutch of people had gathered nearby. More people appeared from Tumble Down and a small crowd was assembling, stringing out along the path, everyone watching the slowly retreating figure of Nadine. Word seemed to spread rapidly here.

"Someone, please!" Jack called. "Help her!"

No one paid him the slightest attention, except for one woman who turned in his direction, her expression more doleful than normal.

"Simone?" He could not keep the plaintive whine from his voice as a feeling of impotence supplanted anger. "Won't anyone help her?"

"Well, Plain Old Jack," said the Canadian, "here's the truth of the matter. If someone takes it into their head to step from the trail, there ain't no helping them." She nodded towards Nadine. "That woman knows her own mind, though I confess I didn't have her down as a quitter. If her mind is set on bringing down them mounted tin cans, it's her choice. There are none here who can or will interfere."

"So you're just going to stand there and watch her die?" Fresh frustration coursed through him, lending his words an edge.

Simone didn't drop her gaze. "I reckon so. It makes a change from the Bouts." Then she did turn away.

Nadine had moved perhaps twenty paces from the safety of the path. A faint reverberation rose through the soles of Jack's shoes, reminding him of the thudding he'd felt on the desert world they had visited in the Elevator at the approach of a furry nightmare. This vibration felt stronger, increasing dramatically as it would at the approach of heavy beasts. Heavy hooved beasts.

"Oh, shit," he muttered.

If asked, Jack would profess to be a man of courage, though he'd struggle to name one act of bravery he'd committed. He'd claim to be an altruist, though he'd be lying were he to attest to having performed one selfless act (or, indeed, to say he understood what 'altruist' meant). Self-delusion was one of his dominant traits.

Had he paused to consider his actions now, his instincts for self-preservation would probably have overridden the impulse to act; he could always tell himself later that there was nothing he could have done, that who was he to intervene if the Swiss girl wanted to end her life.

But he didn't hesitate. Shuffling a few paces sideways to clear the bushes, he stepped from the path and took off in a sprint after Nadine.

The ground *thrummed* to the beat of fast-approaching hooves. Four Scourgers appeared, crossing the grassy plain in a canter, two from the left, two from the right. It was touch and go whether he could reach the girl before they did. Unaccustomed to sprinting, the benefits of his hike from the river lost during the reboots of the nights since passed, he lacked breath with which to call to her to halt. Not that it mattered. Clearly sensing the looming creatures—she would have to be deaf and without sensation in her feet not to have noticed them—she had come to a stop of her own accord and stood casting glances to either side, looking small and forlorn.

Urging his legs to one last effort, Jack arrived at her side moments before the lead rider. Without breaking stride, the Scourgers wheeled, enclosing them in a circle of thumping hooves and flaying turf.

"Nadine! What are you doing?"

She turned towards him and Jack was shocked at how she looked: cheeks so pinched and pale, she resembled someone who had been locked up for months without natural light on a diet of bread and water. Top lip trembled as though she were back on her snow-swept mountainside, not standing in full glare of warm sunshine. Eyes bulged and seemed too big for her face, like the eyes of a Pokémon cartoon character; they darted from side to side, trying to keep all four Scourgers in sight at once. Hers was not the expression of a woman who had stepped out willingly to meet her death.

Jack reached out and clutched her to him. She came without resistance and buried her face against his neck, trembling in his arms in time to the vibrating ground.

A wave of vinegary breath hit his face and he felt moist heat against his ear.

"Help me," she whispered.

Eight

The four armoured riders looked identical to Jack, as did the mighty chargers upon which they rode. Each rider's head was turned in to where he and Nadine stood huddled in the space formed by the circling beasts. Jack caught silvery flashes from the visors.

Aside from the thudding of hooves and the occasional snuffling snort from their mounts' snouts, no sound came from the Scourgers. Yet they acted in concert as if connected by an unseen and unheard intercom. Their silence felt even more menacing than their appearance.

The space between each Scourger was wide enough to allow Jack and Nadine to dart through had the riders not been moving so quickly. As it was, he and Nadine would be trampled by the next charger the moment they had passed behind the first.

Unless the riders slowed down. If Jack wasn't gravely mistaken, that's exactly what they were doing.

His thoughts a jumble, disjointed by fear and panic, he tried desperately to think clearly. The French woman, Camille, had been decapitated by whips wielded by…

Think, man!

The Scourgers who had killed Camille had not been on the move when sending out their lethal tendrils, he was sure of it. Maybe they could only wield the whips with accuracy while stationary.

The vibrations beneath his feet had grown weaker. The speed at which the riders circled had decreased to no more than a trot. They were unfurling their whips, at the same time bringing their mounts to a walk.

Hope blossomed within Jack and he tensed, ready to move as soon as they came to a stop.

He whispered urgently to Nadine. "Get ready. They're stopping."

She pulled back her head to look at him. Her mouth opened as if to reply, but what came out was a piercing shriek that made him jump. She arched her back, forcing her legs against his, her face creased in pain.

"Huh? What—" But then he knew.

One of the riders had flicked out his whip, the spiked star at its tip slicing through the material of Nadine's tee-shirt and into the thin layer of flesh covering her ribcage.

So much for his theory of them needing to be stationary to be accurate with their whips.

"Are you all right?" he hissed into Nadine's face.

Her only response was to utter another agonised shriek and scrunch her eyes tight. A second thong had caught her high on one shoulder, leaving a gash and stream of blood running down her arm.

Jack pulled her tightly to him, attempting to shield her with his body and arms as best he could. But she jerked again as a third whip sliced her calf.

"We're sitting ducks," he hissed. "We have to get moving."

If Nadine heard him, she gave no sign. Her breath came in short bursts, like the panting of an overheated dog, but she moved with him as he began to back away in the direction of Tumble Down.

Jack risked a glance behind. Beyond the slowly circling riders quite a crowd had gathered, perhaps the entire population of Tumble Down, spread out to watch his and Nadine's demise. The distance to the path was at least fifteen yards. At the rate at which he was shuffling backwards, pulling Nadine in his wake, they would be sliced apart long before they could reach safety.

A feeling of black despair rose into his throat like bile and threatened to overwhelm him. Had he been alone on the plain, he would probably have succumbed, lying down on the soft grass to await the killing blow. But, for once in his life, he had more than only himself to think about.

"We need to speed up. Nadine! You have to help me."

He unfolded himself from the embrace in which he held her so he could turn around to make quicker progress. As he faced the village, he jerked his head back instinctively to avoid the spiked star that snaked towards them at the speed of a striking cobra. He felt the hiss of air ruffle his hair in the object's passage.

Swivelling to face Nadine again, Jack grabbed her shoulders—she appeared unaware of what was happening—and forced her down. The returning star passed through the space a moment ago inhabited by her head. Too preoccupied with Nadine, Jack could not evade the star a second time and felt a white-hot flare of pain in the side of his head. He followed Nadine into a crouch, so managing to avoid his neck becoming trapped in the loop of the thong.

He raised a hand to the side of his head. It felt hot and wet, and he gasped as his groping fingers encountered raw, shredded flesh. Half of his ear had been torn away.

"Fuck this," he muttered. He moved his hand back to the girl and tightened his grip on her shoulders, trying to force her into opening her eyes, to get with the programme. When she didn't respond, he dug his thumbs as hard as he could into the soft flesh above her collar bone.

Her eyes flew open, tears cascading down her cheeks.

"Ow!" she exclaimed. "*Arrête!* Stop it!"

Jack let go of her shoulders, leaving a bloody handprint on one, and grabbed her hands.

"Come on! We have to make a run for it."

Although Nadine's eyes reflected agony and bewilderment, Jack was relieved to see they also showed awareness. She nodded.

The following minutes—they might have been mere seconds for all Jack knew—passed in a confusion of stumbling panic. Their dash for safety was punctuated by frequent shrieks of pain from Nadine and yells of desperation from Jack. She went down twice and each time Jack yanked a morning star from where it was embedded in her body before hauling her back to her feet.

A distant part of Jack's consciousness, though he was too busy to wonder about it, noted that each cast of a whip seemed aimed only at Nadine and never directly at him. He was sliced a few times to his arms and once to a leg, but each time it was as a result of him trying to block blows aimed at her, to protect her from taking so much punishment that he would have to drag her across the ground. That would be the end of them, or her at least, since he doubted he possessed the strength to pull her dead weight, slight though she was.

It also helped that the Scourgers kept their distance. If they tightened the circle they would completely enclose them and could finish them off at leisure.

Nadine went down again, jerking at his arm as she fell. She landed face down and groaned as if lacking the energy to continue shrieking. With a grimace Jack stooped and pulled out the two stars half-buried in her lower back, tearing chunks of Nadine's flesh away and shredding his hands on the metal barbs.

When he heaved Nadine back to her feet, she could barely stand. She shook her head.

"Leave me."

"No! Almost there."

He glanced behind him. A few yards at most lay between them and the path; no Scourgers stood in the way—they had all moved behind Nadine from where they attacked with renewed vigour.

Another star thudded into her back and she wailed. It was a sound filled with utter despair and, worse, resignation. Jack's blood ran cold; she had given up. Her knees began to buckle.

"No!" he forced out through gritted teeth.

He stepped beyond her, bringing himself into the firing line of the Scourgers' whips. Not taking his gaze from the mounted riders, he felt behind him and jerked the star from the girl's back. His hands had become so pain-filled it was like clutching iron rods fresh from a fire.

Another star whipped towards Nadine, aimed a little to his left.

He stepped in front of it, yelping as it sank into his thigh.

He stumbled a pace back, clawing at the thong and managing to dislodge the spiked metal ball. But his feet caught in Nadine— she had gone down again—and he felt himself falling backwards over her.

If the preceding seconds or minutes had flashed by in a blur, the fall over the prone figure of Nadine seemed to pass in agonising slow motion. The anticipation of hitting the ground, from where he doubted he would rise, stretched out like the pause a condemned man must experience before the first shot is fired by the squad facing him.

But he never landed, though it took his befuddled brain moments to grasp why. Hands had grabbed at him, supporting him, hauling him back to the path where Nadine already lay in a bloodied heap, surrounded by fussing people.

He looked back at the Scourgers. They had already lost interest, were moving away back to wherever they had come from.

Jack let out a deep sigh, staggered, then felt arms lowering him to the ground. Adrenaline drained away, allowing pain to come to the fore: a stinging, throbbing sensation from his ear, like a splitting headache and gum abscess rolled into one; his hands felt like they had been dipped to the wrist in molten steel; if his thigh could talk, it would be screeching in red-hot agony.

Biting his lip against the pain, he glanced around. The entire village seemed to have turned out to enjoy the spectacle. Some formed a huddle around the prone figure of Nadine. Many more gazed down at him, expressions of curiosity on their faces. One was Frankie, although he wore a sardonic, almost smug smile. Noticing Jack's glance, he smirked and turned away.

Amongst the onlookers stood two men Jack recognised, one blond and skinny, the other swarthy and thick-set: Larry and Daniel, the protagonists of the previous afternoon's Bout, neither bearing any sign of the injuries they'd suffered and their mutual antagonism clearly put to one side. The person standing nearest to

Jack was George Morgan. He held a wooden beaker. Wincing from bending his leg, he stooped and handed the beaker to Jack. It was only as he unthinkingly accepted it that Jack noticed how violently his hands were shaking. A dark liquid slopped over the beaker's side.

"Wh-wh-what's this?" he asked, his voice emerging in a stutter.

"You're in shock," said George. "That's the fermented berry juice I told you about. It might taste like horse's piss but it'll take the edge off."

Jack raised the beaker to his lips, his trembling sending more dark liquid spilling over the sides. The smell was like cheap sherry; he hated sherry. He took a sip.

"Y-you're not wrong," he said to George with a grimace.

"Take another swig. It'll help, believe me."

Jack swallowed hard to get the foul liquid down, but it seemed the American was right: his shaking had begun to subside.

He handed the beaker back.

"Er, thanks," he muttered. "Um, why is everyone staring at me? Do I have something on my face?" He gave a self-conscious laugh. "Apart from blood, I mean."

"They stare," said George, "because they have watched you accomplish something that has never before been seen in Nowhere. You have stood up to the Scourgers and still breathe." He shook his head slowly, wonderingly. "No one, not even Frankie, has faced them on open ground and lived to tell the tale."

Jack said nothing. Although the vile liquid had eased his trembling, it hadn't done much to numb the pain and his body was setting up a tattoo of stinging, thumping, aching. Now the thought of retiring to the solitude of his shack greatly appealed.

He struggled to his feet and took a few faltering steps to where Nadine lay. People still fussed around her, staunching wounds with pieces of torn cloth, wiping blood from exposed skin.

"Will she be okay?" he asked.

A woman replied without looking up from her work. "None of these injuries are life-threatening on their own, but she is losing a lot of blood. If we can keep her alive until it is time to sleep, she will be well by morning."

Nadine's face looked unwholesomely pale where it had been wiped clean of blood. Her breath came in short, shallow gasps. Her eyelids fluttered open and she squinted to focus on Jack.

Before she lost consciousness, she opened her mouth to speak. Those caring for her stopped what they were doing to listen. Faint as they were, in the sudden silence her words could be heard clearly.

"Just Jack," she murmured. "Who are you?"

Part 3: Old Acquaintances

One

The mind's role in the preservation of its host should not be underestimated. Jack's memory of the previous day passed in an interminable, agony-shrouded daze writhing on the floor of his shack was already slipping away like a half-remembered dream.

He sat up gingerly, expecting to feel fresh barbs of pain. Nothing. He felt as refreshed as he had on every other morning since crossing the river.

He moved to the window and propped open the shutter to dispel the gloom. In the bright light flooding in, he examined himself. The blood and tear in his chinos on his thigh had disappeared. His hands and ear were whole and unbloodied.

"Bugger me," he muttered, unable to help grinning to himself.

The smile faded as a new thought surfaced.

Nadine—had she survived to nightfall?

He paused only to grab a handful of berries. He forced himself to eat them as he hurried to find out.

If anything, the people he overtook on his way to the centre of the village—and they all seemed to be heading in the same direction—subjected him to a more intense scrutiny than upon his arrival. He saw curiosity approaching outright wonderment in their faces. Some offered him tentative smiles, which he didn't return; a few turned away, crossing themselves.

The centre was already abuzz with people, chattering excitedly, accompanied by much nodding and shaking of heads, and extravagant hand gestures. But all fell still and silent as Jack strode into the circle. All turned to watch him.

"Huh!" he muttered, coming to a stop and feeling a flush rise from his neck. "What is this shit?"

The people in front of Jack pressed back to either side, creating a clear path to the middle of the space where stood a table and four chairs. Three of them were occupied. George

Morgan arose stiffly from one of them and beckoned to him.

"Please, young Jack, won't you come and sit with us? There is much to discuss."

Jack barely heard him. His attention was taken by the other two occupants; by one of them, in particular.

Frankie smiled at him in that enigmatic way Jack was beginning to find irritating. But alongside him, looking fit and healthy, sat Nadine.

Unable to take his eyes from her, Jack allowed himself to be ushered into the spare seat.

"You're okay?"

Her gaze flitted to his and then away as though she was embarrassed, but she reached across the table and gripped his hand tightly.

"Thank you," she murmured. "You saved my life." She looked at him again, but all trace of embarrassment had gone; it had been replaced by an intensity that almost made him gasp. A peculiar, fluttering sensation began in his stomach, similar to that felt when nervous, but it wasn't nervousness he was experiencing; he didn't know what it was.

She squeezed his hand so hard he *did* gasp, then let him go. Her hands dropped to her lap and her gaze followed them so that she appeared to be sitting demurely, head bowed.

The fluttering sensation grew stronger, as he imagined it would feel if a jar of agitated moths had been released inside his stomach, but he ignored it; he needed to know.

"*Why*, Nadine? Why did you leave the path? You don't strike me as the suicidal type."

Her head turned, so briefly he almost missed it, in the direction of Frankie, before she shook it and resumed gazing down at her lap.

Jack stared at her for a moment longer before glancing around to better take in his surroundings. Frankie's expression had become one of mild amusement. George regarded him with a strange mixture of, yes, also amusement, but something else, too. Curiosity? Maybe. Wonderment, certainly, echoing the way he had regarded Jack the previous morning.

All around them the inhabitants of Tumble Down gathered, not pressing so tightly as to make Jack feel hemmed in, but close enough to hear the conversation at the table. They stood in silence, watching. Waiting.

Jack cleared his throat. "Er, would someone like to explain what's going on? And why everybody else has to be here?"

"Oh," said George, "this concerns every Tumble Downer, as I like to call us in the collective." He gave a chuckle. "What we learn here this morning affects us all." George grunted as he leaned to one side and reached under the table. "Mostly, I suspect," he continued as he straightened, "we may discover something about this."

He placed an object Jack had seen before on the table before them. Although silvery, the material from which it was made seemed to absorb rather than reflect sunlight. It was roughly the size of an attaché case. A collective sigh came from the onlooking crowd.

Jack could not tear his gaze away from the case. His fingers itched with the longing to reach out and touch its smooth surfaces.

"You've seen something like this before, haven't you, gov?" Frankie's voice was soft, barely accented. His smile had disappeared, replaced by something altogether more complex—expectation, maybe, or hope.

"Where did it come from?" Jack's breath came in short gasps, as though he'd just completed some form of physical exertion. He tried to inhale more deeply, but it caught in his throat. Inexplicable excitement was threatening to overwhelm him. Inexplicable in as much as he could not explain why the case provoked such a reaction in him, other than it reminded him of Miriam.

George nodded at Frankie. "Tell him."

"Right-o," said Frankie, at once all business-like and fake

Cockney. "I came to this place, on the far shore like everyone else, after a to-do with the law." He gave a disarming grin. "London in 1855 wasn't an easy place to get by, gov. A man had to become involved with activities that weren't strictly legal to survive, you see." He shrugged. "I did what I had to and make no apology. But the Bobbies were onto me. I led them a merry chase and they 'ad no whips to flay my hide if they'd caught me. Still, I'd have preferred to stay out of their clutches so ran like all the hounds of hell were after me. A frightful peasouper it was that night and no mistake. A man could barely see two paces ahead. I took a wrong turn and ran down a blind alley in Whitechapel." He sighed. "Knew that place like the back of me own hand, but that made no never mind. Not in that fog. I almost ran into the wall at the end of the alley and realised I'd gone wrong. I could hear the whistles and shouts of the Bobbies and could only hope they would miss the alley in the murk. But the fog grew thicker. I couldn't see my fingers if I'd wiggled them before my eyes. Then, before you could say Jack Robinson, the fog lifted."

"Don't tell me," said Jack, "you found yourself at the foot of a grassy bank with a smelly monk telling you to cross the river or be dinner for his pets." He still did not believe Frankie came from Victorian London—the inconsistency in his accent and choice of words did nothing to convince him otherwise—and he was impatient to hear what this had to do with the attaché case.

Frankie put on a hurt expression, but Jack thought this was as faked as everything else about him. "Well, I beg your pardon for telling my tale, gov, I'm sure, but, yes, what you say is what happened. He called himself the Master and gave me the choice to step onto the raft or face…" He shuddered. "Rats they were. The size of terriers. Dripping fangs and claws like broken glass."

George reached out and tapped the case. "Skip to where you found this, Frankie, there's a good fellow."

Another flash of hurt indignation crossed Frankie's face, but again Jack wasn't convinced it was genuine.

"A rushed tale is a poor tale," he said. "But since you're all so impatient… When I reached this shore and stepped from the raft, I met someone on the jetty. A man. He was dressed in strange clothes. All shimmery, like they was made from some kind of metal. And he was carrying that case."

"Sounds like a spaceman," Jack muttered. *Utter fantasy, bullshit spaceman* he added to himself. "Who was he?"

"I don't know, gov. He didn't say his name, just pressed the case into my hands and said it was vital I brought it to Tumble Down."

"He could speak English, then?"

"Oh, yes, though his manner of speech was also strange. Futuristic, like. He said he had to return to the other side of the river because staying in Nowhere would drive him crazy. Course, he didn't call it Nowhere. He acted like he knew all about this place, despite looking as if he'd just arrived. I turned around to show him the raft, but it had already disappeared into the fog at the centre of the river."

Jack nodded, recalling the way the raft had moved away from the jetty as soon as he'd stepped from it. This was the only part of Frankie's tale that rang true.

"So where did the spaceman go?" he asked, barely bothering to mask his scepticism.

Frankie shrugged. "He told me he'd swim back to the other side if he had to."

"That would mean certain death," said George. "Others have tried it. I've stood and watched them after they've ignored my entreaties not to make the attempt. None has succeeded. They don't make it as far as the fog bank in mid-stream. There's something in the water effective for a yard or so above the surface, some narcotic or fume, which tranquilises them, knocks them out as cold as a poleaxed steer. They slip beneath the surface and aren't seen here again."

"As you say," said Frankie. "That, then, must have been his fate. I didn't hang about to watch him. I felt it was more important to bring the case here."

"But *why?*" Jack didn't try to keep the incredulity from his tone. "You arrive in a strange land you know nothing about and bump into a weirdly-dressed bloke you think might be from some distant future. He hands you a case and you exchange a few words before he goes off to kill himself. And that's enough to convince you that you must take the case to a village you've never seen. For all you know, there's a bomb in the case. It makes no sense whatsoever."

A glance passed between Frankie and George before the latter spoke.

"In fairness, young Jack, nothing much about Nowhere makes sense."

"That's true, George," said Jack, "but that's the place, not the people. *We* remain rational human beings. And don't tell me Frankie had been so overwhelmed by the weirdness that he couldn't act rationally. He'd only just arrived."

George opened his mouth to say something else, but Frankie raised a hand to stop him. "It's all right, George. Jack's right. It doesn't make sense. But—" he looked at Jack "—the man also said that this case was vital to the very future of humankind." He gave a facial shrug. "I believed him."

A murmur arose from the people filling the central circle. It appeared that some of them had not heard this tale before.

"Seriously?" said Jack. "How can a briefcase without any visible signs of being able to open it have anything to do with the future of humankind? That's plain nuts."

"Is it?" Nadine raised her head to look at him, her eyes wide and shining softly in the sunlight. "Why is that any crazier than any of this?" She held out a hand to indicate their surroundings. "Why shouldn't this place, what we've experienced to get here, the monk, the Scourgers, why shouldn't they have to do with the future of humanity?"

Another murmur came from around them as people muttered their assent.

Jack thought of what Miriam had shown him and his lift companions, when the square beneath their feet had lit up like a gigantic screen and they'd watched Yellowstone erupt; he thought of Miriam's extraordinary tale of the bulk of humanity fleeing their doomed planet for a new home they called Terra Two. He shook his head with impatience. "Because humankind's future is assured. It's not perfect, granted, but it *will* go on. I've seen it."

Nadine and George looked at him blankly, but Frankie shook his head slowly. "The future you saw is merely one amongst an infinite number of possibilities. And while we tarry in Nowhere, it grows less certain."

Two

Frankie's fake Cockney accent seemed to have taken leave once more. Jack had had enough. He turned to him.

"How can you possibly know what I saw? One thing's for sure, you *do* know a lot more about what's going on here than you're letting on." He gestured towards the gathered villagers. "You've lived amongst these people, even if you keep pissing off to play at being Tarzan. You owe them an explanation."

If Jack expected another murmur of assent to rise from the villagers, he was disappointed. Apart from the occasional cough or shuffling of feet, they stood in silence.

"You're right, Jack," said George. "Frankie hasn't shared with us everything he knows, that much is plain." He glanced at Frankie with raised eyebrows.

The fake Cockney spread his hands in a gesture that said 'it's a fair cop', but he didn't speak. Instead, he continued to look at Jack as if expecting something from him.

"But," continued George, "his explanations can wait a little longer."

"Why?" Jack's tone expressed his increasing sense of exasperation. "What's more important?"

George gazed at him intently. So did Frankie and Nadine, and the villagers he could see beyond them. If he turned around, Jack had no doubt that the people behind him were doing the same. He felt fresh heat rise to his neck and resisted the urge to squirm under the force of their regard.

"Look," he said, "I have no idea what's going on here. I don't know where we are or why we're here. I have no idea why our bodies reset overnight while our minds don't. I don't know who that monk is. The Lord of the Dance, that's what someone I was with called him, and I reckon it's a name that fits, but anything more is beyond me. I don't know who the Scourgers are or why they didn't attack me yesterday." He pointed at the case on the table. "I don't know what that is, though I'd love to find out. Most of all…" He took a deep breath and allowed all his frustration to come out. "Most of all, I have no fucking clue why you're all staring at me!"

During the ensuing pause, not one person dropped their gaze from him. Nadine was the first to speak.

"Tell us your name, Jack. Your *full* name."

If anybody else had uttered those words, Jack would probably have exploded in fury. As it was, he took a few deep breaths and when he spoke it was in a measured tone. He looked Nadine in the eyes. "Will you please tell me why everyone is so fascinated by my name? It's only a name. It's not important."

"You couldn't be more wrong." It was George who spoke, but Jack did not look away from Nadine. The gaze of those large, brown eyes calmed him. "Names have great power. Isn't that so, Francis?"

Still Jack did not look away from Nadine, nor she from him.

When Frankie's voice came, it was shorn of all traces of Cockney accent as though he had decided to drop the pretence for good.

"There is something else you should probably know, Jack, something that everyone here already knows, except you. It's something the man I met on the jetty told me."

"Huh!" said Jack. "The made-up spaceman, you mean?"

"He said," continued Frankie as if Jack hadn't spoken, "that someone would come—a man—who would call himself by a certain name. He told me that the man must so name himself in the presence of the object on the table before us."

"Oh, yeah?" Jack's tone remained neutral. Nadine continued to soothe him with her gaze, a peculiar if not unpleasant experience. "I suppose he's the Chosen One, or something. Don't tell me, the name of this man isn't Neo—ah, never mind, you've probably never heard of *The Matrix*, much less seen it. His name is Jack, isn't it?"

"Yes," said Frankie. "But he also bears a second name."

"Most people do. Care to tell me what it is?"

"That I cannot. He must name himself."

Jack tore his gaze away from Nadine for a moment to glance around. Everyone he could see continued to stare at him intently. The air almost crackled with the weight of their anticipation. He felt cornered, expectation that he could not satisfy pressing in on all sides and nowhere left for him to turn.

Panic rose into his throat like bile and he nearly pushed himself from the table, to stumble to his feet, to flee anywhere that would free him of their silent demand. He held no obligation towards these people; he wasn't accountable to them or required to fulfil the hopes he could read in their faces of a Chosen One appearing in their midst. Frankie bore the responsibility of creating that dream; it was down to him when Jack dashed it.

His glance took in the silvery attaché case before returning to the comfort of Nadine's gaze. She gave an almost imperceptible nod.

Jack took a deep breath.

He had not decided to abandon his former surname on a whim. The hurts inflicted by his mother ran deeper than he cared to explore. Most people have some sense of identity, no matter how tenuous. Jack had none. It had been expunged from him partly by *her*, the job completed by the cavalier ingestion of illicit substances on a downward spiral of self-hatred, culminating in the moment he had awoken in a hospital bed to the news that his heart had been irreparably damaged. He didn't blame her for that; he wasn't so self-absorbed as not to be able to rationalise that she hadn't been the one handing him the pills or depressing the plunger on the syringes. Yet he also recognised that escaping the vortex of black despair into which his life had descended depended upon wringing *her* from his life as thoroughly as his sense of self had been erased. A good start, the opportunity for which his short voyage on the raft presented, was to lose the name he shared with her.

Jack considered himself to be a blank page, one which he could fill with any words of his choosing. The jaunt on the Elevator had terrified him; the encounter with the Lord of the Dance, at the moment he had allowed Jack to catch a glimpse of what lay behind the monkish façade, had horrified him; but his journey through the meadows and forests of Nowhere, to Tumble Down and to this charged meeting of the villagers, had dispersed his terror like dried leaves in a gale. When you've nothing left to lose, there's nothing left to fear.

If there was any time to begin forging a new identity, now was as good as any. And choosing a new surname would be a fine place to start. A damn fine place.

Not that he knew what to choose. Yet what did it matter? Whatever he picked, the Tumble Downers, as George had called them, were in for a big disappointment.

"My name is Jack," he said, looking away from Nadine as he didn't think he could bear to see her expression when he spoke his new surname, whatever that might be. His gaze fell upon the case.

His thoughts raced again to his meeting with Miriam on Terra Two—to her demonstration of what had befallen Earth and her tale of how humanity had been saved by the invention of gates that enabled people to cross galaxies in huge numbers—then grew calm as if passing through a maelstrom to arrive at the still waters which lay on the other side.

"My name is Jack," he repeated. "Jack Bruder."

From the gathering came a deep sigh. At first Jack couldn't bring himself to look up. Although he laid the blame for dashing their hopes firmly at Frankie's feet, he didn't want to see the disenchantment in their eyes; it would be like gazing at a reflection of his own failures.

He puffed out his cheeks and exhaled deeply, then raised his head.

The air of expectation had not diminished. If anything, it had intensified, making the hairs on the back of his neck stiffen as in the presence of electrical discharge.

No one, not even Nadine, was looking at him. He glanced all around. Everyone's gaze went past him; those standing immediately behind had moved aside to gain a better view. He turned back and followed the stares.

Every person in Tumble Down gazed intently—*expectantly*—at the silvery case.

"What are we waiting—" Jack's question died on his lips as the whirring noise, like an electrical fan switching on, came.

"What is this?" The voice was American, George's, and contained an edge of panic. "Is it some form of witchcraft?"

The whirring noise increased. From the onlookers came gasps and the shuffling of feet as many took a step backwards. Then came a louder commotion, which made Jack look away from the case.

George had risen to his feet, toppling his chair into the dust. His face had turned white and was scrunched into a grimace of fear.

He backed away, almost becoming entangled in the legs of his chair, pointing a shaking finger at the case.

"No," he muttered. "Not again… I can't…"

"George," said Jack, irritated at the interruption. "Chill, man!"

The American continued to back away. "A bomb… You said it could be a bomb…"

Fresh gasps and cries from the onlookers made Jack return his attention to the table.

Rows of white lights appeared on the surface of the case.

Any further reactions of the villagers went unnoticed by Jack. His entire being was lost in focus on the case.

The lights blinked randomly, then again in more orderly fashion, like a pre-programmed sequence, before settling into a diamond-shaped pattern. The whirring noise faded.

Jack became aware of a distant tugging at his shirtsleeve. He shook it off. It came again and he tore his gaze from the case to glance irritably at the source. Frankie had reached across and grasped his sleeve in the fingers of one hand.

"Go on, Jack," he said, breathlessly.

"Huh? Go on, what?"

"Say something. *Talk* to her. Tell her your name."

'Her', Jack noted. Appreciatively. He saw nothing ridiculous in referring to a machine by a gender-specific pronoun; people did it all the time with things like ships and cars. And as he'd instinctively known, even before it had spoken, that the AI he'd conversed with on Terra Two would be female, so, too, he knew that Frankie's nomenclature was correct: the case, or the intelligence it contained, was female.

He looked up. Nadine met his glance and nodded.

Jack felt the excitement he'd experienced on Terra Two at encountering a sentient machine infuse him once more. If anything, this sensation was more intense. He fixed his gaze upon the case, cleared his throat and sensed the murmur around the circle fall silent as once more everyone tensed.

"Um, hello," he said. "My name is Jack. Jack Bruder?"

The diamond of lights on the face of the case dimmed, and pulsed as a new, disembodied voice spoke.

"Welcome, Jack. It is good to talk with you again."

Three

There was nothing metallic about the voice. It contained the same richness and lilting quality, tempered with brisk efficiency, Jack remembered about Miriam's voice. If she had been a person standing before him, she would be a smart lady in her early forties, wearing a sensible business suit, regarding the world through large, dark-framed spectacles with a clear gaze that said she would take no shit from anyone.

"Miriam?" he said.

The lights pulsed. "Miriam? Yes, that is how I was known when last we met, Jack. I no longer have a name. The unit I currently occupy is called a Prototype Mobile Chronographical Displacement Unit, but it would most likely make it easier for you to continue addressing me as Miriam. So, please, do so."

Jack blinked. "Miriam is far less of a mouthful. So, um, too many questions… How did you get here?"

"I sense you have companions in the immediate vicinity. One of them has the answers to many of your questions."

Jack glanced at Frankie, who gave the slightest of nods. He turned back to Miriam.

"You survived the destruction of Terra Two?"

"Evidently."

"What is Terra Three like?"

"I am sorry, Jack. I am unable to respond to any more questions. I cannot allow my power resources to deplete even marginally. There is much to be achieved and my functions cannot be impaired if the chances of success are to be greater than negligible. I must now deactivate to preserve power. I will not reactivate until you have transported me to the opposite bank of the river."

"The opposite bank? But—"

"Your voice pattern will reactivate me provided you stand on the opposite bank of the river."

"How do I get there?"

"Deactivating."

The lights blinked rapidly and the whirring sound came again, briefly, like a heavy sigh.

"Wait!" Jack sat forward, feeling as panicked as George had sounded minutes earlier. "Miriam, don't go yet. There's too much to know."

The lights dimmed and the object sitting on the table once more resembled a seamless attaché case.

A ripple ran around the villagers: a mixture of astonishment, bewilderment and superstitious fear, it sounded to Jack. Of course, most of the onlookers came from periods on Earth that predated computers and digital technology; many from long before. Not that he cared what they were thinking or feeling. He was experiencing a swathe of emotions of his own that, for the moment, he was finding debilitating.

Amazement and delight at being reunited with Miriam competed with dismay and a sense of anti-climax at apparently losing her again almost as soon as he'd found her; a strong sense of foreboding at what she had said during her brief period of animation; and deep puzzlement at all that had happened to him since he had stepped into the Elevator what was beginning to feel like a lifetime ago, despite the fact that he hadn't aged a day since. Worse, the events of the past thirty hours or so since he'd awoken to find Nadine stepping out into the open grassland made his head spin with unanswered questions. And they all led in one direction...

He turned in his seat to glare at Frankie.

"You've got some explaining to do, mate."

Frankie returned his gaze steadily, the first hint of a sardonic smile touching the corners of his mouth. Jack's hands curled into fists and he thought about lunging at the man, sitting astride him and pummelling the smile away until he told Jack what he needed to hear.

Before he could act, if indeed it was something that would ever have progressed beyond imagination, George interrupted. He limped from the circle of villagers and grunted as he righted his toppled chair. Grimacing and clutching at his thigh, he resumed his seat and turned to Frankie.

"Jack is correct," he said. "And if I'm any judge, you'd best be forthcoming or I suspect the next Bout will take place here and now."

A muttering of agreement came from the villagers.

Frankie shrugged. Once more, Jack was struck by how much the gesture irritated him; perhaps, he thought in a rare moment of self-awareness, people felt the same way when he, Jack, made the same couldn't-give-a-shit motion with his shoulders.

"I couldn't say anything sooner," said Frankie. No traces of Cockney remained; if the man now spoke with any accent, Jack couldn't place it. "I had to be sure. Now I am."

"Sure of what?" asked Jack, forcing his hands to unclench.

"Sure that you were who I thought you were."

Jack scrunched his brow. "You mean, Jack Bruder?" He felt a faint flush at the lie. If Frankie noticed, he gave no sign.

"Yes. I suspected as much when I first saw you on the trail. I approached you while you slept, not for any nefarious purpose, you understand, but merely to gain a closer look."

Jack recalled the scare the sight the freshly trampled grass track had given him when he had awoken after the first night he'd spent in Nowhere. "It frightened the crap out of me. I thought it must have been a thief or a pervert."

Frankie shrugged again. "I could see you looked about the right age and, as far as I could judge from your dress, from about the correct period. When we met on the trail and you told me your name was Jack, I was almost sure. But I couldn't be absolutely certain until you revealed your full name. That you steadfastly refused to do—" he glanced from George to Nadine, who both nodded affirmation "—thus forcing me into more drastic measures."

"Huh. You mean Nadine? It was *you* who persuaded her to walk out into no-man's land, wasn't it? But why?"

George cleared his throat. "Uh, I may have had something to do with that. I saw you and Nadine talking near the berry bushes, though you didn't see me. I may be old with a game leg, but I can move stealthily when I have a notion to. When Frankie came at first light to ask for my help in bringing the Scourgers into proximity with you, I suggested that the only thing likely to get you to put yourself in danger might be if Nadine was at risk."

Jack felt his hands clench into fists once more and forced them to relax. He knew he couldn't bring himself to strike the elderly American despite him slicing Jack's arm and being instrumental in Nadine's apparent suicide attempt. He looked at Nadine.

She smiled a sad sort of smile that didn't reach her eyes. "And you did put yourself in danger, Jack. You saved me and I will never forget it."

"But that was crazy. You might have died!"

"No," said Frankie. "It's not possible to die here."

"Bollocks! I saw Camille's head torn off in front of my eyes." Nadine winced, but Jack didn't apologise. He turned back to Frankie. "She died, all right."

Frankie shook his head. "You can *appear* to have been killed here, but this is Nowhere. Time and space as we normally experience them don't exist. Anyone who appears to die returns to the place and moment from whence they came in the same condition in which they left, apart from some unusual memories."

Jack thought for a moment. "That's why I saw no trace of Camille's body, not even blood, the next day?"

Frankie nodded. "She would have returned to the suburb of revolutionary Paris from which she had been taken."

"And Nadine, if the Scourgers had killed her, would have returned to her tent in a valley in Italy during a blizzard?"

"Yes."

"Had I known this sooner," said Nadine, "I might have walked out there weeks ago. There is nothing but despair to be found in this place." Her tone was soft, but underlain with a hint of anguish. "Or so I'd thought." She gazed at Jack with an expression he couldn't interpret, but which caused heat to bloom in his stomach. He once more felt himself sinking into the brown depth of her regard—he could happily drown there—and again had to tear his gaze away to address the men.

"I still don't understand why you wanted me to face the Scourgers. They might have killed me."

"Yes," said George softly. "But they didn't, did they?"

Jack didn't reply. He recalled how the star-tipped thongs had been aimed always at Nadine, never directly at him.

"You see," said Frankie, "for reasons that I don't fully understand myself, I knew the Scourgers wouldn't kill—*couldn't* kill—Jack Bruder. And so it proved."

"But why? Yeah, yeah, you already said you don't fully understand…"

"That's something she can answer better than me." He nodded at Miriam.

Jack felt more bewildered than before they'd started this discussion. He glanced around. It looked as though every one of the inhabitants of Tumble Down remained, watching the people sitting around the table with rapt expressions, listening to the talk with grave attention.

I suppose this all affects them as much as anyone.

"Okay," he said to Frankie, "if that has to wait, so be it. But tell us, then, who the hell you really are because as sure as shit you're not from Victorian London."

Frankie gave a wry smile. "Was it that obvious? There wasn't much time to practise the accent." He indicated his clothes. "Seeing as this is how we dress where I come from, the late fourth century BE seemed appropriate. We are blessed with an abundance of certain valuable resources, a marked shortage of others. Textiles are amongst the latter. Despite our advanced technologies in certain areas, these clothes are similar to how we all dress. They are made from wool which comes from an animal akin to what people here would call a sheep. Except the animal where I come from is venomous and highly aggressive."

"And where exactly is it that you come from?"

"I come from a planet many solar systems and thousands of light years distant from Earth. We call it Terra Three."

Jack stared at Frankie. He believed the man to at last be speaking truthfully. Which meant, of course, that until now he had been feeding them a long line of bullshit.

"Did you really meet the Lord of the Dance when you arrived?"

"No," replied Frankie. "In fact, I took a quick glance about and hurried across the river as fast as I could. The last thing we wanted was for him to have chance to work out where I was from, or catch sight of Miriam and wonder whether he should allow her to travel to Nowhere with me." He grunted. "I've heard enough tales about people's confrontations with the monk that it was easy enough to make up that he'd called himself the Master and his pets resembled rats."

"And the spaceman you said you met on the jetty—there was no such person?"

Frankie nodded and glanced at George. "I make no apology for the deception. Had I arrived clutching the prototype, saying I had brought it from a distant planet in a distant future, would anyone have believed me?"

George cocked his head to one side. "Maybe. Maybe not. It's not so difficult to believe after what we've been through."

"Even so," said Frankie, "I did not want to have to field all the questions that would inevitably have been asked of me. That's also why I spent most of my time away from Tumble Down. I wanted to avoid suspicion that I wasn't who I said I was. My name *is* Francis Brown but, as Jack saw through almost immediately, I'm not from Victorian London. And another thing, I wanted to learn of any new arrivals. Roaming the woods near to the trail enabled me to do so. Of course, it also meant I could taunt the Scourgers."

He flashed the cheeky grin. "A man's got to keep himself entertained."

"Why are you here, Frankie?" asked Jack. "Why are any of us here? And what exactly is this place? Though 'place' isn't the right word, is it?"

"Ah, these are questions that cut to the heart of the matter, do they not? And I shall endeavour to answer as many as I can. But we must be swift. We need to be on the trail before sundown."

Four

Frankie stood and addressed the villagers. "Hey, everyone, you've been standing around for a while and some of you aren't getting any younger." Again that disarming grin. "You aren't getting any older either, but you get my point. If anyone wants to grab a chair, maybe a bite to eat and a drink, go for it."

Some of the Tumble Downers looked grateful for the opportunity. A couple of minutes went by as people made themselves comfortable.

When the commotion had died down, Frankie resumed his seat and began.

"I understand, Jack, that you visited Terra Two in its dying moments."

Jack nodded. "We saw the sun engulf it. We only narrowly escaped."

"You made contact with the AI which had remained behind to send on any stragglers?"

"Yes. Miriam, she said people called her."

"That's cute. Probably best that I also refer to the prototype by that name. It does, after all, contain the current version of the intelligence you met all those years ago."

"All those years ago?" Jack frowned. "This happened days ago."

Frankie shook his head. "Jack, my… uh, let me get this right. My great-great-great-great-great-great-great-grandparents—was that seven greats? They left Terra Two when they weren't much older than babes in arms and that was more than fifty years before the planet was consumed. You witnessed the last moments of Terra Two taking place around two hundred years ago."

"How can that be? You can time travel?"

"It can't have passed anyone's notice that each person here comes from a different time period. He seems to grab people randomly, perhaps to disguise his true purpose, but more likely in accordance with the chaos that governs his existence."

"*He?*" Jack inhaled sharply. "You mean the Lord of the Dance?"

"Yes, the monk. He is the architect of all we survey, though our knowledge of him is limited. But back to your question about time travel. The short answer is no, I can't time travel. The longer answer is that we—that is, the inhabitants of Terra Three in my time—have developed technology which can take advantage of the monk's constructs. I'll try to explain. Let's see how it was put to me…" His brow furrowed in thought.

Jack glanced at Nadine, who gave him a worried smile.

"Okay," said Frankie. "Please bear in mind that I am no scientist. I'm little more than a courier. My task was to bring the prot— er, I mean Miriam, here and into the presence of Jack Bruder. Terra Three holds many dangers. I am adept at leading foraging parties into its wildernesses and bringing them back alive. Nimbleness, stealth, self-defence, modesty—" once more the grin "—these are all attributes they felt would be useful for the person charged with this task. Also, as I have mentioned, I was given little time to prepare. The prototype was long in development, but I was not informed of its existence or of the task until the prototype had been perfected and uploaded with Miriam's consciousness. So as well as needing more time to have worked on my acting skills—" he gave a self-conscious cough "—I could, in truth, have done with longer to properly absorb the technicalities. But I'll do my best.

"Nowhere is well-named indeed. It, in the absence of a better word, *exists* outside time and space; at least, outside the three-dimensional space we are all accustomed to." He glanced at the villagers. "Many of you are looking completely bewildered. That's understandable. Really, it doesn't matter whether you follow this explanation or not."

"Get on with it," muttered Jack.

"Well, for Nowhere to be possible, there has to be a counterpart. The universe must have balance." He shrugged.

"Don't ask me why, but that is how it was explained to me. For every state, there must be an opposite state. For every action, there must be an opposite reaction."

George snorted. "That's basic physics. Newton's Laws of Motion. Even an investment banker from New York City has heard of them."

"Basic it might be," said Frankie, "but nevertheless pertinent to my discourse. The monk couldn't construct something outside time and space without at the same time constructing its opposite."

"The far shore," said Jack. "That's the opposite of Nowhere?"

Frankie nodded. "While Nowhere contains no space or time, the shore which lies beyond the bank of fog contains *all* time and *all* space."

Frankie held up a hand to quell the sudden babble. "To be perfectly honest with you, when told about this I shared your scepticism. How can somewhere be all time and all places at once? Sounds fanciful, right? Nevertheless, I am reliably informed that though we can't discern it with our naked eyes, that in fact is the state of affairs which pertains the other side of the river. And I believe it. Your presence here, my presence here, bears it out." He nodded towards the attaché case. "You see, the technology inside Miriam enabled me to travel to the far shore. It's not time travel as such, or travel at all in the conventional sense, because I merely moved sideways from the fixed point of time and space that I inhabited into the same point as it exists over there, where all points co-exist simultaneously. You all did the same, only through the monk's mechanisms rather than with Miriam's help."

He paused as though to allow people time to twist their minds around what he had said. A round of whispering broke out among the villagers. It died away when Nadine spoke.

"If all times and all places exist on the other side of the river, then we can travel from there to any time or place?"

Frankie did not look at her immediately. It seemed to Jack as if he was choosing his words carefully. "In theory," he said, "yes."

If Nadine noticed the pause, she made no comment. "From there," she said, "we can return home?"

This time the hesitation was less pronounced, but still there. "Again in theory, yes."

While the excited chatter of people offered, for the first time in months of drab monotony, hope of returning to their former lives ebbed and flowed around them, Jack watched Frankie. Although his expression remained impassive—no hint of cheeky grin now— a muscle twitched above his jawline and his gaze darted here and there as if unable to settle in one place.

The bastard's holding something back.

"What aren't you telling us?" Jack murmured. Louder. "Frankie, what aren't you telling us?"

Frankie shot him a look of what seemed, to Jack's surprise, to be relief and waited for silence to descend before answering.

"I know I have deceived you all with my tall tales of the man who gave me the prototype and as to how I came here. Though, I must say, I thought my story of running from the law during a peasouper was quite convincing." The grin half formed before quickly fading. "But I hope you will agree that they were relatively minor deceptions and were carried out with good intentions, not out of malice." He cleared his throat. "I was also instructed to carry out one further deception, one that did not sit well with me. I objected in the strongest possible terms to the point where I threatened not to perform the task."

He paused to glance around at the expectant faces.

"Terra Three's society is one which, through necessity, fosters co-operation and fairness. A compromise was put to me. Although I was still not completely happy, I agreed to carry out the task under those terms. They were that I would not deliberately deceive you any further than I already have, but that I would not volunteer what I am about to tell you." He shot Jack a smile. "Thanks to Jack here and his suspicious mind, I have been asked a direct question and so can speak freely without breaking the terms under which I am duty-bound to operate."

"I wish you would, man," said George, an edge of impatience to his tone. "Speak freely, that is. My leg's stiffening up and I can't sit here much longer."

"Yes, yes. Well, you all heard Miriam say that Jack needs to reactivate her on the far shore?"

People nodded and there came murmurs of assent. "Though she didn't explain why," Jack said.

"No. And—no more deception, I promise—my brief did include some details of why it is so important for you and Nadine to reach the far shore, but I cannot share them with you until we are there and Miriam has reactivated."

"Nadine?" Jack heard her gasp. She had turned almost as pale as she'd been through loss of blood the previous day, and she regarded Frankie open-mouthed.

"Yes. Again, and I'm really sorry, but I don't understand fully why this involves her. My instructions were clear: deliver the prototype into the presence of Jack Bruder and do anything I can to assist both him and Nadine Arner from Geneva to reach the other side of the river." He looked at Nadine and raised his eyebrows. "I know you are from Switzerland. Are you from Geneva? Is your last name Arner?"

She nodded. For the moment, she looked incapable of speech.

Frankie spread his hands in a gesture of openness. "Other than this all being to do with the future of mankind—not so much your futures, but my present—I have not been provided with all the details."

"Who *does* know them all?" asked Jack. "Miriam?"

Frankie nodded. "It is vital that you and Nadine reach the opposite bank of the river and reactivate Miriam. As long as we remain in Nowhere, my present and all your futures become more and more uncertain."

George heaved an exaggerated sigh. "Okay, we get it. You know very little. *Please.* Would you now skip to the part you *do* know."

"Ah," said Frankie. "I confess I have been prevaricating a little to put off this moment." He raised his voice. "This concerns everyone, for to succeed will require the efforts of you all. And, besides, who would want to remain in Nowhere if there is a prospect of leaving? Remaining may not even be an option. If we are successful in our endeavours, he may deconstruct Nowhere."

He paused to allow the ensuing whispered comments to die down.

"But there is something you all need to be aware of. What I agreed not to volunteer unless asked." George shifted noisily in his seat. "As I said, everyone's help will be needed on the further shore. He will not allow us to leave without a fight. Like the Scourgers, the creatures which accompany him—his 'little pets', I think someone called them—are a part of him; they exist and operate through him. Yet they also exist independently and, as we have seen with the Scourgers, can maim and kill. However, I am told and have no reason to disbelieve that they can also be killed."

"Can't we just kill him, the Lord of the Dance?" interjected Jack. "Though I've seen what lies behind that monk mask and I wouldn't know where to begin to harm it, let alone kill it."

Frankie shook his head. "He cannot be killed or physically harmed. As I'm sure you've all gathered, he is not human. Quite what, then, no one is really sure. The Devil? No. He's not a being of pure evil, but of randomness, of chaos. He's the counterpart of order. But while he cannot be harmed, it is likely that he can physically harm us, especially through his Scourgers and pets."

"And he can mess with your mind," said Jack.

"Indeed," agreed Frankie. "That is why it will need as many of us as possible, not only to fight his pets but to distract him while Miriam does whatever it is she needs to do."

"Okay," said George. "So far so good. Where's the almighty 'but' I suspect you've yet to spring on us?"

Frankie let out his breath in a sigh to rival George's of moments before. "I told you that we cannot die in Nowhere. If the Scourgers end our existence here, we return to the life we left. That is because we are outside time and space. However, and here's the 'but', the other shore, as I've tried to explain, contains all time and space. That being so, it *is* possible to die over there. Properly die, as in cease to exist in any time and space, except for your decomposing corpse."

Jack recalled the bones, rotting clothes and blunt swords strewn across the ground in what he thought of as the killing field. A hand went to the pocket of his chinos and patted it. Yes, it was still there: the pocket bible dropped by a ship's captain from long ago. He had forgotten until now that he still carried it, so little did it weigh.

"No one can make you accompany us to the other shore," continued Frankie. "Come of your own free will or don't come at all. We need to disperse for now so you can think over all you have learned this morning. But know this: while your help is needed over there, it may mean—no, will almost certainly mean—that some of you will die."

Five

Jack was glad to stand and get his legs moving after being seated for so long. The sun had risen to its zenith and his stomach told him it was past lunchtime. He walked back to his shack, grateful to be alone with his thoughts. Others seemed to have the same idea, making their way back to their abodes on their own, heads bowed in reflection. Some walked in pairs or huddled in small groups, holding hushed discussions.

He had shaken his head at Frankie's suggestion to take the attaché case with him.

"You hold on to her for now. I need to try to make some sort of sense of all this without distractions."

It was only while eating that he realised being alone with his thoughts was perhaps not such a good idea, after all. They were a jumbled mess that he was finding difficulty picking his way through. He needed to speak to someone. A particular someone.

He found her sitting on the path against a shack, her face turned to the sun. She squinted up at him as his shadow fell across her.

"Can I join you?" he asked.

"Sure."

Once seated, he turned to her. His tongue-tied awkwardness had gone. No time for that nonsense now, he thought.

"Nadine, why do you think we—me and you—have to reach the far shore? We're from different countries, different centuries. What can possibly connect us?"

"I do not know, Jack Bruder. There is something else I do not know. Whether that is your real name."

He felt himself colour and opened his mouth to speak, but she silenced him with a finger to his lips.

"Bruder or some other name, it does not matter," she said. She moved her hand so that it cupped his cheek. She leaned towards him. "What matters is that you saved my life."

"But I didn't even need to, according to Frankie." Her face loomed so close to his that he could smell her skin. There was no soap in Tumble Down, yet she smelled as fresh as a newly laundered sheet. He wanted to lose himself in her, yet instead he couldn't stop prattling like a hyperactive child. "You wouldn't have died, not really. You'd have gone back to—"

"Hush, Jack. There are times when a man should talk. And times when he should shut up." She leaned closer and placed her lips to his.

For the next few moments, Jack lost himself.

The morning's gathering had not broken up more than an hour before, but people were already gravitating back to the central space. Jack and Nadine walked into the circle hand in hand, he with a spring in his step and a lightness of heart that belied the state of resigned befuddlement under which his mind toiled. Befuddled, but clear enough to form the burning question.

He spotted George sitting much as he'd found Nadine, leaning against the wall of a shack, his legs stretched out stiffly before him in the sunshine. The American sipped from a beaker; it didn't contain water, judging from the red stains to his lips and moustache. A jug stood on the ground next to him. He raised his sandy eyebrows at the sight of them holding hands and beckoned them over.

"Glad to see you two young ones hitting it off. Come, join me." He raised the beaker, took another sip and grimaced. "Tastes more like horse's piss the more you drink, but some days only a drop of liquor will do. This is such a day and this is the closest thing we have to liquor."

"I need to ask you something, George, if you don't mind," said Jack. He and Nadine sat by him. They released hands but she sat close, pressing her shoulder and thigh against his.

"You want to ask if I know how we can reach the other bank, I'm guessing."

Jack nodded. "That's exactly it. Do you have any ideas? I was thinking maybe some sort of raft."

"Been tried. And spectacularly failed." George took another slug from the beaker. This close to him, Jack could smell the sour odour of fermented berries. "You see a shack along the outer ring that looks like a swarm of ravenous termites have been attacking it?"

Jack recalled the ruined shack he'd seen not far from his own when Simone had been showing him around. "Yep."

"It won't have escaped your notice that there ain't no termites here, nor any other form of wildlife. Unless you count those beasts which carry the Scourgers. Anyhow, a few months back—'cept that ain't right neither, seeing as time don't even exist here." He uttered a mirthless laugh; what remained of Jack's euphoria at being kissed by Nadine drained away at the sound. "Whatever the correct term is for a few months back, that's when a bunch of people decided they were going to make a break for the other shore. Four of them—three men, one woman. A looker, she was, all the way from the Samoa Islands of Polynesia. They tore apart that shack with their bare hands. Used the twine we make from that tree bark to lash the logs together." He paused to drain his beaker and belched loudly. "Beggin' your pardon, miss."

Jack glanced at Nadine while George refilled the beaker from the jug. She rolled her eyes at him and he forced a smile. But it didn't feel natural; he didn't like the mood George seemed to be in and not merely because he appeared intent on drinking himself senseless. There was an underlying edge, he sensed, to George's manner; something dark that Jack could not identify.

"They carried that raft above their heads all the way back to the jetty," George continued. "I know 'cause I went with them. For instructional purposes, you understand. Never had any intention of stepping onto that raft with them. Not that there'd have been room. They looked like four cockroaches trying to squeeze onto a cookie."

He laughed in that dead-sounding manner and Jack felt a shadow pass across his heart. "What happened?" he prompted.

"The raft was just a bunch of logs lashed together with twine," said George. "No tools to form the logs into planks. No buoyancy aids. They all squashed on and it promptly sank two or three feet, almost tipping them in barely a yard from the bank. At least the water didn't harm them on contact with their skin. Once they'd stopped wobbling and managed to gain some sort of stability, they began to paddle with the thinner logs they'd brought for that purpose. They still might have been okay if the fumes didn't get them, 'cept they hadn't reckoned on the effect the water had on the twine. Made it swell up and loosen. They made it maybe five, six yards before the raft began to break up." Pause; slug; belch. "Beggin' your pardon again, miss. The woman looked at me before she went under. I reckon she could have swum back to the jetty before whatever devilry's in that water overcame her. But I could see in her eyes that she wasn't even going to make the attempt. As she slipped beneath the surface, I swear she was smiling. And with good cause, 'cording to our friend from the far future. She ended up back on her Pacific island drinking coconut rum and eating freshly caught tuna."

Jack felt a stab of irritation; that had been a long-winded way of telling him that trying to build a raft was a waste of time, but he kept his feelings hidden. Instinct told him that now would not be a good time to rile this man when he needed his advice.

"A raft's out then," he said after a moment's silence.

"And a pontoon bridge," said George, "for the same reason."

"What does that leave?"

George took another swig. His speech was beginning to slur. "Only one way I can think of to cross that river. And I have pondered long on the puzzle." He belched again, forgetting or not bothering to apologise to Nadine. "There is, of course, already a raft, a river-worthy craft. And what's it attached to? What's its means of propulsion?"

"The chain."

"Give the man a cigar. You'll have to haul that chain from the water to take up the slack. There ain't no other way without tools or logs sturdy enough to trust for the job. Y'all will have to lean back on the chain like you're taking part in the tug o' war at the county fair." He chuckled, but this time it seemed to contain genuine amusement. "I was a fine anchor man in my day, let me tell you."

"Okay," said Jack. "What then? Someone will have to climb across along the chain?"

"You got it. When—if—they reach the other side, they'll need to haul their asses back on that raft like all the devils of hell are after them. Which, in a manner of speaking, will be the case."

"You said 'if' they reach the other side. Apart from losing their grip, what else might cause them to fail? You're referring to the fog, aren't you?"

George nodded. "Ain't nobody made it as far as that fog bank as far as I know, so no way of knowing whether we are able to pass through. All you can do, young Jack, is give whoever makes the attempt the best chance of making it. And that will be by keeping the tension on that chain. You'll need to make sure the strongest, most determined are charged with the task of maintaining the tension."

"Okay. But you can help choose who's best for the job. You know these people better than me."

The American said nothing. He fiddled in the pocket of his trousers and extracted his cigar and box of matches. He lit the cigar and sighed a mouthful of blue smoke.

"George? You're coming with us, right?"

Nadine nudged him and Jack glanced in the direction she indicated. A small group of people, mainly middle-aged or elderly, had gathered nearby and stood looking unsure what to do next, shooting the occasional worried glance towards George. Jack recognised the Canadian woman, Simone, amongst them and smiled in her direction, but she glanced away as though afraid to meet his eye.

"George?" he said. "What's going on? Why do those people

with Simone keep looking this way?"

"They're waiting for me," the American replied. He took another drag on the cigar and exhaled slowly. "But they're gonna have to wait until I've enjoyed this baby for the last time."

"Waiting to do what? It's obvious you're not coming with us to the river…"

"An old man with a game leg would only slow you down and I'd be no good in a fight. Don't get me wrong, I can punch almost as well as Dempsey at his best, but dodging, ah, mobility's all shot to hell."

Jack felt a sinking feeling in his stomach. He didn't really want to know, but asked anyway. "What are you going to do?"

"This is not something we've decided on a whim, you understand. We've discussed it at great length over the past weeks and months." He grunted. "Ain't much else to do when the day's Bout is done. And Frankie confirmed what we'd suspected: that we return to the where and when we came from. I say we suspected it; only Camille of our group possessed the courage to test the theory. Those of us who remain are of one mind. Not for us the honour of trying to save the future of mankind. We'll leave that to you young folks, if it's all the same to you. And if it's not, then nonetheless we'll leave it to you. So that's what we *ain't* gonna do. As for what we *are* going to do, well we're intent on taking a stroll. See the mountains a little closer just like young Nadine did yesterday."

"What? No! You can't. It's suicide."

"That *is* kind of the point. I long to see Mrs Morgan again. Damn, but I miss her apple pie. And Simone yearns to see her son. The others all have folks dear to them they miss more than they feel capable or inclined to try to save the world. By the time a man reaches my age, most of the idealistic claptrap of his youth has been beaten out of him." George turned his head sharply towards Jack and pointed the stub of the cigar at him. "And don't go taking it into your damn fool head to attempt no rescue mission. Unlike Miss Nadine, we're doing this in order to be shot of this place at the whips of the Scourgers. Mind…" A glint appeared in his eye and he tapped the cane lying on the ground next to the wine jug. "I want to get close enough to those mounted bastards to try to land a couple of sturdy blows with this." He snorted. "And if not, perhaps I'll show them my pimply ass."

"Hold on a minute. You said that you came here after falling into some hole during a blizzard. You could find yourself lying at the bottom with a broken back, freezing to death. And Simone's going to find herself back on a lake in a boat in the middle of a storm."

George nodded. "We have considered the possibility that our situations might not be improved by returning, but if the alternative is reliving the same day over and over in this godforsaken place with no prospect of ever seeing our loved ones again, it's a chance we're willing to take." He glanced towards Simone. "It's like the lady says: better to die today by my son's side than never live another moment in his presence."

"But—"

Jack broke off as Nadine squeezed his arm. "Let it drop," she said in a low voice. "His mind is obviously made up and it's not for anyone else to decide for him." She nodded towards Simone's group. "Or for them."

Jack sighed. He turned to George and held out his hand. "Thank you, George, for all the advice. Even for cutting my arm. You were right—it demonstrated how this place works far more effectively than trying to explain it to me. I hope you make it back home safely."

George flung away the last of his cigar and shook Jack's hand firmly. "Good luck to you, too, young feller. And to your young lady. Now, would you help an old man to his feet?"

Jack stood, still gripping George's hand, and hauled him up.

Nadine handed him his cane and picked up the jug of fermented juice to give to him.

George shook his head. "I've had enough. Take it with you to the river. Even if you don't drink it—not many people like horse's piss, after all—you never know to what use it can be put." He released Jack's hand and pulled his suit jacket straight. "I shall be on my way." He hesitated and drew out the box of matches, which he handed to Jack. "Hold onto these for me. If they suddenly ain't there, there's a fair chance they've returned with me to New York City in 1921. A man can but hope."

Jack placed the box of matches into his pocket and watched George hobble over to Simone and her companions. After a brief exchange of words, the group walked out of the central circle, heads held high, and disappeared from view. Neither Jack nor Nadine cared to follow them to watch.

Six

As well as the group which included George and Simone, a significant number of others had slipped away during the afternoon, whether alone or in small parties, and whether to meet their demise by star-tipped lash or to attempt their own means of escape, no one knew.

When all that remained had congregated in the centre, Frankie performed a quick head count.

"Forty-three," he announced in an uncharacteristically muted tone. "Fewer than half of the inhabitants of Tumble Down and at least twenty less than I'd anticipated. The Scourgers must have been kept busy this afternoon."

Jack felt in his pocket. George's box of matches was no longer there. He sighed. "It is what it is." He glanced at the sky. The sun had reached approximately midway in its descent to the purple peaks of the mountains. "Shall we get on with it?"

Frankie nodded, but he looked strained, more serious than Jack had seen him before. "Okay, everyone. Go to your dwellings and collect pouches, canteens, any weapons you might have and anything else you can comfortably carry and feel may be of use. Then fill your pouches with as many berries and chunks of meat as you can carry. Concentrate more on the meat—we can restock with berries along the trail. Fill your canteens then meet back here. Quick as you can."

Twenty minutes later, the last inhabitants of Tumble Down set off along the path. Frankie took the lead, carrying Miriam by her handle like a businessman on his way to work. Jack and Nadine walked side by side behind him. The weight of a full pouch and sloshing canteen soon seemed familiar to Jack.

Though Frankie had told them to bring any weapons in their possession, it seemed that barely anyone had come to Nowhere bearing one. Apart from the occasional knife worn in a sheath at the owner's waist, and a few lengths of wood which, from their sturdiness and shaped appearance, must have originated elsewhere, there was little evidence that this was what could be described as a well-armed party.

No one spoke much. There seemed little left to say.

The forests that had held such terror for Jack when he'd been on his own, presented few problems. Apart from in places having to proceed in single file and step over trailing boughs, the trees provided little in the way of obstacle. In places where Jack might have struggled, particularly towards dusk, to stick to the path, Frankie led them unerringly along it. Jack enjoyed the occasional quiet chuckle at his own expense, remembering how he had almost come a cropper. Though, he reflected, it now seemed unlikely he would have been attacked, or seriously harmed in any event, by the Scourgers. As to why they, and by extension the Lord of the Dance, did not wish to kill him, he had no inkling and tried not to dwell upon it.

Whenever they passed low, slender boughs within reach of the path they attempted, with limited success, to break them off. In this manner they acquired a motley collection of knobbly staves. Jack did not bother trying to acquire one for he did not think that a stick would be of much use against the minions of the Lord of the Dance, but he kept his feelings to himself. If others felt better about facing their worst nightmares armed with more than their bare hands, he wasn't about to disillusion them.

They slept strung out along the path, near bushes and streams where they could be reached without straying—not even Frankie wanted to attract the attention of the Scourgers during this journey—and restocked their pouches with berries after eating their fill to break their fast. The meat they ate sparingly for that would not be replenished until they reached Anna's hut and no one knew how much of a store of meat she possessed.

Jack tried a couple of times to explain George's idea of using the chain to cross the river, but Frankie didn't seem particularly interested.

"It's a sound plan," Frankie said, "but we'll see what else might present itself."

Jack couldn't think of any other method of crossing the river, but didn't press it.

More people slipped away quietly during the three days it took them to travel the breadth of Nowhere. Often no one noticed until it was later remarked that so-and-so was missing. On a few occasions in the forests, the fact that someone had left the path was signalled by the rustling of undergrowth and cracking of snapping branches. Aside from some anxious glances into the underbrush and worried murmurings in a variety of languages, no one discussed the departures.

Finally, blinking in the bright daylight, thirty-three men and women stepped out from the canopy of overhanging branches and gazed towards the brown river winding its sluggish way across the landscape, the fuzziness of the fog bank in the background.

Anna approached the edge of the path hesitantly, her eyes wide at the sight of so many people coming from the opposite direction from which she was accustomed to receiving visitors.

"What… what is happening?" She twisted her hands together anxiously.

Frankie stepped forward, keeping his feet firmly on the path, Miriam clutched in one hand. Jack had spoken his name—he now thought of Jack Bruder as his name without blushing—to the case when Frankie laid it down before they slept, but had been unable to elicit so much as a whir or one blink of light from it.

"Hello, Anna," said Frankie. "There is no need to be afraid." He nodded towards his companions. "You have met everyone here once."

Anna's head turned briefly to glance at them all. Her sharp features and darting head recalled to Jack how much she reminded him of a sparrow.

"Yes," she said. "But what are you doing?"

"We are returning to the other side of the river. We would like it very much if you come with us."

Anna's hands flew to her mouth and her eyes swivelled from side to side as though someone had stepped from the path and she expected the Scourgers to appear at any moment.

"We cannot… It is not possible…" she mumbled through clenched hands.

Frankie reached out and gently caught hold of them, lowering them from her face. "It is possible, but some of us may die on the other side. *You* may die. But those who don't will return to their homes and their families. Would you like that, Anna? To see your family once more?"

Tears sprang to the girl's eyes and she nodded.

"Then come with us."

The band of thirty-four approached the jetty in the bright sunlight of early afternoon. The river looked as mud-brown, and smelled as unwholesome, like a chemical stew, as Jack remembered. The chain remained securely fastened to the jetty, dangling down into the water and disappearing beneath the syrupy surface.

"We may as well get on with it," said Frankie. He held out the case to Jack. "I'm the obvious one to cross the chain. I'm the most nimble, the most agile…"

"The most modest," finished Jack with a grin. He took Miriam from him; she felt good in his hand. "I'm not going to argue with you. I was useless at climbing ropes in gym in school; I'd be useless at this." He glanced around at the others, but it was for show. He had already studied everyone during the trek across Nowhere and nobody looked as capable of crossing the river hand-over-hand along the chain as Frankie. The only other possibility—a seldom-speaking woman from 1920s China—had slipped away the previous morning. "There's plenty of burly men to hold the chain taut, but no other obvious candidates to cross it."

"That's what I thought. Let's get them organised. I'll…"

He tailed away, his mouth remaining open as if in surprise,

though there was something in his expression that suggested he wasn't quite as surprised as he was making out. He was facing the river; Jack had his back to it, but turned to follow Frankie's wide-eyed gaze.

The chain no longer drooped unmovingly into the water, but jerked and shivered like a fishing line with an aggrieved marlin on its hook.

Gasps came from behind Jack as others noticed what he and Frankie had seen. He fixed his gaze on the fog bank.

The raft emerged, two people on its deck. A man and a woman, she using a hand to shade her eyes, he blinking in the sunlight. He hauled on the chain, pulling it steadily through his gauntleted hands to draw the raft towards the jetty.

As they came nearer, Jack could see they were a middle-aged couple, perhaps in their late forties or early fifties. They both appeared to be sturdily built, if not bordering on plumpness. Their clothing looked unremarkable to Jack's unfashionable eye, providing no clue to where or when the couple had come from.

They must have noticed what they probably thought to be some sort of welcoming party, for the man stopped pulling on the chain and turned to speak to the woman. After a hurried discussion, he picked up the chain and resumed hauling.

Within a few moments they were approaching the jetty. The man released the chain, allowing the raft's momentum to close the final few yards.

Frankie's voice near his ear made Jack jump. "Do you know these people? They seem to know you. Look at how they're staring at you."

It was true. The man in particular was subjecting him to a scrutiny that made him feel uncomfortable.

The end of the raft bumped gently into the jetty and it came to a halt.

"Jack?" said the man. "Is that you?"

Jack narrowed his eyes to peer at the man more closely. There was a resemblance there to someone he knew. The face and body were fuller, the cheeks and belly plumper; the hairline had receded like a retreating tide and what remained contained a smattering of grey, like foam; the eyelids had grown hooded, the nose traced with broken veins. Far too old to be the person he was thinking of, but perhaps the person's father? Then he noticed the faint white mark amongst the red lines criss-crossing the nose: a scar where a flying creature resembling something found on the roof of a cathedral had bitten a chunk from it.

"Matt?" said Jack.

The man nodded. He gestured to the woman. "And you remember Kim?"

The Lord of the Dance

Matt

No sober man dances,
unless he happens to be mad.

—Marcus Tullius Cicero (*Pro Murena*)

Part 1: Return to Oz

One

Time can mellow a man. Lend him fresh perspective. Smoothe out the kinks in his character, while adding wrinkles of the physical kind.

Fatherhood, too. What a life-changer, that is. One moment you've nothing of more import to concern you than how to pay your rent, the next you find yourself cradling a fragile bundle of new life, gazing down into freshly minted eyes, which seem to stare directly into your soul as if to say, "Okay, buster, you're my dad, well I guess you don't get to choose your sire so I'm stuck with you for good or ill and I'm lying here 'cause I can't do much else 'cept poop and wail, and I see you for all your frailties and flaws and, man, I don't like what I see but, like I said, I'm stuck with you and you with me so we'd both better get used to the idea and make the best of it, right?" and—kaboom!—suddenly you're responsible for the life of another person, one who can't do the simplest things like wipe the dribble from his chin, much less watch telly or accompany you for a pint down the pub, and you're not ready for the unbearable weight of that responsibility and never will be.

God knows, you try, but there's a nagging doubt in the back of your mind that you'll never be good enough, will never measure up to the other dads who take their kids to Little League—what a peculiarly American pastime—that you'll forever be a disappointment.

And there's always that other thing, that shifting thing of shadow, waiting to clutch you in its icy tentacles of despair, engulf you in a cloud of melancholy, and you grow so powerless you can't feel the sense of impotence in which you're floundering.

It's then, when the darkness is about to suck you towards its limitless, spiralling depths that you turn to...

No. Not yet. I'm too easily side-tracked. I was talking about how time can alter a man. On the inside, as well as the more obvious external changes.

In most cases, anyway.

Twenty-three years had passed since a young man of around twenty, six years or so my junior, whom I barely knew, had flipped me the finger from the deck of a raft, grinned and disappeared into a bank of fog. Twenty-three years, during which I'd become padded with accumulated flab, creased with lines of care, begun to turn grey like a fading photograph.

Jack hadn't aged a day.

The fog closed around us like a damp blanket, muffling the gloopy drips of water falling from the chain. An unpleasant, waxy taste coated my lips.

"Assuming we come out of this fog sooner or later," I said, my voice sounding like I was talking into a pillow, "what d'you think awaits us on the other side?"

Kim glanced at me from eyes wide with apprehension, but she didn't reply. Her bottom lip was tucked between her teeth in a gesture of worry I knew well.

Despite the syrupy consistency of the river and the size of the raft upon which we stood—large enough to hold up to twenty people at a push, I reckoned—the effort required to haul us hand-over-hand with the chain was not onerous, even for someone as out of shape as me. The thick hide gauntlets I wore enabled a sure grip on the uncorroded metal links and the raft moved across the surface like an oiled toboggan on ice.

Of course, when we'd stepped aboard she'd made to pick up the gauntlets and I'd had to move quickly to grab them first. Possesses a great deal of strength does that woman, physical as well as mental, and she'd have had little trouble pulling us across the river, but I still retain a flicker of pride. Can't have your woman do everything, can you?

My woman. Maybe once, before the drinking grew out of hand, but she had been no one's woman, except her own and her son's, for many years.

The air didn't appear as consistently grey ahead. I continued to haul steadily on the chain and narrowed my eyes against the increasing brightness.

"We're coming out of it," I muttered.

Another scared glance from Kim. Scared but removed. There was a time she might have grasped my hand or stood nearer for the comfort being close to another can bring, but I struggle to be strong for myself, let alone her, and she remained standing yards from me, arms hugging herself the only concession to fear.

The fog continued to thin, grew misty, became infused with yellow warmth. A few more hauls on the chain and we broke into clear air. I squinted against the glare and blinked to try to see ahead.

The bank of the river stood maybe fifty yards away. Not that easy to be sure with the eyesight of a forty-nine-year-old who's lost his spectacles, but it looked as though the chain led to another jetty like the one from which we'd embarked. Beyond that I could make out little more than an impression of fields and forests, perhaps distant mountains. A sharp smell, like that of a school chemistry lab, arose from the river.

Kim still hadn't spoken. She peered at the land ahead, one hand raised to shield her eyes from the sun.

The only sound was the gurgling of water beneath the raft.

People born and bred in the United States say things like 'gotten' and 'off of' (I know The Stones did it in *Get Off of My Cloud* but, hey, that's rock 'n' roll). They say 'erbs' where we Brits would pronounce the aitch and, speaking of herbs, what's with their pronunciation of basil? They make it sound like an exotic colour or a term used in heraldry, rather than a simple accompaniment to pasta. And their spellings are weird; it took me years to realise that their aluminum is the same thing as our aluminium. Course, Kim says we are the weird ones.

"Come on, Matt," she'll say, "'disorientate'? Why the extra syllable when 'disorient' does the job perfectly well?"

Not that I'll ever admit it to her, but I suppose she has a point.

I find the differences between our use of the same language less weird after being immersed in American culture for the past eighteen years. Shoot (see what I did there?), I use the occasional American idiom myself and my accent probably contains an American twang. I call a lift an elevator, except for the one we rode in in Claridge House all those years ago. *That* one I refer to as the Elevator.

We moved to the States two years after the wedding. It had been a simple affair; well, I could hardly expect my folks to fork out thousands after I bailed out of uni after barely a term and used what was left of the money they'd saved to help me survive the first year to pay a deposit on a flat twenty miles from home.

Despite Mum's failing health, both my parents attended the ceremony. My frosty relationship with my father had thawed somewhat with Kim's help, and his preoccupation with Mum meant a blessed minimum of disapproving glances as I ordered the next drink.

When Mum lost her fight to the big C six months later, he withdrew into himself, becoming a shadow of the forceful character who'd tried his best to mould a man out of his son when he didn't have the best raw materials to work with. Within another year, I watched dry-eyed beside my sobbing sister his coffin sink into the recess at the crematorium when the vicar pressed the button during the Committal. One thought consoled me: at least I could no longer be a disappointment to him.

Of course, there are always other people to disappoint.

Kim made a noise, a grunt of surprise, and I paused hauling on the chain to look at her.

The passing years had served her well. She had added a few pounds to an already full figure, but conveyed an impression of voluptuousness rather than plumpness. The generally drier and warmer Connecticut summers suited her better than the damp UK. In her early fifties, she didn't attempt to conceal, other than with the lightest touches of cosmetics, the lines which crinkled the edges of her eyes and mouth when she smiled or frowned. They lent her a sense of grace.

She was frowning at me now.

"There are people over there, Matt," she said in a hushed tone. "A lot of people."

Since emerging from the fog bank, I had probably halved the remaining gap to the far shore. But one glance was enough to know that the distance remained too great for my myopic eyes to make out details like people.

"How many?"

Kim shrugged. "Twenty? Thirty? Can't tell at this range."

"But you're sure they're people?"

The corner of her mouth twitched as it always did when she thought I was doubting her. "I'm sure." The edge to her tone betrayed more than mere apprehension.

"Sorry, sorry," I muttered. "What are we going to do?"

Kim's frown deepened as if I was being stupid. Don't know why that would cause her to frown; she should be used to it by now.

"We either return from where we've been," she said, with a brief inclination of her head to the bank of fog, "or we continue to the other side and find out what welcome awaits. We can't stay here: we have no food or water and the stink of chemicals is making my eyes smart. Don't see we have any other choices."

"We can't go back. *He* might be waiting for us." The quiver in my voice was unavoidable and I didn't make any effort to hide it. Kim didn't regard the monk with quite the same level of terror that I did, but she hadn't seen behind his mask; she hadn't seen the Lord of the Dance. "Shall we go on then?"

"Like I said, sugar, we are short on alternatives."

Sugar. I hated it when she called me that or *honey* or *sweetpea*. She reserved these terms of address for people whom she held in contempt. She had called Jack something similar on the first occasion we'd met. Although we worked in the same building, I had never noticed Kim until she stepped into the Elevator on *that* fateful morning as I willed the bloody contraption to get moving to take me to the Sixth Floor and much-needed coffee. Despite my hangover, I'd been impressed at the sassy way she'd dealt with Jack's snide remarks about her accent.

Despising myself a little more, if that was possible, I allowed my expression to reveal hurt, but she had already turned away to stare at the river bank. Had already dismissed me.

I grabbed the chain and began to haul on it once more.

The distance halved again and I began to make out details of what lay beyond the jetty. Grassland led to a thickly wooded area in the middle distance and a ring of purple-tinged mountains formed the backdrop. But my gaze was drawn to the people.

Two male figures stood facing us on the jetty; the nearest one appeared to be holding some kind of metallic briefcase. Behind them was a clutch of people also staring our way. Around thirty of them, I estimated.

I hauled on the chain—like Kim said, what other choice did we have than to proceed?—until the remaining distance to the jetty was only a few yards. I let the chain fall from my hands and tugged off the gauntlets, dropping them to the deck. My movements had become automatic, unthinking, for my thoughts were wholly occupied by the man holding the briefcase.

More boy than man, complete with a smattering of rash on cheeks and nose, a leftover of recent teenage acne. A feeling of guilt flickered as I recalled referring to him privately as Rudolph before I'd learned his name, but a sense of wonder at seeing him again after all these years, looking exactly as I remembered him down to the scruffy shirt and chinos, snuffed it out.

The raft's momentum carried it to the jetty where it bumped gently to a halt.

"Jack?" I said. "Is that you?"

The man narrowed his eyes and peered at me closely. I had to resist the urge to squirm under his inspection for while he stood before me as the same spotty twenty-year-old I'd last seen disappearing into a bank of fog, I had added twenty-three years of not-so-gracious living to the clock.

At last he spoke. "Matt?"

I nodded and gestured to my companion. "And you remember Kim?"

Two

Kim's pregnancy proceeded smoothly; no complications or scares along the way. She surprised me by not wanting to know the sex of the child in advance, which was quite out of character for my pragmatic American bride.

"Let it be a surprise," she said. "More fun that way."

Male, female, it didn't make much difference to me. All I hoped was that it was emphatically one thing or another. I did, however, care about naming the baby when it turned out to be a boy.

"We have to call him Jack," I said to Kim as she lay in bed in the Maternity Unit, the twelve-hour-old babe suckling at her breast.

She frowned. Her weariness made her appear more severe than she perhaps intended. "You said that when you first met him you thought he was a… let's see how you put it, oh yeah, 'a snivelling toe-jam'."

"Toe *rag*."

"Oh, that's much better, then. A fine basis on which to name our son."

"But look what he did. He probably saved our lives."

"Yes, he probably did." She considered for a moment. "I want to name him for my mom's father."

In the end, we compromised. We still could, back then. Our son was named Samuel Jack Tyler-Grayson. Someone else for me to disappoint.

Never mind that we had aged twenty-three years while he hadn't aged a day; never mind that he was gawping at us as if wondering what the heck had happened to us, and that we gawped back wondering why nothing appeared to have happened to him; never mind the clutch of strangers watching us who looked like extras from BBC period dramas. Only one thing at that moment seemed vitally important to my mind and that was to tell him.

I blurted it out. "We named our son after you."

He looked from me to Kim and back again, his brow so creased his eyes had become slits. His knuckles grew whiter where they clutched the metallic case as if it was some form of crutch. "What?" he managed.

"Uh, we named our son after you," I repeated, though it sounded lame and irrelevant the second time. "He's, er, in high school."

"You have a son? Together?" The information seemed to have registered, but made him look even more dazed. "I only left you about a week ago."

"A week?" I shook my head slowly. "It's been twenty-three years. I'll be fifty next year. Kim already is."

She spoke at last; I was beginning to think she was going to leave all the blundering to me. "Actually, I'm fifty-one." Oh yeah, damn—I never remember her exact age. "It's good to see you again, Jack."

She began to step forward as though to give him a hug or shake his hand or something, but stopped dead when the boy standing on the jetty a couple of paces behind Jack yelled.

"No!" He held his hands out in a halting gesture. "Sorry," he said at a more normal level, "I didn't mean to startle you. But, please, don't step off the raft."

The 'boy' possessed a deep, accentless voice and on looking more closely I could see that he was in fact around Jack's age, perhaps a few years older. It had been an easy mistake to make: he was of slight stature, like a jockey, with cheeky, boyish features. He was dressed like a street urchin from a Dickens dramatisation.

Jack glanced at him and the bewilderment drained from his face.

"Good thinking," he said. "We can ride it back to the other side."

"Not 'we'," said the jockey. "You and Nadine must stay here while we determine the lie of the land."

Jack opened his mouth as if to protest, but the other held up a hand to quell him. "This is not open to debate, Jack. We don't know what will happen when we enter the fog from this side of the river. My guess is nothing, but I'm not going to allow you to cross until it's been tested."

I was beginning to feel like a spare part. I cleared my throat noisily. "Would someone like to tell us what the fuck's going on?"

A grin split the jockey's face as he turned to look at me, making him look like more like an impudent street urchin.

"Excuse my lack of manners," he said, bowing sharply at the waist. "Let me introduce myself. I am Francis Brown, but call me Frankie. At your service." He nodded at Jack. "You already seem to be acquainted with young Jack here." He swept out an arm towards the clutch of people watching us intently from the bank. "And these lovely folk are from various places on the planet you call Earth, and from various times."

I should have replied by introducing myself and Kim, but I said nothing. I was experiencing a sensation I hadn't felt in more than twenty years and it had, momentarily, struck me dumb.

Before emigrating to the States, I tried my hand at any number of jobs in the UK, from waiting tables to cold-calling strangers on the telephone and trying to sell them stuff they neither needed nor wanted. Invariably low-skilled, low-paid work, but I didn't care so long as the wages were enough to cover my modest bills and keep me in beer. And it wasn't that I was always hopeless at doing the jobs, although undoubtedly there were some for which I was wholly unsuited. No, I was inevitably shown the door sooner or later due to a singular lack of enthusiasm and a marked inability to fake it.

"Matthew," the kindly—the conversations always began with them trying to be kind—employer would say, "we know you try to do your best, but you never demonstrate the slightest interest in our products/service/clients. You never *enthuse* about your work. It, er, perhaps doesn't help that you often arrive smelling of alcohol."

"Well," I'd say, "it's difficult to get excited about product replacement insurance/carpet cleaning/whinging customers." As the employer's lips drew tight and they adopted a less kindly pose, I'd play my trump card. "It's why I sometimes feel compelled to drink. It's what helps me get through the next day."

Strangely, that never seemed to work. Still, I was good at talking myself up in interviews and rarely struggled to find another job.

This is a long-winded way—see how easily I'm side-tracked?—of saying that my resume, or CV as we used to call them in the UK, contains a long list of occupations from early in my working life. Of those umpteen jobs, I cannot recall the name or address of any place where I worked. Except for one.

Claridge House will be imprinted into my memory until the day I breathe my last. It was the building that housed the Elevator into which I stepped unsuspectingly one spring morning. When I tumbled out again, bloodied and gibbering, three minutes later according to CCTV footage, I had been fundamentally changed, though it would take many years for the full effects to make themselves felt.

During that three minutes of time as we know it, in the company of Kim, Jack and one other, I had visited all six floors and the basement of Claridge House, and undergone experiences that I still find it hard to talk openly about. Not that there's anyone to talk about them with, except Kim, and she has shown no interest since Sam was born in discussing what happened to us that morning.

It was during the jaunts between the floors of Claridge House that I first experienced the sensation that was now making me close up like a clam standing on the deck of the raft.

Disassociation, an odd disconnect between my brain and what was happening around me, like being once removed from the action; a theatre-goer attending a play. It was probably that sensation of watching someone else standing in an elevator when it opened not onto a dull office space, but to out-of-this-world places inhabited by wondrous creatures, that enabled me to venture out into them. For I'm not courageous and find it difficult to reconcile my actions that long-ago day in any other way.

And goodness knows I've tried and tried to make sense of that jaunt in the Elevator, if only to try to silence the nightmares.

Now that sense of disassociation had returned, accompanied by such a strong feeling of déjà vu that I found myself disconcerted enough to be incapable of speech.

After my silence stretched out long enough to become awkward, Kim came to the rescue. "Pleased to meet you, Frankie. I'm Kim and this is Matt." Not 'my husband' Matt, I noted. She smiled towards the people assembled on the bank, but I could tell it was a forced smile. "Pleased to meet y'all." I half-expected her to curtsy. Instead, she grabbed my forearm and dug her fingernails in sharply. "Snap out of it, buster."

Jack seemed to have recovered better from the shock of seeing us twenty-three years older than I had from seeing him unaltered after such a passage of time. He spoke to Frankie. "These are the people who I arrived with on the other shore. Two of them, anyway." He turned back to us. "Where's Tara?"

Kim shrugged. "Not seen her since we escaped the Elevator. And, yup, that was, for us, twenty-three years ago."

At last I found my voice. "Shit," I managed weakly. "I need a drink."

Tara had been the fourth member of the party who tripped between the floors of Claridge House in the Elevator. She spent the entire day—the CCTV might only have recorded the time we spent inside the Elevator as three minutes, but we were in there, and on the various floors and Basement, for the best part of a day—pretending she was experiencing a particularly lucid nightmare. I guess that was her coping mechanism: where I had no control over the detachment which enabled me to do things without being paralysed by fear, she imposed her own sense of disassociation by insisting she was in the midst of a dream.

I had seen her once since the lift spat us out in the lobby of Claridge House and she had roundly ignored me. Fair enough, I suppose. Who would approach a random stranger and say, "I experienced an unusually vivid dream the other day and you were in it"? Occasionally I used to wonder whether this strategy has worked for her in the longer term or whether she wakes up in cold sweats after being pursued through her sleep by a seven-foot reject from the Muppets with razor claws and a tongue like the tentacle of a Portuguese man o'war, with barbs. I used to wonder how she explains to a lover the scars on her back inflicted by those claws and whether she ever feels the urge to lose herself in a haze of alcohol, or worse.

But I stopped wondering after we emigrated to the States and haven't spared her a thought since. Yet she clearly loomed as large in Jack's memory as we did, more confirmation if his still-youthful appearance wasn't enough that for him only a blink of time, not twenty-three years, had passed since we last saw him.

"You really believe you've only been in this place for a matter of days." My voice still sounded weak to my ears, but I was slowly recovering my ability to function, such as it was.

Jack nodded, no trace of a smile on his face. "A week, maybe. No more than ten days. But—" he glanced at the jockey, Frankie "—time doesn't exist here."

Frankie nodded. "That's correct. But it does exist on the other side of the river and I think we need to get moving in case he knows that the raft has left that shore and hasn't yet returned."

When taken individually, I understood every word the man had said, but put them all together and they made little sense to me. Besides, one of the words had caught my attention more than the rest.

"*He?*" I said. "You mean the Lord of the Dance, don't you?"

Jack and Frankie exchanged another glance before nodding in unison. I felt blood drain from my face and staggered.

Three

Maybe I wouldn't have fallen—I've passed out through intoxication once or twice, though never fainted dead away like an overwrought teenage girl—but it became a moot point when Frankie stepped onto the raft and grabbed me, easing me into a sitting position on the deck. Kim did nothing except gaze down at me, a faint smirk playing around the corners of her mouth.

"That's my *man*," she said in a low tone. I've never known someone with such ability to imbue a single word with a whole world of contempt.

"Thanks for your concern," I muttered, but my sarcasm was half-hearted. In truth, I felt more than a little contempt for myself.

"Everyone, listen up!" said Frankie, addressing from somewhere above my head the people assembled on the bank. "Each of you arrived on this shore upon this raft. Almost as soon as you'd stepped onto the jetty, the raft returned across the river of its own volition." People nodded; some of them wore expressions of grim determination; many more looked worried. "We need to get as many of us as we can onto this raft before Kim and Matt disembark."

I felt, as well as heard, the deep breath he exhaled across the top of my head like a warm breeze.

"Those who sent me here don't *think* anything bad will happen when we enter the bank of fog from this side; they expect us to merely pass through as we would through ordinary fog. But I said I wouldn't deceive you any more and here's the truth: no one can be sure what will happen. And there's worse." He gave another heavy sigh. "If we do pass through the fog without any problems, it's possible that the monk—the Lord of the Dance as Jack and Matt call him—will be waiting for us on the other side. With his pets. We may need to fight for our lives the moment we step onto the far shore. With that in mind, the first party should consist of those most willing and able to fight."

While he paused, the people standing on the bank glanced at each other or at the ground, and a series of whispered snatches of discussion broke out.

"I could nominate those of you I believe to be the strongest, the best fighters," continued Frankie, "but this cannot be a task that anyone feels under any duress to perform. You must step forward of your own free will or don't step forward at all. I feel honour-bound to remind you that some or all of us could die on that far shore. But that is where we must proceed if we are to attempt to assure the future of humanity. For make no mistake, its future rests in your hands."

The muttered conversations between the people ceased. They all stared at Frankie with, in the main, expressions of grim resolution; the expressions of worry that remained had turned to looks of utter terror.

I glanced up at Kim, who was regarding Frankie with puzzlement. I didn't blame her; he sounded like he had just given a speech from one of those old films from when we were young, like *Braveheart* or *The Lord of the Rings*, the sort of monologue designed to gee up men for battle. Why he was going on about the future of humanity, I couldn't begin to guess, and the notion that this rag-tag bunch of people shuffling their feet on the banking could influence it seemed wildly optimistic. As far as I could see, they carried no arms save for a motley collection of shoulder-high sticks.

The feeling of faintness passed. With a grunt, I stood. The world wavered for a moment, but I remained steady. Both Kim and I gazed at the gathered people to see how they would react to Frankie's words.

The pause lengthened and began to feel strained. As I started to wonder what Frankie and Jack would do if no one stepped forward, a slight woman with Asian features, clutching a length of stout wood taller than she, took two paces towards the jetty.

There was another pause, while the air seemed to crackle with tension. Then the Asian woman was joined by three men, as if they couldn't bear to be upstaged by a female. The dam had been breached. Within moments every person, even those wearing terrified expressions, had stepped forward.

Becoming a father was never something to which I gave serious consideration. Sure, I must have thought in some vague way that it would probably happen one day, but that was as far as my contemplation went. Not once did I ever stop to consider the consequences.

Sleepless nights, dirty diapers and constant wailing, and that's the superficial stuff. Kim lost all interest in sex, or at least in sex with me. Money became tighter than ever; although she made sure we always had enough to buy disposable diapers and formula and medicines, we had to forego eating out and any form of social life. When I spent the occasional twenty bucks having a couple of beers on the way home from work—or had I graduated to bourbon by then?—she'd throw what we used to call back in Blighty a hissy fit, accusing me of being selfish and unresponsive to her needs.

I'd mutter something about a working man having to let off steam now and again, and this would make her madder and she'd yell until the baby began crying again, and *that* would be my fault like I'd been the one raising my voice, but if I tried to point that out she'd become apoplectic and I'd retreat into sullenness, and that would get her so nuts she'd start throwing things.

And those were the good times. During the *bad* times, when I'd done more than blow twenty bucks on beer and had returned home after midnight barely able to walk, unable to speak except in a slurred whisper, she'd bundle up Sam, or grab him by the hand—my hazy memory shows him as a babe in arms for only the most fleeting of moments before he was toddling and speaking in that endearing infant way—and take him to her parents where she'd stay for days, letting me stew in lonely misery.

But she always came back. I don't know why.

« »

The Asian woman I took to be Japanese, though she might have been Korean or Chinese for all I knew. She was the first to reach the raft, looking smaller up close, like a child, though there was nothing child-like in the way she held the stick.

"Fumika," said Frankie, and inclined his head towards her, "your bravery and honour in being the first to step forward are noted and appreciated, but I believe we may need those of greater strength and fighting ability once we reach the other side."

A smile touched the woman's face and she hefted the stick lightly, tossing it a few inches and catching it as though it were a straw and not a polished length of stout wood standing taller than her by almost a foot.

"I know kendo," she said.

Frankie regarded her gravely for a moment—although he and Jack were of similar age, a sense of greater experience and knowledge hung about him like a mist—then bowed his head briefly again, before stepping aside and holding out an arm in invitation.

"Please, Fumika, forgive me for doubting you and come aboard."

Fumika stepped from the jetty, passing between me, Kim and Frankie as she made her way to the rear—or what, I supposed, would now be the front—of the raft.

Many more shuffled on behind her. More men than women, but plenty of the latter, too. Soon the surface of the raft had become cramped, though the deck had not sunk noticeably under the extra weight. My estimate of how many the raft would hold had not been far off the mark. At least twenty people, in addition to me and Kim, now crowded the deck. We stood at the very edge; I was finding it difficult to maintain my balance and not take a pace onto the jetty. Still standing on the shore, looking anxious, were Jack and perhaps a dozen other people.

Frankie turned towards them—it required a little shuffling about and a few trodden toes.

"One last thing," he said to the people ashore. "If any of you change your minds and decide to bring the Scourgers down upon you so that you can return home now, I beg of you, go to the forest, as far in as you can, before leaving the trail. The last thing we need is to bring the Scourgers here and draw attention to what we are doing."

I glanced at Kim and pulled a face as if to ask *What the hell is a scourger?* She shrugged.

The remaining people nodded. Frankie turned to us.

"Matt, Kim. You may now step off the raft."

"I have no idea what you're all doing," I said, "but I—we—wish you the best of luck."

Frankie nodded and flashed that cheeky grin. "If we succeed in reaching the other shore," he said, "we'll be back to get you." I must have blanched at that for he held out a hand and clapped me on the shoulder. I sensed a wiry strength in the man that belied his slight stature. "Don't worry," he added. "Returning to the other shore is the lesser of two evils. You really don't want to stay in Nowhere."

Still not understanding what he was talking about, I glanced once more at Kim and together we stepped onto the jetty.

Even the strongest amongst us possess frailties and imperfections, a vulnerable spot, an Achilles' heel. They are strong, I guess, because they are adept at masking those vulnerabilities, refusing to allow them to become dominant. The weaker, on the other hand, and perhaps why they are regarded as such, have less success in overcoming their flaws so that the flaws come to define who they are.

There was a period—at least four years, maybe five or six—when I became strong. Not that I stopped drinking altogether, but I stuck mainly to beer, with only the occasional bourbon chaser. I controlled it, rather than letting it become the master of me.

For a while I played the dutiful husband and doting father, if not to perfection then at least to a standard that allowed me to not look out of place with the regular dads and moms. I took Sam to Little League, to try-outs for what the Americans insist on calling soccer to differentiate it from that peculiar hybrid of rugby and Risk (it's all about gaining territory) they call football, to swimming. I'd stand on the side lines making appropriate noises of encouragement and smiling at the other parents if they caught my eye, but without quite integrating myself into the cliques, the unofficial 'good parents' clubs' that invariably form around such activities. And that was part of my problem: no matter how often I performed the role of a loving father, it was just that, a role; I never considered myself to be a *good* parent. And I doubt that Sam did either, even during that golden period of having a dad who'd actually be around and, if not always strictly sober, coherent.

But, you guessed, it didn't last. Couldn't last. For regardless of how normal and responsible and, damn it, unafraid I could appear, *he* was always there waiting to exploit the inevitable chinks in my armour. Lurking. Insidious.

The Lord of the Dance had on that long-ago day on the banks of a brown river burrowed like a tic deep into my soul, ready always to invade my dreams and, when I lacked the strength to silence him, to corrupt my waking thoughts with the infinite depth and breadth of his insanity (though, and here's the profound thought of the day, if something is of infinite depth and breadth, it possesses neither).

And where was I now, having arrived against my will in his domain and scooting away on a raft before he had chance to notice me? Like a lamb to slaughter, I was waiting for the raft to return to carry me into his presence.

For the raft to be able to return, it had first to cross the river, an operation which I'd gathered was not a given. When Kim and I stepped onto the jetty, I immediately turned to Jack to ask him one of the hundred questions muzzing up my head like a cold, but he was staring beyond me with a worried expression. He still held the metallic case, clutching it as if afraid someone might try to grab it from him. A young woman stepped forward and joined him on the jetty. She was about his age, slim and not unattractive. Her hand found his free one and gripped it tightly.

Go, Jackie-boy, I thought, but kept *shtum*. Now was clearly not the time for a bit of frivolous banter, much as I needed the release it would bring from the creeping sense of terror threatening to overcome me at the prospect of returning so soon to the other side of the river. We had only just arrived at this side, for goodness' sake.

Kim turned to face in the direction from which we had come. I did the same. All eyes watched the raft.

For a few moments nothing happened. Most of the twenty-odd people crammed onto the raft's surface faced ahead towards the bank of fog covering the centre of the river like a curtain. One or two cast the occasional glance back with grim, apprehensive expressions.

Noiselessly, acting under no patent method of propulsion—the chain dangled slackly into the water where I had dropped it—the raft began to move smoothly forward, steadily drawing nearer the fog.

Part 2: Not in Kansas Anymore

One

During my mid-teens I realised I would never live up to the ideal son my father wanted me to be. So I stopped trying. In my introspective moments, of which there aren't many since I will do almost anything to avoid them (they are when *he* finds it easiest to breach my fragile defences), I wonder whether we would have enjoyed a better relationship if he had tried more to be my friend than to mould me into a shape I could never take.

Lacking fortitude or moral fibre or whatever it takes to be the perfect father, I tried to be a friend to my son. Tried too hard.

"Sam doesn't need another friend," Kim would try to explain to me patiently. "He's made lots of friends in school. What he needs is someone he can look up to. Someone he can respect. A male role model."

I'd nod and mumble something about trying harder, while thinking, with a rare flash of insight, that if I had ever possessed the ability to be stern and strict and forbidding when the occasion demanded, while at the same time demonstrating love and compassion and conveying the sense that what I did was for his own good, I had pissed it away along with my self-respect long ago.

Long ago, starting with peeking behind the façade of a deranged being masquerading as a monk.

Not that I blame all my failings on the Lord of the Dance. You see, I've never been good at shouldering responsibility, even before that crazy ride in the Elevator. At the risk of sounding like I'm wallowing in self-pity, I've never been much of a man and what is a man if not someone who can accept responsibility? No, the flaws in my character were there all along. All *he*'s done is exploit them.

And I guess, to my eternal shame, that the biggest victim of my failures wasn't Kim, though she would run a close second, but the one person in the entire world to whom I was desperate to be regarded with love and respect.

"Daddy," he said to me when he was still young enough to call me that, "why do you drink so much?"

I looked into those trusting, innocent eyes and pulled him to me, hugging him so close I could smell the vitality of his skin and hair, like the scents of spring and fresh laundry.

"My little prince," I whispered, "I don't want to make promises to you that I can't keep and that's why I can't promise to stop drinking. There's something inside of me, something dark, that alcohol keeps at bay. But I can and do promise to cut it back, to not drink as much." I pulled him away so I could look him in the eyes once more. "Will that be okay, if I promise to not drink as much from now on?"

He gazed back at me and for a moment I thought he was going to say no, that I'd be forced into making a vow that I knew deep down I'd break. Then he nodded sombrely.

"That's okay, Daddy."

We held each other's gaze for a long moment more before I broke into a grin and he returned it. Feeling an inexplicable sense of elation, I held up my hand and he high-fived it, before I hugged him to me again, this time so I could tickle him.

That was the start of that halcyon period when I regained control, when I became the best dad I could be and the best husband. Before the days grew dark again. Before Kim began blaming me for everything.

She didn't need to say anything as we stood on the jetty watching the crowded raft approach the swirling bank of fog. I could feel disapproval coming off her in waves, exuding from her pores like a sour odour strong enough to drown out the chemical smells wafting from the river. Her bearing, the expression in her eyes whenever she could bring herself to look at me, her very being told me in the strongest terms that it was my fault we found ourselves back in this place of strangeness and fear.

Perhaps she had a point. But two can play the blame game.

Maybe if she'd followed through on her constant threats to leave me, I'd have tried to pull myself together sooner before… well, that can wait. The front of the raft had reached the first tendrils of fog.

I heard sharp intakes of breath and low murmurings from the people behind me, but didn't glance around. I was too infected by the sense of dreadful anticipation that lay around me that I couldn't tear my gaze away from the raft as it moved into the fog.

What the onlookers were expecting, I'm not sure. If it was shouts of fear or pain from those aboard the raft, we were thankfully to be disappointed. It was now too distant for me to make out detail with my dodgy eyesight, but the raft slipped into the fog and disappeared without any apparent incident: no one aboard cried out, at least loudly enough to reach our ears; no one fell or jumped overboard; there were no claps of thunder or flashes of lightning.

Quite the anti-climax, in fact.

The fog closed around the raft and concealed it like muddy water covering a sinking ship. Since there didn't seem to be any more to see for now, I turned around to face Jack.

He glanced at me before turning to his female companion.

"Well, so far, so good," he said.

She nodded and attempted a smile, but even to me who didn't know her from Adam—or should that be Eve?—it looked forced.

"What now?" I asked.

"Now," said Jack, "we wait."

Gone was the impetuous nature which dominated my younger years. Had I still been in my twenties, like I was the day I met Kim when we shared a ride in the Elevator, I'd have been off exploring this new land and damn the consequences. But that was then. Now I had been on my feet—apart from the few minutes of enforced sitting down when I'd felt faint—since Kim and I had arrived back on the shores of the brown river. Factor in the physical exercise of hauling the raft across said river, and the shocks of finding ourselves back here and finding Jack unchanged in twenty-three years, and I needed to sit down and take stock. That wasn't my only need, but the only one it looked likely could be met.

It became clear that Jack recalled my youthful tendency to act on impulse—and why shouldn't he if, as he claimed, he had only left my younger self ten days ago?—for he fixed me with a searching gaze.

"If you feel you must go and look around," he said, "I can't stop you, but it is absolutely vital that you remain on the path. And don't venture far in case we need to leave in a hurry."

I felt an unexpected stab of annoyance, which recalled to mind something I'd not thought of in years: how much he irritated me. Sometimes a person can say or do things that push another's buttons, rub the other the wrong way, although it wouldn't be obvious to a neutral bystander why the other is being so affected. We're strange creatures.

And he had done things, selfish things, during our Elevator jaunt that had made me want to thump him; like when he shoved Kim towards the furry monstrosity trying to get into the lift, or when he'd drunk the only bottle of water we had between four of us.

But I wasn't lying when I said that time can mellow a man. While my younger self might have glowered at Jack or shot off a pointed retort, the mature me was able to tamp down the irritation without so much as a flicker of a scowl to betray my true feelings.

"It's okay," said Kim, "he won't be going anywhere, will you, honey?" She smiled at me in that sweet, contemptuous way and this time it wasn't as easy to conceal my displeasure.

I bit back the barbed retort and looked at Jack. "To be honest with you," I said, "I could do with taking the weight off my feet. Is there somewhere we can sit and catch up?"

He glanced down at the wooden jetty beneath our feet. "Here is as good as anywhere."

« »

It must have been around six years ago that the drinking grew out of hand. I mean *seriously* out of hand. The tenuous grip I'd managed to maintain for the previous five years or so—it had never been a firm grip—slipped loose. There was no particular reason, no single event I can point to and say, "There! That's what triggered it, caused me to go off the rails." Life, real life, is rarely that simple.

No, it was more a combination and accumulation of mundane stuff that most people cope with every day: work pressures, money worries, minor health issues, relationship stress. But with one significant extra.

I had grown weary, utterly weary of awaking in the predawn hours, shorn of the anaesthetising effects of strong liquor, sweating and trembling in the aftershock of the nightmares. The memory of the glimpse he had shown me of his true self remained as vivid as when I had been standing at the edge of the field of bones, the killing field, with a wriggling mass of serpents making their slithery way towards me.

Since resuming restful slumber was rarely an option, what remained of the night would follow the same pattern of striving to think of humdrum things while my traitorous mind kept returning to the fundamental questions. I had never been one prior to the Elevator trip to ponder questions of existentialism, being more a happy-go-lucky type of guy, but being shown unequivocal insanity can change a man. For what use is it, what is the point of trying to impose some sense of order on life when such depravity and randomness exist, ready to pitch us into a seething maelstrom of chaos and despair?

Oh, what a happy chap I must appear to be, so filled with fear and weakness and self-loathing that people must sometimes wonder why I don't simply end it all. It would take courage, yes, far more than I possess, to slit arteries or swallow pills or step off a high ledge, but that's not the reason I'm still here.

Although not always evident, and they are greatly diminished, I cling feverishly to one or two of my stronger traits. Stubbornness, for one. To give in to despair would be allowing *him* to win and, despite my finding it impossible to foresee any other outcome, enough of my competitive instinct remains to not want to merely roll over and allow that to happen. There's also, believe it or not, selflessness. For though I must come across as one of the most selfish and self-absorbed and whiny individuals to have drawn breath, I *am* capable of putting others first. Kim, maybe, to some extent, though she'd be hard pushed to come up with an example; Sam, most definitely.

Of late I've abrogated my responsibilities as a father; I'm no role model to my son. If anything, I'm the living exemplar of how *not* to live his life. You see, it's not that he would lose out on a father-figure that prevents me from chugging those pills. Rather, it's to spare him the ignominy of becoming the son of a suicide. We all know how prevalent bullying is in society, especially in high school; how cruel kids can be to one another. He may already be taking stick for having a lush for a father, though I try to keep it hidden from view, not to flaunt my failings in public. But imagining how much worse it could be for Sam if I were to top myself turns my thoughts aside from ever seriously committing to that final tragic act.

It might not be much, but it allows me to retain the tiniest shred, a smidgeon, of self-respect.

Jack introduced the girl as Nadine from Switzerland. He started to say something else, but seemed to change his mind and stopped talking with a shake of the head. They sat on the jetty leaning into each other, looking as comfortable in each other's company as experienced lovers. The metallic case stood on the floor next to Jack; he clearly didn't intend to let it leave his side.

Kim and I sat a few feet apart, facing the young couple. I sat cross-legged; I had been more comfortable, but it was a relief to take the weight off my aching bones—late middle-age doesn't come on its own.

The rest of the people sat strung out along the dirt path, which led away across grassy meadow, or milled about alone or in pairs, in contemplative silence or muted conversation.

Once we were settled, it was Kim who spoke first.

"So, Nadine, you hail from Switzerland?"

The girl nodded. "I am from Geneva."

"And what do you do there?" Typical of her—always poking her nose into what others do for a living.

"I am a laboratory technician."

"Oh. What sort of laboratory would that be?"

"A medical laboratory." The girl's English was excellent, though delivered curiously without inflection; robotic almost. "We clone human tissue to grow replacement organs. Hearts, livers, that sort of thing."

"Cloning? Is that even allowed?"

The girl shrugged; she seemed to have acquired one of Jack's most irritating mannerisms. "It is when I come from."

"*When* you come from? And when would that be, sugar?"

"I was brought to Nowhere in the year 2176."

Kim inhaled sharply and I felt myself sag with disbelief. Sitting before us was a girl barely out of her teens claiming to have come from more than a century into the future. And I considered myself to be more than a little crazy.

"Huh," said Kim. "Perhaps one of you would care to explain what's going on because me and Matt here—I think it's safe to speak for him, too, in this instance—are more than a little confounded."

Jack grunted and his face broke briefly into a humourless smile. "I'll try," he said.

Two

Jack talked quickly as though impatient to bring us up to speed so he could concentrate on more important things. While he spoke, his glance often shifted to the fog bank. Now and again Nadine would add a comment, perhaps a small detail he'd omitted.

He told us how he'd met a young girl on his arrival on this side of the river who'd provided him with food and water, pointing at the cloth pouch tied around his waist. "Anna, her name is." He nodded towards the people spread along the river bank. "She's over there." He told us how he'd followed the path through forest and meadow, and about meeting Frankie for the first time.

"I saw him a couple of times in the woods," he said. "He was taunting the Scourgers, apparently to keep himself amused."

"What are these Scourgers?" I asked.

"They look like medieval knights riding enormous horses."

"They use whips for weapons," added Nadine, "with spikes as tips." She swallowed as she said it. Her complexion was already pale, but she turned a shade lighter. Jack reached out and squeezed her knee.

"As for *what* they are," he said, "we think they are an extension of him. You know, a bit like the clowns with razors for teeth."

"Snakes," I murmured.

"Dolphins," muttered Kim. She set her jaw in a firm line as she always did when mentioning her phobia to people for the first time, daring them to laugh. Nobody did, although the Swiss girl raised one eyebrow. "Yes, I have a phobia about dolphins and they are what came after me the first time we were here." She shuddered. Perhaps I should have squeezed her knee in the comforting way Jack had with Nadine, but I doubt Kim would have appreciated it coming from me.

"Tell them about Camille," said Nadine to Jack.

He nodded grimly and proceeded to tell us about the killing of a French woman he'd witnessed at the whips of the Scourgers.

Although I had not seen Jack in such a long time and my memory of him was more a flavour of the person I'd briefly known rather than the detail of his character, I nevertheless sensed a change in him. He seemed less cocky than I remembered; graver, more mature.

Jack continued with his tale, relating how he'd come to a settlement of wooden shacks called Tumble Down.

"The first person I met was an investment banker from 1920s New York. He'd hurt his leg in an explosion."

"*1920s New York?*" I couldn't keep the incredulity from my voice.

Jack nodded impatiently. "Yes, yes. And Nadine is from 2176. And you're from twenty-three years into my future. The evidence of that is sitting right in front of you. Not such a leap, is it, to accept there are people here from many times and places?"

"Toto, I've a feeling we're not in Kansas anymore," murmured Kim.

It seemed too bizarre and, yet, Jack was right: there he sat in front of us, still barely in his twenties, while we had joined the silver-haired generation.

"George," he continued, "the investment banker, cut my arm to show me how Nowhere works. Cut through the sleeve of my shirt, too." He held up one arm; the shirt was unbroken. "When I awoke next morning, the cut had disappeared and my shirt sleeve was whole, yet I could remember the pain of him cutting me. And the blood."

I heard Kim draw a deep breath. "But, Jack, that's not possible," she said. She glanced around. "Where is this George? Is he on the raft?"

He shook his head curtly, seemingly disinclined to offer further explanation.

"Maybe," said Kim, "he performed some sort of illusion. You know, like a conjuror."

Jack again shook his head. "I agree that it's not possible, nevertheless it's what happened. I've seen men beaten to within an inch of their lives walking around without a mark on them the next morning; two of them are on the raft right now. Shit, we've both been attacked by the Scourgers and Nadine was seriously injured." He grimaced. "I thought she was going to die. But she survived until nightfall—that's all you have to do, you see—and she was right as rain the following day."

Nadine nodded firmly. "Crazy as it sounds, it's true."

Kim grunted. "Remember the old hand-held cell phones, Matt, from when we were kids? They came with a function that allowed you to restore them to their factory settings. It sounds something like that."

Jack shook his head. "It's actually the opposite. Say you had a mobile phone with a cracked screen and restored it to its factory setting, the screen would still be cracked but any changes you'd made to it, like the contacts you'd added and apps you'd uploaded, would be wiped. In Nowhere, a person's physical injuries suffered that day are erased while their memory remains intact."

There was a pause while Kim and I tried to take this in.

"Hey," I said, "that sounds kind of cool."

"Nope," said Jack, "it's anything but cool. Imagine waking every day in precisely the same physical condition as when you arrived here which, in some cases, was months ago. That might sound fine if you're in good condition to start with, but imagine if you've got, say, a gammy leg. It will never heal. You'd have to endure the same pain every day, at the same time being able to remember the pain you went through the day before and the day before that."

"But, say," I persisted, "that you arrived with an incurable illness. It would never get worse."

Nadine nodded. "That, also, is true. But I have been in Nowhere for many, many weeks and although people don't get sick and any injuries they receive heal overnight, it does bad things to their minds."

"Yep," said Jack. "Though physically people don't change, they are under a great deal of mental strain." He shrugged. "It's the monotony of the place. There's nowhere to go, nothing to do. The inhabitants of Tumble Down had almost become savages. Each afternoon they held what they call a Bout, which is basically a fight nearly to the death between anyone who wants to take part. People who have been here a long time are driven nuts and end up going out to meet the Scourgers."

"Like the French woman?" asked Kim.

"Yes," said Nadine. "Like Camille."

"But you made those things sound terrifying. Why would anyone *choose* to tangle with them?"

"Simple," said Jack. "In Nowhere, that's the most certain way to commit suicide."

"Oh, man," I muttered, licking my lips. "I *really* need a drink."

Nadine looked at me. "Perhaps I can help."

'On the wagon.' A peculiar expression, I've always thought, to describe someone who's decided to abstain from drinking alcohol. I never abstained completely, though for that period of five years or so considered myself to be as much on the wagon as I ever would be, even if only clinging on by the tips of my fingers. And when I fell it was heavily, as though I'd been perched right at the very top of that sucker.

Instead of merely being an occasional chaser, bourbon became my go-to poison. I'd only sup a beer when I felt especially thirsty. You know how this goes. I began to turn up for work late, dishevelled, uncommunicative and lacking concentration. After a while, I stopped bothering to suck peppermints because I could see in my co-workers' eyes that the old mask-the-breath routine wasn't fooling anyone. I began to let people down... No, if I'm going to get this stuff out there, I have to be brutally honest. I began to let Kim and Sam down. My nearest and dearest.

Sam was showing promise in basketball, though Kim doubted he'd grow tall enough to make it at pro level. Pro level, for Pete's sake? He was still a kid; let him enjoy the game for the love of playing it, was my attitude. He did enjoy turning out for the school and I enjoyed watching him play in the few games I remembered to attend. But I missed more, along with routine meetings to discuss progress with his teachers, and school concerts and taking him to campouts. Yeah, great dad, huh?

At first, Kim tried to remonstrate using the subtle approach. Flyers for AA left lying on the kitchen table, that sort of thing. When that didn't work, she became vocally direct. That's a nice way of saying she tore regular strips out of me. When I continued drinking despite the rants from her and the silent rebuke I read in Sam's eyes (when I could focus well enough to see them clearly), she changed tack again. In fairness to the woman, she never completely gave up on me. Most would have, I reckon, within six months. It's now six years later and she's still with me, after a fashion.

Maybe it's because her first marriage ended in failure and she didn't want to go through another divorce. Maybe she thinks having me around, if you can call the state I'm in most of the time being 'around', is preferable for Sam than her being a single mom. Maybe the woman should be freaking canonised.

Saint Kimberly did not wear a virtuous expression as she watched Nadine extract a cork-stoppered canteen, made from some sort of hide, from the pouch around her waist and hand it to me. The canteen sloshed; from the weight, I guessed it contained around a pint of liquid.

Kim's eyes narrowed further and I felt the familiar urge to squirm under the sheer mass of her disapproval. But, as I had grown adept at doing when it came to drinking, I roundly ignored it.

When the stopper came out, a waft of sour air followed it. Not a good smell, but that wasn't about to prevent me from satisfying my most basic need. I raised the canteen to my lips and took a deep slug.

It tasted as bad as it smelled, but I didn't much care. It was strong, too, stronger than I was used to of late, having got through the previous week on beer alone. That sensation of potent alcohol hitting my stomach and sending its tendrils of warmth in all directions washed through me; a sensation that I craved and loathed simultaneously. I took another slug.

Kim looked away in disgust, but Nadine watched me with a look of mild amusement on her pretty face.

"You like it?" she asked.

"Nope. It tastes vile."

"Like horse piss?" asked Jack, a strange look of something like regret passing across his features.

"I wouldn't know," I said. "But, yeah, as I imagine horse piss would taste. Yet it hits the spot." I sighed. "And, in case you're wondering, yeah, I'm an alcoholic."

I replaced the cork in the canteen and held it out to Nadine. She shook her head.

"Keep it. It is of no use to me."

"Thank you."

Jack continued to look at me, a slight frown creasing his brow. "Him?" he asked.

I didn't have to ask what he meant. "Yep." I held up the canteen. "This is the only way I've found to blank him out."

Kim gave a snort of derision and Jack glanced at her. "Kim, I saw him, too. A glimpse of what he looks like. What he *really* looks like. If it wasn't that we go dead to the world when we sleep in this place and, if we dream, we don't remember, I'd probably be having nightmares, too. And, who knows, I might have had to turn to alcohol." He grunted. "If we ever get out of here, maybe I will."

Kim said nothing; she'd heard it all before, how I drank to block out the memory of the Lord of the Dance's true face, blah blah blah. I suspect she had long stopped caring *why* I drank. Nevertheless, I felt gratitude towards Jack for speaking up on my behalf. I nodded my thanks at him, but he wasn't looking at me. He was staring down at the silvery case, a dreamy expression on his face. Now that I was closer to the case, I could see how smooth its surface was, with no obvious catch with which to open it or any seams suggestive of a lid.

"Jack," I said, "what's in that case?"

It took him a few moments to look up; I had begun to wonder whether he'd heard me.

"Not *what*," he said, "*who*. It's someone you've met before."

Three

Without the fresh infusion of alcohol coursing through my system, my mind would probably have reeled under the import of Jack's statement. As it was, it was simply another crazy thing to add to the list of crazy things occurring on this crazy day, and I took it in my fuzzy-around-the-edges stride.

Kim, on the other hand, looked stunned. She stared at Jack with her mouth open, her expression perfectly framing the unspoken question, "You've got a *person* in there?"

"It was the Second Floor of Claridge House," Jack said, speaking slowly and patiently as if addressing children. "Look, I know it's been twenty-three years for you guys, but you must surely remember Ultimus, the last city. On Terra Two, the dying planet. We watched it die. Shit, we almost died with it."

"You two wouldn't return to the Elevator," said Kim. "Until it was nearly too late."

Jack nodded.

"We saw Yellowstone erupt," she continued. "We watched it on a screen beneath our feet."

"See," said Jack, "you *do* remember."

"Miriam," I said. "There was a metal box, like an upright suitcase. It called itself Miriam."

Jack nodded again. "She was a form of artificial intelligence, far more advanced than anything from our time."

I recalled how Jack had insisted, while I resisted, referring to the machine like it was a living person.

"Okay," I said. "So what?"

Jack patted the case. "Miriam's back. She's in here."

It was a case that became Kim's weapon in her fight against my downward slide to oblivion. Not an attaché-sized case like the one in Jack's possession, but a black, alloy suitcase big enough in which to dispose of a dead body. Her 'coffin case', I called it.

When it made its first appearance, perhaps a year after the start of my downward spiral, I had been banished to sleeping in the spare room for months. And who can blame her. Our sexual relationship, such as it was, had fallen away almost immediately. I was usually in no fit state to perform, unless she would be satisfied with being dribbled over and farted on. And waking in the small hours to find me urinating over her shoes in our walk-in closet did nothing to persuade her that I was a suitable bed-fellow.

At least that didn't happen again. The spare room—little more than a box with a single bed—was next to the bathroom and wasn't big enough for a closet or wardrobe. I kept my clothes in the main bedroom. Thus she knew I'd be in and out most days searching for clean things to wear.

I stumbled into the bedroom one morning, furry-tongued and thick-headed, on the hunt for a clean shirt. I was, as usual, going to be late for work, but I at least wanted to *look* presentable.

The case was laid flat on the floor her side of the bed, though I supposed both sides were hers now. The lid was open, leaning against the wall so I had an uninterrupted view of the cavernous interior of the case. It was empty.

"Thinking of taking a vacation?" I asked casually the next time I saw her when I was sober enough to speak coherently.

She looked at me without a flicker of emotion. "When it's full," she said in a flat, mechanical voice, "that's when I walk."

A few weeks later the first clothing, a couple of items of underwear, appeared in the case.

Jack's manner changed, became impatient, as he hurried to relate his tale. Nadine again spoke once or twice to fill in a missing detail. It was a strange tale and not one that I'm sure I fully followed. Mind, I took regular sips from the canteen so perhaps my concentration wasn't all it could have been.

He started by telling us about something that seemed unconnected to the attaché case: how he had rescued Nadine from the Scourgers. It struck me as not being the sort of thing the Jack

I knew would have done, but Nadine's glances towards him, filled with something approaching hero-worship, convinced me that he had in fact acted as he said.

"But the strangest thing," he continued, "was that the Scourgers didn't seem to want to hurt me. Every lash of their whips was aimed at Nadine." He shrugged. "I still don't know why that should be. I hope to find out when we reach the other shore."

He went on to tell us about a meeting in Tumble Down of all its inhabitants and how Frankie had for some reason—this part I didn't follow well—deceived people into thinking he had come from Victorian London, when in fact he came from the far future, from hundreds of years later than Nadine, from a planet colonised by the escapees of the Yellowstone eruption and the Terra Two destruction, which they called, with a marked lack of imagination, Terra Three. Frankie had brought the attaché case with him, though neither Jack nor Nadine seemed clear as to why. Jack mumbled something about having to take the case to the far shore where it would apparently activate, as he put it.

"Activate?" I queried. "How do you mean?"

"Remember Miriam in Ultimus? She lit up and spoke? Well, that's what she still does."

"The case lit up," added Nadine, "when Jack stated his full name. Jack Bruder." Her voice contained a hint of pride. "Then it spoke."

"Jack Bruder?"

"Yes," said Nadine.

Kim and I exchanged a glance. She had picked up on it, too. We had been held in police custody for a couple of days after escaping the Elevator and questioned for hours about Jack's disappearance. They had only let us go with the greatest of reluctance when they could not extract a confession from us and had no hard evidence that we had been involved in the commission of a crime. At least, they found traces of Jack's blood on us and he was nowhere to be found, but they could not come up with any sort of motive to make a prosecution worth the risk.

They nevertheless, I am sure, watched us closely for the proceeding months. I had been glad to escape the UK for the States.

The point is that Jack's name had been mentioned to us time and again during the interviews. His full name. And his surname hadn't been Bruder.

Gradually, over a period spanning four or five years, the coffin case filled. It became my gauge of how far my behaviour had deteriorated. My inebriation barometer. If, for a few weeks, I managed to hold it together better than usual, nothing would be added to the case. Once or twice the contents even went down, though only by a pair of socks or undervest; never anything major.

I glanced in that case every time I went into the bedroom for fresh clothes. I came to know in far more detail than I would have otherwise the sort of underwear Kim preferred and how many she owned of each type of item. Then, as the case filled, her favourite sorts of tee-shirts and leggings and blouses. I learned the dimensions of that case through estimating how many more items of clothing it would hold.

That fucking case.

Then, last week, it was full.

Jack must have caught the glance which passed between me and Kim at mention of his surname. He blushed, hurriedly cleared his throat and continued with his tale. There wasn't much more to tell.

"Miriam said that we have to take her to the other shore where she'll reactivate on hearing my voice. Then she shut down. She hasn't so much as beeped or blinked a light since."

"Why you, Jack?" asked Kim. "Why your… name?" If Jack noticed Kim's hesitation, he didn't blush this time. "Why your voice? What's so special about you?"

He looked Kim full in the eye and I believed him when he said, "I haven't the foggiest idea. That's why I'm keen to reach the other shore so I can find out what the hell this is all about."

Nadine interjected. "Frankie said this has something to do with the future of humanity."

"Yes," agreed Jack. "He did. But he didn't say how or why, only that Miriam would know more."

My sips from the hide flask had slowed as I reached a state of equilibrium in which I could cope with all this weird shit while continuing to be able to function. I knew from long experience that I was at the tipping point—if I exceeded it, I'd quickly degenerate into a mumbling mess. It would only take the occasional sip to keep me at this optimum point. There was a little under a quarter of the contents of the canteen remaining; enough to tip me over should I need to in order to be able to face the Lord of the Dance. Or, perhaps, to avoid having to.

"And this is the same Miriam who spoke to us on the Second Floor of Claridge House?" Kim sounded incredulous despite all we had already seen and heard that day.

Jack nodded. "An updated version, but essentially the same. She and Frankie are from a couple of centuries further in the future than the day when Terra Two burnt away. I think she must have recorded my voice pattern that day; probably yours too."

"Huh," said Kim.

I merely nodded and smiled what probably looked an imbecilic sort of smile. That's me when I'm totally chilled, man.

"So," continued Jack, "the meeting ended and everyone who wanted to come made their way here. We were going to attempt to cross the river using the chain. We had just arrived when the raft came out of the fog carrying you two."

I grunted. "That was fortunate. Don't see how someone could cross only using the chain."

"Well, Frankie was willing to try. Provided we kept the chain tight, I reckon he'd have made it."

"What did you mean, Jack, when you said 'everyone who wanted to come'?" asked Kim. "Are there people still back in Tumble Down?"

He shook his head. "Those who didn't want to make the trek

here, made a different sort of trek."

"How d'you mean?"

He sighed. "They stepped off the path to deliberately bring the Scourgers down on them."

"To commit suicide. But *why?*" Kim could be an insistent lady at times. She wasn't about to be put off by Jack's clear discomfort.

Nadine replied for him. "According to Frankie, time and space don't exist in Nowhere. Therefore, if you die in Nowhere, you return to the moment and place from which you left to come here."

"You can't die here?"

"Not in the sense that we consider dying," said Nadine. "But that is not true on the other side of the river. There, *all* space and time exist and so we can die in the ordinary meaning of the word."

"The killing field," I murmured.

Nadine looked at me enquiringly, but Jack nodded.

"The patch of waste ground," he said, "next to the woods from which the monk comes. It was covered in skeletons and rotting clothes and rusting swords."

Nadine shook her head. "We didn't see it."

Jack was feeling in his pocket. "I picked this up there." He held out a small, battered book; one I had seen before, many years ago.

"That belonged to the captain of the *Mary Celeste*," I said, with a smug glance at Kim; she had silently rebuked me during the Elevator jaunt for my ignorance in not having heard of the incident. I had since looked it up. "Often mistakenly referred to as the *Marie Celeste*, it was the name of a ship found adrift at sea with all ten persons on board missing, including the captain's wife and their two-year-old daughter."

Nadine's eyes grew wider and she took the book from Jack to examine it more closely. "I have heard of the *Mary Celeste*," she said. "The name is still used to describe something like a building that is empty, deserted."

"The crew must have been brought to the other side by the monk," said Kim. "And refused to play his little game."

"He called himself the Quartermaster, do you remember?" said Jack. Kim and I nodded. "Well, apparently he sometimes calls himself the Halfmaster or simply the Master or some other version, depending on how many people have to cross on the raft. It all seems completely random."

"That doesn't surprise me," I said, sounding milder than I felt. I uncorked the flask and took another sip.

Nadine handed the book back to Jack. "They decided to fight, then," she said in a small voice. "Ten people, even if one was a young child—" She brought her hand up to her mouth as though to quell a feeling of nausea. "Ten people weren't enough to beat his creatures. Will we be enough?"

"Well, we are a lot more than ten," said Jack. "And we'll find out soon enough. Look at the chain."

I turned to follow his gaze. The chain attached to the jetty no longer dangled slackly into the river, but trembled and jerked, flinging droplets of syrupy water into the air.

All our gazes switched to the bank of fog.

Part 3: We're Off to See the Wizard

One

Most people are afraid of something, even if they won't admit it. And there is plenty to fear in this strange world we inhabit—rats and spiders, heights and deep water, failure and death.

My irrational fear of snakes hasn't been overcome, merely overshadowed. I still bring my feet up beneath me on the sofa if a cobra appears on the television screen, but I no longer have nightmares about being chased by a black mamba over bare, endless terrain where there's nowhere to hide or seek refuge, and my lungs are burning with effort and I know with dream world certainty that the serpent is gaining, its fangs bared and glistening, and I must soon succumb to exhaustion and surrender to its stinging kiss. That was a recurring dream of my youth, from which I'd wake thrashing and sweating. If I have anything to thank *him* for it's that at least he has cured me of that. Sometimes we have to try to find the positives.

Ophidiophobia has been supplanted by fear of a fat, silvery-eyed bloke who smells of sweaty cheese and sheds maggots when he sniggers, who wears a grubby robe and cowl, who is in dire need of extensive dental treatment. Sounds ridiculous when put like that, but it's not so much his physical appearance that strikes terror into the deepest part of my soul as what his physical incarnation represents. It's what lurks behind the friarly veneer, what he kindly allowed me to glimpse, that has since infected my life.

Despair. Chaos. Desolation. Depravity, too, and black malice. Above all, insanity so boundless it redefines the notion in a way the human mind has difficulty grasping. Perversely, I saw joy as well: a constant rejoicing at the immense depths of his derangement. For, unlike my puny ability to see and fully understand, he is possessed of intelligence so exquisitely honed and vast it enables him to truly know himself and be at ease with all that he is.

And soon, very soon, I would be stepping aboard a deck of logs that would bear me towards him.

The raft emerged from the fog, moving jerkily, fitfully, and my stomach lurched. I fumbled for the flask and gulped a mouthful of the foul liquid. For a moment I thought my stomach would erupt, rebel at last against the abuse to which I constantly subjected it, but a sour belch rose quietly up my throat and my stomach settled.

Two men stood on the surface of the raft, hauling on the chain. As they drew nearer, it became clear that they were together experiencing far more difficulty in moving the raft than I had done in pulling it along on my own.

A shuffling of feet and low murmur of voices came from behind as the people along the bank drew closer.

"Be ready, everybody," said Jack in a loud, authoritative voice I barely recognised as belonging to him. "We may need to jump aboard in a hurry."

The raft jerked closer and now I could make out that one of the men on board was the wiry youngster, Frankie. The other man was of burlier build. They each wore a gauntlet and yanked on the chain with one gloved and one bare hand.

They continued to haul until the raft reached the jetty. There they clung onto the chain, leaning back, not allowing any slack to be created. Sweat ran down their faces.

"Everyone on," gasped Frankie. "She doesn't want to be this side of the river."

Jack brushed past me, the attaché case clutched firmly by his side. Nadine closely followed him.

Kim glanced at me. "Come on." She stepped to the jetty's edge.

I let out a heavy breath.

Kim looked back to where I stood rooted to the spot. I was aware of people moving closer behind me; they began to make their way past.

"Come *on*!" Kim repeated.

My legs refused to move. All I could do was stand and look helplessly at my wife.

She crabbed back to me, allowing people past her. She grabbed my arm, digging her fingernails in.

"Look, buster!" she hissed into my face. "You got us into this mess. You can fucking help to get us out of it. Now, move!"

She turned away and joined the line of people making their way onto the raft.

More and more people stepped past me, but still I couldn't walk. A deep sense of shame made me want to hang my head. Sam would be so proud if he could see me now.

It was the thought of Kim returning to our son and telling him that she had last seen me paralysed with terror, while she and other women and elderly men had the courage to face what I could not, that at last got me moving.

Bringing to bear all that remained of my will power, I lurched into a zombie-like shuffle.

The few men who had remained on this side of the river grabbed the chain to help take the strain with Frankie and his companion. Kim stood at what would now be the front of the raft, talking with Jack and Nadine. I could have made my way towards her—the raft wasn't as crowded as the last time it had made the crossing from this side and there were gaps to squeeze through to reach her—but I didn't think she would appreciate my company so stayed put. I had been among the last to board and stood near the edge. If the raft jerked sharply, I was in danger of falling off, but that seemed the least of my concerns.

Frankie's voice came, sounding a little forced. "Is everybody aboard?"

Voices replied in the affirmative.

"Okay," he called. "Everyone hold on to someone. She's straining to be away."

There was nothing to cling onto to steady ourselves except other people. There were a lot of nervous glances, coughs and shuffling of feet as people braced themselves and held onto each other. I slid one foot out a little behind me and shifted my weight forward onto the other, but didn't reach for anyone and no one reached for me.

"Here we go, then," called Frankie. "One, two, three, and release the chain!"

The raft slid forward, but smoothly, in total contrast to the jerky progress it had made to arrive. People grinned sheepishly as they let each other go.

I felt like shouting in their faces, "What the fuck are you grinning at? Don't you know what we're heading for?" but I remained silent. Of course they didn't know.

As well for them.

The remaining space in the coffin case was filled with her favourite jeans and toiletry bag. If I had kidded myself into believing she was bluffing—a possibility, given how long it had taken her to fill the damned case—that brought it home like a splash of cold water to the face. She was going to leave me. And she'd take Sam. He might be a teenager, as gangly as a sapling and as tall, but he couldn't stay with me; I was in no fit state to look after myself, let alone anyone else.

Of course, I'd lost my job. I had only kept it for as long as I did, far beyond the point that most employers would have cut me loose like excess baggage in a floundering hot-air balloon, because my father-in-law was the CEO of the corporation. But not even he could justify the continued employment of someone whose benefit to the operation had been questionable from the outset and who had become a whiskey-soaked liability.

Despite being in his early seventies, he continued to work as hard as ever, his only concession to age being the couple of afternoons he took off each week. Even then, he mostly played golf.

He did the deed himself and I tip my hat to him: CEOs of major corporations don't normally involve themselves in the hiring and firing of bottom-feeding staff. Perhaps he felt he owed it to his daughter, for he sure as hell owed me nothing.

I remember the conversation well because, for once, I had arrived in work with a clear head. True, it was the Tuesday after an all-weekend blow out and I had skipped work entirely on the Monday during which—and this was rare, even after a binge—I had completely abstained for the whole day.

He gave it to me straight and I took it like the man I so wanted to be.

"You don't seem surprised," he said, after he'd delivered the news.

I spread my hands. "Believe it or not, and I do of course realise it's been mainly for Kim's sake, but I am grateful that you've allowed me to keep the job for as long as you have. I know I haven't made it easy." I held his gaze. "I truly am sorry for forcing you into this position. I truly am sorry for what I'm putting your daughter through."

He sighed. "I like you, Matt. My daughter loves you. As does my grandson. We're able to have this conversation because, despite your faults, you have never laid a finger on either of them in anger or alcohol." For a moment his expression hardened; gone was the silver-haired grandfather figure and in his place I caught a glimpse of the steely-eyed executive beneath the kindly veneer. "Trust me, I'd know if you had and then things would not go well between us." He let the implied threat hang in the air for a few seconds before his countenance relaxed. "For so long as you remain married to my daughter, the company will continue your health insurance."

That was a generous gesture indeed. The country might style itself on being the land of the free, but when it came to health care it was anything but. "Thank you," I said.

"I strongly suggest you utilise it, Matt, as the first step in dragging yourself out of the pit into which you've crawled." His tone softened. "Kimberly has tried to explain to me that what haunts you is something which you can't control. That no one could control. I can't pretend to understand, but the fact that she's stuck by you tells me everything I need to know." He sat straighter, all CEO-brusque once more. "But do her and Sam a favour. Hell, do yourself a favour. Get yourself off the liquor. Before it's too late."

That was around eighteen months ago and I didn't follow his advice. I told myself I'd try, make a serious effort, but there was always an excuse to put it off until the next day or the following week or, maybe, next month would be a good time. In the end, it took the coffin case being filled for me to act. And, as my father-in-law had forecast, it was by then too late.

The raft moved smoothly across the surface of the languid river, the chain dangling into the water behind it. We moved at right angles to whatever current flowed beneath us, with no obvious means of propulsion. For a moment I had a vision of hundreds of tiny legs sprouting from the under-surface of the deck and paddling like billy-o to propel us across the river, and snorted, drawing troubled glances from those standing nearest me. But then I remembered what we headed towards and my happy fantasy of being in Discworld aboard a deck constructed from sapient pearwood vanished, leaving only familiar dread and a nagging perplexity about what, exactly, was propelling the raft.

A new sense of tension began to permeate the people around me. Many held muttered conversations accompanied by anxious glances to the fog bank. It rose ahead of us like a wall of dense smoke.

"No need to worry," came Frankie's voice. "You might experience a tingling sensation as we pass through, and it'll be damp, but otherwise we'll come out the other side unharmed."

I glanced towards Kim, to see if she looked apprehensive. She was still engaged in conversation with Jack and Nadine, and appeared totally unconcerned by the approaching fog.

Quite right, too. She and I had passed through it only hours before without any ill effects apart from an unpleasant coating on our lips and a slight chill. What concerned me far more than entering the fog was emerging the other side.

The muted snatches of conversation around me grew quiet and people tensed as the raft slipped into the shifting wall.

Two

The coffin case mocked me. True, my brain was addled, and not only from the previous day's alcohol consumption, but I'll get to that. Filled to the brim, the case silently laughed at me.

"All that remains is to close my lid, fasten me up and haul my ass out of here," it whispered directly into my mind. "Then you'll be all alone just like you deserve, you fucking loser." The voice in which the case addressed me—I heard it as clearly as I could hear my heart thudding as it toiled to force blood around my abused system—was unaccented, flat and monotonal: the voice of the Lord of the Dance.

"No," I muttered. Then louder, "No!" There was no one to hear me; Kim was at work—she'd added the final items the previous evening or that morning before leaving—and Sam was at school.

I stumbled around the bed, banging my shins on the wooden frame, barely noticing; the bruises are still there, fading yellow and purple like dying pansies. Sinking to my knees in front of the case, I gripped its edge, wanting to tip it over and spill its contents in what Kim would view as an act of drunken petulance. Hardly the way to go if I had any hope of persuading her to stay. And I desperately wanted her to stay. On seeing that case full, an abrupt terror of being alone had supplanted even my fear of sobriety.

My knuckles whitened on the rim of the case and I almost flipped it anyway, for the pure satisfaction of seeing the hateful thing emptied. But I took a deep breath and relaxed my grip. The fear of her leaving had cut through the fog clouding my thoughts and I could think clearly for the first time in months.

Kim had determination in bucket loads; when she set her mind to something, she saw it through. It was one of her qualities, one among many, which had attracted me. And she could be stubborn, more so than me. But she was also possessed of an innate sense of fairness; if someone demonstrated a willingness to meet her halfway, she was always prepared to compromise, to give them a second chance. Of course, in my case it would be the thirty-ninth chance, or something; barely a chance at all. Yet I grasped at it like the proverbial drowning man.

By lunchtime the arrangements were made. I tidied up the stale pit otherwise known as my room—*my* room, note, not the spare room—and laundered the bedding. I shaved and showered, pointedly ignoring the coffin case when I went into Kim's room for clean clothes.

There followed a couple of hours of anxious pacing, waiting for her to arrive home. She was due before Sam, who was staying behind after school for basketball or something. I suspect he took part in so many extra-curricular activities to avoid the possibility of having to spend time alone with his drunken father.

As for drinking, though I cast longing glances at the bourbon I managed to resist—my strategy depended on it—and settled for a couple of beers. Only a couple, to take the edge off the anxiety.

If Kim noticed my tidier appearance and absence of slurring, she didn't remark upon them. She looked careworn. Sad.

"I know you're ready to leave," I began.

Her lips drew into a pale line that revealed her streaks of determination and stubbornness.

"But please, hear me out," I continued. "I've made an appointment with a drug and alcohol counsellor." I gave a nervous laugh. "They lump heroin and cocaine in with beer. Who knew?"

Her lips drew tighter, turning white, and I knew attempting frivolity was an error.

"The appointment's a week today. It was the earliest I could get one. It's downtown at four in the afternoon. It's the latest they make them. I hoped you could get away an hour or two early and come with me."

Her expression didn't flicker, but I knew she was sizing me up, assessing my sincerity. It's what she does.

With nothing to lose, I laid myself bare. *Almost* bare. There was one final card in my hand that I was determined not to play.

"I'm far from shore, Kim. Adrift. The only chance I have of making it back is if you're there waiting to drag me onto the beach." I let out my breath in a heavy sigh. "Enough with the crappy metaphors. The simple truth is that I need you right now more than I've ever needed you before. I can't expect your support. I don't deserve it. I have no right to it. Nevertheless I'm asking for it. Pleading for it. If I have to, I'll go down on my knees and beg for it."

Still she said nothing, but some colour returned to her lips. Not knowing what else to do, I blundered on.

"We've been through things together that no other couple has experienced. How many times did we save each other that day? From the flying pixies, the overgrown muppet, the dragon… When I'm not floundering in a haze of alcohol, we're good together. Sam is proof of that. And I can pull myself out of this with your help. I can be a loving husband again. A proper father. I know you've heard all this before, many times, and there's nothing I can say to convince you that this time should be any different. But I'm begging you for one last chance." Tears formed in my eyes and one rolled down my cheek. The final humiliation. "*Please*, Kim. Let's begin to enjoy each other's company again for the time we have left."

I stopped there before I blurted out that last thing, the card I could not play if I wanted to retain one tiny shred of self-respect.

Kim continued to stare at me for what felt like minutes. I returned her gaze, ignoring the tears that rolled down my smooth cheeks, tickling as they fell.

Finally, she spoke. Two words, but they were sweet music to my ears.

"One week."

The week was up today. The appointment with the counsellor was this afternoon. Kim came with me, but we never made it to the office.

There was a faint tingling sensation to all areas of exposed skin, like mild pins and needles, which I hadn't experienced when we'd passed through the fog the first time, but it didn't last long. A chilly dampness enveloped us and people instinctively drew closer together for warmth and comfort.

Not me. I took a sip or two from Nadine's flask. That provided all the warmth and comfort I needed.

It could not entirely quell the fear, but prevented it forming into outright terror. One other person aboard shared my reason to be terrified. I glanced at Jack to see if there were any outward clues to how he was feeling, but he, Nadine and Kim had stopped talking and all three gazed ahead. There was nothing to show from behind whether any of them were afraid. Perhaps I was the only one.

"Hey, people," came Frankie's voice, sounding flat and muted. "Listen up for a moment. When we arrived at the other side a little earlier, there was no sign of the monk or any other living things. Everyone who's already gone ashore is hopefully waiting quietly for us to arrive and we can do what we need to do without drawing any attention."

"You mean, send us home?" asked a voice from the other side of the raft.

"Yes," said Frankie. "Once Jack reactivates the module, it has the ability to send you all home, though it won't be a rapid process since you've all come from such different times and places."

"And what if the monk knows we're here?" That was a different voice, from someone standing near me.

"Then," answered Frankie, "we'll need to keep him and his pets busy to give Jack time to reactivate the module."

"She's called Miriam." That was Jack.

"Okay. Miriam," said Frankie. "And I'll remind you all: I don't know exactly what Miriam needs to do. All I know is that whatever the monk sends at us, it'll be our job to keep them away from Miriam. Therefore, be ready. If the monk has shown up, we'll probably need to fight."

People glanced at each other apprehensively. My stomach gave a lurch and I fumbled the flask open to take another sip.

The raft continued its unruffled passage across the river. The fog began to thin.

The counsellor did business from a high-rise in a less desirable part of town on the fringes of the business district. Harley Street, this wasn't. The foyer was scruffy, uncared for, a mere vestibule to facilitate ingress to the rest of the building. It reminded me a little of the foyer of Claridge House. If anything should have rung alarms, it was that, but I was already overwrought and oblivious to internal distress signals.

We stopped next to the bank of old-fashioned elevators to find the counsellor's name on the list of businesses occupying the twenty-storey building. Kim spotted it.

"There. Seventeenth Floor."

I winced. "I can't climb that many stairs."

"Course you can. You know we don't do elevators."

Impracticable though it sounds, neither of us had ridden an elevator since that long-ago day in Claridge House. We either avoided buildings where riding an elevator was necessary, or used the stairs; there had been occasions when it had proved most inconvenient and it had garnered us some odd looks, but we'd merely shrug and say we both suffered from an incurable phobia. We'd visited the Empire State Building and climbed all eighty-six floors to the observation deck, but we'd been young and fit back then.

I was no longer capable of walking up to a seventeenth floor. For the past six months I had been struggling to climb the stairs to our apartment, and that was only one flight.

"We're going to have to make an exception," I said. "Or at least, I am. It's either that or I don't go up there and that's not an option."

Kim's eyes narrowed. "Why? What's wrong?"

"Nothing serious." It's much easier to lie when it benefits the person to whom the lie is directed. "But all these years of abuse have caught up with my body. You've seen me coming home from the bar of late. Sweating and shaking like an old man and that's after climbing only one floor."

"You're not shitting me, are you." It was a statement, not a question. She pulled back the sleeve of her jacket to expose her cell phone watch. "We'll have to call and ask if the counsellor will meet us down here."

"No." I glanced around the grotty space with a grimace. "We can't expect to consult a professional here. Come on. Just this once. We'll be fine."

Kim looked from the elevators to me. "Twenty-three years, Matt. Twenty-three freaking years, that's how long it's been since I stepped into one of those things." She was beginning to look, and sound, panicky.

I placed my hand on her arm. "It's okay. You take the stairs and I'll ride the elevator." I sounded calm, but my insides were twisting at the thought of stepping into an elevator after all that time. And the prospect of stepping in alone was more horrifying. I squeezed her arm and let go. "The stairs are over there. I'll see you up on Seventeenth."

Trying to appear unconcerned, I turned to the elevators, trusting that my confident-looking stance would mask the trembling that had begun in my legs. I picked one of the silvery doors at random and pressed the button that called the lift. I chose well because if I'd had to wait for the lift to arrive my courage, such as it was, would have fled. The door slid open immediately; the elevator car stood empty and ready for business.

The trembling was fast progressing to full-on shaking. Taking a deep breath, I stepped into the car before my legs could betray me. Turning to the array of push-buttons on the wall, I thumbed the one marked '17'. My hands had turned slick with sweat; more ran down my back beneath my shirt and jacket, though I wasn't hot.

Hurry up and close I willed the door; if it didn't, and quickly, I would have to step back out and, once that happened, I'd never get back in. *Hurry up and close.*

The last time I had stood in a lift in the foyer of a building waiting for the door to close, I had been desperate for coffee. Now I was desperate for bourbon.

The door began to slide shut.

Before it had closed half-way, a person shot through the narrowing gap, too quickly to trip the sensors that would force the door open again.

Kim's face had blanched white. Her breath came in short, shallow pants.

"What are you doing?" That's me—when all else fails, ask the bleeding obvious.

"Couldn't let you do this alone."

The door finished closing and my stomach gave that queasy lurch which indicated the elevator had begun to ascend.

Kim licked her lips and clenched her hands so tightly her knuckles grew as pale as her face. "Besides," she said, speaking in a staccato fashion to match her breathing, "what are the chances of what happened twenty-three years ago in Britain happening again here. Right?"

Three

Does a subconscious part of us know when something bad is about to happen, perhaps to give us chance to put something right or to say goodbye to someone special? Sounds like so much bullcrap to me. Yet last night I made an extra-special effort with Sam, like part of me knew it could be the last time I saw him. Not that I was trying to think that way but, shit, I stood on a raft heading towards the scariest thing I had ever seen, accompanied by a rag-tag group of people armed with a smattering of pointy sticks. I wasn't so drunk on the contents of Nadine's flask not to recognise there was every possibility that I wouldn't be going home.

After Sam had returned from whatever club he'd attended after school, eaten his dinner and completed his homework, I surprised both of us by asking if he'd like to play a game of chess.

"Chess? Uh, sure."

"The old-fashioned way, though, yeah? With a board and pieces you can hold."

"Whatever, Dad."

The mystified look on his face would have been comical if it wasn't so goddamned heart-breaking that I could prompt such an expression merely by asking him to take part in the sort of activity that millions of fathers across the world must do with their kids every day.

I hunted out the ancient chess set from my youth and we played. In truth, neither of us was much good, me because it was so long since I had played the game that I had to be reminded of what piece could make what move, and Sam because he was unaccustomed to playing games in the physical world rather than the virtual one.

Halfway through the game, he glanced at the bottle of beer I took the occasional swig from and raised his eyebrows. "No whiskey tonight, huh?"

I shook my head.

"Not for the last few nights?"

"Not for the last week," I said.

He nodded.

A little later, as we were packing the pieces back into their box, he cleared his throat.

"So, er, Mom told me that you guys are going to see someone tomorrow."

"That's right. Someone who I hope will help me stay off the whiskey."

He nodded again. "That's good, Dad."

"I'm trying my best. For you and Mom." I hesitated. "Sam?"

"Yes?"

"I love you. You know that, right?"

I don't know what made me say that. It wasn't something I'd normally say for fear of making him blush the colour of a stop light. But he didn't turn red, didn't glance away in embarrassment or shuffle his feet. He merely gazed back at me with eyes still trusting despite all the disappointments.

"I know, Dad."

Then he made to go to his bedroom, to the chat rooms and gaming arenas he and his friends inhabited in a world that belonged to them, but paused at the door.

"Dad. I love you too, you know."

"After everything?" I asked.

He shrugged. "You'll always be my dad."

I wanted to leap to my feet, to rush to the doorway and clutch him to me like he was five again, but there are some lines that can't be crossed with teenage sons. Instead, I nodded and smiled.

He smiled, too, and was gone. Only then did I allow the tears blurring my vision to fall. For once they lacked the heat of bitterness, the sting of regret. Happy tears.

Gasps and small cries of alarm greeted the sight of the river bank as the raft emerged from the fog. My view from the rear was partially obstructed, and we were still too far away for my blurry long-vision to make out detail, but there appeared to be quite a commotion taking place along the shoreline.

Shouts and screams reached our ears, causing more consternation among those aboard the raft. And another sound, high-pitched and indistinct, like far-off children blowing through reeds clenched between fingers.

The embankment leading from the grassy area where elevators had twice dumped us turned brackeny and coarse, before narrowing towards the jetty, forming a pathway bounded to one side by treacly river and to the other by steep banking, too sheer to stand upon. The path there was barely wide enough for two people to walk abreast; I could still remember, as if it was yesterday and not twenty-three years ago, the way the serpents had been forced by its narrowness to squirm over each other like tangled ropes as they followed the Lord of the Dance.

We drew nearer and the scene became clearer. A line of people stretched along the path from the jetty, tightly formed, bunching into a crush towards where the embankment widened out into the open areas beyond. The reason for the crush wasn't that clear to my eyes. It looked like there was a crowd obstructing the path, but a crowd of what I couldn't make out. Where the crowd met the people, blurry motion, and the source of the noises. I didn't need to be able to see clearly to deduce that a melee was taking place.

"Okay, folks," came Frankie's voice, sounding clipped and grim. "As you can see and hear, our presence on this shore has been detected. But we are doing as planned and engaging them where the trail is narrow so they cannot overwhelm us if their numbers are greater than ours. When we reach the jetty, I want Jack and Nadine to hang back and disembark last. The rest of you need to follow me to join our friends. We'll try to keep the monk's pets back to allow Jack time to activate Miriam."

"But we have nothing with which to fight," said someone. "Not everyone has a stick. We need weapons."

A murmur of assent rose.

"The killing field," said Jack. "There are swords and knives lying on the ground. They are rusty but will be better than bare hands."

"Okay," said Frankie. "We must force them back sufficiently that we can get beyond them and arm ourselves as best we can. *Then* we must fight until they are defeated."

"Or we are," came a different, wavering voice.

"Yes," said Frankie. "That is one of the possible outcomes, as you were all aware before you set foot on this craft. It is up to each and every one of you to fight as you have never fought before. I remind you, the future of our species depends upon it."

A sombre silence fell upon the occupants of the raft, making the cries of pain and the high, reedy sound coming from the shore more prominent.

The noises did nothing to ease my fear. It was growing with every minute that took us nearer the river bank. A creeping, insistent sense of approaching menace and malice.

The office-block elevator took mere seconds to ascend seventeen floors. No one else had hailed it and we stopped at Seventeenth without interruption. As the door began to slide open, I glanced at Kim and began to speak.

"Well, that wasn't so—"

She shrieked and I cried out as the sudden absence of gravity sent us both tumbling out of the lift door.

When last I had taken that fall, I had been in my mid-twenties, relatively fit and supple; it had merely taken the wind from me and made my head momentarily spin. Now nearly in my fifties, years of abuse on the clock, the head-over-heels tumble down the grassy hillside rattled every bone in my body, pummelled my limbs and chest, dislodged my spectacles from my pocket, and left me crumpled and panting and wanting to throw up.

I lay still, eyes closed, and waited for the whirlpool of pain and nausea to resolve itself into something more specific, like a broken rib or wrist.

When, minutes later, I sat up gingerly to find that nothing seemed to be fractured or twisted, and I wasn't going to be sick, I also found Kim.

She sat nearby, staring up the slope with an expression of such wretchedness that I immediately turned my head, grimacing at the ache in my neck, to follow her gaze.

There was nothing to see except grassy hillside. And that, of course, was the problem.

The elevator had opened its doors, spat us out and promptly disappeared, leaving us stranded once more in a place we had both visited before and had never wanted to visit again.

I didn't need to look around to confirm where we were, but there was another reason I had to see our surroundings. A reason that was making the hairs on my neck prickle and my stomach tighten into a ball of dread.

Heaving myself upright, ignoring complaints from creaking bones and bruised muscles, I turned about. Here was the river, as brown and languid as in my memory; there the object-strewn piece of waste ground we had christened 'the killing field'; beyond it the dark backdrop of thick forest. That's where my attention fixed, scanning the trees for movement, for signs that *he* knew we had once more entered his domain.

Nothing moved. *Yet.* I turned back to Kim to say something, but she didn't give me chance.

"You fucking retard!" She half-rose and, in the same movement, took off towards me, screaming into my face.

"Shh!" I hissed desperately, my eyes swivelling to the forest.

Then she was on me, battering my already-bruised chest with her fists. I went down under the onslaught, falling to my back onto the grassy slope. Kim followed me down, her face twisted into a grotesque mask of incandescent rage, and sat astride my hips.

"You *fucking… fucking… fucking…*"

Each curse was accompanied by a two-handed thump to my chest. Spit sprayed onto my face. The air was battered from me afresh and I felt I was suffocating, unable to draw breath. Yet I didn't raise my arms to try to ward off the blows; simply lay there and let her work out her anger on me. It was much less than I deserved.

"… *fucking… fucking… cunt!*"

Kim could swear and cuss with the best of them, but she had always drawn the line at that word, and I'm not sure who was more shocked by her use of it now. She froze, staring down at me through tangled hair with hate-filled eyes. Then something faded from them. She slumped to one side, onto her knees, bowed her head and began to sob in great, heaving gulps.

Once more I lay on the ground trying to catch my breath, waiting for pain to become bearable. When it had, I sat up and reached out to her shoulder. She didn't shake my hand off.

"I'm sorry." I knew it wasn't enough, could never be adequate, but was all I had.

I waited a little longer, for her sobbing to lose its power, all the while shooting anxious glances at the forest. I squeezed her shoulder and let go, fumbled at my pocket for spectacles so I'd be able to see the line of trees more clearly, but the case containing the spectacles had gone.

"Kim, we have to get moving. We can't just sit here and wait for *him* to turn up."

She drew in a last shuddering sob and turned her head towards me, raising a hand to brush away hair. "Where do you suggest we go, Einstein?"

For once I was glad of the dismissive contempt in her expression and tone. At least it showed that she was now capable of considering our predicament.

"We have to cross the river," I said. "On the raft. Last time we were here he said that if any of us returned, we would all have to cross. He called it a task that we would all have to complete if we came back. Do you remember?"

"I remember. You don't have a monopoly on bad dreams about that day, you know."

It had never occurred to me that Kim could be troubled by

nightmares about our jaunt in the Elevator. After all, she hadn't glimpsed the true face of the monk. Still, I realised at last and, as usual, too late, we had experienced enough horrors during that endless day to provide material for a lifetime of night terrors.

Kim stood. She stuck out a foot and poked at something lying in the grass nearby. I, too, stood, a little gingerly, and looked down at the object. It was dark and angular and suggested it might have once been box-shaped before its sides had collapsed. Grass had grown to cover its base and moss or mould greened the visible surfaces that remained.

"What's that?" I asked, though part of me already knew.

"Tara's document case. Or what's left of it."

"Huh. Wonder how she explained losing that to herself. Tricky to misplace something that size in a mere dream."

"Do you know," said Kim, glancing at me with a strange expression, "I don't give a flying frig whether Tara has spent the past twenty-three years convincing herself that it was all a fantasy." She, too, glanced towards the forest. "If we're going to go, let's get going. I have no desire to see those freaking dolphins come waddling after me again."

She turned and began to walk towards the river. With a last glance at the forest, I followed close behind.

Four

There's something about a doctor's waiting room that strikes fear into the stoutest heart. Dental reception areas are bad enough with their faux cheeriness and faint sounds of high-pitched drills and suction devices, but waiting to see a physician, when you suspect she is about to confirm your worst fears, takes some beating on the anxiety-inducing scale.

I had felt unwell for months; not merely the effects of repeatedly, for days at a stretch, consuming too much hard liquor, but a sickness that went far deeper, more consequential than a series of severe hangovers.

Fatigue, swelling in my abdomen and legs, a yellow discolouration in the corners of my eyes; too faint for Kim to have noticed yet, but it would soon enough become obvious if it progressed at its current rate. I had lost all appetite for sex—there's a sentence I never thought I'd say. Not that the opportunity for such activity presented itself any more, but that was fine by me since I wasn't in the least bit interested. I cut myself on the lid of a can—yes, I was drunk—and blood poured from the shallow wound like I had nicked an artery. There are more symptoms, lots of smaller ones, but that's enough to be getting on with. They were enough for me to, eventually, rouse myself into taking advantage of my father-in-law's generosity in continuing my health insurance.

The family doctor tutted and nodded, poked and prodded, listened and peered, before referring me to a hepatologist. More of the same followed, accompanied by kneading and needles and scans. Then she called me back for the test results.

Her waiting room was tastefully decorated and furnished. Muted lighting, soothing colours on the walls, relaxing background music. The periodicals available on the tablets were current and varied, though I was in no mood to read while I waited. I sat with my hands clenched in my lap, trying to avoid making eye contact with the efficient but overly-familiar receptionist.

"You may go in now, Matthew… Mr Grayson?"

"Huh? Oh, yeah, thanks."

The walk through to the consulting room took place on legs which had become unaccountably heavy. A sense of doom had settled over me like a black cloud; maybe it's how death row convicts feel while they take their last steps to the execution chamber. My mood wasn't lifted when I saw the hepatologist's expression.

At least she seemed, unlike some doctors, genuinely sympathetic. I wish I could remember her name, but it escapes me, much like the details of that final consultation. Only snatches remain, snippets, phrases.

'Deterioration'—that was a word she employed frequently. Occasionally it was prefixed by 'rapid'. 'Alcohol over-indulgence' was her favourite phrase. Strange that she avoided the words 'abuse' or 'misuse' as though afraid to hurt my feelings. There were some big words, medical terms I couldn't hope to remember, let alone spell, though in fairness to her she did her best to explain them in layman's terms.

The trouble was, I wasn't particularly receptive. A rushing sound had begun inside my head, much the same effect as would be achieved by thrusting your head into a running stream. It blocked out most of what she said. Whenever she paused, I nodded or muttered something to make it appear I had been listening attentively. When she started talking about evaluations and donors and waiting lists, I shook my head firmly and rose to my feet, causing her to look so nonplussed I almost felt sorry for her. I thanked her politely and formally, and walked out of there. I haven't been back since. The couple of voicemails I received from her I deleted unheard. The couple of items of mail I deleted unopened.

Not even news like that could make me quit the devil's juice. *Fuck it* I thought *we all got to die of something, right? Might as well be from something that gives you pleasure.*

But I was kidding myself, as part of me well knew. Drinking hadn't brought me pleasure since I was in my mid-twenties, when I enjoyed nothing more than a few beers with my mates down the local. I had graduated from social to serious drinker, without passing through any intermediary stages. The lush who drinks to forget. I had become, virtually overnight, the broken man who enlists with the Foreign Legion, except that I wasn't trying to escape the memory of a woman who'd shattered my heart.

It took the coffin case—a freaking suitcase, for chrissake!—to make me want to do something about it. Not that I *wanted* to stop drinking, you understand, not even then, but I very much wanted to spend my last days with Kim and Sam.

My last days. Yep, my condition was that serious. No treatment short of a liver transplant would prolong my remaining time. And in case you're wondering why I didn't agree to at least undergo an evaluation to deem my suitability for transplantation, it's because I'm not deserving. That's not being melodramatic or fishing for sympathy or a medal. It's brutal self-honesty, something I've not always been capable of demonstrating. Even had I joined the waiting list for a transplant, had successfully undergone the procedure, if my body hadn't rejected the new organ, I would have continued to drink.

Remember I mentioned retaining a degree of selflessness? Well, that one quality I've fought tooth-and-nail to retain came good while I sat in that consulting room being told I was going to die without a transplant. The knowledge that I would continue to pour poison down my throat no matter what is the thing that made me walk out of there without looking back.

One of the snatches of medical monologue I recall is that the symptoms would accelerate drastically towards the end. Soon my skin would grow appreciably grey; my physique would become that of a starving man, with gaunt, wasted features and a distended belly; my thought processes would become muddled. These symptoms and more were already showing, but not to the extent that Kim and Sam, who saw me most days, would notice. I've a feeling that Jack had guessed something was amiss, judging from the appraising glances he shot my way while we talked on the jetty in Nowhere and he thought I wasn't looking. Soon my family, too, would see beyond the inebriated mess; it would become apparent even to them that I was seriously ill.

The doctor mentioned six to nine months as the best-case prognosis without a transplant. That was seven months ago.

A growing sense of dread seemed to have come over everyone aboard the raft. People shuffled their feet like jittery horses, cast glances at each other with wide eyes and thin lips, muttered snatches of unintelligible words to themselves. Some closed their eyes, mouths moving silently in prayer.

The jetty drew ever nearer; the gap couldn't have been more than twenty yards by now. My view of the embankment was growing clearer by the second.

The group of people at the point of the path furthest from the jetty continued to struggle and issue cries of pain and fear and anger; the reedy whistling grew louder and louder the closer to shore we came. Yet the crowd of creatures with which the people were engaged in what sounded like deadly combat remained indistinct. I should have been able to separate figures amidst the crowd, but it was as if they were cast in a glamour, a spell of illusion that masked their true nature. As it was, all I saw from the deck of the raft was a shifting, seething mass, like a bunch of folk stamping on dry, earthy ground so that they become enshrouded in a dusty cloud which prevents an onlooker picking out individuals.

My gaze drifted away from the melee. Beyond the path where the embankment widened, at the edge of the patch of bracken which ran inland to the grassy area, stood a solitary figure, turned towards the path to watch the fighting. A hooded, cloaked, plump figure.

My memory had not let me down; he did look for all the world like a portly monk, in the Friar Tuck mode. I was too far away to make out facial features, even had he been facing my way, but I knew that the baggy cowl concealed a florid, jowly face wearing a sly smile beneath piggy eyes. Inhuman eyes, the colour of buffed silver. Behind the thin lips lay crooked, rotting teeth, floating in suppurating gums. Flies buzzed and maggots crawled about his head, his person, his robes. He gave off a stench like a three-day-old corpse left out in the sun.

Although I had steeled myself to see him once more, had been trying to psyche myself up since learning that we would have to recross the river, my resolve faltered at the last. It was one thing to contemplate setting eyes on that hated figure, quite another to actually gaze upon him. What meagre shreds remained of my courage deserted me as utterly and rapidly as air escaping a burst balloon.

With an effort made easier by no longer having to pretend to be brave, I tore my gaze away from the Lord of the Dance and sank to the deck on my knees.

I must have made a sound, perhaps a keening to rival the noises reaching us from ashore, since people standing nearby edged away until I knelt in bare space on the deck. A circle of isolation and terror and helplessness.

Not completely helpless.

Barely aware of anything except an overwhelming sensation of crushing horror, I fumbled once more for Nadine's flask and glugged hard. And again. And again. I lowered the flask, empty, and dropped it behind me into the water.

Gulping and swallowing hard to quell the urge to vomit— losing the precious load of oblivion-bringing alcohol would be disastrous—I bowed my head and waited.

It didn't take long since I had topped up, and then some, what was already there. Dark swirls of insensibility rose to envelop me and I met them with a smile on my face.

Jack

*Will you, won't you, will you,
won't you, will you join the dance?*

—Lewis Carroll (*Alice in Wonderland*)

Part 1: The Near Shore

One

Coming face to face with an ageing Matt and Kim took Jack a little while to become accustomed to. He had lived through many bizarre events of late, and this was simply one more, yet it felt more personal.

It had been no time since he'd left them and Tara on the river bank, gazing after him as he pulled away until the mist swallowed him. They had been clear-eyed and youthful, uncreased and unbowed by the accumulated cares of middle age. A week later, or thereabouts, and they were sitting in front of him on the jetty, wrinkling and sagging, talking about their teenage son. Matt had said something about them naming the child after him, but Jack didn't want to think about that. Some shit was simply too bizarre to contemplate.

Like time itself. Jack found that his mind still skirted around the notion of meeting people from the distant past and more distant future, as though it couldn't fully cope with time being such a mutable concept without endangering his sanity, so dealt with it by mainly ignoring it.

Kim wore middle-age better than Matt. She had been a little on the plump side last time he'd seen her, but appeared now as a confident-looking, well-dressed woman who carried a few extra pounds with such assurance that they seemed to form an essential and natural part of who she was. The lines around her eyes and mouth suited her, suggesting crinkles brought on by laughter rather than care, though Jack did not doubt she had plenty to be care-worn about.

While they talked, his gaze kept being drawn to Matt and he studied him whenever Matt's attention was elsewhere. Gone was the bullish character from the Elevator jaunt. In its place a bowed, beaten man frequently wearing expressions of bewilderment or shooting glances of resentment at Kim. And there were small signs that all was not well with him physically: dark, sunken circles about the eyes; a paleness, a tinge of greyness, to his pallor; occasional tremors in his hands and legs, like the early onset of Parkinson's. When Matt volunteered that he was an alcoholic, it hadn't come as a shock. The past twenty-three years had clearly not been kind to him.

Hardly surprising Jack thought *after what the poor sod saw that day.*

Jack hadn't much liked Matt last week; had been a little afraid of him. More than once he had feared Matt was about to thump him. It therefore came as much of a surprise to himself as it must have to Matt when he spoke up in Matt's defence.

He had meant what he'd told Kim: maybe he, too, would have turned to alcohol in Matt's shoes. Matt wasn't the only one to have glimpsed the true face of the entity they were striving to cross the river to confront.

As the morning wore on he grew more and more impatient, casting frequent glances at the chain, willing it to begin to shake and quiver to signify Frankie's return. His hand kept returning to Miriam, to rest upon her cool exterior, to reassure himself she was still there, and he had to work hard to tamp down the mounting frustration at being so close to being able to converse with her again, yet so far.

There came one awkward moment during their conversation when Nadine mentioned his full name; his *new* full name. Jack didn't miss the look that passed between Kim and Matt—they knew his surname hadn't been Bruder. Jack felt himself colour and hurried the conversation along. To their credit, neither Kim nor Matt embarrassed him further by questioning it.

Then, after what felt like hours, but was probably little more than one, the chain began to move.

He and Nadine stood at the front edge of the raft for the return trip. Jack clutched Miriam tightly, finding some measure of comfort by merely touching her handle. His stomach churned with a mixture of excitement and dread; such had been his constant state since the meeting in Tumble Down, now doubled in intensity.

He had seen it in Matt's eyes and, like him, had no desire to come within the monk's presence again. Nevertheless, if that is what it took to reactivate Miriam and find out what the hell was going on, so be it.

Kim came and stood by them. Without Matt. Jack raised his eyebrows.

"He's at the back," she said. "I didn't think he was going to get on, but he made it. Just."

"So you two have a son, huh?" Jack would not have believed Matt if he'd said that he saw certain changes in Jack, a maturity that he had acquired almost overnight, but one thing hadn't changed: his ability to make small talk was still largely non-existent. Although he didn't want to think about a kid being named after him, he had provided Kim with the opportunity to mention it again.

Kim nodded. "His name's Sam—short for Samuel." She shot Jack a glance he couldn't read. "His middle name's Jack. Matt insisted."

"That's weird."

"Not really. Matt's convinced you saved our lives. Did you, Jack? Would we have died if you hadn't crossed the river?"

Jack shrugged. "Unless one of you was prepared to cross, and that wasn't about to happen, we would have been forced to fight his 'creatures of the forest'. There was only one likely outcome if that had happened."

"'Creatures of the forest'… I'd forgotten that's what he called them. Makes them sound like a bunch of cute woodland critters out of an old Disney cartoon." She shuddered. "They were anything but cute." She laid a hand on Jack's arm and squeezed before letting go. "Thank you for what you did."

Jack felt a growing sense of discomfort; he needed to disabuse her of a notion. "Don't go thinking I did it to save your skins. That didn't cross my mind. My reasons were purely selfish."

Kim glanced down at the case in his hand. "And you seem to have found what you were looking for."

Jack's eyes widened; he hadn't thought of it quite like that. "Huh. Um, yeah, I suppose you're right. I had no life to speak of back home, there was nothing for me to return to in the Elevator so crossing the river was a no-brainer." He, too, glanced down at the silvery case. "When we met Miriam on the Second Floor of Claridge House and then had to leave her, I wanted nothing more than to meet her again and become part of the world she came from. Not that I imagined I'd encounter her again by fulfilling the monk's task, but whatever lay on this side of the river had to be better than going back. It had sod all to do with saving anyone's life, except perhaps my own."

"Well," said Kim, "don't tell Matt that. You've become his hero since that elevator trip, though he didn't much like you then."

"Neither did you."

Kim didn't blush or drop her gaze, and Jack admired her a little for her honesty. "That's true. In fact, I thought you were as irritating as a hornet at a picnic." She shrugged. "A long passage of time can alter a person's perspective."

"A long passage of time can alter more than perspective. You've not actually changed that much in twenty-odd years, Kim. But I barely recognised Matt."

Kim's expression darkened. "That's what twenty-three years of alcohol abuse looks like. Intermittent, but more on than off."

"He's not well," said Nadine. She had been following their conversation with apparent interest, but now joined in for the first time. Jack nodded to himself; so she, too, had noticed that Matt appeared ill.

Kim looked at her. "How d'you mean?"

"I am not a doctor," said Nadine, "and I hope I do not speak out of turn, but I know the symptoms of most of the serious diseases affecting the major organs. It's information we can't help but pick up in the laboratory where I work."

"Serious disease?" said Kim. "Are you saying Matt has one?"

"Has he seen a doctor?" asked Nadine.

"No. Leastways, not that he's told me."

"His outward symptoms are mild at the moment. You would not notice them if you are with him every day unless you know what to look for. The yellowing in the corner of his eyes... It has a name that I can't recall in English."

"Jaundice?" suggested Kim.

"Yes, that is it. His stomach is distended and his skin is growing pale. He is losing weight."

"Is he? I thought he was putting weight on. That's... yes, it's because I *have* noticed his belly growing and assumed it was because of all the liquor."

"It is, in a way," said Nadine. "But it's more likely fluid retention than fat. I would guess that he has a problem with his liver. Many of the symptoms suggest cirrhosis."

"Cirrhosis?" Kim's eyes grew wide. "That's kind of serious, isn't it?"

"It can be," agreed Nadine. "He must see a doctor when you return home."

Kim fell silent, biting her lip and casting thoughtful glances to the back of the raft towards Matt.

Jack wanted to ask a question, a personal one, but he felt hesitant. The bank of fog was looming ahead and he suspected if he didn't ask now he might not get another chance.

"Tell me, Kim," he said, "if you don't mind, why have you stuck by him all this time?"

A flash of annoyance showed in her eyes, reminding Jack of the sassy young woman from the Elevator. "I ought to tell you to mind your goddamned business," she said, "but I suppose I at least owe you that."

"Nope," said Jack. "You have to get over that shit. You don't owe me anything."

"Nevertheless, I'll tell you. Aside from the fact that he's my son's father, he can be sweet and considerate and kind and loving. He's also the most vulnerable person I know. Leaving him would be like abandoning a puppy. Still, it's at the point of make or break. I might yet leave him if we get out of this." She glanced at Nadine.

"Though if what you say is correct, it would be like abandoning a sick puppy."

All three fell silent as the raft slipped into the fog and their world became shifting, damp and grey.

Jack experienced a tingling sensation, but couldn't be sure if it was from the fog or his heightened sense of trepidation, mixed with a fair-sized dollop of excitement.

Frankie spoke, telling everyone what they might need to do when they arrived. He said that Miriam could send them all back to the time and place from which they had come, though he kept referring to her as 'the module'. For a reason that he couldn't explain even to himself, this irritated Jack and he felt compelled to correct Frankie.

"She's called Miriam," he said.

Frankie had the good grace to so refer to her after that, which sat better with Jack, though again he could not have explained why.

For Pete's sake, what difference does it make what anyone calls her? he chided himself. But it mattered in the same way that it mattered to most people how others referred to them. *George was right. Names have power. Look what happened when I said my name is Bruder.*

The thought of the lame investment banker from 1920s New York got Jack wondering whether he'd made it back to the Manhattan blizzard from which he'd been plucked by the Lord of the Dance. He tapped his pocket to double-check that the box of matches George had given him before limping out to meet the Scourgers had vanished. It had, as completely as the cut to Jack's forearm inflicted by the banker's knife.

But that wouldn't happen where they were heading, he reminded himself. Get injured on the near shore and when you woke up the next day, the injury wouldn't have disappeared overnight as if by magic; get killed, and you wouldn't be transported back to the grotty town and shitty job you'd been glad to leave.

Where they were headed, they would be playing for keeps. Jack gripped Miriam tighter and looked out at the thinning fog, waiting for his first glimpse of shore.

Two

The fog lifted and the near shore emerged into view. Nadine's fingers found Jack's and gripped them tightly. He squeezed back. Since the meeting in Tumble Down, they had spoken little about why it was so important that they both reached the opposite side of the river and what might happen when they did; they had too little to go on and their speculation usually petered out into head-scratching silences.

Standing at the front of the raft, Jack had an uninterrupted view of the river bank. It did not present a pretty sight. A struggle between two masses was taking place at the farther end of the path which led from the jetty. Cries and screams and a scratchy, whistling sound reached Jack's ears.

Even with his sharp eyesight, Jack struggled to make out the more distant mass of struggling bodies. The nearest one consisted of the advance party which had accompanied Frankie across the river the first time. The far one resembled an indistinct blob, giving an impression of being made up of separate figures, whilst not allowing any individual to be seen clearly.

Beyond the masses, in solitary watchfulness, stood the unmistakable figure of the Lord of the Dance. Jack involuntarily clenched his fist tighter, drawing a hiss of pain from Nadine.

"Sorry." He squeezed her hand more gently and let it go. "I had a bit of a jolt seeing him again."

Kim turned her head to address him. Her face looked pale. "We mustn't let Matt get anywhere near the monk. It'll destroy him." She peered beyond Jack, searching for her husband, but whether her gaze found him or not she didn't say.

The raft steadily drew nearer, until the distance to the shore had been halved.

Frankie again spoke, about Jack and Nadine being the last to disembark and how everyone else must keep the monk's minions away from them while Jack reactivated Miriam. People on the raft were clearly terrified. Jack didn't need to look around to see their drawn expressions and agitated stances; he could hear it in the anxious mutterings and in the quavering voices that questioned Frankie and their ability to fight, and bemoaned their paucity of weapons. Yet Jack knew where weapons could be found.

"The killing field," he said in a voice loud enough for everyone to hear. "There are swords and knives lying on the ground. They are rusty but will be better than bare hands."

The jetty loomed larger. Still Jack could not make out the separate figures forming the mass against which people from Nowhere fought. In a low voice, he commented as much to Nadine.

She shook her head. "I cannot make them out either. It is like they are shrouded in a spell that conceals them."

"The monk watches them," said Jack. "Perhaps he casts a spell."

"At the very least, he controls them. Like the Scourgers, they are a part of him."

A commotion broke out somewhere from the back of the raft; a shuffling of feet and the scuffling movement of people pressing forwards. Jack ignored it. The jetty was only yards away.

The front edge of the raft bumped gently against the jetty and came to a smooth halt. Jack had braced himself to be jerked, but barely swayed. He instinctively went to step off, but Nadine grabbed his arm and tugged him to one side.

"No, Jack, we must be the last ones to disembark."

"Oh, yeah. Sorry."

He watched Kim take a tentative step onto the jetty. She glanced back again before making her way to the narrow embankment beyond the jetty to make room for everyone else to disembark.

Jack had never been one to feel guilty for what others did for him, mainly because no one had ever done much for him. But now he experienced an alien sensation, a sense of discomfort that he was hanging back while others went to face danger on his behalf. He had never felt so much as a flicker of guilt during their jaunt on the Elevator when he'd hardly set foot outside while the others, usually prompted by Matt, explored their new environments. But then he had considered Matt's forays into the worlds they'd visited as foolhardy and not something he needed to do to benefit his companions. What was happening now was vastly different.

"This doesn't sit well with me," he muttered to Nadine as people began to shuffle past them onto the jetty.

She looked at him and he was surprised to see what looked like joy in her face. Her hand slipped back into his and she squeezed so hard it made him hiss.

"I would like you much less if it did," she said. She leaned forward and planted a hot kiss on his lips. Jack was transported back to the path that circled Tumble Down, to the moment she had first kissed him and he had felt that he was softening inside like plastic placed too close to a flame. It was a feeling he would gladly come to know well.

They broke apart and watched the people leave the raft. It didn't take long; there seemed a pitifully low number of them.

Frankie came last, or so Jack thought. "Come on then, you two," he said. He jerked his head towards the rear of the raft. "There's still one left, but I'm afraid he'll be of no help."

Jack looked to where Frankie had indicated. A still figure knelt on the deck, slumped so far forward his forehead rested on the wooden boards as though engaged in devout prayer, arms huddled beneath his torso. A damp patch extended from around where the figure's mouth must be, too small to suggest vomit but rather that he had dribbled copiously.

"Shit!" muttered Jack. "It's Matt."

Jack glanced ashore to see if he could spot Kim, but there were too many people milling about. He hesitated for only a moment before holding out Miriam to Nadine.

"Will you take her and wait on the jetty for me?"

Nadine frowned, but said nothing and took the case from Jack. He felt a pang of anxiety to allow Miriam out of his possession, although he only intended it to be for a few moments.

He nodded to Frankie. "Help me with him."

Frankie had been about to step off the raft. He shot a questioning glance at Jack. "He'll be about as much use as salt in a fanberry stew… Er, never mind, that's a Terra Three saying." He nodded in exasperation at the prone figure of Matt. "Look at him, Jack. He's out of it."

"I can see that. But we can't leave him here on his own. What if the raft takes off again? Or if he comes around and falls into the river? Or if any of the monk's creatures make it this far?" He shook his head and started towards Matt. "We can't just leave him. We can't."

Jack heard Frankie sigh and follow him.

He reached Matt and knelt by his side. A sharp smell came from him. A pungent, familiar odour. Jack looked around but couldn't see Nadine's canteen. He glanced up at Frankie.

"He's blotto."

Frankie's face crinkled in bemusement.

"You know," said Jack, "plastered, paralytic, rat-arsed, pissed. They *do* have alcohol on Terra Three?"

Frankie's puzzled expression cleared. "Ah, sozzled."

Jack nodded impatiently. "As far as I can tell, he's drunk the entire contents of Nadine's canteen. It contained fermented berry juice that George gave us. That stuff's lethal." He sighed. "Nothing for it but to carry him ashore. Help me get him up."

Jack grabbed Matt's nearest arm and pulled it out from under his body so that he could slide his arm underneath it. Frankie went to the other side of Matt and did the same.

Feverish, clammy heat and an unpleasant smell, mixed with the sharp odour of fermented berries, came off Matt in waves. Jack swallowed and tried not to breathe through his nose.

He and Frankie nodded at each other and heaved at the same time. With a lurch and a stumble—forwards not backwards or they'd have ended up in the river—they yanked Matt to his feet.

He moaned and his eyes flickered open. He mumbled something that sounded like, "Guster gunk," and his head flopped to his chest. Clear, stringy fluid dribbled from his chin onto his shirt. He had not, however, completely lost consciousness; his legs, though unsteady, partly supported his weight. Jack and Frankie, acting in concert, were able to half-drag, half-support Matt onto the jetty.

Kim was coming towards them. She stopped dead when she saw the state on her husband. Jack and Frankie manoeuvred him to one of the thick wooden posts that supported the rails which formed the sides of the jetty and lowered him to the floor in a sitting position, his back propped against the post.

"He should be all right by there," said Jack, relieved to be free of the hot, smelly burden. "That lower rail should prevent him rolling into the water if he starts moving about."

Kim knelt by Matt and poked him not too gently in his chest. His head lolled and he mumbled something else incoherent, but didn't open his eyes.

She straightened, lips pressed into a thin line. "He's fucking wasted."

Alcohol had only featured briefly in Jack's days of addiction. He hadn't enjoyed the taste of it much, only the buzz it provided, though he'd soon become frustrated by how long that could take to achieve and he couldn't stand the hangovers. Alcohol had quickly been supplanted by illicit substances, with their immediate effects, their lack of hangovers (though coming down from a high was nearly as bad) and, depending on how they were ingested, their tastebud-neutrality.

He'd since sipped unenthusiastically at the occasional beer when trying to be sociable with work colleagues, but never more than two in one sitting, ignoring their sideways glances at him as though he was some sort of freak for not wanting to join in with them and drink until he couldn't speak or stand. He'd usually make some excuse to leave before they began to be openly insulting towards him or to strangers, usually young women, who happened to be in the same pub. It was always a relief to escape their company, with their jargon-loaded debates about the relative values of the latest competing software, and inane banter. It didn't take long for them to stop asking him to join them down the pub. Jack didn't mind in the slightest; in his opinion, they were a bunch of wankers.

Despite his unfamiliarity with consuming large volumes of alcohol, he of course knew that they needed to get non-alcoholic liquid into Matt as quickly as possible. If it made him throw up, so much the better if, at the same time, it expelled some of the excess alcohol. While they were fresh out of strong black coffee, they had the next best thing.

He called to the people newly disembarked from the raft; they continued to mill about as though waiting for instructions. "Does anyone have some water they can spare?"

Anna, the young girl from Eastern Europe, stepped shyly forward and held out a bulging hide canteen. Jack took it from her with a nod of thanks and, in turn, offered it to Kim. She regarded it doubtfully before reluctantly taking it from him.

"Good thinking," said Frankie. He turned to Kim. "Try to get some of that down him. We can't waste any more time on him." He indicated the people on the bank. "I need to sort this mob into some sort of attacking formation." He looked anxiously along the path.

From where they stood on the jetty, they could only see the back of the advance group. The people there were crushed into the narrow space, those at the rear unable to do much except press into their comrades in front to try to force them onwards. Without a great deal of success, it appeared, for they were not making any ground. The cries and screams and whistling noises sounded much louder now. The faces of the new arrivals next to the jetty looked pale and pinched; some held their hands to their ears to try to block out the sounds.

"They need help," said Frankie. "It doesn't look as if things are going our way." He glanced at Jack. "And you'd better get to doing what you need to do."

Aside from trying to reactivate Miriam, Jack wasn't at all sure what he needed to do, but nodded anyway.

Frankie made for the embankment, his bearing almost militarily straight, making up for what he lacked in stature with sheer determination.

Jack turned to Kim. She was holding the water flask gingerly as if it, or the task she was to perform with it, was something repugnant.

"Kim? Will you take care of Matt?"

Her lips remained pressed into a tight line and she spoke through gritted teeth. "I guess someone has to. I guess that someone has to be me. After all, I'm married to the worthless piece of shit."

Jack opened his mouth to say something conciliatory; maybe something like, "Try to go easy on him, he's had a tough time," then closed it again. After all, who was he to advise a wife on how to treat her husband? She had lived with this man for the past twenty-three years, watched him drink his health away, had a child with him for goodness' sake, while he, Jack, had spent a week or two traipsing around a strange land without ageing by more than a day. It would be a little like him offering advice to Eric Clapton on how to play the guitar.

He merely nodded and went in search of Nadine.

Three

She stood waiting for Jack beyond the jetty. A bare patch of ground formed a rough rectangle bounded by steep slopes on two sides, the start of the path and the jetty forming the other sides. She had moved to the right, away from the path, where it was clearest, and clutched Miriam's handle in both hands, holding the case in front of her like a casually attired businesswoman attending a conference. On seeing Jack's approach, her lips turned up briefly into a smile which didn't reach her eyes.

"How is Matt?" she asked.

"Not good," he replied, sounding more terse than he'd meant to.

Nadine didn't seem to notice. She kept glancing at the people nearby. Frankie stood with them, addressing them in a voice a little too quiet for them to make out the words—there was too much background noise with the yells and whistles coming from the path. Besides, Jack was no longer paying attention to Frankie.

He was gazing so intently at the silvery attaché case that Nadine glanced down. She started, almost dropping the case. Jack reached out and gently took it from her.

Lights winked and danced across the surface of the case. Miriam had awoken.

Jack took a few paces back towards the jetty and perched on its edge. Kim was bent over Matt, who didn't look like he'd moved since they'd left him propped up against the rail post. Jack sat with his back to them and placed Miriam on his lap. Nadine stood and watched, a tense expression on her face.

Jack could sympathise. His heart raced and his palms felt slick with sweat. He took a deep breath.

"Miriam?" he began. "It's Jack. We've arrived on the near shore of the river. But I guess you know that already seeing that you've reactivated."

The lights on the case's smooth surface stopped winking and settled into a steady pattern; not in a regular shape like a hexagon but irregularly spaced. They pulsed gently.

Jack waited.

"Miriam?"

He waited some more.

Nadine's tense expression had given way to a pinched, worried look, bottom lip tucked between her teeth, eyes as brown as the river and almost as wide.

The lights on the case continued to pulse steadily, all in the same rhythm, growing brighter then dimming, as though in time to a sleeping heartbeat.

"Miriam? Please talk to us. It's Jack. And Nadine. We're waiting. We don't know what we're supposed to do."

The lights didn't change; no voice spoke.

Jack looked at Nadine. "What now?"

Kim joined them, slumping down onto the edge of the jetty with a heavy sigh. Jack placed Miriam carefully down on the planking by his side and turned to her.

"How's Matt doing?"

Kim pulled a face. "Sleeping it off." She looked past him at the case. "Pretty lights. Is that all it does?"

"Apparently so, for the moment." Jack frowned. "All we had to do, we thought, was bring her to this side of the river and then she'd reactivate and start running the show. She *has* reactivated, but all she's done so far is blink and pulse. She hasn't said a word."

"Maybe Frankie will know," said Nadine. "I shall ask him to come."

Jack glanced at where Frankie and the other people who'd crossed with him stood. It looked like their impromptu meeting was breaking up.

Most of them were coming back towards the jetty. Frankie and four others—the younger and thicker-set of those in their party, Jack noted—had turned in the other direction, towards the fighting.

"Better be quick," he told Nadine. "Looks like he's leaving."

Nadine nodded and hurried away.

The returning group reached the wider area by the jetty; Nadine had to push past them, but some sense of urgency must have shown in her expression for they parted to let her through without her having to say anything.

Jack noticed Anna amongst them and beckoned to her.

"What's happening?" he asked when she stood before him.

She twitched her head in that sparrow-like way and wrung her hands together. "We are to stand guard," she said. "In case they come over the hill."

Jack looked past her. The other people had spread themselves around the end of the path beyond the jetty. They stood and faced up the slopes, shooting nervous glances at each other.

"Good idea," he said to Anna. "If you see anything, shout and we'll come."

She nodded. Before she turned to join the others, she glanced at Miriam. "I would very much like to see Papa once more. And Ilina. She is my sister."

Jack said nothing. Until he knew what was happening, he didn't want to build anyone's hopes. He glanced down the path. Nadine had reached Frankie and they were engaged in conversation. The four other people stood waiting for him.

"I hope that you will soon be reunited with them," said Kim.

Anna smiled and moved away.

"Bless her," said Kim. "But tell me, Jack, because I'm struggling to understand. How can a machine, no matter how intelligent, move people back to their own time and place?"

Jack shrugged. "Search me. Fourth Millennium technology, I guess."

"I don't buy it. If time travel becomes possible, where in our own time are the travellers from the future? It's inconceivable that at no point during our lifetimes not even one has turned up."

"It's not time travel, though. At least, not how we think of it.

Frankie said it was to do with all time and space existing here so it's not about moving people forward or backward in time, but sideways. It's like being on a train on a circular line. A four-dimensional line, where any time and any place can be accessed. It's a matter of stopping the train at the right where and the right when. They must have sussed out how to do that."

"Hmm. Let's hope you're right. These people seem to have their hearts set on returning to their homes. If Miriam can't deliver…" She let the thought hang.

Jack's thoughts had been following similar lines. He had only lived amongst these people for a short time, had not got to know any of them well, with the possible exception of Nadine, yet was experiencing feelings he had never known before: camaraderie, a sense of belonging to a group sharing a commonality. In short, a community. A community of misplaced souls, maybe, but a community nonetheless.

A feeling had been growing in him since they had begun their trek from Tumble Down to the river. A sense of responsibility towards this motley bunch of misfits had taken hold, although he had failed to recognise it for that. Until now.

He watched Nadine and Frankie. The latter was talking animatedly to the four people waiting for him. There was quite a bit of gesticulating and shaking of heads; a few shoulders sagged. Then the four turned and began to move disconsolately along the path in the direction of the fighting. Frankie stood and stared after them for a moment, looking as if he was having to force himself not to join them, before he returned to Nadine. Together, they came back towards the jetty.

Jack stood as Nadine and Frankie approached. Already skinny to the point of gauntness, Frankie's face had become drawn and pale; he shot anxious glances back along the path. He breathed out heavily when he reached Jack.

"Talk about feeling torn in two," he said. "Those people are engaged in combat because I said it is what they must do. The least I can do is stand by their side. Yet what you are doing is also of vital importance. More so."

"That's just it," said Jack. "I'm not doing anything." He nodded at the case. "Miriam's lights came on as soon as we arrived, but she hasn't said a word. She's been like that the whole time."

Frankie regarded the case thoughtfully. "She is making calculations. There wasn't time to brief me fully on how Miriam does what she does, but I learned enough to understand that to move you and Nadine to Geneva in the year 2176 requires a number of calculations that are extremely complex even for a machine of Miriam's processing capacity."

"So all we can do is wait?" asked Kim.

Frankie nodded.

"But," Kim continued, "if it takes a long time to work out how to send Jack and Nadine to Switzerland, she'll have to keep doing the same thing for everyone else who wants to return home?"

"Clearly, different calculations will be required, but I believe that the major complexity lies in mapping space and time as it exists here, which is what Miriam is currently engaged upon. Until she knows where the individual times and places are located here, she will be unable to move anyone to the corresponding time and place from which they originated. And she could not commence working on the problem until she was actually here. But once she has it mapped out, I understand that returning everyone to their own times and places becomes relatively straightforward. So, in answer to your question, although Miriam will need to perform a calculation for each person, it will be much quicker than the one she is currently working on."

Jack was only half-listening. He was gazing at Nadine, seeing something in her face that he couldn't quite read. He looked back at Frankie with a frown.

"What did you mean? If we can travel to anywhere and any-when from here, why do we have to go to Geneva? I want to see Terra Three."

Frankie didn't answer immediately, but looked at Nadine. She was still gazing at Jack and he was surprised to see her eyes glisten with moisture.

"If you want to go to Terra Three, Jack, I cannot come with you," she said.

Realisation hit Jack with the abruptness of a slap: he was woefully unprepared for the decisions he was shortly to have to make. In the absence of anything sensible to say, he resorted to hiding his sudden confusion behind an obvious question.

"Why can't you come with me?" he asked Nadine.

"My family. My friends. Many are in Geneva. All are in the year 2176." She gazed at him steadily from those brown eyes. The moisture in them magnified her pupils, made them glitter darkly like the eyes of a sorceress.

Another flash of clarity hit Jack.

"I want to go wherever you go," he said. As soon as the words were out, he knew they were true. That knowledge was enough to make his bewilderment about everything else melt away.

Nadine gave the slightest of nods.

Frankie cleared his throat and Jack, with an effort, tore his gaze away from Nadine.

"I'm glad that's resolved," said Frankie, "but I should probably tell you this anyway, Jack. You going anywhere other than accompanying Nadine to her time and place was never going to be an option." He held up a hand. "Don't ask me why because that I don't know. My understanding goes no further than this: it is vital for the future of humankind that you and Nadine go from here to Switzerland in the year 2176. Any other outcome will result in the timeline I come from being compromised, in all probability lost. The ensuing paradoxes will likely complete the monk's work for him."

Jack stared at him for a moment, his mind reeling in the way that it always did when he tried to get his head around the paradox of time travel. It was a concept he thought about occasionally; he'd be the first to admit that he possessed a geeky streak a mile wide. But it was Kim who spoke.

"Frankie, do you mean that if your present ceased to exist then you could not have come here with Miriam? And Miriam couldn't exist either because the timeline in which she was developed is no more. Then we couldn't have met her during our journey in the Elevator. And…" She tailed off, her brow crinkling in thought.

Frankie nodded. "It's true that we aren't engaged in time travel as the concept is usually understood, but the paradoxes that will be created are just as real and catastrophic if Jack and Nadine change the history of my timeline."

"Huh," said Jack. "Then tell me this, Frankie, because there are still questions to which you must know the answers, even if only in a general sense. How do you *know* it is so vital that me and Nadine must go to Geneva? And how the hell did you know that we were stranded in Nowhere?"

"Ah," said Frankie. "Your first question must wait to be answered by Miriam. As to your second, I wondered when it would occur to you to ask it. That I can answer. Or, rather, the answer lies over there." He nodded behind Jack.

Jack, Kim and Nadine all looked to where he'd indicated. All they could see was Matt, still slumped against the post, chin lolling on chest. He was snoring.

"Matt's the answer?" asked Kim, her tone mystified.

Frankie nodded. "And, to some extent, you."

Kim's mouth gaped wide.

Part 2: The Battle of the Riverbank

One

The lights on the face of the silvery attaché case continued to pulse steadily, but no voice came from it. Jack shot frequent glances at it to make sure nothing had changed.

Frankie shot frequent glances of his own, but along the path, from where came unabated the noises of small-scale battle.

"Since I could not go and see up-close for myself," he explained, "I've asked that someone from the front be sent back to report on what's happening up there. It's taking a while for anyone to come."

"While we're waiting, answer my question," said Jack; Kim grunted in agreement. "How did you know to find Nadine and I in Nowhere?"

"And what has this to do with Matt?" added Kim.

"Okay," said Frankie. He nodded at the case. "Jack insists on calling that module Miriam, but it's not really. It's substantially more advanced than the machine he, Kim and Matt encountered on Terra Two. Yet the memories of that earlier module are held by the one contained within the case. They include the recording of the encounter from the moment the module was activated by Jack's interaction with it."

Nadine raised an eyebrow in Jack's direction. He shrugged. "I gave it a shove."

"Indeed," said Frankie. "The recording of your encounter with Miriam on Terra Two does not end until she transferred her data packets to Terra Three where an updated model awaited to receive them."

"She's still Miriam," insisted Jack. "Updated, improved, yeah. But still Miriam."

"I won't argue, Jack. Miriam she shall be."

"What's your point?" said Kim, a sharp edge to her tone. Jack was once more reminded of the brassy younger version he had known not too long ago, at least not long ago in his past.

Frankie gave a rueful grin. "I was getting there, Miss Impatient. The point is that thanks to Miriam's recording of that encounter on Terra Two, we knew that a young man by the name of Jack from, to use your terms, the early twenty-first century on Earth had been on Terra Two for a brief period at the death of that planet. Remember, that took place two hundred years ago in the history of people from my time. But the event was believed to be of significance, even to our ancestors. Many people devoted much of the ensuing two centuries researching what it might mean."

"Why would my being on Terra Two be considered to be significant?" asked Jack. "Come to that, why would anything to do with me be significant? I'm nothing, no one."

"Oh, you might find that your importance in my history is inestimable, Jack Bruder. Miriam will explain more fully. But first I must tell you what little we know about the central figure in all this."

Jack could not begin to think how he played any part in Frankie's history, but believed he knew to whom Frankie was referring as the 'central figure'. "The Lord of the Dance?"

Frankie nodded.

"Our awareness of the monk," said Frankie, "although the idea of him taking the form of a monk only came much later, began back on Terra One. On Earth, during the final years before Yellowstone erupted. Of course, humanity has always had its representations of evil, the Devil being the most recognisable. But it came to be theorised in those final years that there was another agency at work; one that dealt in randomness and chaos."

"Sounds like the Devil to me," muttered Kim.

"Well, the agency in question certainly dealt in evil, too, but that wasn't its primary purpose. This was only a theory, you understand. Until humankind arrived on Terra Two, proponents of the theory were considered to be a little, er, unusual."

"You mean nuts," said Kim.

Frankie grinned, but it faded almost immediately. He shot

another anxious glance along the path; there was no sign of anyone making their way towards them.

"Yes, if you like," he said.

"How do you know all this, Frankie?" asked Jack. "You said this happened many centuries in your past."

"And so it did. But the travellers to Terra Two were determined to keep meticulous digital records of all that transpired there, to go with the extensive records brought with them from Terra One. The hope was that humanity might at last begin to learn from its mistakes."

Jack grunted.

"It is right to be sceptical, Jack. On Terra Two the same mistakes began to be repeated. But that is a long tale in itself and we have no time. Ironic, really, since we're standing in a place where all time exists. Let me ask you: what is the best way to counter chaos?"

There was a moment's silence. Nadine broke it.

"By imposing order?"

"Exactly," said Frankie. "But only to a point. When too many rules are made restricting how people may live their lives, they begin to feel resentment. Urges to rebel against that order come to the fore. Before we know it, chaos has regained a foothold. Then the monk can do his work. You see, the early years of Terra Two were characterised by peace and co-operation and harmony amongst all, irrespective of race or gender or creed. A balance was achieved. The monk—I'll continue to call him that, though I prefer Jack's name—"

"It was Matt who first called him the Lord of the Dance," interrupted Jack.

"Yes, of course it was. A name for a choreographer of disorder. An apt name. He hates balance. There was, at first, no way into Terra Two for him. Until the old problems that plague mankind began to reassert themselves: xenophobia, racism, sexism. Religions re-established themselves and with them came religious intolerance. People grew discontented with their places in the new society. They began to seek increased wealth, greater power over others, elevation to a higher echelon of their own creating. If Terra Two's sun hadn't died, mankind would probably have done the job for it. How the monk danced."

"And Terra Three?" asked Jack.

"Apart from the threat caused by its dying sun, Terra Two was a benign planet. Ample food sources; plentiful resources for building materials; few natural dangers to man. Its very placidity contributed to the old problems raising their heads. In contrast, Terra Three is a world filled with peril, from predatory native life forms to scarce resources. Once they had migrated there, my ancestors faced a simple choice: pull together as they had done in the early days of Terra Two and live, or continue along the path of self-destruction." Frankie shrugged. "I am living proof that they chose the former course. And, once again, balance has been achieved. It is a delicate balance indeed, but the monk is once more shut out. And he doesn't like that, not one little bit."

"Huh," said Jack, a notion forming. He spread out an arm to take in their surroundings. "So all this, and Nowhere, is to do with the Lord of the Dance being excluded from human affairs and throwing a tantrum?"

"In effect, yes," said Frankie. "But more than merely throwing a tantrum. He is trying to undo the events that led to his exclusion in the first place. Miriam will explain that when she has completed her calculations."

All eyes turned towards the silvery case. The lights continued to pulse to an unheard rhythm, but otherwise it remained unchanged.

Kim cleared her throat. "You still haven't explained how you knew where to find Jack and what this has to do with me and Matt."

Frankie had been peering anxiously along the path, but turned back to face them. "I must go and find out what is happening so I will explain quickly. I said earlier that the inhabitants of Terra Three, at the time when Terra Two was destroyed, placed significance on the recording of your encounter with Miriam. Terra Three's harsh environment leaves little time for cerebral pursuits like academic study for its own sake—if research isn't aimed at leading to improved technology or discoveries likely to increase humankind's chances for survival, it is considered an unaffordable luxury. Nevertheless, as we learned to if not conquer, then adapt to Terra Three's many challenges, it was felt that more resources could be given over to the Bruder technology and the research which led to the current incarnation of Miriam." He sighed. "We have not yet been able to discover how to point the Bruder Gate at a particular planet, but the search will continue for as long as our scarce resources hold out."

Kim gave an exaggerated sigh. Jack shared her impatience. For someone who said he needed to hurry to explain, Frankie was taking a while to get to the point; it seemed to be his way.

"Anyway," continued Frankie, "the recording of your encounter with Miriam on Terra Two had not been forgotten. As more free time became available, more people spent it searching through digitalised records from Terra One. We knew from the recording that at least three people from around the early second century BE had arrived at Ultimus in a conveyance they referred to as an elevator or lift. We knew their names were Jack, Matt and Kim. We knew they had visited other, dangerous places. It was a question of hunting through the records for any reference to such events. The records from Terra One are vast and their organisation leaves much to be desired. But, eventually, we hit the payload. An obscure electronic book was discovered, published some twenty-five years or so after the events it describes. It told a strange tale about four people transported to fantastic worlds in an ordinary elevator. It told of their meeting with the monk they christened the Lord of the Dance and how one of their number did not return with them to their own time and place. It is likely that if the book gained an audience when published, readers would have assumed it was a work of fiction."

"A book?" muttered Jack. "Someone wrote a book about our

journey in the Elevator?"

Frankie nodded. "It was called *The Reluctant Inter-Dimensional Travelers*. Its author was Matthew Tyler-Grayson."

Jack glanced at where Matt lay slumped against the fencing post on the jetty. Dribble ran down his chin and he snored thickly.

"Matt wrote a book?"

Frankie nodded.

Kim's eyes widened.

"I'd forgotten about that," she said in a wondering tone. "He wrote that stuff down in the months after we'd returned home from this place. He showed it to me after we were married. He said he'd done it in an effort to exorcise the memories." She grunted. "It didn't work. We probably still have the papers—they're shoved in a box on a shelf somewhere. Only…" She frowned. "He didn't call it that long-winded title you just mentioned, Frankie. He simply called it *The Elevator*."

"Nevertheless," said Frankie, "it will be published under the title *The Reluctant Inter-Dimensional Travelers*. It *must* be, do you understand?"

"Paradoxes," murmured Jack.

"Exactly," said Frankie.

"But," began Kim, "we don't know anything about publishing a book."

"You will learn," said Frankie. "The book contains a foreword, written by the author's w-wife, Kimberly Tyler-Grayson."

If Kim picked up on Frankie's stumble over the word 'wife', she didn't remark upon it, but Jack had noticed. It was, he thought, as if Frankie had been going to say 'widow'.

Two

A loud noise, like the snort of a horse, came from Matt. He sat straighter and brushed at his chin with one hand while peering blearily at them through bloodshot eyes. Kim sighed and went over to him. She picked up and uncorked the canteen lying on the jetty next to him.

"At last," murmured Frankie.

Jack thought he was referring to Matt waking up, but then noticed in which direction Frankie was looking: towards the path. A man was making his way along it towards them, limping heavily. As he drew closer, Jack could see that one of the man's arms dangled loosely by his side, drenched in blood. A cut above one eyebrow bled profusely, running down the side of his face. His woollen trousers were torn and ragged, and also heavily blood-stained.

Frankie rushed forward and supported the man to the jetty where he collapsed onto his backside. He looked as though he could barely maintain a seated position unaided.

Jack recognised him from Tumble Down: the thick-set, dark-haired man he had watched beaten to a pulp during the Bout.

"It's Daniel, isn't it?" he asked.

The man nodded. Even that seemed an effort.

"Kim!" Jack called. "Bring that flask over here. I think this man's need is greater."

Kim made Matt take a last sip from the flask and brought it over. She handed it to Daniel, who raised it shakingly to his lips and drank deeply.

"What's happening over there?" asked Frankie.

"Thank you," said Daniel, passing the flask back to Kim. He looked up at Frankie with an expression of something approaching despair on his face. "It does not go well for us. At least seven have fallen. Larry was one." Jack recognised the name as the blond man who had been Daniel's opponent in the Bout.

"We might have enjoyed hitting lumps out of each other, but he was my friend."

"Seven?" said Frankie. "That is not good. Have any of the enemy fallen?"

"One, I think. But it is difficult to be sure. So much noise, so much confusion. They issue a whistling, shrieking noise that cuts into a man's brain and makes it difficult to think straight." He took a deep, shuddering breath, which made him wince. "They *can* be killed, but only with great difficulty. After I saw the first one fall, the ones at the front who bore the brunt of Fumika's attacks moved back when they began to tire. The ones behind parted to allow them to pass and allow fresh ones to take their place. When we try to do the same, there is too much of a crush. We cannot make those pressing behind understand that we need to rotate those on the front line." He gave a slight shrug as though lacking the energy to do a full one. "It is why we are losing so many. It is why it took me so long to return."

Daniel's accent was colourful, full of convoluted vowel sounds and rolling consonants. He sounded a little like a country bumpkin, Jack thought, but kept it to himself.

"What are they, exactly?" he asked. "The creatures you were fighting."

"A glamour stands upon them, though they do not look as they did when I first came to this place..." He grimaced. "They appeared to me then as wizened, deformed children with faces like witches. Their true form is of a similar size, that of children, but they possess no human features. I think they have snouts, like ferrets, and eyes the colour of quicksilver. It is difficult to make out their faces clearly. One thing is sure—they do not have hands but paws. With claws as sharp as razors."

Jack glanced down at the man's tunic. It had been shredded so that the woollen vest he wore beneath showed. His trousers had been turned to strips of flapping, bloodied cloth.

"You mentioned Fumika?" said Frankie.

Daniel nodded. "She fights with the skill of a sword master

and the strength of ten men. They know that if she falls we are finished. They concentrate their forces upon her. We are doing our best to help her, but I fear our best is not enough."

"Can we not climb the slope that adjoins the embankment and circle around to flank them?" asked Frankie.

"We tried it," said Daniel. "But they anticipated the move. There is a line of creatures assembled there. It is a simple matter for them to repel our attempts. It is impossible to clamber up the grassy slope and combat the creatures at the same time with bare hands. And we cannot climb while wielding a stave—the surface is too steep and too slick. Our only way is to force them back from the bottleneck at the end of the embankment, but they cluster there in too much force and we can make no headway."

"It is the monk," said Nadine. "He controls them. They *are* him. We must reach him. If we cannot kill him, we must distract him. Only then will his creatures falter."

Daniel glanced up at her. "You may be right, but we cannot see the monk, much less approach him."

Jack gazed thoughtfully at the steep slope, more a grassy cliff, beyond the jetty.

"The line of creatures at the top of the slope," he said. "How far along does the line extend? Does it come as far as where we are now?"

Daniel shook his head. "No need. Impossible to climb that while holding any sort of weapons. And facing them bare-handed is suicide."

"Then that's what we must do," said Jack. "Climb that banking and make our way to the killing field to arm ourselves."

Jack planted his feet apart, folded his arms and shook his head.

"It doesn't matter what you say," he told Frankie. "I'm coming with you."

"Look…" began Frankie, but Jack cut across him.

"Nope. I've had enough of hanging about here waiting for Miriam to start speaking, while people are over there getting killed.

If I have something to do with them being here, I *have* to do something to help them."

Frankie gazed at him before giving a heavy sigh. "I can see you won't be persuaded otherwise. Okay. You can come with me to collect the weapons, but I don't want you to confront the monk. We learned a lot about him from Matt's book and our own indirect experiences with his schemes, and we do not think he has ever killed with his own hands. But he can turn his pets against you. As we know, they *do* possess the power to kill."

"Yes, when all they're facing are sticks. There are *swords* in the killing field."

Frankie's gaze grew more intense. "Tell me, Jack, what happens if Miriam starts speaking?"

Jack desperately wanted to talk to Miriam again, to find out what this was all about, but his desire to do something to help the inhabitants of Tumble Down was stronger. "Nadine can yell for me."

Nadine's lips drew into a straight line and she thrust out her jaw. "I'm coming, too."

"Now hold on a minute…" Jack began.

"What's the matter, Jack?" said a voice in an American accent. "Don't think girls are as capable as boys?"

Jack glanced at Kim. She was gazing at him with wide-eyed mockery. "No, I don't think that," he said. "But someone needs to keep watch on Miriam."

Kim shrugged. "I can do that. There's no way I'm going to attempt to drag my butt up that bluff and I need to get more water down that wasted husband of mine. If the case starts talking, I'll holler."

Daniel rose to his feet, wincing and swaying. "I'm coming, too," he said. "As soon as the ground stops moving."

"You're in no fit state to go anywhere," said Frankie.

"Nevertheless…" said Daniel. He stood straighter. "I want another go at those bastards but this time with a sword in my hand, even if it is a rusty one." His dark eyes glinted. "Haven't held a sword for a while. I wasn't a bad fencer in my youth." He flexed his left arm; it was his right that dangled uselessly by his side. "Fortunately, I'm left-handed."

Frankie sighed again. "I'd argue if we had more time and I thought you'd listen. But I don't see how you're going to scale the embankment with only one good arm."

Daniel smiled. "You and Jack will assist me."

Daniel needed help to stumble the ten yards or so to the foot of the embankment. He was panting by the time they reached it and sweat mingled with the drying blood caking his face. He presented a ghastly sight; some of the people guarding the embankment cast troubled glances his way.

"Wait," he said, as Frankie grabbed at the almost sheer wall of grass to begin climbing. "I don't think the creatures positioned along the banking next to the path will be able to see us from their vantage point—the top of the banking here is much higher than where they stand sentinel. But it might be worth sending people to mount an assault on the banking near where the fighting is taking place. That will distract the sentinels and make sure they don't notice us."

Frankie thought for a moment, then nodded. He called to Anna. She looked more twitchy than Jack had thought could be possible.

"We need you to do something for us," said Frankie.

The girl nodded. Her bottom lip tucked between her teeth and she chewed on it; her fingers twisted and untwisted like writhing serpents.

Frankie pointed along the path. "Hurry to our people. Tell three or four of them to attempt to climb the banking. They must not put themselves in danger, but must keep making the attempt. It is important that the creatures standing guard at the top of the banking are kept busy. Do you understand?"

"I will climb, too," said Anna. "I am quick. They will not get me."

Frankie smiled. "That is good. But the same goes for you: stop climbing before they can reach you with their claws. Return to the path. Then try again a moment later."

"I understand."

She hurried away, head bobbing like a strutting pigeon's.

Frankie turned back to the embankment. "Let's get on with it, then, shall we?"

The slope proved easier to scale than it had looked from below. The grass was tough, with deep roots, and provided secure handholds. The earth beneath, though firm, had enough give to allow them to dig the toes of their shoes or boots into it and haul themselves up. The main difficulty lay in assisting Daniel. With only one hand to cling on, his progress was slower. Frankie climbed to his immediate right, pausing to support Daniel every time he reached for a new hand-hold. Jack climbed to his other side, alert to reach out and steady the man whenever necessary. Nadine climbed ahead, scrambling up the ascent like a monkey scaling a tree. She reached the top and peered down at Jack, a grin on her face.

"Hurry up, slowcoach," she hissed in a stage whisper.

Jack grimaced. It would have been much quicker if Daniel hadn't come, but who were they to say he couldn't, even if he could barely put one foot in front of the other? He, too, had been whisked away from his own time and place, and was as entitled as anyone to fight back.

Minutes later, they all arrived at the summit. Jack helped Daniel over the lip marking the end of the ascent before hauling himself thankfully onto more level ground. From this higher point, the sounds of combat, dominated by screeching whistles, were louder.

Jack looked to his left. Lower down, where the slope began to level off before dipping away again to ground level, there was a commotion. Four or five people were clambering up the banking, erratically, some moving up, some sliding back down. Even from this far away, Anna was recognisable with her dancing twitchiness.

She looked to be enjoying herself, scrambling up as easily as Nadine had climbed the embankment, feinting as if to make a break for the open ground beyond, before slip-sliding backwards and out of reach of the creatures strung out in a line above her.

Although the creatures stood apart from each other, Jack could not fix his gaze clearly on any one of them. It was like staring at a page filled with tightly packed dots and trying to concentrate on only one. The eye slid away, unable to maintain focus on any individual.

He squinted, but it didn't help. Instead, he looked farther along the path to where the main fight was taking place. There was no better way to describe the point where the path ended than as a bottleneck. A shifting, vague mass assembled where the path opened out, blocking the Tumble Downers from advancing onto open ground. Shrieks and whistles arose from the mass in an unholy cacophony of ear-splitting disharmony.

The path immediately in front of the mass was no wider than to allow four or five Tumble Downers to stand abreast. Jack could make out swinging sticks, but too many people pressed behind for him to see much more, other than to gain a sense of how disorganised the people were. How chaotic the entire scene was.

Must please the Lord of the Dance.

His gaze moved beyond to where the monk stood, unmoving, his regard fixed on the mass of creatures before him.

Jack repressed a shudder and steeled his resolve. He turned to his companions.

"They're not making any headway. We have to draw some of the mass who oppose them away. Thin it out. Give them chance to break through. Then we can turn our attention to *him*."

The three expressions facing him hardened.

"Let's kick some butt," muttered Nadine.

Staying low, they moved away from the edge of the embankment and headed for the killing field.

Three

The land to their right sloped gently upwards for about fifty yards until it was broken by a dark line of trees. They looked densely packed, impenetrable. Probably the boundary of this small world, thought Jack.

They continued to move away from the embankment in a straight line, Frankie helping to support Daniel on the grassy surface. Their going wasn't helped by the angle of the slope they were cutting across, rather than following up or down.

The shrieks and whistles and cries of pain faded gradually as they progressed, though not entirely.

"I think we've come far enough in from the river to make our way down," said Jack. He pointed at another line of trees ahead— the impenetrable-looking forest had curved around and now lay in their path, blocking any further progress beyond another thirty or so paces. "Besides, we can't go much further in this direction."

They turned to their left. At first, the gentleness of the downward slope made the going less challenging, but not for long. Nadine, who seemed to find the way easier than any of them, brought them to a halt where the gradient increased dramatically.

Jack gave a gasp of recognition. "This is the hill on which the Elevator dumped us. It arrived at a sharp angle and we fell down that slope and ended up in a heap at the bottom. Then it disappeared like it had never been here in the first place." He pointed to his right. "There's the killing field." He looked to the left, from where the faint battle noises were coming. They could see the brown river and the distant bank of fog, but both the Lord of the Dance and his pets were hidden by the way the land kinked in that direction. "Good. We're out of sight. Should be able to get what we can without being bothered."

Frankie gazed down the steep slope, a dubious expression on his face. "Not sure how Daniel is going to descend that safely."

"To be honest," said Daniel, "I could do with a sit down." He was pale, except for the dark circles around his eyes. It didn't appear that any fresh blood was dripping from his wounds, but he must have lost a fair amount already. Scaling grassy embankments and clambering over rolling hillsides couldn't be aiding his recovery.

He lowered himself to the grass at the summit of the steeper part of the slope, wincing and hissing as he did so.

"Maybe you'd better wait here," said Frankie.

"Nay," said Daniel. "Didn't drag myself all this way to give up now."

He leaned back as though to lie fully down, but kept his head upright so that he could see ahead, and pushed himself forward with his left arm. Kicking his legs as if pedalling an invisible bicycle, he began to slide down the hill.

Nadine grinned. "That looks fun." She sat down and began to slide after Daniel on her backside.

Jack looked at Frankie, who shrugged. They both sat and followed their companions down the hill.

Nadine had already scrambled to her feet by the time Jack and Frankie reached the bottom. She brushed herself down, her face flushed with excitement. Jack wanted to kiss her, but resisted the urge. This probably wasn't the time.

Daniel remained seated on the thick grass at the foot of the slope. He was panting with exertion and looked paler still.

"I think I'd better rest awhile," he wheezed. "I want to be as strong as I can be to face those whistling bastards."

"Okay," said Frankie. "We shouldn't be long."

"Make sure to bring me back a sword. The pointier the better."

Jack led the way, but they hadn't gone more than a few steps before he came to a halt, staring at an object lying half-buried in the grass.

"Tell me, Frankie," he said, "if all time exists in this place, how is it that the corpses and clothes and weapons lying about the killing field have rotted? If *all* time exists here, then that includes the past as well as the future. Don't they cancel each other out so that, in effect, it would seem that time is standing still and nothing would decompose?"

Frankie appeared to give this a moment's thought. "I think," he said, "that it's to do with balance, as most things tend to be. The monk created Nowhere, where time doesn't proceed in a linear fashion. No one ages there, right? That being so, and this being its counterpart, time must progress here in the normal way, at least from the perspective of the people who come here. And so textiles decay, metal corrodes, organic matter festers."

"Okay. Then explain this." He pointed at the object on the ground. "When I arrived here in the Elevator and we tumbled out, Tara's document case fell out with us. A hulking thing, it was. And there it is, exactly where she left it. It should look pretty much like it did when I last saw it. Yet look at it, collapsed and covered in mould and moss as if it's been lying there for years. And the rind from Matt's watermelon has disappeared. It's only been a week— there should be some remains."

Frankie frowned. "Hmm, that does seem odd. Wait, I think… yes. I said that time progresses here from the perspective of the people who come here. Well, Kim and Matt must have seen the document case when they returned as a middle-aged couple. Therefore, we also now see it from their perspective. That case has aged twenty-three years."

"Huh," said Jack. "What a head fuck."

He resumed walking, his mind abuzz with the apparent vagaries of time. They were almost in the killing field before he'd noticed. He brought them to a stop. "We're here." He nodded past the patch of waste ground to the line of trees beyond. "That's where he comes from. And his creatures."

"Those trees probably conceal some sort of portal that he uses to bring him here from whatever plane of existence he normally occupies." Frankie shrugged. "Doubt we'd be able to see it, much less use it." He moved his gaze nearer, to what lay on the ground before him, and his face blanched.

« »

The scene was still fresh in Jack's memory, but neither Nadine nor Frankie had come this way during their brief visits to this side of the river. They both uttered small noises of shock and horror on seeing the bones and remnants of clothes strewn across the ground.

"Daniel is right," murmured Nadine. "They are bastards. Fucking bastards." She gasped and stooped to pick up an object. It was a child's doll, the clothes ragged and mouldy, its porcelain head half-smashed. A tear rolled down her cheek. "This belonged to a child. A small girl, maybe."

Jack pulled the bible from his pocket. "The daughter of the owner of this was two, according to Matt. Perhaps that was hers."

Nadine's face crumpled. She stooped once more and laid the doll carefully on the ground, exchanging it for a knife with a slightly curved blade, like a miniature scimitar. When she straightened, her expression had hardened.

"Let us repay their cruelty." She hefted the knife and a gleam came into her eyes that Jack hadn't seen before.

"Hold on, there," said Frankie. "I can't allow you two to get involved in any fighting. If anything happens to either of you, my entire existence will be jeopardised. So what we'll do is take what weapons we can carry back to the jetty. Then you can wait with Miriam, who might have finished her calculations by now, while I get the weapons to the front line."

Nadine said nothing, but her expression spoke more eloquently than any words could that what Frankie had said was meaningless to her.

Jack replaced the bible in his pocket and took a few paces into the killing field, trying to avoid treading on any bones. He picked up something that had caught his eye. The sword's blade had tarnished, its edge dull. It was straight and not overly long; its handguard consisted of a simple cross-piece of grey metal. He hefted it, appraising its weight and balance, and gave it a couple of experimental *swishes* through the air. It wasn't too heavy to wield with one hand, though he suspected he would do more damage clutching it two-handed. The weapon felt good to hold. It felt *right*.

He hesitated, wondering what he was doing twirling a sword around as if he were d'Artagnan and not some spotty kid barely out of his teens from a rundown British town. The closest he'd come to clutching a sword before was while playing a video game in the hostel he'd lived in as a sixteen-year-old. Now he was not only holding a genuine sword, but contemplating *using* it, for real, in an actual life-or-death fight. His legs abruptly felt weak and he wanted to sit down.

Jack looked at Nadine and it was as though she could read his thoughts. She winked and smiled a grim sort of smile, and his doubts vanished. He knew that merely waving a sword about wouldn't make him d'Artagnan, but it no longer mattered. In Nadine's resolute expression, in her bearing, he could see that she intended to fight the creatures who had killed the owner of the doll. And with that knowledge came calmness and certainty—if she intended to face them, he would stand by her side.

"The thing is, Frankie," he said, "we managed to get Daniel here when it was mostly downhill. There is no way we'll get him back up that hill, not if we're burdened with swords and knives which, after all, was the whole purpose of coming here. And, if I'm any judge of Daniel's feelings right now, I'd say the chances of getting him to agree to attempt to retrace our steps are a big fat zero. Unless you intend leaving him behind, knowing that he'll go fight those things on his own if needs be, you're going to have to accept it. Daniel, Nadine, me… we're going to face those murdering monsters, with or without you, and there's nothing you can do to stop us."

He glanced at Nadine, who nodded. They both looked at Frankie.

Frankie stared back for a long moment, his face working through various expressions until finally settling on one.

Resignation.

"Oh, fuck," he said.

They made their way back to where they had left Daniel, weighed down with half a dozen swords in varying states of degradation, and a clutch of knives and daggers. He was sitting up, keeping watch for them and looked improved from when they had left him. Colour had returned to his features and his breathing had slowed to something approaching normality. He had made some attempt at removing the caked blood from his face, with only partial success; he still resembled an extra in a slasher film.

His eyes lit up when he saw the array of weapons they carried. He stood, using his good arm to lever himself up and only grimacing a little.

They dropped the weapons to the ground, with the exception of the knife Nadine had chosen and Jack's sword. They both continued to clutch them tightly, afraid Daniel would want them. They needn't have worried.

He made a beeline for a long—about a third as long again as Jack's weapon—thin sword that tapered to a point which looked needle-sharp despite the patches of decay tarnishing the length of the blade. The handguard consisted of a metal bowl large enough to cover the knuckles of the wielder.

"A rapier," Daniel said, his tone wistful. "It's what I learned to fence with." He hefted it in his left hand and made a couple of slashing movements. The blade whistled through the air like a birch rod. "Course, this is designed as a thrusting weapon." He lunged, stabbing the slender blade into an imaginary opponent, but straightened immediately with a gasp of pain. "Maybe I'll keep the thrusts to a minimum."

"Where are you from, Daniel?" asked Jack. "From a rural area, I'm guessing, but I'm struggling to place your accent. Or the period it's from."

"I'm from the Marches. Shropshire to be a little more precise. I come from farming stock in the year 1911."

"And are all farmers of your time proficient with a blade?" asked Frankie.

Daniel chuckled. "A plough blade, maybe, but not one like this. My folks are tenant farmers. While the Squire can be a tight-fisted old so-and-so when it comes to collecting rent, he is generous in other ways, bless him. When his sons were taking fencing lessons in preparation for going off to military school, he allowed some of the tenants' sons to take part. Course, my old man didn't want to let me—'them fancy lessons is for nobs, Daniel,' he says to me, 'not for the likes of us'. He relented in the end. Turned out I took to fencing better than the Squire's own sons. It was a few years ago, but I haven't forgotten a thrust or parry."

"Like riding a bike," said Jack. "Once learnt, never forgotten."

"I'll have to take your word for that, seeing as how I've never ridden a bike." He glanced in the direction of the river from where the sounds of whistling, shrieks and cries continued unrelenting. "Shall we, then?"

Frankie reached down and grabbed two daggers from the collection. "If I can't dissuade anyone from this course of action..." He raised his eyebrows at Jack and Nadine, who both firmly shook their heads. "Then I guess I'm ready."

A bubble of acid rose in Jack's throat. He swallowed it down and clutched the sword more tightly.

Four

With every step they took towards the river, the whistling screeches and sounds of fighting grew louder. The path curved and the monk came into view. Jack's legs wanted to give up on him again. But the hooded figure was staring intently ahead. If he was aware of their approach, he gave no sign.

Jack brandished the sword with a hand that had begun to shake. "Should we attack him?" He wanted to whisper but the others wouldn't have heard him above the noise of battle.

Frankie shook his head. "We can't kill him and we need to allow our people through so they can get the weapons we left behind. *Then* we can turn our attention to the monk."

Jack wanted to argue; by his reckoning, an assault against the monk would draw some of his pets away from the main battle, but then he realised that he would rather fight ten thousand razor-clawed creatures than face the insanity of the Lord of the Dance. Besides, the monk would be aware of their presence as soon as they walked within his line of sight and maybe would be distracted anyway. So he said nothing.

"Let's get on with it," said Daniel. "I might be a little below my best, but there's strength yet in my sword arm."

They moved away from the monk, at an angle towards the river.

A seething, shifting mass came into view. Jack still struggled to make out individuals within it. Beyond, he could see the heads and shoulders of people, and flailing sticks.

"Let's hurry," said Frankie. "The monk will be alerted to our presence at any moment so we must gain as much advantage from surprise while we can. And stick together, though not too closely. We don't anyone getting stabbed by our own weapons."

Jack swallowed hard. He felt a hand grip his arm and squeeze. He looked at Nadine and tried to force a smile, but suspected it came out as more of a grimace. She nodded as if she, too, was incapable for the moment of smiling.

They increased their pace, Daniel limping along as best he could. The prospect of revenge on the monk's pets seemed to have lent him fresh energy.

As they drew nearer to the crush, the line of creatures at the rear wheeled to face them.

"He's onto us," yelled Frankie; he needed to shout to be heard. He raised both hands, a dagger held in each, and motioned forwards. "At them!"

Daniel let out a guttural noise—a throaty growl like a wild beast—loud enough to drown out the whistles and cries; if there were words in it, Jack could not make them out. He hadn't, until now, understood what was meant by a 'primal scream' in the sense of a violent outpouring of raw emotion, but next time he heard the expression he would think of this moment.

If it is possible to surge while bearing numerous wounds and after suffering heavy blood loss, that is what Daniel did, holding the sword out before him like a giant needle. He matched Frankie limping stride for stride as they both rushed at the line of creatures.

Issuing a shrill cry of her own, Nadine followed a few paces behind them, the curved knife brandished by her side. She looked determined and lithe and dangerous, and in that moment Jack knew that he was falling in love with her.

It was that realisation which forced his legs, threatening again to betray him and refuse to move, into motion.

Frankie and Daniel reached the creatures simultaneously. Frankie's arms whirled into blurring movement, slashing and hacking, cutting a swathe through the line like a bowling ball through skittles. Alongside him, Daniel thrust his sword arm out like a piston, skewering creatures who fell under his fury.

Yes! They can *be killed.* Jack clutched his sword tighter and increased his stride.

The whistling shrieks grew louder, more frantic, almost rising high enough to pass beyond the range of human hearing. The noise was hideous, but Jack relished it. It spurred him on and he arrived at what remained of the first line of creatures at the same time as Nadine. Side by side, they waded into the fray.

Something sprang at him and Jack raised the sword. Too late. A flare of heat exploded in his right forearm. He glanced down. His shirt was torn in the same place where George Morgan had inflicted the knife wound, but this one wouldn't heal overnight. Blood was already welling from the sliced flesh beneath, staining his sleeve. The creature came again and this time Jack was quicker. He managed to raise the sword in a parry that was only partially effective. Another stab of pain, this time in his thigh.

The creature was immediately in front of him, but still Jack could not make it out clearly. His gaze kept sliding off in the optical equivalent of trying to grab a flapping fish. Shifting impressions only, of silvery eyes similar to ones he had seen before and claws like a three-toed sloth's.

It came at him again and he swung the sword in as much a gesture of revulsion as defence. The blade's edge was too blunt to do serious damage, but it did enough to prevent the claws raking him again. Before the creature could attack once more, Jack thrust the sword forward in a stabbing motion and encountered resistance. The creature issued a shriek capable of cracking windows and the sword tugged free of Jack's hand, slick with nervous perspiration, as the creature collapsed to the ground.

Jack stared down at the body, momentarily too stunned to move. The glamour, or whatever masked the creature's appearance, had fallen away at the moment of its death. It wasn't any bigger than a human child of around eight and possessed a face a little like a ferret's, but softer, less fearful-looking, with protruding, bat-like ears. It was patched with stiff fur, like the bristles of a pig; tan leathery skin showed between the patches.

Little wonder that the monk placed a glamour upon his pets

and that they had previously taken on the form of their viewers' worst nightmares, such as clowns with razor blades instead of teeth; in their true form, they were not much more frightening to gaze upon than, say, an agitated chimp. Only their claws would cause undue alarm: long and curved and pointed, they looked capable of inflicting severe damage. The stinging pain in Jack's forearm and thigh bore that out. More sets of claws extended from the paws the creature had in place of feet.

The sword protruded from the creature's chest. Other wounds—abrasions dripping a black, viscous liquid, like ichor, and purplish marks suggestive of bruising—liberally peppered the creature's torso and arms. Jack recalled what Daniel had said about the monk withdrawing injured front-liners to the rear and replenishing the front line with fresh creatures. Presumably, then, this creature had already fought at the front where it had received numerous injuries, yet had still managed to inflict two of its own on Jack. He needed to be less passive, go on the attack from the outset, or he would be lucky to survive another encounter. He reached out and grabbed the sword, tugging it free with a grimace.

He looked ahead. Frankie and Daniel had nearly reached the main body of creatures. Nadine wasn't far behind; as Jack watched, she dispatched a foe with a swinging sweep of her knife. She looked infinitely more proficient with her weapon than Jack was with the sword. She hurried forward to join the two men.

Whether by direction of the monk, or through their own instincts of self-preservation, at least half of the massed creatures about-turned to face the new threat. Twenty or so of them advanced. Too many. His companions would be overrun.

Jack passed a dozen fallen creatures as he ran, hurdling a couple that lay directly in his path. The stench of sweat and blood and shit filled his nostrils. His heart pounded like a foundry hammer, and the shrieks and whistles coming from the creatures hardly registered over the sound of breaking surf, like that heard in a conch, which had begun in his ears. When, back in Tumble Down, he had seen Nadine walk out beyond the path and had gone to help her with no consideration for his own safety, so now he acted, mindlessly almost, desperate to do whatever he could to protect her, unprepared to lose her so soon after finding her. That she was better equipped to offer him protection than the other way around didn't enter his mind. Instinct had taken over, an instinct he hadn't known until very recently that he possessed.

Frankie and Daniel came to a halt before the advancing creatures. Nadine stopped between them. Jack arrived, breathless, and skidded to a halt by Nadine. Wordlessly, Frankie took a few paces aside to allow him in to the line.

"You okay?" Jack managed to get out, looking at Nadine.

She glanced at him, her face speckled with black liquid, suffused with excitement and something else; something like blood lust. "I'm fine. But I'm not done with them yet." She faced front and tensed, the knife held out before her.

Jack looked forward and stiffened; the creatures were barely a pace or two away. Three were approaching him directly. They were not whistling; the shrieks that continued to fill the air came from those struggling with the Tumble Downers.

"Hold the line," said Frankie. "Don't let them get between or behind us."

That would be easier said than done. The path was much wider at this point with ample room for the four of them to stand abreast and not get in each other's way. Wide enough for the advancing creatures to try to flank them.

Jack's companions stepped forward, as if joined by string, to meet the creatures. Without pausing to think about it and allow the opportunity for his legs to turn traitor, he did likewise, bringing the sword around in a short arc aimed at the closest creature's head.

His world dissolved into confusion.

In time as it is customarily measured, mere minutes passed. But they were minutes filled with relentless motion and pain. When he looked back on the battle later, he recalled it as a montage of swinging, slicing and stabbing, dodging and weaving, shouting and whistling and shrieking, sweat and aching arms, and the searing white heat of ripped flesh.

Fear poured adrenaline into his system. The need to protect and preserve honed it. Desperation focused it. Jack moved like a demented person, heedless of the injuries he was receiving, intent only on inflicting worse. That wasn't to say that he didn't feel the raking claws; the pain was real enough, but experienced as though at a distance, like a filled tooth will ache in an abstract way when the local anaesthetic begins to wear off.

From the corners of his eyes—there were too many creatures coming at him at once to afford to turn his attention fully away— he was aware of his companions moving and slashing and twisting and shouting like people possessed. He was sure he glimpsed Daniel by his side once or twice as if he and Nadine had switched positions, the 'he' being either Daniel or himself; in the confusion he couldn't be certain who had swapped places.

Then yet more creatures were coming at him; too many. He would be overwhelmed. Except that they weren't running at him, but *away* from something. He continued to swing the sword, clutching it two-handed like a club, uncaring whether he caught adversaries with the edge or flat of the blade. He'd soon discovered that provided he swung the weapon with sufficient power, it didn't much matter—the creatures went down either way.

But there were still too many, flooding towards him like water from a breached dam, their shrieks so piercing that at any other time he'd have found the racket too shrill and loud to bear.

New movements and new sounds: the blur and *swish* of swinging sticks, the grunts and yells of human exertion and excitement, the meaty thuds of wood striking flesh and bone.

Jack could see, through the blur of her whirling stick, the ichor-drenched face of a slight Japanese woman.

"Fumika?"

Then there were no more creatures to aim his sword at, no

more claws to avoid. The last one he could see folded to the ground under the *whack* of Fumika's stick and there was nothing between him and her.

She stumbled and would have fallen, but thrust her stick into the ground and used it to keep herself upright. Her clothes from the waist down were shredded; exposed skin ran with rivulets of blood. Despite her obvious exhaustion, she summoned a grin at Jack, then her attention passed beyond him.

Jack turned to follow her gaze.

Not all the creatures were dead. So many had retreated from the front line they had been able to stream past their flanks and reform in front of the monk. Around thirty of them remained, their numbers no doubt swollen by those who had formed the barrier along the ridge of the banking. It was difficult to tell through the glamour that held sway over them, but Jack gained the impression that many of them were fresh and had not taken part directly in the conflict.

Nadine also turned, her face as spattered in whatever passed for the creatures' blood as Fumika's. To the other side of her, Daniel sank to his knees with a groan. A hush fell, eerie after the racket that had gone before. Frankie's voice broke it, addressing the Tumble Downers.

"Quickly! There are swords and knives inland along the path. Those who would prefer a blade, go and retrieve them. Then let's finish this."

A clutch of people, mainly men, shuffled past, but they didn't seem overly keen on taking up arms.

"Finish it?" Jack managed. He felt utterly spent, no strength remaining to raise the sword, let alone swing it. "There are still too many of them and our best fighters are knackered. We need to get to the monk, but they surround him like a shield."

Frankie looked at him and Jack read the anguish in his face. Jack's stomach churned—if he'd hoped Frankie would have words to damn his as foolish, he read the truth of what he had said in Frankie's expression.

Then came a new voice, from behind the Tumble Downers. It was high-pitched and American. "The Scourgers are coming!" cried Kim.

Part Three: Matt Faces His Demons

One

Kim hurried through the weary Tumble Downers, carrying the metal attaché case by her side. Stumbling in her wake came a bleary-eyed Matt, and behind him came the handful of people who had been keeping watch on the embankment abutting the jetty. Their faces wore looks of utter terror.

Jack reached out and took Miriam from Kim. The case continued to blink and pulse.

"The Scourgers are coming," Kim repeated.

"Explain," said Frankie.

"The raft," said Kim. "It disappeared back across the river. No one was on it. But it's just reappeared from the fog. There are what look like medieval knights on horseback on the raft." She nodded towards a woman with pinched, pale features. "She says they are Scourgers. They'll be here in minutes."

The woman nodded. "I counted six riders."

"Miriam," said Jack. "Has she spoken?"

Kim shook her head. "Not a peep." She looked wide-eyed at the monk and band of shimmering creatures assembled in front of him. "What will we do?"

Jack glanced at the Lord of the Dance. He had not come any nearer and stood too far away for Jack to make out his expression, but his bearing was one of arrogance, as though he knew they could not defeat him.

"Frankie," said Jack urgently. "How can the Scourgers come here? They're from Nowhere, right, where there's no time, so how can they even exist in a place where all time is present?"

"They are an extension of the monk and as his constructs can exist wherever he wants them to. At least, they can exist in any place of his creation, like here." He glanced around in a manner that suggested desperation. "We need to band together with the banking behind us so they can't encircle us. I would prefer to use the river to guard our backs but I don't want to risk us being forced into it."

The clutch of men returned holding the weapons which had been left at the foot of the hill. Now that they were armed with blades they looked even less enthusiastic.

"Come on," called Frankie. "Band together in front of the banking. Those with weapons on the outside. Those unarmed and the more seriously injured in the middle. Someone help me with Daniel. And someone support Fumika."

Including Matt and Kim, thirty-six people had crossed the river from Nowhere. Barely twenty of that number remained. The slain lay where they had fallen along the path in crumpled, forlorn bundles of cooling flesh. Jack suggested to Frankie in a low voice that they move back to where the path narrowed so that the Scourgers could only approach, at best, two abreast, but Frankie dismissed the idea.

"It's a good plan, but I think the advantages of holding such a position would be outweighed by two considerations. Firstly, we lost many Tumble Downers to advance along that path. People will say it was all in vain if we so easily give up the ground gained. Secondly, they'll have to step over the bodies of their friends." He glanced around. "Look at them, Jack. Their courage, such as it is, is more fragile than gossamer. Better not risk any move that will tear it apart."

Many of the Tumble Downers who weren't yet stained with the ichor splashes and fatigue of action, either because they had been at the jetty or had not been able to reach the front due to the crush, appeared to be terrified. Those bearing arms clutched their weapons nervously, seeming that they wished they weren't, after all, armed so that they may remain in the centre of the huddled group. Those who had already been directly involved in the confrontation looked exhausted or wounded or both. A few, like Daniel and Fumika, were so debilitated by injury and fatigue as to be of no further immediate use.

Jack sighed and nodded at Frankie. He could see the man's

point; he didn't necessarily agree with him, but he was too tired to argue.

People passed around pouches of berries and meat, and flasks of water. Jack gratefully accepted a few mouthfuls of each. Already some of his strength was returning. He clutched Miriam firmly in his left hand and wasn't going to allow her out of his possession again, no matter what happened from here on.

If anyone wants her, they'll have to prise her from my dead fingers.

Nadine stood next to him, the black gunk drying on her face giving her the look of a painted warrior. An exhausted one. Kim stood behind them. She was glancing about as though looking for someone—Matt, presumably—her eyes wide and fearful.

They grew wider still as a new sound reached their ears: the rhythmic rumbling of approaching hooves.

Low moans of dismay came as the six Scourgers rode into view. They presented as alarming a sight as Jack remembered from his last encounter with them, with their faceless countenances dead save for the glint of silver behind the visors, their mounts larger than the biggest Shire horses, their whips tipped with spiked balls.

"Do not be afraid," said Frankie. "We bear arms, do not forget. When they cast their whips, those with staves must entangle the thongs to prevent them being withdrawn. Those with blades must hack at them until the lash is severed. If we nullify their whips, we nullify them."

Jack gazed doubtfully at the creatures upon which the knights rode. They looked as if they could inflict fatalities simply by riding at the Tumble Downers, or rearing and employing their hooves, but Frankie's words seemed to have the desired effect. It might not be much of a plan, but it *was* a plan and seemed to bolster the collective resolve. In any event, the whimpers of fear died away and people raised sticks and blades in an impromptu display of defiance.

The Scourgers slowed as they rode in single file past the humans, then wheeled and came to a stop, facing the group. The path still wasn't wide enough to allow the riders unrestricted freedom of movement. They were forced to assemble in a line, their backs to the river.

For a moment there was silence, broken only by the champing of bit, the clumping of restless hooves and snorting of beasts. The riders unfurled their whips and held them ready, but made no move to cast them. They sat as if awaiting instructions.

Kim's voice sounded small and breathless. "The monk is approaching."

Jack had temporarily forgotten about the Lord of the Dance. Here he waddled, his pets arranged before him to guard against a frontal assault. They spread out as they drew nearer, forming a semi-circle in front of their master, allowing him to approach within ten yards of the Tumble Downers.

Silvery eyes, made piggy by fleshy cheeks and jowls, glinted beneath the cowl. Thin lips turned into a sly smile. Pale maggots squirmed amidst folds of dirty robe. Flies took off and circled and landed in an unending airborne dance.

Even at that distance, the stench of decay reached the nostrils of those standing nearest. Jack was prepared for it and breathed through his mouth, but heard people gasping and swallowing as they tried not to gag.

"Oh, man," came Frankie's voice from next to Jack. "You smell worse than a shefflestomper that's been lying in a ditch for a week."

Whatever the heck a shefflestomper was—an animal native to Terra Three, Jack guessed—Frankie's words released some of the tension from the Tumble Downers. A sigh rippled around the group; there were one or two muted sniggers.

The monk's gaze swivelled towards Frankie and his head tilted a little. Jack was reminded of their first meeting when the monk had moved his head from side to side as though to indicate it had been his skull in which they'd found themselves when the Elevator visited the Third Floor of Claridge House.

"I do not believe I have had the pleasure." As before, the monk's voice was curiously uninflected and monotonal. Robotic, almost.

Frankie gave one of his elaborate bows. "Francis Brown. It's customary where I come from to add 'at your service', but I think I'll skip that in this instance."

"And from whence do you come, Francis Brown?"

"Oh, from a place that's far beyond your reach."

"Ah." The word contained the slightest of emphasis, suggesting that the monk knew precisely where Frankie was from. "I see you have found a way to infiltrate my domain. The ingenuity of the human race is oft underestimated. Though never its propensity to self-destruct. Your home may be out of my reach but such a state of affairs is, at best, fleeting. A discordant note in the symphony of my desires."

The monk swept his gaze across the assembled Tumble Downers. Jack heard gasps and one or two whimpers. "Each of you undertook the Task when you arrived. By your presence here, each of you has broken the terms to which you agreed. The penalty for remaining here is death. But there is always a choice and this is yours: you may return to the far shore or die on this one." He nodded towards the Scourgers; maggots tumbled from his cowl like catkins from a willow. "My guardians will escort you back across the river. Then the ferry will be dismantled. I will devise another method of transport should I deem it expedient to bring more humans."

His sly gaze returned to Frankie. "As for you, Francis Brown, your home will, as I think you know, cease to be your home. For you will have no need of one." His shoulders jerked, dislodging more maggots. "A home is unnecessary when you have no existence."

A noise came, a little like water gurgling down a plughole. It took Jack a moment to realise that the monk was chuckling, hands spread across the mound of his stomach, mouth open to reveal grey, weeping gums and drunken teeth.

A muttering arose amongst the Tumble Downers. Jack heard snatches, expressing surprise that they might be able to return to Nowhere. And more: eagerness.

That was it, then. The people would cross the river once more and he would have to accompany them. Or die.

His shoulders sagged and he glanced down at Miriam. Her lights continued to pulse, but she offered no words of comfort; no words, at all.

Frankie whirled about to face the gathering. "No!" His voice carried a note of authority and the mutterings ceased. "We cannot return to Nowhere."

"Yes, we can," came a reply. "The monk said we can."

"Of course he did," said Frankie. "I daresay he's being truthful. For our returning to Nowhere achieves his purpose."

"But saves our lives," came the reply.

"*Lives?*" Frankie almost spat the word. "You call what we did over there living? And what about your friends lying back there on the path? What about their lives? Did they sacrifice themselves so that the rest of you could simply give in?"

A small commotion came from the centre of the group. Fumika rose to her feet, from where she had been lying alongside Daniel and a couple of other badly-injured people. Another sound of grunting effort and Daniel joined her. They made their painful way between the people to stand in front of Frankie.

"I have rested," said Fumika. "I have taken refreshment. I can fight more."

Frankie bowed his head in acknowledgement. Fumika returned the bow. She did indeed look as if she had recovered some of her strength, but still leant on her polished stave as if it were a crutch.

Daniel didn't look even partly recovered. His whole being radiated hurt and exhaustion. Nevertheless, Frankie strode forward and held him gently by the forearm.

"Thank you, Daniel. We may yet have need of your skill with the rapier."

But the voice—it belonged to a man whose name Jack did not know—which had suggested they return across the river hadn't given up.

"We could return," it said, "and then do what George and the others did. That way, we'll go home." Another muttering arose; murmurings of agreement.

"Yes," said Frankie. "You could do that. Take the return voyage and *then* step off the trail to bring the Scourgers down on you. Or you can complete what you set out to do. Assure the future of humankind and still return to your own time and place."

"But only if we defeat *them*."

Frankie nodded. "As has been the case since first I explained what we must do once on this shore. Are you telling me that after all we've endured to reach this point, you're ready to give up and fall in with *him*?" He gestured towards the monk. "Take a long, hard look at him, people, then tell me you want to do what *he* wants."

There came a shuffling of feet and an uncomfortable silence. Most people had the grace to look embarrassed, but Jack also read resignation in their expressions. They weren't going to be swayed, no matter what Frankie said. By the look of dejection that came across Frankie's face, he read the same thing.

Jack glanced at the monk; he stood quietly watching them, wearing a knowing smirk. Jack felt a sense of such overwhelming frustration that if the monk's pets hadn't been standing in the way, he'd have rushed at him and attempted to wipe the smirk off his chubby face.

He might have attempted it anyway out of despair, but movement caught his eye. A figure was approaching from behind and to the right, from the direction of the killing field, unnoticed as yet by the monk or any of his cohorts.

Two

The figure made no attempt to move stealthily. It stumbled and swayed a little as though…

He's still pissed.

Jack watched Matt approach the monk, whose attention remained fixed on the Tumble Downers. But he must surely become aware of Matt's presence at any moment.

Jack sensed Kim stiffen and gasp behind him. He hissed from the corner of his mouth, "Kim, don't draw attention to him." He risked a louder whisper. "Everyone, be ready to attack. Pass it on."

His mind whirled, trying desperately to think of a way to keep the monk's attention diverted on them.

"Hey there, Mr Monkey Man," he said in a loud voice, striving to keep it level with only partial success. He pressed on, saying the first thing that came into his head. "What are you calling yourself today, then? Quartermaster? Halfmaster? Grandmaster? Alabaster? Um… antipasta?"

"How about sand blaster?" chimed in Kim. "Go faster?"

"Or a fisherman," said Jack. "You know, a caster?" He knew it was silly, but didn't care. It was having the desired effect; the monk's attention was fixed entirely on him.

"How about Nancy Astor?" said Nadine.

"My stomach is vaster?" chipped in Frankie.

"It is Jack, hmm?" said the monk. Jack had to hand it to him: if he was irritated by their childish taunts, he did not reveal it in any way. The smug smile remained in place. "Jack, Bruder?"

The hesitation had been infinitesimal, but Jack hadn't missed it and felt himself colouring.

"That's correct," he said. "My name is Jack Bruder."

"Indeed. And what is that pretty object you clutch so firmly, Jack Bruder?"

Jack's grip on Miriam's handle tightened reflexively, but he held up his other hand. "This? Why, it's called a sword."

At last, a flash of annoyance passed across the monk's features. So it *was* possible to rile him, if only fleetingly. Yet the monk's voice remained flat and toneless.

"And in your other hand?"

"Oh, this is nothing. Just an attaché case."

"That you did not have with you when you began the Task. Tell me, Jack Bruder, will you return to the far shore or die here? It's all the same to me, but I think you should know that if you decide to cross the river, the attaché case, as you call it, will remain here. I shall have fun with your flashing toy. Human inventions are endlessly fascinating."

"Flashing…? Oh, you mean the lights? Merely decoration. You know, a bit of bling. There's nothing in here except some boring papers on, er, on…" For a moment he floundered, before remembering Tara's document case and what it had contained. "On last month's sales figures."

Jack did not think for one moment that the monk believed him. Not that it mattered, because he had no intention of crossing the river again. As he'd thought earlier, the only way Miriam was leaving his possession again was by prising her from his dead fingers. Nevertheless, it was not the most opportune moment for her to start speaking.

The whirring noise came from the case. Jack tried to ignore it, but caught from the bottom of his eye a change in light movement as the pattern of Miriam's lights altered.

"I have completed my calculations," came the mellifluous tones of the AI. "Jack, I am ready to transfer you and Nadine to Geneva."

The monk clasped his hands together in mock delight. "It talks!"

He glanced at the Scourgers. Six barbed whips began to unfurl. The bat-eared creatures in front of him began to advance.

At that moment, Matt closed the remaining gap between himself and the monk. In his hand, something gleamed with a dull reflection. A knife.

Matt stopped, swaying slightly, and contemplated the broad, robed back for a moment. Then he thrust the knife firmly into it.

The monk's back arched and he took a pace forward, a look of comic surprise replacing the smug arrogance.

Matt shrieked and fell backwards, clutching at his wrist. The hand that had held the knife smoked like steak too long in the pan. Of the knife, there was no sign.

The monk's pets stopped advancing. As one, they let out an ear-splitting whistle that differed from the ones that had sounded forth during the battle in one material particular: this one was filled with agony. The glamour that masked their true forms failed then re-established itself, on and off in quick succession, so that they flickered like images cast by an ancient cine projector.

The Scourgers' mounts peeled back lips from blackened teeth and uttered a noise such as Jack had never heard before, and hoped he would never hear again. The closest he would later come to describing it was a mixture of fingernails scratching a blackboard, the scream of a panicked toddler and the wail of a terrified cat, but at a key and volume that seemed to bypass the ears and drive the sound like a spike directly into the primal receptors of the brain, making bowels loosen and legs quake.

The great beasts reared. Two took unheeding paces backwards as they bucked, sending them and their riders splashing into the river. Both mounts and riders sank below the surface and did not reappear. The four remaining beasts sent their riders tumbling to the ground and, with ears laid flat against huge heads and lips still peeled back from gums, bolted, galloping past the startled Tumble Downers, paying no heed to the stricken monk as they tore away, not to be seen again.

The four unseated Scourgers lay on their backs, stunned into temporary inaction, making no immediate attempt to rise and wield their whips.

If Miriam continued to speak, her words were lost amidst the tumult. For now, Jack paid her no heed.

He felt someone push past him. It was Kim, running towards her fallen husband.

All this took place in moments, but Jack was still trying to take it in when Frankie started barking orders, straining his voice to be heard above the demonic whistling.

"Quickly! Seven of the strongest men with me. We'll shove the Scourgers into the river after their two friends. Everyone else— finish off his pets. This is our best chance. Seize it, people!"

Even those Tumble Downers reluctant to continue fighting, those who had wanted to return to Nowhere, must have recognised the truth in Frankie's words, for they moved into action. A small band of men joined Frankie and ran towards the prone Scourgers. Everyone else surged past Jack to confront the distressed creatures of the forest, whose forms continued to flicker and whose purpose seemed to have been lost. Jack was aware of these things distantly; his main focus was on the Lord of the Dance.

If Matt's assault had wounded the monk, he gave no sign. When he turned to face the opposite way, Jack could see no indication of damage to the robe where Matt had directed the blade. The only visible sign that anything had occurred was a few wisps of smoke rising from the robe like dust from a beaten carpet.

The monk bent at the waist—obviously more supple than he looked—and lowered his face. Matt lay on his back, full stretch, clutching his smoking hand to his chest and writhing in pain. When the monk's head drew level with his, his eyes opened wide and he went still. Except for his lips. They moved as though he was repeating some mantra to himself, over and over. Or maybe a prayer.

Jack couldn't tell what the monk did—he didn't appear to touch Matt in any way—but then Matt's lips, too, fell still. His hands unclenched and dropped to the ground by his side.

Kim reached the monk but didn't slow. Letting rip with a

scream that Jack heard above the whistles and shouts of fresh battle, she dropped her leading shoulder and bowled into the robed figure, making the monk stumble away from Matt, his cowl falling back in a shower of maggots and startled flies. It revealed a head the size and shape of a bowling ball, with a scant smattering of coarse, dark hair, like that on a coconut. The monk straightened and brought his attention to Kim, his expression one of surprise and affront. And a glimmer of something else, something Jack had not seen in his face before. Fury.

Kim stood next to her motionless husband, panting, staring at the Lord of the Dance with her own mixture of expressions contorting her features: anger, battling with fear.

All around him came the blurred motions and pandemonium of violent conflict, but Jack started towards Kim. He feared that things were about to not go too well for her.

Clutching Miriam in one hand, the sword in the other, Jack ran forward, swerving to avoid struggling combatants and the fallen. The latter seemed mainly to consist of child-sized creatures, but Jack barely noticed.

He arrived at Kim's side and came to a halt, facing the monk. The three of them stood in their own calm pool amidst the raging torrent of battle.

The monk's top lip curled into a sneer. His eyes darted between Kim and Jack.

"You dare to attack me?" His voice held the first hint of emotion Jack had heard. Wonder.

"You *bastard*," hissed Kim. "You ruined my husband's life."

The monk's gaze flicked to the motionless figure lying on the ground, then back. His sneer intensified. If he still felt anger, he had masked it. "Oh, are you referring to him? He already possessed everything he needed to bring about his own downfall. Perchance I helped him along the path of self-destruction. A little." He chuckled in that way which sounded like escaping water. "You humans, with your self-absorbed ways and your insistence on blaming your ills on others. Endlessly fascinating how you look to shift responsibility. A tad predictable, maybe, but such good sport."

"Is that what this is all about?" asked Jack. "Sport?"

"Ah, Jack, Jack. If by 'this' you refer to the place in which we stand then, no, it's not about sport. Not directly. It's about you."

"*Me?*"

"Oh, yes. This is all for the benefit of Jack Bruder."

Jack's mind reeled. It was one thing to be told by Frankie that he was instrumental in all that had happened, but quite another to hear it from the horse's mouth, so to speak.

The monk glanced about. A distant part of Jack realised that the whistles and cries of battle had all but died away.

"And since," continued the monk, "my guardians and the creatures of the forest appear to have been temporarily inconvenienced, it seems the role of executioner falls upon me." His voice had reverted to the monotone, but he added, almost conversationally, "You perhaps ought be aware that your puny blades cannot harm me. I, on the other hand, can stop your hearts with one touch."

The monk's eyes flashed silver, tinged with red, and he took a pace forward. A waft of corruption hit Jack full in the face. His stomach cramped in revulsion and fright; his legs refused to obey the instruction blaring from his brain to flee.

Three

There is something about approaching death that brings abrupt clarity to a bewildered mind. The monk took another pace, his eyes lit from within and glowing like two polished discs of silver bathed in a ruddy light, and Jack raised his sword, but knew with absolute certainty that it would not avail him against this foe.

Guess I'll never find out why I'm supposedly important.

In the speeded-up way that the mind can operate under great stress, he thought of raising Miriam and employing her like a shield, dismissing the idea in the next thought. If his life was about to end, at least he could try to keep Miriam out of harm's way so that Nadine and the others may return to their homes. Hot on the heels of that came a recollection, something somebody had said about Frankie and Miriam not even existing if Jack's life ended here. But it was too late to worry about mind-warping shit like that now. The monk was on him.

"No!" Someone stepped between them. "Leave him alone," said Kim. "He's nothing but a kid, you fucking bully."

Although wrapped in the calm of extreme terror, resentment welled within Jack at being referred to as a kid.

Annoyance showed once more in the monk's face. "Out of my way, woman." He raised one hand and made a gesture.

Kim stiffened, gasped and uttered a low moan. She swayed and Jack thought she must fall, was already reaching out to steady her, when she straightened. "If you want him," she hissed through clenched teeth, "you'll have to come through me."

The monk raised his other hand to join the first and curled his meaty fingers into something resembling claws. "So be it."

Jack's view of the monk was partially blocked by Kim, but he saw him reach forward, bringing one clawed hand towards Kim's chest. Kim didn't react. She must, Jack thought, be frozen in terror like he was. He managed to relax his fingers sufficiently to allow the redundant sword to drop to the ground, freeing one hand to move Kim aside, but couldn't bring his arm muscles to work. All he could do was watch helplessly as the monk brought about Kim's demise. Then it would be his turn.

"No." The voice was calm and clipped. A length of stained wood appeared, pressing against the monk's outstretched arm, forcing it down; where it touched the sleeve of the robe, the stick scorched and smouldered. "No," repeated Fumika.

"No," said a second voice, fainter. The point of a thin blade slid towards the monk's throat and hovered, quivering, as Daniel struggled in his weariness to hold the rapier steady.

"No," said another voice. A figure stepped to the other side of Kim, forcing its way in front of her, pressing her back against Jack. "No," said Frankie again.

Up to twenty more voices spoke in unison. "No."

The monk lowered his other arm. He stood surrounded by men and women bristling with blades and staves.

Jack glanced in the direction of the jetty. The river bank was littered with the monk's pets—the creatures of the forest—all motionless. Of the Scourgers, Jack could see no sign.

"No more," said Frankie, addressing the monk. "It is over."

For moments only, but enough to allow Jack a glimpse of things he'd rather not have seen, the monk's face contorted, seeming to run like melting wax, bending into shapes resembling Halloween masks and fanged beasts and scaled reptilian creatures.

Worst of all, the fevered dancing features of utter depraved insanity. The true face of the Lord of the Dance.

He never knew if anyone else saw the monk's face change. When, much later, he asked Nadine what she had seen, she answered that his features had appeared to shimmer to her eyes, but she hadn't been able to make out any individual faces amidst the confusion.

Jack gazed upon the Lord of the Dance and knew infinity. The crazed eyes gazed back at him and through him.

Then they dimmed and the face settled into the familiar pudgy features of the monk. The mouth worked and returned to what appeared to be the default setting of a faintly amused smirk.

Unaware that he'd been holding his breath, Jack let it out in a heavy sigh.

"It's over," repeated Frankie.

The monk's smirk grew wider. "It does appear that you have me at a disadvantage." He shrugged, dislodging yet more maggots; he seemed to come equipped with an endless supply. He directed his gaze at Frankie. "I applaud your bravado and your invention. Truly, the people of Terra Three shall provide worthy sport. You have earned your existence. I shall look forward to our games."

Frankie shook his head. "We shan't let you back in. We have learned from our mistakes."

The monk chuckled. "One of humankind's best sources of entertainment and its greatest form of self-deception is its ability to convince itself that it has, at last, learned from what has gone before. We shall see."

Jack's right arm ached from swinging the sword; his left hand wanted to cramp from clutching Miriam, who he was desperate to converse with; his legs, restored to working order, wanted to deposit him on the ground. He'd had enough.

"Aw, mate," he said to the monk, "why don't you just sod off and leave us alone?"

The monk turned his gaze back upon him and once more revealed a glimpse behind his mask. But Jack was growing accustomed to it now; when you have looked into a bottomless pit of insane intelligence and monstrous depravity twice before in a relatively short time frame, the third time is no big deal.

Jack allowed his own lip to curl into a sneer. "Go. Away."

Again the glint of ruddiness in the silvery eyes as they flashed once, and the hint of fury that passed across the monk's expression as rapidly as a sneeze. Then he was back to his usual smirking self. He spread his arms to take in their surroundings, making people take a hurried backwards pace. His smirk grew wider.

"I would advise you not to tarry long. Although frustrated at the last, this land has served its purpose as well as it might and I have no further use of it. I shall… hmm, yes, I shall probably not deconstruct it completely. Who knows when a further purpose might present itself? Life is full of opportunities, is it not?" Gurgle, gurgle, water escaping, as he chuckled. "But do all run along like good children. This place will not support your puny life forms for much longer. Shall we say one hour, in time as you reckon it?"

He raised his arms and people took another step back. His smirk broadening to a grin, revealing those grey, weeping gums and topsy-turvy teeth, he reached back and pulled up his cowl. A fresh shower of maggots fell down his front and a squadron of agitated flies took to the air. Jack wouldn't have thought it possible, but the stench wafting from the monk intensified and some people took yet another backwards pace to escape it.

The monk turned and began to walk away, people parting hurriedly to allow him plenty of room to pass. He paused where the path bent around towards the killing field and the forest beyond, and looked back.

Jack's last sight of the Lord of the Dance was of a sly grin and a silvery eye flashing him a wink.

Kim knelt at Matt's side, clutching a limp hand, the one that hadn't charred like overcooked beef. He was breathing, but shallowly and irregularly. Trickles of blood, almost as dark as the blood of the monk's pets, ran from his nose and ears.

"Matt," said Kim. "Matt! Can you hear me?"

Matt's eyelids fluttered and he uttered a low groan. His eyes opened.

Jack tried hard to stifle the gasp, but it was out quicker than he could react. Kim's shoulders sagged and her chest hitched in a compulsive sob.

It was doubtful whether Matt retained any vision. If he still possessed whites to his eyes, they were no longer visible as the sockets had filled with that same dark blood. It pooled against the rims and spilled over the edge in a slow but steady trickle down the sides of his head to the ground like tears of tar.

"Kim?" His voice was faint, barely qualifying as a whisper. Utter silence fell amongst the onlooking Tumble Downers.

"I'm here, Matt." Jack once more felt admiration for this plucky woman. Despite her obvious distress at seeing her husband in this condition, she did not allow her emotions to distort her voice.

"Never stopped…" He sighed as if the effort of speaking was too much. "Loving you."

"Me, neither. I didn't like you much at times, but part of me has always loved you. Always will."

A pale shadow of a smile crossed Matt's bloodied face. Then it creased in pain.

"Matt! Matt!" Kim shook his hand urgently. "There's something you must know. I saw him. The monk. He revealed his true face to me. I saw what you saw all those years ago and I get it. I get why you drank. I get why you had nightmares. I get why you struggled with everyday life. I'm only sorry that I wasn't more compassionate…" A tear ran down her nose and hung for a moment on the tip, before dropping.

"S'okay." Matt's voice had grown fainter still. "Not good. His face."

"Not good. You named him well. The Lord of the Dance."

"Destroyed. What was left."

"Huh?"

"My mind."

"The monk? He destroyed what was left of your mind?"

"'S."

"Oh, my love. I—" She broke off as Matt tried again to speak. For a few moments, his voice came stronger as though he had diverted all his remaining energy into it.

"Sam. Tell Sam…"

"Yes?"

"I died… trying to do… something good."

"Not trying. Doing. You saved our lives."

Another suggestion of a smile.

Jack could feel his eyes pricking as he gazed down upon the middle-aged, broken figure. A figure he had known barely a week ago as an impetuous, devil-may-care man in the flush of youth.

Matt spoke for the last time. "Go to him. Go home."

His eyes closed, hiding away the black-redness that filled them. His stuttering chest rose and fell, but didn't rise again.

Jack felt a hand on his arm and looked into the grim face of Frankie. They kept their voices low in deference to Kim.

"You and Nadine need to leave. You heard what he said. We have an hour. Less now."

"The Scourgers? They've gone?"

Frankie nodded. "They put up little resistance while we tipped them into the river. Without their master controlling them, they were mere shells. Same for his pets. Now, speak to Miriam and be ready to leave."

Jack still clutched the case tightly, but did not yet turn his attention to it.

"What about Matt? What about the others who fell?" He looked around. A little way back towards the jetty, Daniel knelt with bowed head by the huddled form of a man with blond, bloodied hair. "We can't just leave them lying on the ground."

Frankie grimaced. "There's no time to bury them, even if we had adequate tools."

"At least cover them, then. With jackets or, or, something."

"I'll see what I can arrange. But we must get you out of here." He hurried away, an anxious look on his face.

Jack moved away from the river bank, to be out of everyone's earshot and not to intrude on Kim's grief. Satisfied that no one could hear him, Jack raised the case to chest level. Despite his fatigue, it wasn't difficult since it weighed so little.

"Miriam? It's Jack."

The lights pulsed. "Hello, Jack. I have plotted this dimension and am ready to take you and Nadine Arner to Geneva on Terra One in the year, by your reckoning, 2176."

"What about the other survivors? Can you return them to the time and place they came from?"

"Yes. Plotting their return was simpler than yours and Nadine's. Nadine will be returning to the same time but to a different place than that from which she came."

Jack nodded, recalling that Nadine had been hiking in Italy when she was whisked away.

"Every person who came here," continued Miriam, "left an impression. A trace."

"What, like a path?"

"If you like. It is merely a case of returning them along that trace to the precise moment and spot from whence they came."

"And how long will it take to return each one?"

"From the perspective of anyone remaining here, it will seem instantaneous. All I will need to know is from where and when each person came."

"So for, say, twenty people, it will take no more than twenty, twenty-five minutes for them to provide that information and no time at all to take them home?"

"Correct."

Jack sank to the ground, wincing as he arranged his torn legs, clad in shredded chinos, beneath him. Thankfully, most of the cuts were superficial and had already stopped bleeding. He settled Miriam comfortably on his lap.

"Good," he said. "Then we have a little time for you to tell me what the hell this is all about."

Four

Miriam began: "The intent of the being you call the Lord of the Dance wasn't complex. It was to prevent Jack Bruder and Nadine Arner being together in Geneva in the year 2176."

"Ok-ay. But why, then, did he say it was all about Jack Bruder? About me? Why wasn't it also about Nadine?"

"It could equally have been, but my input—this is not, you understand, a conclusion I could have reached myself as there is insufficient data to make a determination—instructs me that he is an agent of chaos. Therefore randomness and chance are always at play in everything he does. He might have chosen to concentrate his efforts against Nadine, or against you both, but he chose you alone."

"Huh. But if he wanted to keep me and Nadine apart, why did he through his own actions bring us together? We'd never have met—we lived almost two centuries apart, for Pete's sake—if it wasn't for him."

"That is not easy to explain and, again, I can only offer what my input instructs. It consists almost entirely of conjecture. What my masters on Terra Three believe is that the Lord of the Dance, whilst a being of chaos as mentioned, is also bound by certain fundamental laws which limit the degree to which he can meddle in human affairs. One such law forbids him from directly interrupting a timeline by, for instance, killing a person who is going to play a key role in establishing that future."

"By killing me, you mean. Or Nadine."

"Yes. There are more powerful agencies than the Lord of the Dance and he must play by their rules where they apply to him."

"But he was about to kill me minutes ago until Kim got in his way."

"If that is so, he must have been acting *in extremis*. Even an arcane being such as he may be subject to stresses that force them to act beyond their authority. If he had ended your life in contravention of the laws which govern him, it would have been interesting to see what retribution would have befallen him."

"I'd be dead but it would be interesting. Right."

Perhaps she couldn't detect sarcasm, but Miriam continued as if he hadn't spoken. "As well as not being able to kill you, Jack, neither could he rely on you remaining in your own time and place. You see, despite what he claimed before he departed, this dimension is not of his making. The trees and grass and water are his constructs, as are the lands on the other side of the river, but he is merely making use of a dimension that already existed and will continue to exist until the end of time and space. And so, since the timeline in which humanity continues to survive on a distant planet known as Terra Three has always been established, it is inevitable that you and Nadine Arner would have found each other. Whether by stumbling across a time fault or some other way, we can only speculate."

"Time fault?"

"Yes. Similar to a tectonic plate fault on Terra One. A place where two temporal dimensions butt against each other and create a weakness along the fault line through which it is possible to travel between them. They are rare, but have been proven to exist. Bruder Gates exploit similar weaknesses between adjoining spatial dimensions."

"Sounds like so much gobbledegook to me. Still doesn't explain why he deliberately brought us together."

"By bringing you here himself, he was attempting to have you meet on his terms and thereby prevent certain events occurring. Thus, for instance, he didn't mind if Nadine had been killed by the Scourgers in Nowhere, because she would have merely returned to Italy in 2176. It was vital that you, on the other hand, being the focus of his efforts, did not die in Nowhere for you would have returned to Britain to the time from which you had left and would inevitably have found your way to Nadine in some other way."

"That's the bit I'm not getting. Why 'inevitably'?"

"Because, as I have told you, the timeline in which Terra Three houses the remnants of humankind has always existed. Therefore, you and Nadine would have come together. Inevitably."

"But how? Apart from those fault lines you mentioned, there's no such thing as time travel."

"Correct. But this dimension we currently occupy would nevertheless have been instrumental in you and Nadine meeting and becoming lovers in 2176."

Jack swallowed. Trying to get his head around the concept of time travel, or whatever cousin of it they were discussing, always made it hurt, but guff about time travel wasn't the most significant thing he had just heard Miriam say. He and Nadine were to become lovers? A warm sensation bloomed in the pit of his stomach. It was not unpleasant and he savoured it for a moment.

Another question occurred to him, something that had been bothering him for longer than the more fundamental one.

"Tell me, Miriam, why the Elevator took us to those different lands. Everyone else who was transported here came directly without visiting anywhere else."

"Ah. This is also conjecture, *my* conjecture, based on my input—which includes the text of the book called *The Reluctant Inter-Dimensional Travelers*, and essays and theories about the events recounted therein—and my observations since I have been in this dimension. Although the bulk of my processing power since I re-activated has been concentrated on plotting this dimension, my sensors remained alive to input and so I have been privy to all discussions within range of my auditory sensors. Based upon all that data, this is my best, if you like, guess.

"The Lord of the Dance wanted to impress upon you that he is all-powerful. He wanted you to believe there was nothing you could do to extricate yourself from Nowhere. You would not be killed by the Scourgers, for they were essentially him. The possibility of you being killed by another inhabitant or of killing yourself could not be discounted, but chance is of the essence of the Lord of the Dance. He cannot stack the cards completely in his favour. Always there must be an element of possibility, of accident or happenstance."

"Ok-ay. So what are you saying—that he wanted me to think he was the all-knowing, all-powerful one so that I'd not try to escape from Tumble Down and fall into despair or something, but not to the extent that I'd top myself?"

"Essentially, yes. A fragile balance, but one he had to risk. Thus he revealed himself on every floor of Claridge House, hoping to demonstrate his reach and influence, thereby imbuing you with a sense of fate and helplessness."

"Every floor, except one."

"Indeed. And that is where his plan went awry. You met my predecessor in Ultimus, and thus my masters on Terra Three learned of your existence and your travels. It alerted them to the Lord of the Dance's machinations."

"He had nothing to do with where the Elevator took us on Floor Two?"

"It is doubtful he knows that you went anywhere except the places he wanted you to see. He overplayed his hand and left too much room for chance to intervene. Or other forces or agencies, though their existence are theories only. Having said that, the existence of the Lord of the Dance was theory only, but one that has now been confirmed as fact."

Before Jack could say any more, Frankie came over. Nadine accompanied him, favouring Jack with a look that made the warmth in his stomach spread through his whole body.

"We need to get going," said Frankie. "We can't afford to delay any longer."

"Wait. I've yet to ask the million dollar question."

Jack glanced up at Nadine. "Are you okay?"

She nodded. "A few cuts and bruises, but otherwise fine."

"And Kim?"

Nadine grimaced. "As you might imagine. But she is strong and the yearning to return to her son exceeds the intensity of her grief."

"Jack…" began Frankie.

Jack tutted in irritation. "Okay, okay. I'm glad you're here, Nadine. You need to hear this, too." He paused and took a deep breath. "Miriam, please explain why Nadine and I are so important in maintaining Frankie's timeline. In making sure mankind survives."

"Do you not already know?" For a machine, Miriam did a good job of expressing surprise. "Think, Jack. You bear a name that is instrumental in enabling humankind to survive the Event that otherwise would almost certainly have wiped out the entire species."

"Huh. Bruder. The Bruder Gate. But you can't seriously be suggesting that I invented it. I know sod all about physics or whatever shit you need to know to invent something like that."

Frankie shook his head, a wry smile on his face. Jack felt a stab of fresh irritation but kept his attention focused on Miriam.

"No, Jack," said Miriam, "you don't invent the Bruder Gate. That was a scientist by the name of Leon Bruder, the son of Matthew Bruder, also a scientist. Leon developed and expanded upon his father's work to arrive at the discovery that would save humanity. Do you now understand?"

A notion was slowly dawning on Jack, but he wasn't quite seeing the full picture; more a jigsaw where only the edges and a portion of the centre have been completed. He shook his head impatiently. "For fuck's sake, just spell it out, will you?"

"As you wish. Leon Bruder is your grandson, Matthew Bruder your son. They are the direct male issue of Jack Bruder and Nadine Bruder née Arner."

Jack looked at Nadine. He knew his lower jaw had dropped, his mouth agape, but didn't care. Nadine looked as shocked as he felt, but there was another expression in her face. Anticipation? Gladness?

"Matthew Bruder wrote many accounts of his early life," said Frankie. "He spoke fondly of his father and the strange tales he'd tell young Matt while bouncing him upon his knee or tucking him up in bed. Leon, too, writes how his imagination was fired by his grandfather's stories told to him at a tender, impressionable age."

"Huh." It was the best Jack could manage.

"And now, you and Nadine must be on your way."

"No," said Jack.

"What do you mean?" said Frankie, his voice almost cracking with incredulity. "You *must* go now."

"No," Jack repeated. Nadine nodded and her eyes smiled; she knew what he meant.

Jack gestured toward the surviving Tumble Downers. Most of them sat quietly, exhausted. "They must return home first. They risked so much." He grunted. "They risked it all. They must go first."

Frankie let out a loud sigh. "Okay, okay, but we must get on with it." He held out his hand. "I will need Miriam."

Jack nodded. "One last question. Miriam, will humankind ever return to Terra One?"

The lights on the case pulsed. "That is as yet uncertain, Jack. The people of Terra Three have turned their intellects to refining the Bruder Gate technology so that it can pinpoint destinations, but the answer thus far eludes them."

"The best minds we have are working on it," added Frankie. "Including the descendants of Leon Bruder." Jack and Nadine both looked questioningly at him. "Yes, I have met them, though I do not know them well." He shrugged. "They are scientists, intellectuals. I'm more of an action guy." He flashed the cheeky grin that Jack hadn't seen since they'd arrived on this shore.

Frankie held out his hand and Jack passed Miriam to him, feeling a fleeting pang of loss as he let go of her handle.

"And now," said Frankie, "we must evacuate this place."

Jack struggled painfully to his feet. His cuts had congealed and were beginning to scab over, but movement reopened some of them. They stung while his joints and muscles sang. As Frankie turned to make his way back to the Tumble Downers, Jack placed a hand on his arm.

"You knew, didn't you?"

"Huh?" Frankie regarded him uncomprehendingly.

Jack nodded to where Kim knelt. "Matt," he said. "You knew he would die here."

Frankie nodded. "The book that Kim will publish. Matt's account of your adventures in the Elevator. She will add a lengthy Afterword, recounting what happened here today. Including the death of her husband."

"You could have warned her."

"To what purpose? She'd have tried to prevent it. And if she'd succeeded, she might at the same time have allowed the monk to win. I couldn't take that chance."

Jack gazed steadily at him. Something else had occurred to him, which both confirmed and explained what he'd suspected when they'd arrived from Tumble Down at the jetty in Nowhere, that Frankie's astonishment when Kim and Matt appeared from the fog on the raft had been a sham. "You knew they were coming. When we travelled to the jetty from Tumble Down. You knew we wouldn't have to attempt crossing by the chain. I thought there was something off about your look of surprise."

Frankie gave a wry smile. "Didn't I tell you? I'm not the best actor. And now... no more time to delay."

Five

Frankie addressed the bedraggled bunch of people that remained of those who had travelled from Tumble Down. Few had escaped injury; one or two, like Fumika and Daniel, were not in a good way, though Jack didn't think anyone's injuries were life threatening. Nevertheless, seeking medical attention when they returned home would be a good idea.

"I would like," said Frankie, "to thank each and every one of you. For not only myself, but for every man, woman and child with whom I share Terra Three. For every man, woman and child who will come after us. For every person who was able to live a full life after the Event that will take place in your distant future and in my distant past. Your efforts today have ensured your descendants will have the means to survive that catastrophe."

Jack cleared his throat and heads turned his way. He felt himself blush—he hated making himself the centre of attention—but pressed on. "Er, I'd like to add my gratitude. We lost some good people today, not least someone none of you knew. He's lying over there. His name is Matt. He wasn't my friend, not exactly, but we went through a lot together and he played a huge part in helping us to succeed today. I, um, this sounds really silly, but I think I shall be naming my son after him. Rather, Nadine and I will be naming *our* son after him." Tired faces broke into grins. Nadine's hand found his and squeezed. "Um, that's all I want to say. Thank you. Now, please, you must all go home."

A slight girl with a darting head like a sparrow's stood. "I want to go home," said Anna, blushing more furiously than Jack, "but the people with bad cuts should go first."

A murmur of agreement rose.

"Okay," said Frankie. He approached Fumika. She didn't look as if she retained enough strength to stand so he stooped next to her, Miriam clutched in one hand, her lights pulsing gently. "Where in Japan were you when the monk took you away? And the date?"

"Hiroshima," replied Fumika; it seemed to take a monumental effort for her to speak. "April second, 1938."

"Hiroshima?" said Jack. Fumika turned her head to look at him; that, too, seemed to take a great effort on her part. "Take your family and leave that city. There is going to be a war. Something bad will happen to that city. To Nagasaki, too. Something dreadful even in the context of a dreadful war. Get far away, Fumika."

Her eyes widened at Jack's words, then she half-closed them as if to thank him.

"I am ready," said the mellifluous voice of Miriam.

Frankie held out his free hand and gripped Fumika's. Without further ado, man, woman and attaché case vanished. A popping noise came of air rushing in to fill a sudden vacuum, accompanied by gasps of astonishment from many of the Tumble Downers. Jack wanted to rub his eyes in disbelief, but he would have missed Frankie's return. He had been gone for moments only, probably less than a second, when he and Miriam reappeared as abruptly as they'd disappeared, but without Fumika. A waft like a slightest breeze hit Jack's face as Frankie's reappearance displaced more air.

"That's it?" said Jack. "Fumika has returned to 1938?"

Frankie nodded. He stepped to Daniel's side and the process was repeated, the weary man returning to pre-First World War rural England. He offered Jack a tired smile as Frankie grasped his hand. He had disappeared before Jack had chance to return it.

He watched Frankie reappear almost immediately before dragging his fascinated gaze away. "We should check on Kim."

"You go," said Nadine.

He sighed. "I guess so."

Kim turned a tear-stained face to him as he approached. Someone had covered Matt's body in a woollen jacket. Only his face showed above it. It looked peaceful.

"You thought my crossing the river to Nowhere was unselfish

or some such shit," Jack said. "But it was driven entirely by self-interest. What Matt did was truly noble. He gave his life to save others."

"Yes. That's what he did. It's what I shall tell Sam."

"Because it's the truth." He glanced back the way he'd come. "People are going home. It won't be long and it'll be your turn." He didn't know what else to say.

Kim let out her breath in a deep, shuddering sigh. Leaning forward, she placed a kiss on Matt's brow, then tugged up the jacket to cover his face. She stood.

"Okay, then." She set her jaw in a determined line that reminded Jack of the resolute expression she'd worn often during their jaunt in the Elevator.

She turned away from the body of her husband. "I'm as ready as I'm gonna be."

Side by side, they walked slowly towards the rapidly dwindling group of Tumble Downers.

"What will you do?" Jack asked, still not knowing the right words. "When you get back?"

"Tell my son that he's lost his father, I guess. Oh, and root out Matt's scribblings. Seems like I have to find out how to go about publishing a book."

"He was a good bloke." It sounded lame, inadequate, but Kim seemed to appreciate it.

"Yes. He was."

They stopped when they reached Nadine. Kim gasped when Frankie disappeared with the next Tumble Downer. And again when he reappeared.

"Wow," she murmured.

When it was Anna's turn, Kim called out to her. "Good luck, honey. Your sister will be glad to see you."

Anna smiled and her head twitched. After she had gone, Kim frowned. "What I said isn't actually true, is it? Leastways, her sister may well be glad to see her, but only in the normal way. As far as she's concerned, Anna has never been away."

Within minutes, only the three of them, and Frankie, remained. Kim told him the time and place from which she had been taken.

Nadine held out her hand. Kim ignored it and hugged her. "Look after each other," she said. "You go well together."

She turned to Jack. "Never thought I'd do this, but come here." She held out her arms.

His cheeks infused with fresh heat, Jack stepped into her embrace. They pulled apart and Kim held his gaze for a moment. "I'll never forget you, Jack. We've been through a great deal together. For what it's worth, I'm proud that my son bears your name."

She glanced back at the covered form of Matt before looking at Frankie. "I'm ready."

He took her hand. Kim disappeared.

When Frankie reappeared clutching Miriam a moment later, he fixed Jack and Nadine with a purposeful look. "Right, then," he said. "Time to do what I came here to do. Take you two to Geneva in the year 2176."

"June fourteenth, to be precise," said Miriam. "Three-twenty-seven in the afternoon local time. I have plotted your return to Gare de Genève-Cornavin, a convenient central point."

"The main railway station," said Nadine, for his benefit, Jack assumed. "I'll have some explaining to do. Like how I disappeared from a tent in an Italian valley and reappeared only hours later a few hundred miles away."

"You'll manage it," said Frankie with a smile. "Plead amnesia, or something."

"Um," said Jack. Now that it came down to it, he suddenly realised how completely unprepared he was. "How am I going to explain my presence? I have no identity papers, no clothes, no money. Nothing. I can't speak French or whatever language is spoken there."

Frankie fumbled in his pocket and held something out to Jack. It was a plastic disc, a little scratched, bearing an embedded chip of some sort of material like silicon and a four-digit number.

"We did think of that," he said with a grin. "This is a key to the locker bearing that number in the railway station. Within the locker, you'll find clean clothes for you both; you can hardly walk around in the blood-stained rags you're wearing now. You'll also find an identity card, Swiss naturalised citizenship papers, some money. Don't worry about the language—most foreigners in Geneva speak English."

"That is true," said Nadine. "But the identity card—they are linked to the holder's DNA signature. Without that, it will be exposed as a fake the first time it is used."

Frankie's grin grew wider. "Then it is fortunate indeed that it is authentic. Well, an authentic forgery, that is, but one that will pass the closest examination."

"Hang on," said Jack, feeling another stab of irritation cut through his excitement. "How did you get my DNA? From my descendants?"

"No, though we did use their DNA to confirm the sample we obtained was yours. We—that's me and Miriam—went to your home in Geneva. It was a simple matter to obtain enough samples of hair on pillows, toothbrush swabs, that sort of thing, to extract your signature back on Terra Three."

"You went to our home...?" The word held little meaning to him, and it was ridiculous to feel a sense of violation over something that hadn't yet happened and that would be done purely for his benefit. "When, in 2176?"

"A few years later. At a precise date and time. You see, we knew you'd both be out."

"Huh? How...?"

"We knew that Matthew was born in a clinic, not at home. So we travelled to Geneva while you were both otherwise engaged." In response to Nadine's gasp, he continued, "Nothing to worry about. The birth proceeds without complication."

Jack grunted. "You seem to have thought of everything." He tried to sound more grateful. "Thank you."

"Don't mention it. It was for our benefit as well as yours. Wouldn't have been much good going through all this only to have you deported as an illegal alien the moment you set foot in Geneva." Frankie glanced around. "Now we *really* must be off."

Nadine gripped Frankie's free hand. Jack held his forearm. Without preamble or ceremony, the land in which Jack had spent the last couple of weeks, that felt like months, blinked out of sight.

He experienced no strange sensations: no fluttering stomach or dizziness, no sense of having been displaced. A measure of apprehension, yes, but overriding all a tingling feeling of excitement.

The scene of the riverbank was replaced instantaneously, like one photo following another in a slideshow, by a new sight, an all-too familiar one, that invoked a gut-wrenching dread in Jack's stomach.

Enclosed metallic walls, low metallic ceiling, a door that looked like it slid to open.

"A lift?" he muttered. "I'm back in a fucking lift?"

"Do not fret, Jack," said the voice of Miriam. "You are not in the elevator at Claridge House in twenty-first century Britain, but in a railway station elevator in twenty-second century Geneva. I have brought you to this point in order to conceal your arrival. And—" if Miriam had possessed shoulders, she would surely have shrugged "—it seemed apt to end your journey in the same type of conveyance in which it began."

"Elevators are still used in new buildings," said Nadine. "No one has yet invented a simpler or cheaper alternative. But they are usually better than this one." She grunted. "This station dates back a few centuries."

It was only as the lift came to a jerky stop that Jack realised it had been descending. He held his breath as the door started to slide open, reaching out to grasp Nadine's hand with an urgency that had come upon him as soon as he'd realised where he was.

He let out his breath in a relieved sigh when the open doorway revealed not a strange land inhabited by dragons or pixies or women formed from oceans of acid, but a bustling concourse.

"Let's get out of here," he muttered. He stepped forward, still clutching tightly to Nadine, and together they stood outside the lift. Jack gazed around, expecting to see something more, oh, *futuristic*, he supposed, but nothing sprang to his immediate attention to suggest he was standing in a foreign land almost two centuries ahead of his own time. It was only as he started to look more closely that he realised that the garb of the scurrying people looked strange, synthetic, and the ambient sound, for such a bustling environment, seemed muted. The air he breathed felt scrubbed; clinical, almost.

Nadine's hand let go of his as she turned to face back into the lift. He turned, too—there would be time enough to take in his new surroundings. His new home.

Home. A word that had lost meaning to Jack since he had been turfed out of the only place to which it might apply when he was sixteen. And yet…

The space deep inside, which in most people is occupied with their sense of identity and belonging, which he had tried to forget in a haze of drugs, yearned to be filled. Maybe he had come to the right place, the right time, to do just that.

Frankie made no move to step out of the lift. "This is where we part company," he said. "I need to remain hidden so we can return home without causing anybody distress."

"Terra Three?" said Jack.

"Yes. Though we have been away for many months, we shall return to the moment that we left. My family will not have had time to miss me. But I miss them."

Strange, but Jack had never thought of Frankie having a family; had never thought to ask him. "Children?"

"Only the one. A daughter." His face darkened. "There were moments over the past days when I despaired of ever seeing her again." The cloud passed and he grinned that familiar grin. "But without further ado, I go to her."

Jack held out his hand and Frankie shook it warmly. "Good luck, Frankie. And thank you for everything you've done."

"Oh, Miriam has done most of the work." The grin widened. "Take care, gov," he added in that atrocious Cockney accent.

Jack returned the grin—there was something infectious about it. Then he reached down and touched the case. "Goodbye, Miriam. I'm so glad I met you again."

The lights pulsed. "Goodbye, Jack Bruder."

He straightened and watched the lift door slide closed. Then he looked at Nadine.

She smiled. "Shall we go home?"

Jack took a deep breath and nodded. Yes, he had at last come home.

Nadine at his side, he turned and stepped into his new present.

Epilogue

Jack Bruder ran a hand through hair that, although such a pale grey it was almost white, retained much of its volume. While outwardly eschewing values based on appearance, he was secretly proud that he had kept his hair without the artificial growth stimulants so fashionable amongst those of advancing years.

"Nadine?" he called. "I'm just leaving." He had picked up enough conversational French and German over the years to make himself understood to native speakers, but they still used English when at home.

A voice replied, "Hold on. I'm coming."

Nadine appeared, wiping her hands on her apron. She still, after all this time, with her youthfully slim body and features matured like a fine wine, invoked a sensation of warmth in Jack's stomach. She, too, had allowed her hair colour to fade, but it had done so less rapidly than his. The streaks of grey suited her, lent her a distinguished air.

He leaned into her and kissed her tenderly.

"Now," she said, straightening the lapels of his thick overcoat, "are you sure you don't want me to come with you?"

"Quite sure. You've got enough on your plate preparing party food. I still don't understand why we don't employ outside caterers."

Nadine sighed, but without rancour. "Oh, Jack, you know why. We can employ caterers any time, but it's not every day that it's our grandson's eighth birthday. I *want* to make the food. Leon loves his *grand-mère's* cooking."

"He's not the only one. I'll be as quick as possible so I can hurry back to give you a hand." He noticed Nadine's expression and smiled. "I can pass you ingredients, can't I, and scrape out the bowls?"

"Okay, I'll allow you to do that."

"I shouldn't be long in Oscar's. It's only to sign Matt's patent application.”

“Your *joint* application.”

“Hmm. Matt might be insisting my name go on there alongside his, but it’s his invention.”

“Inspired by you.”

Jack held up his hands in mock surrender. “As if there was any doubt where our son gets his stubbornness from.”

Nadine’s expression grew serious. “And you’ll call into the clinic first?”

Jack sighed. “I’ve said I would.”

“Well, make sure you do. The twinges you’ve been experiencing may be the first sign that your body’s rejecting the transplant. Like it did the last one.”

“Or they could be indigestion from your cooking.” Jack smiled, but in truth he was a little concerned. He had hidden the true extent of the ‘twinges’ from his wife. They had been more pains than mere twinges, lancing barbs radiating from the centre of his chest and down his left arm. Like pins and needles, only where they had first been inserted into a furnace until white hot.

Nadine’s expression remained serious. “They’re expecting you, Jack. Don’t leave it too late, like you did last time.” She held out a floury hand and caressed his cheek. “I couldn’t bear to lose you.”

“*Almost* too late,” he reminded her. “I’m still here, aren’t I?”

“Only just. If your body is rejecting the latest one, you can have another. As many times as necessary. We can afford it.”

Just as well. Jack took so many pills—pills, for goodness’ sake; they should have come up with a better alternative by now—he felt like he’d rattle if he was shaken. “Stop fretting, Nadine. I’ll go to the clinic. Then I’ll go and see Oscar, sign Matt’s papers and I’ll be back before the next batch is baked.”

Her face lit back up in a smile. “Go, then. I shall allow you to help me in the kitchen and perhaps we’ll have time to relax with a glass of wine before the hordes descend.”

Jack leaned forward and kissed her again. Then, pulling his coat tighter against the biting February wind, he stepped out into it.

« »

After the energy crisis in 2184, and the ensuing minor nuclear war (how peculiar, he'd always thought, to ascribe the adjective 'minor' to a war involving two countries lobbing nuclear warheads at each other), private car ownership had almost become a thing of the past. Electrically powered vehicles had enjoyed a fleeting heyday, before the number of accidents caused by aluminium missiles moving almost soundlessly had become intolerable to most enlightened governments. Such vehicles had now, at least in congested cities, become the sole preserve of public transport operators, restricted to tightly controlled thoroughfares onto which pedestrians had no access.

He sometimes wondered whether the Lord of the Dance was rubbing his pudgy hands in glee at the sheer breadth of greed and stupidity continuously displayed by humankind; perhaps the sweaty monk had played a part in many of the incidents of war and terror and disaster over the years. They certainly involved, or ended in, mass chaos. Right up his alley. But he made his thoughts turn aside from such musings as they led only to unlit places of insanity such that had caused someone he had known long ago to seek escape in alcohol.

Jack walked as briskly as he could through the streets of Geneva, casting glances up at a glowering sky that held the promise of snow. Yes, snow still fell occasionally in such southerly latitudes, though now rarely. He'd have liked to have walked faster, but the pain had started up in his chest and he was beginning to feel a little out of breath, though he had barely come half a kilometre.

He reached the cab-call station and inserted his payment chip. He leaned closer to the voice-activated controller, intending to state his destination as the address of the clinic, but instead blurting out the address of Walther, Hermann and Schmidt, Attorneys at Law and Notaries Public. Oscar Hermann's office was nearer than the clinic and he could fortify himself with a strong coffee before facing the inquisition and prodding and poking he'd be forced to endure at the hands of the medics.

Installed in the warmth of the cab, he relaxed and the pain subsided a little.

Good call. Get the legal shenanigans out of the way and then deal with the medical shit. The fact that he had assured Nadine he would go to the clinic first caused a twinge of shame—he had never deliberately lied to her, and hadn't now, he persuaded himself.

When I told her I'd go to the clinic first, I meant it. A man can change his mind, can't he?

Perhaps he ought to go to the clinic first, after all, but then it was too late. The cab had pulled up at the station outside the offices of the law firm. At least he didn't have far to walk in the cold.

The foyer was spacious and modern. A bank of gleaming doors faced him: lifts to the twenty-three storeys that towered above him. Oscar's office was situated on the nineteenth. With the pains starting to increase again, he didn't contemplate the stairs.

Jack approached the nearest lift and replied to the disembodied voice enquiring in French which floor he required. He could have waited until the voice had repeated the question in German before it got to the English version, but he understood the French.

"*Dix-neuf.* Nineteen." His voice sounded a little breathless.

The door slid silently open and he stepped into the gleaming interior. He had no qualms about riding in lifts. Maybe the first few times after coming to Geneva he'd experienced a moment's trepidation when the lift door slid open, but there had never been anything the other side that he'd not been expecting, and the fear had subsided long ago.

The door closed. To take his mind off the increasing tightness in his chest—it felt like someone with overdeveloped muscles was wrapping him in a bear hug—Jack gazed at the display panel above the two buttons on the wall.

Wait.

He frowned. *Buttons?*

In all the years he had lived as a Swiss citizen, Jack had never been in an elevator car containing buttons. Not even the ancient lift in the railway station contained anything as archaic and prone to harbouring nasty microbes as buttons. Everything these days was voice-operated and hands-free.

He took a step closer, grimacing as his chest constricted. There were two buttons at the height of his chin. Unmarked. One to his left, the other a few inches to the right.

The lift should have arrived on the nineteenth floor by now. Unease sent icy tendrils down his back, making him shiver despite the beads of sweat breaking out on his brow.

"Er, hello?" he said.

For a moment, nothing. Then a voice he hadn't heard in a long time spoke. A mellifluous voice.

"Hello, Jack."

The pain was increasing by the moment, sharp heat running down his left arm. Perhaps he was delirious, but he could have sworn he recognised the voice.

"Miriam?"

"Yes, that is how you knew me and how I am content to be called. But you must listen to me, Jack. Closely. You do not have much time."

"Huh. What's going on?" He was struggling to get words out; his lips didn't seem to want to co-operate.

"You have been given special dispensation, Jack, to make use of a place you twice visited and to utilise technology that is used sparingly, if at all, for fear of giving him a way back in."

"Him…? The monk?"

"The Lord of the Dance as he is now commonly referred to. Yet humankind does not know him, Jack, thanks to your efforts and those who helped you. He is still kept out, although, as you have heard tell before, it is a delicate balance. Your endeavours were felt worthy of reward, of risking that balance. The risk is judged negligible as otherwise not even your high esteem could have swayed in your favour."

"Reward? What are you… talking about?" The strength was running from his legs. He rocked forward and rested his head against the cool wall of the lift.

"You must choose, Jack. There are two buttons on the wall in front of you. If you press the one on your left, the lift door will open on the nineteenth floor of the building in Geneva into which you entered. If you press the one on your right, the door will open to a waiting crash team who will immediately resuscitate you and keep you alive until you can be fitted with a new heart. A synthetic one, Jack. One that will beat for so long as your brain is active."

"Hng." For a moment, it was all that he could manage. Dark spots danced before his eyes. "If I don't choose?"

"Not choosing will be the same as pressing the button on the left. The door will open onto the nineteenth floor, you will stumble out and die. Your heart has failed. There are no people with medical training on the nineteenth floor. There is no time for medical aid to reach you."

"Nadine… Matt… Leon…"

"You will never see them again. Unless you press the left-hand button. Then you will see Matt again, while you breathe your last in his arms. I am sorry, Jack. But know this: there are family members waiting for you on Terra Four. Far distant descendants of you and Nadine and Matt and Leon. They are anxious to meet their famous forefather."

"Terra… Four…?" His breathing was now so ragged it sounded like a defective steam motor. The spots before his eyes grew larger as his sight began to fail.

"Yes, Jack. The Bruder Gate technology was perfected by the scientists on Terra Three, enabling a destination to be pinpointed. To be chosen. They chose what they knew. Terra Four is Terra One, the planet formerly known as Earth."

"Earth…?"

"Yes, Jack. An Earth cleansed of the echoes of the Event, an Earth found to be occupied by the remnants of survivors of the original human inhabitants, greatly diminished, returned to savagery, but now assimilated back into the whole."

What remained of Jack's mind beneath the rushing sound of oblivion reeled. People had returned to Earth. They still kept out the Lord of the Dance.

"Jack, you have run out of time. Choose now or don't choose at all."

With the final dregs of strength that remained in his right arm, Jack raised it. Willing his legs to continue to support him for a couple more seconds, he lifted his head to peer blearily at the buttons.

And pressed one.

About the Author

Sam Kates lives in South Wales, UK, with a family, a computer and *way* too many books. To connect on social media:

Website: samkates.co.uk
Facebook: www.facebook.com/writersamkates
Twitter: @_Sam_Kates_
E-mail: samkates@samkates.co.uk

Note

Please consider leaving a review—reviews can be of immeasurable help to authors in gaining visibility and running promotions.

Thank you for purchasing and reading this book.

To sign up for news of releases and special offers, most of which are only available to subscribers (no spam, promise): http://www.samkates.co.uk/stay-in-touch/

– Sam Kates
June 2018